compulsion

compulsion

HEIRS OF WATSON ISLAND

MARTINA BOONE

Simon Pulse
NEW YORK   LONDON   TORONTO   SYDNEY   NEW DELHI

SIMON PULSE
An imprint of Simon & Schuster Children's Publishing Division
1230 Avenue of the Americas, New York, NY 10020
First Simon Pulse hardcover edition October 2014
Text copyright © 2014 by Martina Boone
Jacket photograph copyright © 2014 by Oleg Oprisco/Trevillion Images
All rights reserved, including the right of reproduction in whole or in part in any form.
SIMON PULSE and colophon are registered trademarks of Simon & Schuster, Inc.
For information about special discounts for bulk purchases, please contact
Simon & Schuster Special Sales at 1-866-506-1949 or business@simonandschuster.com.
The Simon & Schuster Speakers Bureau can bring authors to your live event. For more
information or to book an event, contact the Simon & Schuster Speakers Bureau at
1-866-248-3049 or visit our website at www.simonspeakers.com.
Jacket design by Regina Flath
Interior design by Hilary Zarycky
The text of this book was set in Granjon.
Manufactured in the United States of America
2 4 6 8 10 9 7 5 3 1
Full CIP data is available from the Library of Congress.
ISBN 978-1-4814-1122-6 (hc)
ISBN 978-1-4814-1124-0 (eBook)

To my family with all my love.
To my husband, who knew the odds and still supported me.
To my son, who encouraged me.
And most of all to my daughter,
without whom I would never have rediscovered
young adult literature and found my writing heart.

CHAPTER ONE

The heat that crept into the airport baggage area whenever the door opened should have told Barrie Watson that she had arrived in hell. But it wasn't the Charleston weather, or the fact that her mother's sister, who she'd never even heard of before the funeral, was three hours late picking her up. Neither of those things kept Barrie's butt glued on top of her suitcase and her eyes on the door.

It was hope that kept her stuck, that stole her breath and made her eyes smart every time some likely looking woman rushed in and scanned the nearly empty area around the luggage carousels. Barrie hated hope. Too often, it was a Go Directly to Jail card that led to disappointment.

The latest candidate through the door did seem promising, though. Blond. Midthirties. The mile-high heels of Barrie's purple sandals left fresh dents in her suitcase as she leaned forward to search for some tug of recognition or family connection. But the woman ignored her and ran to embrace a man in madras shorts at carousel number two.

Around Barrie, the walls tunneled in. The whole day, the whole week, had been hell, and now her chest was tight and her heart was racing. She sucked in a deep, calming breath. Then she wiped her palms on the thighs of her capris and got ready to redial the number the lawyer had given her for Watson's Landing. Yet again. She nearly dropped the phone when it suddenly vibrated in her hand.

For an instant, she couldn't help but hope. The screen showed her godfather's number, though. And now what? Mark would worry himself sick—sick*er*—if she told him Aunt Pru hadn't come. Barrie couldn't add to his worries. She had to be cheerful.

She was *going* to be cheerful.

"Hi, Mark!" she chirped.

Great. Now she sounded like a demented cheerleader.

"Don't you 'Hi, Mark' me, Miss Thing. Do you know how long it's been since your plane landed? Since when don't you call when you're supposed to?"

Barrie's eyes closed at the love in his voice. That rich timbre with its hint of a lisp was at the heart of her every memory: Mark making her laugh, soothing her, teasing her out of being afraid. With her eyes closed she could keep him closer, see him in the size-fourteen pumps and yellow dress he had worn to drop her at the airport that morning, see the strain in his red-lipstick smile and in the pallor of his dark brown skin as he'd pulled her in for one last hug. As he'd fussed over her. Waved to her. Sent her away.

No. She wasn't going to cry. Barrie was through with tears.

Cradling the phone against her shoulder, she laid both palms flat against the suitcase and told him the literal truth: "I just this minute put my hands on my luggage." Her voice cracked, but she pulled herself together. "How are you feeling? You're not overdoing it, are you? Yelling at the movers? Flirting with them?"

"No more than they deserve." Mark's smile was audible. "Now tell me everything, baby girl. Were you okay on the flight? No panic attacks? How's your aunt Pru? Is she anything like Lula? Are you going to like her, do you think?"

"You aren't supposed to be worrying about me—"

"Of course I'm going to worry. Now, what's wrong? You don't like it there. I can tell—"

"You can't tell a thing." Barrie sat up indignantly. "I haven't even seen the place. But I've got to go. Aunt Pru just got back with the car. I'll have to call you later."

It was only a little lie. It slipped out without Barrie's permission, but the weight of it settled around her shoulders when they'd said their good-byes. What if her aunt never came? Barrie couldn't call Mark back and tell him she had lied. She refused to let that be one of the last conversations they ever got to have.

All right. Fine. She would find the place by herself, and once she got there . . . No, she wouldn't think of that just yet. Aunt Pru had to let her stay long enough to finish high school. That was all there was to it. There were no other relatives to take her in.

The thought finally pushed Barrie to her feet. She wobbled briefly on the skyscraper sandals Mark had talked her into wearing that morning for extra confidence. Towing her luggage behind her, she stepped through the exit door into a curtain of humidity that made her long yet again for San Francisco.

A dispatcher materialized beside her. "Cab, miss?"

"Yes, please." Barrie blew a wilting strand of blond curls from her eyes.

The dispatcher waved a taxi to the curb. Barrie slid into the back while the driver loped around to stow her suitcases. The trunk slammed closed. The cab shook, and rocked again when the driver wedged himself behind the wheel.

"So, where we goin'?" he asked, studying her in the rear-view mirror.

"Watson Island."

"That's a good hour, dependin' on traffic." His gaze slid from the three diamond-encrusted keys on Barrie's necklace to the oversize gold watch Mark had slipped onto her wrist that morning. Once he had finally decided she was good for the fare, the driver nodded. "You have an address?" he asked.

"Watson's Landing Plantation." Barrie hated the heat that crawled up her cheeks. "Just go to the island. I can find it."

That was one thing Barrie could always count on. Finding things was the Watson gift. Barrie could find anything—had to find it, really—and the pressure that built in her head whenever she was near something lost had seemed stronger since her mother's death. Even now, an object on the floor of the taxi tugged at her attention, squeezing her temples in a rapidly increasing ache.

The driver lurched out into traffic. Barrie bent and groped under his seat until she freed something small and round from beneath the rails. A wedding ring. The gold was cool against her fingers and scratched thin from years of wear.

"Excuse me." She tapped the driver on his shoulder. "Is this yours?"

He turned and a grin split his face. "I thought I'd never see that again. Lord, thank you. Thank you."

Barrie dropped the ring into his palm and sighed at the familiar click in her head, like a puzzle piece snapping into place. The pressure vanished.

The cab gathered speed. Barrie rested her cheek against the window. Miles of sky and saltwater marsh sped past, interrupted by stands of pines swathed in palmetto skirts, and houses buffered by masses of pink and yellow flowers. Even in June, San Francisco cloaked itself in cool, protective layers of fog, but here the landscape overwhelmed her like the crowds at the airport. It was all too open, too bright, too much. She distracted herself from her nerves by imagining how she would paint the scenery—in bold, broad strokes with lots of white—and that made the time pass faster. Almost before she knew it, before she was ready, the cab drove over the bridge to Watson Island.

"Can't be long now," the driver said. "There's a signpost for the plantation there."

According to the arrows, the town of Watson's Point was to the left and Watson's Landing was to the right. The driver nosed the cab onto a road shadowed on both sides by trees dripping Spanish moss. They drove a few miles before crossing a shallow creek via a smaller, wooden bridge, and immediately a historical marker stood at the edge of a tall brick wall. About all Barrie caught was the word "Watson" before the cab moved past.

"Wait. Stop!" The command came out louder than she'd intended, and her cheeks went warm again as the driver slammed on the brakes. "I'm sorry," she said. "Could you please back up?"

The driver gave her a long-suffering look, but he backed the cab to the marker.

> Watson's Landing Plantation was established in
> 1692 by a grant to Thomas Watson, captain of the
> privateer vessel *Loyal Jamaica*, and has remained
> in the Watson family without interruption. It is one of
> the oldest rice plantations on the Santisto River, and
> the original house, constructed of locally made brick,
> remains intact.

Privateers and rice plantations. Wonderful. More details Lula had never bothered to share about their family. Barrie tucked her hands beneath her thighs to keep from rubbing Mark's watch as if it were Aladdin's lamp.

The brick wall, too tall to see over, continued alongside the road as the cab drove on. Above it, expanses of sky alternated with oak and cypress woods until, after what must have been several miles, bursts of camellias and roses appeared, climbing over the top of the bricks as if trying to escape.

7

The driver swung the cab into a driveway. A gold *W* hung in the center of the scrollwork above a closed black iron gate, and a plaque embedded in one of the brick end posts read:

Private property. No trespassing.
Gardens and Tearoom
Open 1:00 p.m.–6:00 p.m., Thurs to Sun

Open. As in, to the public.

The idea brought a slick of moisture to Barrie's palms. Strangers walking around, peering in the windows . . . How could anyone live like that?

"You sure this is where you want to go?" the driver asked.

"Yes," Barrie lied.

The driver continued to watch her expectantly, as if there were something she was missing. Finally he said, "It's closed Wednesdays."

Barrie stared at him another moment before realizing he meant that the gardens and tearoom were closed. What if there was no one to let her in?

"I'll go buzz the intercom," she said with an inward sigh.

She forced herself out of the cab and picked her way across the crushed oyster shells and gravel. Beyond the gate, a sunken lane ran between two rows of live oaks so old, their branches mingled overhead. Claws of light tore through the leaves and drapes of Spanish moss, creating mottled patches of shade on the ground. No house was visible. Barrie pressed the antiquated buzzer and steadied herself against the gatepost.

The moment her skin made contact with the bricks, the Watson gift gave its familiar returning click, and she felt an easing of pressure, as if a headache she hadn't even been aware of had suddenly released its grip. Yet she hadn't returned anything. Nothing except herself, and she hadn't been lost. She wasn't even staying unless someone *answered the stupid intercom.*

All right. Stay calm. Barrie gulped in another breath. She reached for the buzzer again, then paused. The gate was open half an inch. Had it been like that before? She gave it an experimental shove, and it slid across the driveway with a metallic screech. After waving the driver through, she closed the gate behind him and climbed back into the cab. Foot jiggling with nerves, she peered ahead while they crawled down the lane.

The house emerged slowly from behind the violet-shadowed trees. Where at first there was only an impression of whitewashed bricks, fluted columns, and gabled roofs, once the taxi neared the end of the lane, the branches pulled back to reveal a beautifully proportioned mansion framed by blooming gardens. The lawn stretched to meet the woods and sloped gently toward a river where the sun reflected on tar-dark water.

Barrie gasped. Not at the size, not at the age, not even at the *fact* of the plantation. What struck her most was how much the house reminded her of Lula's house in San Francisco.

"This is where my mother grew up," she whispered, surprising herself. She'd never called Lula "mother," not out loud. Lula had hated the word. But then, Lula had never told Barrie about Pru or Watson's Landing, or anything at all, really, so to hell with what Lula'd wanted.

"My mother died last week," Barrie said, testing the sound of those words too.

"I'm sorry." The driver's eyes met hers in the rearview mirror.

Barrie nodded and looked away. The cab pulled up to the house and rolled to a stop behind an ancient Mercedes with a live albino peacock perched on the hood like some bizarre kind of ornament. The bird shrieked, flew down, and landed beside a woman seated on the steps. Purse clutched on her knees in a white-knuckle grip, the woman stared at Barrie.

This had to be Lula's sister. Lula's *twin*. The woman resembled Barrie enough to make that clear. Unlike Barrie's mother, though, she had no burn scars to hide behind a wig and veil. She wasn't stooped in pain. She was pretty. Beautiful, almost.

Was this what Lula would have looked like if fate had been kinder all those years ago? Barrie studied her aunt's full cheeks, her neat triangular chin, the liquid play of emotions across her face. Slowly, she climbed out of the cab.

"Aunt Pru?" Barrie asked.

The woman struggled to her feet, scrubbing at eyes as gray as Barrie's, as pale as Lula's. She smoothed back her blond curls, and with her gaze locked on Barrie, she took a shaky step. That was as far as she got, as if she didn't have the strength to descend the remaining stairs.

"Barrie?" she asked. "Is that you?"

Barrie ran a few steps, then stopped. A handshake seemed too formal, but she had never hugged anyone except for Mark, and a hug felt awkward when she and her aunt had never met. She clasped her hands behind her and licked her lips. "I kept trying to call you, but no one answered."

"I was on my way to get you." Her aunt's words trickled out like they weren't in a hurry, a syllable at a time. "I—I was going to the airport. I just sat down a moment to catch my breath. . . ."

Barrie glanced at her watch. "It's four fifteen—"

"Four fifteen?" Pru checked her own watch. "Oh, goodness. It is." She sank back down on the step, wrapping her arms around herself as though she felt cold despite the afternoon heat. "You must have thought I'd abandoned you—"

"No. It was fine," Barrie cut in before her aunt could burst into tears.

Of course it wasn't fine. The problem wasn't only that Pru hadn't come for her. Something about her aunt, and the whole situation, was off. Pru's clothes seemed more like what a teenage girl might have worn years ago, instead of a woman of thirty-six. The sundress was ironed stiff, as if Pru had taken trouble with it, but the pattern was so faded, Barrie couldn't tell if the fruit on it had begun as apples or apricots. And Pru's scuffed, old-fashioned Mary Janes would have made Mark groan. Overall the look was more can't-afford-anything-new than vintage chic.

In that, Barrie's aunt matched the house. A shutter hung drunkenly on a nearby window like it was going to crash down at any moment. Paint peeled from one of the tall columns, and mortar had crumbled from between the bricks.

Unlike the manicured gardens around it, the house looked neglected, as if no one cared enough to maintain it. The opposite of Lula's obsession to have every room and knickknack perfect.

The driver handed Barrie the charge slip to sign. "You sure you're goin' to be all right here, child?" He nodded his chin in her aunt's direction and added softly, "I can still take you back. No trouble."

Barrie shook her head. Now that she was here, she couldn't

leave. Her aunt was undeniably strange, but Pru's features added up to familiarity, to family. And the house, while run-down, was magnificent. It was *Watson's* Landing. Lula's history. Barrie's own history.

"I'm going to be fine here," she said, as if determination could make that true.

CHAPTER TWO

Inside, Watson's Landing reminded Barrie of an aging beauty, all sagging skin over lovely bones. Even the smell was ancient. The air stank of jasmine, decay, and dust. And the furniture, like the outside of the house, was an eerie echo of Lula's mansion in San Francisco.

Pru carried one of Barrie's heavy suitcases up the mahogany staircase with surprising ease, as if her wiry arms were stronger than they looked. Barrie trailed her aunt more slowly, dragging the other suitcase one step at a time. She tried not to be alarmed that Pru's breath still came in shuddering little gulps, or that Pru had yet to explain why she had sat outside for hours and forgotten to pick Barrie up.

Who *did* that?

Well, Lula's sister apparently.

Maybe Pru was as nuts as Lula.

Barrie was searching for a way to ask her aunt why she hadn't gone to the airport, when halfway to the narrow landing between the first floor and the second, her suitcase caught. She stumbled and grabbed the banister. The spindles swayed beneath her weight. Planting her feet, she fought for balance.

Excellent. She'd been here five minutes, and she'd nearly killed herself.

"Stop it! That's enough!" Pru's face went white, almost blue around her lips, and her eyes were directed toward the ceiling.

Barrie hastened to apologize. "I'm sorry. I didn't mean to—"

"What?" Pru gave her a startled glance, and color flooded into her cheeks as if she, too, blushed at every little thing. "No, not you, sugar. It's this hellhole of a house. I can't keep up with everything that breaks around here."

The way Pru's gaze avoided contact suggested she was lying. Or insane. Or possibly both.

Maybe crazy ran in the family, which was par for the course, because Barrie was starting to feel unhinged.

She edged up the stairs to the landing, let her suitcase drop on the scarred floorboards, and opened and closed her hands to get the circulation back. A full-length portrait of a weather-beaten Watson ancestor hung on the wall in front of her in grim detail. A ship sank in a boiling sea behind him. The frame held an inscription that read: *Thomas Watson, 1692.*

"If that suitcase is too heavy for you, you can leave it there on the landing. I'll come back down for it—"

Pru's voice cut off as the doorbell rang. Her hands flew to her cheeks and the tear tracks beneath her reddened eyes. "That'll be Seven. Oh, Lord! I can't let him see me like this."

"Seven?" Barrie asked.

Pru stared down at the front door like she wished it would spontaneously combust. "Beaufort," she said, and Barrie couldn't quite tell if it was a name or a curse. "He handled the papers with Lula's lawyer."

"Mr. Ferguson?"

"Yes, the one who did the will. He—Seven—said he might come by to introduce you to Eight, but he can't know I didn't get you at the airport. He'll think I'm certifiable. Which is what you must be thinking, finding me on the steps like that. Maybe I *am* losing my mind—"

The bell chimed again, and whatever else Pru had been going to say was swallowed by another wave of tears. She looked so small and trapped that Barrie wanted to run and hold her. Which was strange.

Pru wiped her eyes again and vacillated on the step.

Anyone who saw her would know that she'd been crying. What if the lawyer actually thought Pru *was* crazy? He might try to ship Barrie back to San Francisco. Mark would panic all over again—

"It can be our secret," Barrie blurted. "No one has to know. You go hide, Aunt Pru, and I'll get the door and tell them you're in the shower."

Pru gave her a grateful nod. "Ask them to come back after dinner. Say I have to finish the baking for the tearoom, but I'll make a peanut butter whoopie pie cake if they come back later. That always used to work on Seven."

The bell rang for longer this time, and then chimed at short intervals. Barrie waited until Pru was out of sight before walking down to yank the door open.

The Beauforts loomed on the stoop, their shoulders swallowing all the light. The older man, brown-haired and hard-edged, stood poised to jab the bell as though he were used to mashing the world beneath his thumb and making it obey. His green eyes were narrowed in concern. Or maybe temper.

His smile came slowly, but it transformed him enough to make Barrie slightly less inclined to slam the door. "You must be Pru's niece." He held out his hand. "I'm Charles Beaufort— Seven, people call me. And this is Eight, my son."

"Nice to meet you." Barrie shook Seven's hand awkwardly,

and finding another hand thrust out at her, reached for that one too, before she looked up at its owner. Eight grinned down at her, a half-moon flash in his tanned face, electric green eyes blazing as if so much life had been crammed inside him that it was pushing to get out.

Barrie's brain telegraphed an only slightly milder version of the returning click she had felt when she'd first touched the bricks by the gate. The air felt clearer, lighter, as if a layer of static interference had been peeled away.

Whether he felt it or was reacting to her reaction, Eight's slouch and his grin both disappeared. Barrie tried to will herself not to turn the same pink as his rumpled oxford shirt. Her cheeks didn't listen. She pulled back her hand and tucked it behind her, pasting on what she hoped would pass for an honest smile.

"Aunt Pru's in the shower," she said, "and she's behind getting ready for tomorrow. She asked if you could maybe postpone until after dinner. Sorry. That's my fault, not hers. We got to talking, and . . ."

Seven's frown deepened the lines around his eyes. "I was hoping Eight and I could take you both out to eat for your first night here."

"Pru said she'll make you a peanut butter cake if you're willing to come back later," Barrie said, praying he wouldn't argue—he seemed the type to argue.

"One of her whoopie pie cakes?" Seven waited a beat before he continued, "Is eight thirty late enough?"

Barrie gave a manic nod and waved good-bye. Then she closed the door and leaned against it until her legs stopped shaking.

"Was he mad?" Pru leaned over the top of the banister. She suddenly looked too familiar: the curve of her shoulders, the angle of her neck. Barrie had seen her mother peer down from the second floor like that a million times at home.

Lula's twin.

The realization struck Barrie all over again, and she tried to memorize everything about the moment so she could sketch it later. If not for the scars, Lula might have looked like this. Years ago, Barrie's mother might have bent over the upstairs railing here, the same way Pru was leaning over it now. Lula might have looked down to greet whoever had come through the door to stand in the foyer. Maybe she had smiled and been happy to see—who? A boyfriend? A best friend?

For the hundredth time since the reading of her mother's will, Barrie wondered why Lula had left. Why had she run away to San Francisco and stayed there even after the fire that had killed her husband? Why had she let everyone on Watson Island believe she had died too, instead of letting them know she was horribly burned and had a newborn baby she couldn't care for?

The answers had to be here at Watson's Landing. Barrie could find them if she stayed. And however strange it all seemed, she was going to stay. Mark wanted her to. Pru clearly needed someone. No one in all her life had ever needed Barrie before. Not really. Not enough.

She fought to keep her voice even as she spoke to Pru. "They said they'd be back at eight thirty."

"They'll be early. Seven never waits," Pru said, too bitterly for someone discussing dinner plans.

Barrie climbed to the second floor. The staircase opened onto a gallery with corridors on either end leading into the two wings of the house. Pru carried Barrie's suitcase toward the one on the right, but a stomach-clenching sense of loss pulled Barrie in the opposite direction. Rubbing her head, she stopped and peered into the gloom of the unlit corridor.

"Are you coming, sugar?" Pru called behind her.

Barrie edged closer to the hallway. "What's down this way?" she asked.

Her aunt glanced back. "It's best you stay clear of that whole wing up here. It's dangerous, and I haven't gotten around to doing any repairs. Really, there's not much point, when I've got too many rooms to clean as it is."

Barrie studied Pru's back as she followed her aunt down a hallway hung with brooding portraits of more Watson ancestors. Pru's battered Mary Janes moved evenly over the Oriental runners. Didn't she feel the awful pull pulsing from the other end of the house? Or the other pings of loss from behind the closed doors they were passing?

It shouldn't have been possible for anything to be lost at Watson's Landing. But the crushing pull from the other wing faded the farther Barrie walked, and whatever was lost behind the other doors didn't hold much significance. By the time her aunt stopped near the end of the hallway, Barrie could almost forget that the finding gift had exerted itself at all.

Pru threw one of the doors open with a flourish. "This has the best view of all the bedrooms, I think. The French doors open onto the balcony. Your mama used to love to sit out there and watch the river." Fresh tears slipped down her cheeks, and she wiped them away with the back of her hand. "Lord, what a first impression I'm giving you, sugar. I swear, I'm not like this all the time."

"It's all right. Lula was your sister," Barrie said. "I understand."

And maybe for the first time, she was starting to. Learning that Lula had survived the fire must have been a shock after all this time. Especially if Pru had loved her twin.

One phone call. One letter. That was all it would have taken for Lula to spare Pru years of grief.

For that matter, Lula could have come home and gotten help after the fire. Barrie would have given anything to have a sister or a brother. Someone of her own to love and fight with, grow with. So why had Lula thrown away her twin without a second thought?

Barrie stepped into the bedroom. It was even bigger than her old one in San Francisco. Another tattered Oriental rug softened her footsteps, its faded silk colors echoing in the drapes, the embroidered canopy of the four-poster bed, and the two armchairs squatting in the corner. She parked her suitcase beside a desk that held a basket of bougainvillea, which Pru must have picked fresh that morning, and crossed to the balcony. Beyond the French doors, the gardens sprawled toward a marsh and a gleaming river live with birds and singing frogs. Across the water a second mansion commanded a shallow hill.

Eight Beaufort was wrangling a sailboat down at the Watson dock. Unmistakable even from the back, he stooped to untie the lines, then stepped onto the deck and settled himself beside his father, who yanked the outboard motor to life in a puff of smoke.

"This is your closet here. Your bathroom's through there on the right," Pru said. "Be careful with the faucet in the bathtub. It came loose this morning. It should be all right as long as you don't turn it fast or yank it, but make sure the water isn't too hot before you get in. I don't want you scalding yourself."

A yellow Labrador paced the end of the dock across the

river. He gave a bark that Barrie could see but couldn't hear, trying to hurry the Beauforts across. Or warn them away.

"Is that where Seven and Eight live?" Barrie asked as Pru came to stand beside her. "The house over there?"

Pru's gaze fastened on Seven with an expression between pain and hunger. "Yes, that's Beaufort Hall. Now, you should clean up and unpack before they come back. I'll leave you to it and go fix supper."

"And a pie cake," Barrie said, smiling.

"And a pie cake." With a rusty laugh Pru threw her arms around Barrie and gave her a hug. "Oh, I *am* glad you're here, sugar. Lula's daughter. Imagine that."

Pru held her tight, and Barrie felt the returning click again. She stood stiffly at first, then relaxed into the embrace and squeezed back harder than she intended.

"Come down whenever you're ready," Pru said when she pulled away at last. "Turn right at the bottom of the stairs and go to the end of the hallway. That'll be the kitchen." She crossed the room, and her footsteps retreated down the hallway.

Barrie turned back to the French doors and the view. The small boat had crossed the river and pulled alongside the Beaufort dock. Eight jumped out to tie it off while his father hurried toward the house. After meeting Eight with a wagging tail, a dropped ball, and a silent bark, the Labrador bounded away in invitation. Eight picked up the ball from the wooden planks and threw it.

He used a pitcher's throw, arm and leg coming up, his whole body fluid. The dog ran an impossibly long distance before retrieving the ball. Eight meanwhile kicked off his flip-flops and stripped off his shirt. Barrie caught her breath. Eight Beaufort would make any girl catch her breath.

Almost as if he'd heard her thoughts, he looked toward her window. Could he see her all the way from there? Guiltily, as if he'd caught her spying, Barrie ducked back behind the curtains and kept watching.

With the dog at his heels, Eight sprang into a run. He pounded down the dock toward the river, but the dog reached the water first and jumped in with a splash. Eight launched into the air, knees clutched to his chest. Barrie didn't breathe until both he and the dog had bobbed back to the surface. She could almost hear Mark giving that beautiful body a nine on a scale of ten. But only because Mark didn't believe in giving tens.

Mark had to be frantic about her by now. Barrie had to call him. Get it over with. She had so much to hide, she wasn't sure how to keep him from making her confess, but she dug her phone out of her purse and dialed the number.

"It's about damn time," Mark answered. Then his voice turned velvet on a sigh. "You doing all right, baby girl? All settled in? How's your aunt? What did you think of her? Is she anything like Lula?"

"Pru is great," Barrie said. "She seems . . . nice. More grounded than Lula."

"Well, that wouldn't be exactly hard. Now, tell me you're going to be happy. I need you to be happy."

"I love you," Barrie whispered. "I miss you."

There was a long pause, and then Mark said: "I miss you more than you can possibly imagine."

Barrie needed to get a grip. She couldn't let Mark down. Sinking to the floor, she wrapped her arms around her knees as if that would hold her together. "So," she said, channeling cheerful Barbie for all she was worth, "there's not much to tell yet. The house *is* great."

"Ooooh, you have to send me pics. I need to compare it—"

"Compare it to what?" Barrie's trouble-meter pinged to high alert. "What do you know that I don't?" Already she was smiling, picturing Mark's graceful fingers drumming against his leg, impatient to share whatever he was keeping secret. "What are you up to now?"

"I've been going through the attic. Who knew Lula was hoarding stuff up there all these years? Trunks full of clothes, and the shoes . . . Don't even get me started on the shoes. Of course, not a speck of wear on any of them. You should let me send you the shoes."

"Hey—"

"Well, I *know* you two didn't wear the same size, but it's a crime to give shoes like these away."

"You got me plenty of shoes. Now, what else did you find?"

"Oh, no. You deserve to be tortured for making me wait today. Besides, you'll see soon enough. I already mailed it to you. Trust me, you'll be floored when you get the package."

Barrie drank in the excitement in Mark's voice. She could almost believe he was the pre-cancer Mark. The words were only a little breathier, a little weaker.

How much weaker?

Barrie's hands began to shake. She'd been having nightmare thoughts like this ever since Mark had broken the news, since the initial shock and Lula's— Well, after *all* the shocks. How was she supposed to track Mark's decline from clear across the country? How was she supposed to know how much time he had left? She hadn't even seen how sick he was when she'd been right there with him.

If she had noticed and made him go to the doctor sooner . . . If they had caught the cancer earlier . . .

But the doctor had said that pancreatic cancer had hardly any symptoms. Not until it had been too late to save Mark. Why did it have to be too late? How was that even fair?

Barrie pushed back the questions that only left her bleeding. She couldn't help Mark anymore. She could help her aunt, though. The idea sprang fully formed into Barrie's head, and she blurted it out before she could reason it through or ask Pru if it would be all right.

"Is it too late to cancel the auction?" she asked. "I think I want Lula's things."

"I said you would regret not taking anything. I've got just a few more closets to sort through, and the rest of the attic. Tell me what you want."

"Everything. The furniture. Lula's clothes. Don't sort anything else. Just call the movers and have them take it all."

"Is that going to be okay with your aunt?" The phone line crackled, as if Barrie's words had knocked the connection off frequency. "Is there even room?"

Barrie couldn't explain what the place was like. The loose banister, the falling shutter, the broken faucet. Pru had talked about cleaning the house herself. Barrie could help with that, but if they had Lula's furniture, they could replace the scratched and faded stuff, sell whatever was left, and use that money to fix Watson's Landing. It was a great idea. Best of all, it wouldn't involve lawyers or the complicated trust fund Lula had left for her.

"I'd like to go through Lula's things myself," she said. "I know I said I didn't care, and I'm a pain in the ass—"

"Yeah, you are."

"But I'm *your* pain in the ass. So you'll do it?" In the long silence Barrie imagined Mark pursing his mouth and drawing slow circles on the table with his crimson-tipped index finger.

"You know I'll make it work," he said, "if you're sure it's what you want."

Pain sliced through Barrie, a bitter blue pang of homesickness and nostalgia and guilt. "*Please* let me come back and take care of you," she said, breaking all her resolutions again. "Don't make me stay away. I don't mind going to the hospice, and I don't mind coming back here after school has started."

"We've been over this a hundred times, baby girl. I need to know you're settled before I . . . go. And I have no intention of letting you change my diapers and fluff my pillows while I gasp out my last breaths on a morphine drip. Anyway, it's all arranged. I even won a vintage bed jacket on eBay this morning. I'll be the best-dressed queen in the place, and I'll be as happy as a . . . Hell, I don't know what's happy anymore. Clams sure aren't. But I'll make friends. Imagine that! I'll finally have people my own age to talk to."

Barrie pressed her fist to her mouth to block the sob bubbling up her throat.

"I'll be happy knowing you are happy," Mark said. "So concentrate on settling in like I asked. Get ready for your senior year. Art classes, boys, homecoming, college applications, prom, graduation. All that. You promised, remember?"

Across the river, Eight Beaufort pulled himself onto the dock and tossed his hair to get the water out. Beside him the dog shook all over, while Eight threw his head back, laughing.

"I've found a hottie already," Barrie said, turning from the window. "Dark hair, acres of shoulders. You'd love him."

"Prove it. Send me pictures. Put some wear and tear on those shoes of yours for me."

"All the places you've always wanted to go. I know," Barrie said. "I won't forget my promise."

CHAPTER THREE

The armoire smelled of jasmine and magnolias from the sachets Pru had left inside it. Trying to shove the conversation with Mark out of her head, Barrie set a speed record for unpacking and stowed her empty suitcases in the corner of the room. Then she washed her face and headed toward the stairs.

Every sound seemed magnified. Watson's Landing was quieter than Lula's house. No soap operas emoted from Mark's television; no beach music bounced defiantly under the door of Lula's room. There was only the reverberation of Barrie's heels and the groan of old wood, as if the house itself protested her intrusion. Even the portraits hanging along the hall looked disapproving.

She paused at the top of the steps, where the pull from the unoccupied wing grew sickeningly strong. What kind of lost thing created an ache like that? Barrie stared down the dark hallway, fighting the need to go investigate.

How could Pru ignore this feeling? Walk past it day in and day out, as if she didn't even feel it?

Was it possible Pru didn't have the gift? Barrie had no idea how it passed from one family member to another. Maybe it didn't go to everyone.

There were so many things she didn't know. Even worse, she suspected she didn't know what she didn't know. Which made it hard to look for answers.

She clomped down the staircase without touching the banister, trying not to make too much noise but sounding like a six-legged horse in spite of herself. At the bottom, she turned down a long wood-paneled corridor. The scent of ground beef, tomato, onion, garlic, and oregano led her through a swinging door into a time warp of a kitchen that hadn't been updated since whenever avocado-ugly had still been in style.

"I was beginning to think the house had swallowed you, sugar." Pru glanced over her shoulder as she stirred a pot bubbling on the antique stove. "Did you find everything all right? Are you all unpacked?"

"Yes, thanks. Should I set the table?"

"That would be wonderful. The plates and glasses are there." Pru pointed to a nearby cabinet with the spoon, splattering red sauce on the floor. "The silver is through the door in the butler's pantry. Third drawer on the right, opposite the freezer."

The pantry was larger than Barrie had expected. A swinging door on the opposite end led into the tearoom, which was empty except for linen-covered tables and shelves lined with sweetgrass baskets, small art prints, and various jars of jams and pickled vegetables for sale.

Barrie let the door fall closed again and retrieved the forks and knives. Those were actual silver, the same familiar pattern she had eaten with all her life. The blue and white plates she took from the kitchen cabinet were identical to Lula's too, as if her mother had tried to re-create Watson's Landing in San Francisco, only newer, better, less damaged.

There was nothing new in Pru's kitchen. No dishwasher or microwave, nothing modern. As for damage, one of the cabinets had a hole where the knob would have screwed in, and two of the drawer pulls were missing. On the back door the lock had torn free and now dangled uselessly from the security chain. It all had an air of faded respectability that was only underscored by the spotless cloth and cut-glass vase of apricot roses Pru had placed on the round oak table.

The more Barrie saw of Watson's Landing, the more she was glad she had asked Mark to send Lula's things. But how was she supposed to tell Pru she had arranged to have a houseful of furniture delivered? That would sound like she thought what Pru had here wasn't good enough, which wasn't what she'd meant at all. And she'd had no right to make arrangements on Pru's behalf.

"I didn't know what kind of food you would like." Pru brought a bowl of steaming noodles and meatballs to the table and settled herself across from Barrie. "I hope you're all right with pasta. To be honest, it's not much fun cooking for myself. I usually eat whatever's left over from the tearoom."

"I could help—I love to cook."

"I'll bet a Sunday supper it wasn't Lula who taught you that."

"No." Barrie almost smiled. She couldn't imagine Lula near a stove. "Mark and I had a weekend ritual where we'd order takeout from a restaurant and try to copy the recipe. Between that and watching the Cooking Channel, I'm pretty good. I could help you in the tearoom. Or clean, do dishes. Whatever."

"Just keep your own things in order, sugar. That'll be plenty. Don't worry. There's not as much work as you'd think. The garden takes care of itself, and Mary comes in at noon to handle the tearoom. One way or another the work all gets done."

"But I honestly don't mind."

"Why don't you take time to settle in before we decide anything? September will be here before you can blink. Do you have any of your school shopping done yet?" Pru glanced dubiously at Barrie's purple heels. "The kids might not wear the same clothes as they do in San Francisco. We tend less toward fancy and more toward comfortable around here."

Comfortable? Barrie wasn't going to be comfortable no matter what she wore. The thought of school practically made her start to hyperventilate, and these shoes and the rest of her clothes would be the last things she and Mark ever bought together. Spaghetti slithered off her fork faster than she could wind it around.

"Mark is sending all my things," she said. And Lula's. She tried to scrape up the courage to say those two little words aloud.

How would Pru react? Barrie needed to call Mark and tell him she had changed her mind. Except she hadn't. She wanted Lula's things, and Pru needed Lula's things, even if Pru didn't know it yet.

The click of silver on porcelain was like a metronome counting out the silence. Looking up, Barrie found her aunt watching her with the fixed stare of someone who isn't seeing the present.

Barrie cleared her throat. "This is wonderful spaghetti, Aunt Pru."

Pru shook her head as if mentally changing the subject. "Good. That's good," she said. "Now, did Lula ever mention

Mary to you? I'm sure she must have, and the woman's been like a cat on hot bricks ever since she found out you were coming."

"Mary?" Barrie stiffened at the thought of more stray relatives she'd never heard of. "Is she another aunt?"

"She used to work here at the house, back when your mama and I were little. But Lula was always her favorite. Mary'll tell you all kinds of stories about the trouble your mother would get up to."

"I can't picture Lula getting into trouble. Were you identical twins?"

"Lord, no. Lula got all the looks in the family—and she was always the first to say so. I can't imagine she'd have changed that much. Did you bring any pictures with you?"

Barrie stared at her aunt in shock, then hastily looked away. Pru didn't know about the scars, she realized. But of course Pru couldn't know. Unless the lawyer had mentioned it, and why would he?

Barrie reached for her glass and set it back down again when she discovered her hand was shaking. How did she even start to explain?

Lula would *never* have let a camera near her. Barrie had always known that her mother's scars had to be bad, but she hadn't *understood*. Not until the paramedics had taken off the wig and veil after the heart attack while trying to save Lula's life.

The scars, the tight plastic skin . . . Barrie laced her hands painfully in her lap.

"There aren't any pictures," she said, her voice sounding thick and swollen. "I don't have any."

"Oh. Well," Pru said, too brightly, "it doesn't matter. I'm sure she never looked much different than she did the last time I saw her. Lula was always primping—that's what Daddy used to call it. Did she show you the pictures of herself in her pageant tiaras? I don't even know if she took any of those with her."

Even a simple "no" wouldn't slide past the knot forming in Barrie's throat.

"She was homecoming queen, too." Pru paused with her fork in midair. "I can't get over how long ago it all was. The days slip into one another. You blink, and a year has passed, and next thing you know, decades are gone." The fork clattered against her plate.

"Maybe you could show me some pictures of you two growing up," Barrie said.

"The historical society or someone in town should have a yearbook. I could ask."

Barrie leaned forward. "What about here? Photographs? Anything."

"Daddy threw all that away. Anything with Lula in it." Pru's eyes met Barrie's, then slid to the clock on the wall. "Lord, would you look at the time? Seven and Eight will be here in a few minutes, and I haven't started on that whoopie pie cake. I'll have to use something from the freezer."

She scurried toward the butler's pantry. Barrie stared after her, then carried the dishes from the table to the counter. Turning the tap to hot, she let the water run while she squeezed a green stream of soap into the sink.

It was too quiet in the other room. Finally the freezer slammed, and Pru emerged red-eyed with a foil-wrapped package glazed in frost, which she set down on the counter.

"Oh, don't you worry about these." Pru nudged her aside. "Go sit down. Relax. I have to let the cake thaw a few minutes anyway."

"At least let me dry."

Outside, the light was fading. Pru's bent head reflected in the window as she scraped spaghetti into the trash.

"Mr. Fergusen mentioned a heart attack," she said, so softly, Barrie almost couldn't hear it. "Did Lula suffer much?"

Barrie sucked in a breath, trying to think about how to answer that. How much did Pru need to know? In her shoes, would Barrie have wanted to know the truth?

Hip braced against the counter, Barrie twisted the soft cotton cloth between her fingers. "How much did Lula's lawyer tell you?" she asked.

Pru glanced at her sharply. "What about?"

"About the fire that killed my father." The dishcloth was wound so tight in Barrie's fingers, the skin on her knuckles turned pale. She let it go and concentrated on smoothing it against her thigh. "Lula was in the bedroom when it started. She tried to climb out to the fire escape, but she was eight months pregnant with me. She couldn't get the window open far enough. Her hair and clothes burned before the firemen reached her. Even after all the surgeries . . . The scars, the way she looked—"

"The way she looked?" Pru slowly repeated Barrie's words. "Her hair . . . her *face?* Oh, Lord. No." The plate slipped from her hands and shattered on the floor. She swayed as her knees gave out.

Barrie lunged to catch her aunt. She struggled to hold Pru up, but the dead weight carried them both to the ground. Pru burrowed her face in Barrie's shoulder, shuddering with silent tears.

"Here, let me get her." Seven's deep voice came from the kitchen door, along with a whisper of cooling air. Footsteps scratched on the broken porcelain, and he raised Pru to her feet. "What have you done to yourself now, woman? Look at you. You're bleeding." He guided Pru to the table and lowered her into the nearest chair. Accepting the napkin Barrie had hurriedly dampened, he dabbed at the cuts on Pru's knees and the blood running in rivulets down her shins.

There had to be clean towels somewhere. Barrie turned

to search for them, and pulled up short when she saw Eight standing in the open doorway watching Pru and Seven with narrow-eyed intensity. When he caught Barrie looking at him, he pushed a hand through his thatch of sun-streaked hair and gave her a grin that lit him up.

"Hello again," he said.

The greeting might as well have been in Swahili. Barrie's tongue wouldn't cooperate to answer. She nodded and made herself keep moving until she had found a clean towel and handed it to Seven.

He wiped Pru's knees again, then sat back on his heels so he and Pru were eye level. "Thank goodness none of these cuts are deep enough for stitches, but I'd like to put a butterfly bandage on a couple of them. Do you still keep the first aid kit in the butler's pantry?"

"On the counter by the door," Pru said.

"I'll go get it." Eight hurried across the kitchen.

Seven's attention was still on Pru. His eyes slid from her trembling lip to the hands she was folding and unfolding. His heart was naked, the way Pru's had been when she'd watched him from the upstairs window. Then he surged up to tower over Pru as if he'd suddenly turned into a different person.

"Now, do you want to tell me what harebrained thing you were thinking, woman, kneeling in broken china?"

"What?" Pru stood and snatched the bloodstained towel

from his hand. "I did it to give you something to complain about, of course. Knowing you were coming over and how much you like to play white knight and all."

"You know that isn't what I meant—"

"Then what? You thought I'd stop crying if you insulted me? You never could stand to see a woman cry. I haven't forgotten that."

His voice dropped in warning. "Pru—"

"Don't," she said. "Don't you start."

"Then talk to me. We can do better than this."

"Can we? I thought we were friends once."

"We are friends."

"We were. Twenty years ago. But clearly my father was right."

Barrie backed away as they argued, wishing herself invisible the way she had wished herself invisible a million times when Lula had screamed at Mark. It wasn't until Eight came out of the pantry carrying the box of first aid supplies that either Pru or Seven appeared to remember they had an audience. Pru gave Seven a pointed stare and nodded in Barrie's direction.

Seven didn't take his eyes off Pru. "Eight," he said, "I don't think Barrie's had a chance to see the gardens yet. You should show her."

"Don't you go anywhere, Barrie, sugar. You stay right

here with me." Pru looked stricken, determined, and mad all at once.

Eight dropped the box onto the table beside his father so fast, a roll of gauze bounced out. He crossed the kitchen and gestured Barrie toward the door. "Come on. I'll show you the path down to the river."

Barrie's knees locked in indecision, remembering Pru's earlier panic.

"In case you haven't picked up on our quaint local customs yet, that was our cue to get out and let them talk."

Eight stood so close, Barrie could feel his words on her cheek and smell his skin, like cloves and cherries and root beer. He held the door open and followed her outside to the terrace.

Their arms brushed. Barrie jerked away.

Did he feel it too? The *not*-lostness when they touched? Or was she the only one?

"Shhh," he said. "Quit moving around. I can't hear what they're saying." He hadn't quite closed the kitchen door behind them, and he motioned Barrie out of the line of sight while he ducked flat against the house to listen.

"You came out here to eavesdrop?"

"Like you've never done it."

Barrie shook her head. Mark and Lula's fights had always been knock-down, drag-out loud with no concern for privacy.

41

"Seriously?" Eight grinned down at her. "Knowing everybody's business is practically a point of pride around here. You must have been raised by nuns or something."

Barrie thought of Mark in the Halloween costume he always trotted out in when they watched *Sister Act*. Mark doing his Whoopi-Goldberg-as-Deloris impression, arms up and butt out, shaking all six-foot-two-plus-heels of himself to "Hail Holy Queen." A barrage of different emotions, too many to process, all punched Barrie at once. She rushed across the brick-covered terrace to get away from Eight, from the memory.

"Hey, hold on." Eight hurried after her. "I'm sorry. Whatever I said, I didn't mean it."

"Just leave me alone." Barrie's footsteps quickened. She heard him behind her, then beside her again, but she didn't stop. She wasn't going to be responsible for anything that came out of her mouth just then.

She didn't want to be at Watson's Landing listening to other people's arguments. Dropped into lives already in progress, like a television program she'd switched on halfway through. Lives that had nothing to do with her. She wanted to be home with Mark. Except *home* didn't exist anymore. Did she even know what the word meant? Had she ever known?

She walked faster, rushing past the tearoom in the glassed-in portion of the porch, down a lighted staircase to the lower terrace, and into a maze made up of low boxwood hedges. Eight's leather flip-flops smacked the soles of his feet beside her, and crunched as the brick walkway became an oyster-shell-and-gravel path leading to a three-tiered fountain at the maze's center.

He was there to steady her when she tripped. "Where exactly are you going?" he asked.

Where *was* she going? Barrie took deep breaths to ward off panic. Too much in her life was never going to be the same. Too much was new and strange.

Even the garden looked arcane. Hundreds, thousands of fairy lights winked along the terraces and glowed among the trees, casting macabre shadows on the ground. Beyond the hedges, the river had turned the color of nothing in the twilight, mirroring the emptiness Barrie felt inside. But downstream, closer to where the Santisto emptied into the ocean, the lights of a subdivision were already coming on, spilling gold and red reflections like wounds across the water.

There was no escape by the river, and too much light in the maze. Barrie veered across the lawn, giving in to the pull of the darkened woods.

CHAPTER FOUR

"Wait." Trying to make eye contact with Barrie, Eight walked backward across the grass. "Would you please stop? I'm a jackass, okay? Don't be mad. Come back to the house. Whatever I said, I'm sorry."

He was apologizing, but he looked confused. He deserved to be confused. Barrie herself didn't know what she was doing. Running with nowhere to go. Running from herself.

"You're fine," she said on a long, slow sigh. "It's been a nightmare week."

Instead of relaxing, Eight's face creased, and he stuffed his hands into the pockets of his shorts. "You haven't had a chance to process yet. Dad says I holed up in a closet for three weeks after my mother died." He turned to walk beside her, his shoulders hunched up as if to deflect the memory, and it took him a few beats before he continued: "I was ten. Apparently they hauled me out once in a while, hosed me off, fed me, and let me crawl back in because they knew I needed time."

Did his mother's death still hurt as much? Or did dead-motherness eventually wear off?

For Barrie, Lula's death was all tangled up with Mark's cancer. She couldn't say where grief ended for one and started for the other, grief and love and unfairness. Why Mark? Why either of them?

"At least you knew your mother. You know how to remember her." The words came from the scraped-out, dark place inside Barrie. "I'll bet she was wonderful, wasn't she? The kind of mother who baked oatmeal cookies. Put cartoon character Band-Aids on your knees. Walked you to the bus stop every morning. Or do you not have bus stops around here?"

Eight's chin lifted, but the rest of him stilled to attention. "I take it your mother wasn't like that."

"Lula? No." Barrie's breath hitched on the last syllable and she paused beside him. "She was the kind of mother who locked herself in her room and surfed online auctions for designer clothes no one would ever see her wear because she hadn't left the house in seventeen years. The kind who didn't let anyone, not even me, see her scars. Who didn't tell her twin sister she was still alive. Who dropped dead of a heart attack when her best friend—her only friend—told her he was dying of cancer, so she wasn't there for him the one time he really needed her."

Grinding to a halt, she shook her head. Eight's mouth hung open—literally open, like a fish on a hook. He probably thought she was psycho. She rubbed her temple to relieve the pressure.

"Okay. You have a little baggage." Eight rocked back on his heels.

"You have *no* idea."

"Come here." He pulled her against him gently, and held her. His heart beat, strong and steady, against her ear until her breathing and her own heart slowed and the world shifted back to solid beneath her feet.

How had she not realized how furious she was at Lula? For dying and stealing the last months of Mark's life. For dying and leaving only unanswered questions to mark her passing.

"I thought I was doing okay," Barrie whispered.

There had been so much to do. Making funeral arrangements. Finding the hospice. Dreading the days until she had to say good-bye to Mark. Struggling not to run back to him as she shuffled between too many people in the long security line at the airport. Trying not to hyperventilate when she was buckled into her seat and forced to sit still while the plane took off.

She had been fine until she'd stopped moving.

She couldn't stop moving. If she stopped, the loss, the change, the newness, would all catch up with her. Head down, refusing to look at Eight, she set herself in motion again. One foot and then the other.

"What was going on back there in the kitchen anyway?" she asked, because Eight was still watching her with a puzzled expression. "What were you hoping to overhear?"

"Explanations," he said, as if he'd expected the change of subject. "There's no way my dad should have known where to find the first aid kit. Or that Pru should have known peanut butter whoopie pie cake is Dad's favorite dessert."

"So? They were friends."

"That's just it. I don't think they were. Or they shouldn't have been."

"Why not?" Barrie asked, and when he didn't answer right away, she paused to study him, which wasn't a hardship by any means. His solid jaw was a little stubborn, but it spoke of steadiness, and in contrast his eyes were kind. And worried.

He smiled abashedly when he caught her watching, and gave a one-shouldered shrug. "You have to understand. Watson Island is all about history, and the Beauforts and Watsons had been friends since the Stone Age. But that ended when my great-aunt Twila ran off with your great-uncle Luke. As far as I know, until your aunt called my dad about the legal work for your move, they hadn't spoken since they were in school together. Not that anyone speaks to your aunt very much."

"What? Why?" It was an odd way to phrase it.

"No one sees her much." Eight took a moment to arrange his thoughts. "Look, from what I've heard, Emmett—your grandfather—was strange after Twila left. The two of them had been engaged, but Twila broke it off to run away with Emmett's brother. Then when Lula took off too, someone else running away from him, I guess Emmett really lost it. They all holed up here on the plantation, and no one saw much of them after that." He paused, and his lips tipped in a wry smile. "Now it's your turn. Why was your aunt kneeling on broken china?"

He had the whole good-guy thing down to an art; Barrie had to hand it to him. He walked beside her without pressing her, as if he knew she needed space, as if he knew exactly what she needed. Which probably meant he wasn't a good guy at all.

"Pru didn't know Lula was scarred from the fire that killed my father. I knew she'd been gorgeous before the fire; Mark told me that much. But I never stopped to wonder what it had to be like for her to go from being beautiful to having those awful scars. The way Pru reacted, it was as if being pretty was all Lula cared about."

"Was it?"

"I don't know. I didn't know her well enough." It was hard to admit that to herself, much less to say it aloud. "I didn't even know she grew up here. That she had a twin or any relatives."

"There might have been a reason she kept it quiet."

"What do you mean?" Barrie stopped walking.

"Your grandfather told everyone she died in the fire that killed your father."

"Are you saying he knew she didn't? That he knew she was alive?"

"I'm not sure I know what I'm saying. Except that either there's an empty casket in the Watson cemetery or they buried someone else in your mother's place."

"Mistaken identity," Barrie said.

But that made no sense either. There had been only two people in the fire.

Eight pushed his hands deeper into his pockets. "Emmett would have had to go out to San Francisco to provide an identification. Or he sent them DNA or dental records. Something. They wouldn't have shipped the wrong body all the way out here for the funeral."

The droning buzz of mosquitoes had grown loud in Barrie's ears. "How do you know there even *was* a funeral?" she asked.

"Because this is Watson Island. Everyone around here knows everything about everyone. Especially about you. About *us*. The three founding families. We're the island's favorite hobby."

Barrie rubbed her temples with clammy fingers. The ache

had become too insistent to ignore, but it was more than the horror of Eight's words making her head hurt. Something lost had been pulling on her Watson senses.

"Hey! What are you doing?" Eight blocked her path before she could set off toward the trees. "You can't go into the woods."

"Why not?"

His jaw clenched and then unclenched. His eyes slid toward the right.

As a tell, that was damning. You could never trust a guy who told a lie too fast or a truth too slow—Mark had taught Barrie that. Of course, there was a third option. A slow lie, the kind that made it clear the teller was winging it as he went. Barrie suspected Eight was too experienced a liar for that.

He nodded toward her shoes. "You aren't dressed to play in the woods at night," he said, "and there are snakes, and alligators that come up from the river. Anyway, your aunt will be wanting us back."

The truth. Too much truth, and told too slow.

All right, so he was not a natural liar. But finding pull or not, it *was* darker beneath the trees. And Barrie was no fan of snakes.

Eight's eyes caught hers. He studied her, keenly, strangely, as though he were reading what was going on inside her. No one had ever looked at her like that. As if she held the answers to the mysteries of the universe, every star, moon, and planet. Then his face shuttered tight, and he strode toward the house.

Moisture sprang to Barrie's eyes, turning the fairy lights into shimmering ribbons. God, why couldn't she stop wanting to cry? As if Eight didn't already think she was a nutcase. She curled her fingers into her palms and dug in deep, exhaling and willing herself calm. It helped when the pressure in her head grew fainter as they left the woods behind and approached the boxwood maze.

In the open, the shadows had deepened on the ground, and the river had become a Turner painting of liquid moonlight. Between Beaufort Hall and the subdivision downstream, an engine sputtered. Eight stopped walking and turned toward the sound.

A darkened speedboat glided toward an almost invisible dock. On the hill above it, spotlights lit the skeleton of another mansion: three jagged chimneys, wide stairs, and eight tall, white columns, partially blocked from view by a stage or some kind of scaffolding. Farther back on the property the windows of a smaller house glowed like eyes.

The ruined mansion would have been eerie anywhere. Downriver from Beaufort Hall, downriver from Watson's Landing, it reminded Barrie of the aftermath of a tornado. Damage with no context, no reason, no logic. Two great houses survived while a third lay crushed and broken.

"You mentioned three founding families," she said. "I assume that meant three plantations. Is that what those ruins are?"

"Eight? Barrie? Come on back. You've been out long enough." Seven's voice carried across the garden.

Eight had been scowling, but at the sound of Seven's voice, he broke his stare and took Barrie's hand again.

She was sick of nonanswers. Tired of him pulling her around. She folded her arms across her chest. "Why can't you answer a simple question?"

"It's complicated—"

"Nothing's that complicated."

"It's Colesworth Place." He watched her expectantly while he said the name.

"Colesworth?" Barrie's mental landscape shook with the rumble of things falling into place. How had she not guessed? "So my father grew up here too? He and Lula went out to San Francisco together?"

"You didn't know?" He looked at her with sympathy that set her teeth on edge.

The idea of her mother and father eloping together made no sense within the context of Lula's hatred. Barrie shook her head, and the movement didn't feel connected to her, as if she weren't controlling her motions.

"What happened to the mansion?"

"Burned by Yankees. Sherman on his march to Columbia. Wyatt—that's your uncle, your father's brother—is trying to rebuild it, which is certifiably crazy."

Eight's pity made Barrie feel even smaller than usual. She was used to being small, and not unused to being pitied, but coming from Eight, with his beautiful-boy, pink-shirted confidence, it was hard to take.

"Don't look at me like that. I don't know anything, okay? My mother didn't tell me anything about this place."

The lighted ruins shone against the sky. Barrie could almost picture the mansion burning.

It struck her that fire had been a theme in her father's life. Maybe that was appropriate. Lula had always said she'd hoped Wade burned in hell.

Her mother had seen to it that Barrie was officially, legally, a Watson, so it was only Barrie's first name, her real name—Lombard—that served as a reminder of Lula's bitterness. Lombard, after San Francisco's crooked street, and in memory of Wade Colesworth, Barrie's crooked father. Lula had meant the name as a warning, according to Mark, a reminder not to fall in love with charming, deceitful men.

"Does Wyatt have any family?" Barrie asked.

Eight put his hands back into his pockets. Another delaying gesture.

"Please? Tell me." Barrie had never had family. Only

Mark, who counted for everything but blood, and Lula, who'd counted for blood and not much else. Now there was Pru, and an uncle . . .

Eight waited another beat, then two, as if he couldn't decide, and just when she thought he wasn't going to answer at all, he sighed. "Your cousin Cassie will be in your class next year," he said. "Sydney's a year younger, so she'll be a junior."

Two cousins. Girls. Sisters. Barrie's toes gave a little bounce. "What are they like? Do they know about me? I can't wait to meet them."

"Hold on. I wouldn't count on being friends with them."

"Why not?"

Eight cast a skeptical glance at his father's long frame silhouetted by the light spilling from the kitchen. "Can you please stop dawdling and come back to the house?"

Barrie started walking. Eight fell in beside her, his strides slowed to match her shorter ones. "Basically, think of any feud you can name. Montagues and Capulets, Hatfields and McCoys. It was Colesworths versus Watsons and Beauforts around here for three hundred years, before Luke Watson and Twila Beaufort ran off. Now it's just the Colesworths against everybody else in town."

He glanced at her, gauging her reaction, but she didn't really know what to think. "It all sounds very hyped up, but kind of romantic. Very Romeo and Juliet," she said. "Anyway, what does any of it have to do with my cousins?"

Eight tensed, and if he wasn't good at deceiving, he was even worse at hiding how he felt. "Don't dismiss it just because it sounds silly. You haven't lived here long enough to understand. The Colesworths have been pissed off for centuries, so they're dangerous. And Wyatt has been asking questions about you and Lula. Dad thinks he's hoping to get his hands on Lula's money—your money—since he's your uncle. That would be the typical Colesworth reaction. Figuring the angle, working out what's in it for them."

Mist from the fountain cooled on Barrie's skin. "You do realize I'm a Colesworth too?"

"That isn't what I meant."

"What did you mean?"

"You're different."

Different. And there it was.

All her life Barrie had been on the receiving end of *different*. Even once she'd learned to disguise the Watson gift, she'd still been the daughter of a woman who stood at the window and glared at people on the street from behind a curtain. The goddaughter of the ex-drag-queen who went to parent-teacher conferences dressed in vintage suits and designer shoes. Barrie had been judged or pitied by strangers, by teachers, by parents, and by classmates. By people she had hoped would be her friends. Being a Watson, being herself, had been hard enough that it had barely occurred to her that she wasn't just a Watson.

Eight cut her off when she tried to walk around him. "I meant different from Wyatt, that's all. Finding out about the Colesworths doesn't mean anything has changed."

Everything had changed.

And how did Eight always know exactly what she was thinking? Was it written on her face in Magic Marker? "I still want to meet my cousins," she said.

"Don't push it. Your aunt and my dad would have a fit."

"Come on. It's a small town. We're bound to bump into them by accident. Or we can make it an accident. Where do they hang out?"

Barrie waited for Eight to answer, but he seemed lost in thought. How was it possible for him to have so much life inside him and go so still? As if he were taking her apart, weighing the individual pieces, memorizing them, and putting her back together.

"Please?" she asked. "Help me meet them, or I'll have to figure out another way." She wasn't going to let ancient history get in the way of family.

"You realize my dad will skin me alive when he finds out. And he will find out. You're sure you want to do this?" He ran a hand across the back of his neck and watched Barrie until she nodded. "Fine. Cassie works at a restaurant in town. I'll take you there for lunch tomorrow."

CHAPTER FIVE

Too anxious to sleep, Barrie carried her sketchbook out onto the balcony. Sitting on the rough-painted wooden slats, she leaned back against the house and let the magnolia-scented night settle in around her. Across the river, the lights of Beaufort Hall shone steadily on the hill, and the ruins of the house downriver shone like jewels lit to tempt a thief.

The idea startled Barrie. Was it the sneaking around behind Pru's back that bothered her?

There hadn't been any actual sneaking yet. Pru had gone to bed with a headache by the time Barrie and Eight had made it back to the kitchen, and Seven had been too focused on getting home to ask many questions.

Barrie thought about meeting Cassie, and it made her smile. Cousins. She had two cousins. Possibly more, if Luke

Watson and Twila Beaufort had children somewhere. Those cousins would be related to both Eight and Barrie, which seemed strange since she and Eight weren't related to each other. She kind of liked that, though, the idea that she and Eight were linked in some way. She found a clean sheet of paper and started drawing a family tree to show connections between relatives she had never—until today—even heard of.

The more she sketched, the more certain Barrie became that meeting Cassie wasn't wrong, whatever Eight or Pru might think. She and her cousins weren't responsible for anything that had happened between the families before they'd been born. Barrie wanted, needed, to stay at Watson's Landing until she graduated. If she and Cassie were going to live in the same small town, be in the same class, they couldn't be enemies.

Pru was going to be furious, though, wasn't she? If Barrie went behind her back. Mad enough to send Barrie away?

Lula would have.

How much was Pru like Lula?

Below the balcony the river sparkled in the glow of the moon and a breeze stirred the leaves and sent the shadows racing. Barrie tried to sketch the scene: the dock, the marsh grass, the river flowing toward the ocean. Her pencil refused to behave, and the round face of the moon became Pru's face. The moss hanging from the trees turned into an image of Lula

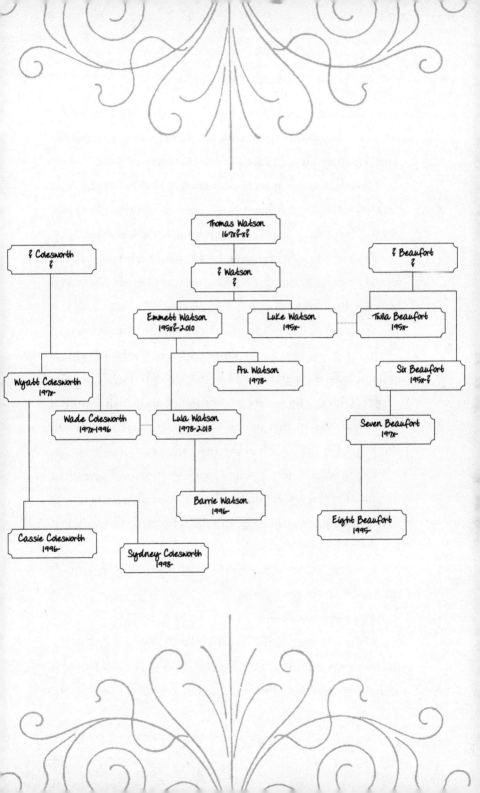

in her concealing veils. Even the picture of the dock showed a boy and a dog jumping off into the water. Barrie tore out the page, crumpled it, and threw it onto the balcony floor.

Downstairs, the grandfather clock tolled midnight. The light reflecting on the water brightened, as if a thin cloud had cleared the moon. Except no clouds hung in the star-dusted sky.

The night turned orange and gold, and even brighter. Barrie leaned forward, grasping the railing to steady herself. She pulled herself to her knees.

Where the edge of the marsh skirted the Watson woods, a ball of fire hovered a foot above the river, shedding threads of flame onto the water like a ball of yarn unrolling. The river grew brighter. The sphere grew smaller and smaller until a faint glow was all that remained where it floated in midair. But behind it, the river had been cast aflame.

Barrie closed her eyes and reopened them. The railing dug into her fingers, reminding her that she wasn't dreaming. The flaking paint crumbled, and the splintered wood pricked her skin. She *wasn't* dreaming. She wasn't.

So what, then? What was it? Ball lightning? A will-o'-the-wisp? Marsh gas igniting?

The river was *burning*.

Flames blanketed the water from the Watson side to the midpoint between Watson's Landing and Beaufort Hall, as if an invisible wall kept the fire from burning all the way across.

Both the flames and the unseen barrier ran upstream as far as Barrie could see, and downstream almost to the Colesworth dock, where the fire turned inland at the shallow creek and blazed toward the wooden bridge.

Barrie jumped to her feet. She had to call someone. Alert the fire department. But there was no smoke. No burning smell. No sound of flames crackling in the quiet night. A hallucination, then? Too much excitement?

Or too much Watson crazy.

It was beautiful, whatever it was, and it compelled, *impelled*, Barrie closer. She tiptoed along the balcony. The old wood creaked, the sound impossibly loud in the stillness. Not that a hallucination would pay attention.

And yet, it did.

A shadowed figure of a man took shape where no one had been before. Lit by the flames on the river, he stood in three-quarter profile, and the sputtering ember, all that remained of the fireball, was cupped in his hands. A cloak of black feathers covered his back and shoulders, and a matching feathered headdress melded into his long, dark hair.

He turned suddenly and looked at Barrie—straight *into* her—with eyes that were only lighter spots in a face painted with a war mask of black and red. Barrie felt the stare. Felt him searching inside her, weighing her the way Eight had weighed her earlier, though that was impossible.

How could she see eyes, features, from this distance?

She couldn't breathe until the figure turned away. Then she blinked and he was gone, leaving only the burning river and the remaining wisps of the sphere hovering in the air.

Her heart was a drumbeat in her throat, war drums pounding, pounding a retreat. The fire on the water shimmered, flared higher, then surged back toward the shore, converging where the figure had been and spooling itself into a dense, fiery ball. When the sphere was once more as bright and large as it had been when it started, the river was dark except for the drifting moonlight. The fireball hovered for another breathless moment, then floated slowly back into the Watson woods and wove itself between the trees.

Whatever spell had held Barrie in place released her. She raced to the far end of the balcony, suddenly desperate to keep the fire in sight. But it moved deeper into the woods, illuminating the trees and underbrush, and creating illusions of eerily moving shadows as it passed.

She rubbed her arms, leaning over the balcony and craning her head to keep the light in view. Eventually she lost sight of it. Or it vanished. Or the flames went out.

Had it been there at all? Flames on the river. Under the water. Rushes in the marsh that glowed but never burned. A ghostly hallucination that reacted to her—interacted with her.

She hurried back into her room and latched the door to

the balcony behind herself, as if she could lock out the memory of the river on fire, shut out everything that had happened since Mark had made his cancerous announcement. It was all too much. She had to be going crazy. Maybe there was something in the air here that made people hallucinate.

No wonder Lula had run away.

Shivering despite the summer heat, she crawled into bed and huddled with the quilt wrapped around her, watching the river, waiting for the water to turn to fire again. The clock chimed one, then two, and the moon and stars cast the only light.

She dreamed. The river and the marsh were burning, and Lula was screaming, running from the flames, always a few steps out of Barrie's reach.

CHAPTER SIX

Waking up on West Coast time, Barrie's eyes were gummy, and nightmares had left her brain feeling bruised. Her first thought was about caffeine. She needed coffee. Vats of it.

Still in her sleep shirt and pajama shorts, she pushed through the swinging door into an empty kitchen. A plate of croissants, a basket of tea bags, a thermos of coffee, and a note from Pru waited on the counter:

> *Hope you got some rest! Sorry about last night.*
> *I'm out in the garden. Come and find me when*
> *you're ready.*

Barrie poured herself a cup and wandered out the back door. Dipping the croissant into the steaming coffee, she stopped at the railing to look out beyond the lower terrace at the river that had turned to fire at midnight, and at the woods where the flaming sphere had disappeared. The woods where Eight had told her not to go.

Was that a coincidence?

Not very likely.

She searched the garden for her aunt. Spotting Pru by the fountain, she waved, staring with a puzzled frown at the enormous blue ceramic bowl Pru was lugging along. The bowl was so large, Pru had it braced against her hip.

"Hello, Aunt Pru. Good morning!"

Looking up, Pru paused. She beckoned for Barrie to come down, then took off the floppy wide-brimmed hat she was wearing and tossed it into the empty bowl.

Barrie started down the stairs. She heard Eight before she saw him: the *slap-slap* of his flip-flops, the crunch of the gravel path, the song he whistled softly as he rounded the rosebushes at the corner of the house. There was no time to sprint back up to the kitchen and duck inside. Halfway down the steps, she stopped in all her pajama-clad, barefooted, bed-headed glory, and cringed as he saw her.

He burst into a grin that made her feel like someone had hit her in the chest, and a returning click went off in her head. She scowled at him, wishing he would go away.

His smile disappeared. "Hey. Whoa. What did I do?" He

broke off a white rose from a bush by the stairs and waved it in the air. "White flag. Truce, all right?"

"That's a flower, not a flag." Barrie glanced over at Pru, but her aunt had gone back to work. Deliberately, Barrie suspected.

Eight bounded up the stairs and presented the rose with a flourish. "A peace offering, then."

No one had ever given Barrie a flower before. She took it gingerly. It smelled like moonlight: enigmatic and full of possibility.

"What are you doing here so early?" she asked, trying not to stutter.

"I thought we had a date for lunch."

"Yes, *lunch*." She waved her croissant at him. "I'm just having breakfast."

Eight brushed that aside with a one-shouldered shrug and a grin that had probably given him whatever he wanted since before he'd sprouted teeth. "I thought I'd give you the grand tour of the island. We're going to need an excuse to go out that Pru won't question. On the other hand, we could skip seeing Cassie altogether and only do the tour."

He turned up the wattage on his grin, blinding Barrie until she almost found herself agreeing. It would be so much easier to agree than to argue. But going into town with Eight without a purpose . . . Going anywhere with Eight. For the first time the enormity of that sank in. It would be hard enough meeting her cousin on her own. The more Barrie thought about meeting Cassie, going into Watson's Point at all, the more she wanted to lock herself in her bedroom and hide like Lula.

There were so many ways in which a meeting with her cousin could go wrong. Cassie might hate her for being a Watson. Or just plain hate her. Cassie had grown up here, after all. She had friends here. Eight had said the whole town took sides in the Colesworth-Watson-Beaufort feud. Barrie could already picture walking down the hall on the first day of school while Cassie and her friends whispered together behind her back. And what if Pru found out Barrie had snuck off to meet Cassie on her first day in town? Pru would have every right to send her packing.

"Of course I still want to go." Barrie took a sip of cooling coffee to avoid the dissecting look Eight gave her. It reminded her of the way the figure by the river had watched her the night before. The hallucination. It had to have been a hallucination. In daylight, it was easier to believe her mind had been playing tricks. She glanced up and caught Eight still watching her. "Would you stop looking at me like that?"

"Like what?" he asked.

"Like you're pulling my brain out through my skull."

He laughed, but then crossed his arms over his chest. "You can't make everyone happy all the time. You know that, right?

And you shouldn't feel guilty for wanting things of your own, separate from Pru."

"Would you stop making pronouncements about what you *think* I want? What is it with you?" Barrie turned and stomped up the stairs.

"Where are you going?" he called after her.

"To change. Do you mind?"

"A little bit, yes. I'm not actually opposed to what you're wearing now."

The note in his voice made her look back at him, and he ran a slow and pointed survey from her curls down to her bare legs and rainbow-painted toenails. His eyes laughed up at her. "You know what would make that outfit even better? You could add those purple shoes you were wearing yesterday."

Barrie's face heated another ten degrees. "You're a pig," she said conversationally. "And just for that, I'll let *you* figure out what to tell Pru about this grand tour you're going to give me."

She hurried into the house before he could argue, but halfway up the stairs to the second floor, she tripped on a wobbly step and grabbed the banister before she remembered it was loose. She nearly went flying when it lurched. Her coffee did go flying. She barely saved the cup.

The house was definitely out to get her.

Puddles of milk-lightened coffee were slowly widening on the steps. Since no one else was around, she stripped off her pajama shorts to mop the spill. Then she sprinted the rest of the way to her room in her underwear, and put on a halter top, a clean pair of capris, and the shoes she had worn the day before. Her choice of shoes had nothing to do with Eight mentioning them. At all. They just happened to be her favorites.

On her way out the door, she stopped to get her phone off the charger, but it wasn't there. Or anywhere on the desk. Thinking maybe she had left it on the bed, Barrie patted down the quilt and then checked her purse, and searched the floor, the drawers, the armoire, the bathroom, and both her empty suitcases.

She tried concentrating on the phone, picturing it and mentally reaching for it. That had never worked for her very well, but she'd seen Lula do it plenty of times. It didn't surprise her when she felt nothing. She definitely hadn't taken the phone downstairs this morning, though, and upstairs she hadn't been anywhere except her room. Which meant the phone was *lost*, and if it was lost, and it was anywhere nearby, then she should have already felt the pull.

That left only Pru. Why would Pru have taken her phone?

More confused than ever, Barrie pushed the suitcases under the bed and out of sight, and stepped out into the corridor. Small tugs of loss came to her from behind several doors, including Pru's bedroom at the end of the hall. She opened the door, then hesitated on the threshold, queasy at the idea of invading

Pru's space. On the other hand the room didn't quite look like it belonged to Pru either, or to anyone. Nothing personal lay scattered on the dressers, no sign of individual taste. From the four-poster bed hung with white lace to the floral paintings on the walls, the bedroom could have been a guest room decorated a hundred years ago, or three hundred years ago.

Reminding herself that Eight was waiting, she pushed her feet forward and followed a ping of finding pressure to the floor behind the nightstand. She found a gold earring and an aspirin tablet there. Two bobby pins, a ponytail holder, and three different kinds of buttons under Pru's dresser also whispered for her attention. By themselves, they were all small things, but still it shocked her to find anything lost in Pru's room.

How could Pru sleep with loss all around her?

Shaking her head, Barrie moved on to search the other bedrooms, and found a pen, a bookmark, and a pill bottle filled in 1969, along with a few more buttons. The closer she drew toward the staircase, the more she felt the aching waves emanating from the empty wing. Beads of sweat pricked on her lip. It made no sense that Pru could walk past a loss this powerful, day in and day out, without being compelled to lay it to rest. None of this made sense.

Much later than she'd intended given that Eight was waiting, Barrie hurried downstairs and back outside. At the top of the terrace steps, she smoothed her shirt and pasted on a smile, ready to fake her way through whatever excuse he had concocted to explain their tour. But as she approached the fountain, she began to suspect her aunt hadn't fallen for either his story or his charm.

Pru knelt in a flower bed, decapitating wilted flowers with angry snips of her shears. Standing beside her, Eight was emphasizing whatever point he was making with his hands, his movements short and sharp. Pru shook her finger at him as she retorted. Barrie strained to hear what they were arguing about, but by the time she drew close enough, both Pru and Eight had seen her and fallen silent.

Pushing back the floppy hat, Pru smiled a bit forlornly. "Eight says you two want to go into town. I had hoped you and I could talk this morning. Wouldn't you like to stay here with me instead of having him drag you off before you've even gotten settled?"

Barrie's mouth opened to say, *Of course*, the way she had agreed to stay a thousand times when Lula had asked. Or ordered. Until this last year Barrie had always stayed. She'd spent her whole life feeling guilty every time she wanted to leave the house.

That wasn't the person she wanted to be anymore, and there was no point setting precedents she had no intention of keeping. She was seventeen. She wasn't going to ask permission to go into town with Eight. *Pru* was the one who had gone to bed early and left her alone last night, Barrie's first night at Watson's Landing. If talking hadn't been important to Pru then, it couldn't be that important now.

Raising her chin, Barrie made herself look Pru in the eye. "It wouldn't be polite for me not to go when Eight is already here. We can catch up this afternoon, can't we?"

Her aunt's reluctance warred with what Mark had always referred to as Lula's "Southern upbringing"—but manners eventually won out.

"I suppose we can," Pru said. Rising, she dusted soil from knobby knees made vulnerable by the bandages Seven had applied. She stepped closer, intent as if she were going to say something. Instead she reached for the clasp of Barrie's necklace and pulled it gently around to rest on the nape of Barrie's neck, where it belonged. "But you be careful of yourself, sugar, and don't be bothered by anything you hear in town. Folks around here are full of nonsense and superstition."

"All right." Barrie made a mental note to ask Eight what Pru had meant.

"You see you keep your promise, Eight Beaufort." Pru spoke to him without taking her eyes from Barrie.

"I will, Miss Pru." Eight tugged at Barrie's wrist, and leaned in to whisper into her ear: "Let's go quick, before she changes her mind."

Barrie had to walk fast to keep up with him. "What did

she mean? What promise?" she asked. "Oh, hold on. I forgot to ask her something."

"Did you decide to stay after all?" Pru was still standing at the edge of the flower bed when Barrie reached her.

"You haven't seen my phone anywhere, have you?" Barrie asked. "I thought I left it in my room, but it isn't there."

Pru lowered the brim of her hat and turned toward the bushes. "No, I haven't seen it. I'm sure it's around here somewhere, though."

Barrie stood a moment waiting for Pru to say something else, then shrugged and hurried toward the front of the house. She tried to convince herself it was disappointment rather than anger that had strained her aunt's voice. But clearly, she was going to have to walk a fine line between keeping Pru happy and having no social life. Still.

Rounding the corner, she found Eight leaning against a silver Mercedes convertible, looking almost as ornamental as the white peacock that was on Pru's hood again with its tail fanned out. A pair of gray peahens pecking for worms on the lawn nearby seemed to be unimpressed by either male.

Nerves fluttered in Barrie's stomach. She climbed into the car. The temperature in full sun was already close to scorching, but the oak lane was cool and dim. Silver-lace tendrils of moss waved overhead as the car passed, as if the trees, like Pru, were reluctant to let Barrie go. It was a disquieting thought. She shifted in her seat to look back at the house.

Someone—Pru?—had fixed the shutter that had hung crookedly beside the front door when Barrie had arrived the day before, but now a shutter on the other side had fallen off.

"It's dying, isn't it?" Barrie winced at her melodramatic word choice, but it felt all too accurate. The house was beginning to feel like a person to her, a personality. A presence.

"What's dying?"

"Watson's Landing. I don't—" She stopped herself mid-sentence.

"Don't what?" Eight prompted.

She had started to say she didn't understand how money could be a problem for any Watson. Eight wouldn't understand, though, and she didn't want to try explaining. He had never been exposed to Lula's glares, or Mark's fussing. He didn't know about the finding gift. As far as Eight knew, Barrie was normal.

Normal.

What an exhilarating, freeing thought. Here on Watson Island, Barrie was a blank canvas. She could color in the rest of her life in any way she wanted. When Eight stopped at the end of the lane, she hopped out of the car feeling light enough to float. But dropping back into the passenger seat on the other side of the gate, the strange ache she had felt when she'd first arrived on the island pressed against her temples.

Eight eased the car out onto the road. "Was the gate unlocked all night?" he asked. "It was open when I got here."

"I have no idea." Barrie clicked the seat belt closed.

"Dad asked me to mention it because Pru got mad when he brought it up. He was worried about you two being here by yourselves."

"It's unlocked for visitors when the garden and tearoom are open anyway."

"That's different from being open in the dark so someone can drive right in," Eight said.

Mouth opened to retort that Pru had managed fine on her own for years, Barrie caught herself. She didn't want to pick a fight with Eight. How had her good mood evaporated so quickly? A second ago she'd been happy to go into town, and now she was antsy, itchy, as if her skin were pulled too tight. She had no right to be mad at him, or even at Seven, and she had no reason to feel guilty at the thought of leaving Pru alone.

Slowing to take the car across the wooden bridge, Eight glanced over at her. "Dad is right, you know," he said. "It's not a good idea to leave the gate open."

"What did Pru make you promise this morning?" Barrie retorted.

He tapped the steering wheel without answering and sped up again as the car cleared the bridge.

Barrie sent him a withering glare. "You don't get to ignore me when I ask a question."

"Like you didn't just ignore me a second ago?" He cocked his eyebrow at her, managing to look half-disapproving and half-amused. "It's not like I'm not on your side. It's just . . ."

"Let me guess. Complicated?" Barrie spoke through gritted teeth.

Eight said something under his breath, but with the top and windows down, the wind ripped his voice away. Well, who needed to hear him anyway? He was irritating. Barrie reached over and cranked up the stereo.

The station was playing beach music, one of Lula's favorites: "Be Young, Be Foolish, Be Happy" by the Tams. Barrie had even caught Lula dancing to it once, her mother's movements stiff and painfully off the beat. It had been one of the few times Barrie had seen Lula almost happy. Now with the volume up, the bass of the music pounded painfully through Barrie's head, but the song reminded her she wasn't in the mood to be mad, or sad. She was tired of being afraid of every new experience, tired of the sour-apple taste that anxiety left in the back of her throat.

Maybe it *was* reckless, and totally unlike her, to sneak behind Pru's back to meet her cousin. She wondered if Lula had felt the same sense of scared anticipation, the same rush of being alive, when she had snuck off to meet a Colesworth in spite of the feud. Had that been the attraction? The knowledge that Wade was forbidden? But Lula must have loved Wade to run off with him.

Wrapping her hand around her necklace, Barrie leaned forward in her seat. She thought of the way Lula had watched her, for hours sometimes, without saying a word. With Lula's expression invisible beneath her veils, that furious, silent scrutiny had felt like hate. It shamed Barrie to realize she had never wondered *why* her mother would feel like that.

"Why do the families hate one another?" she shouted to Eight over the music and the wind. "What began the feud?"

Eight's shoulders stiffened visibly. He glanced at her, then snapped his attention back to the road as a truck whipped past them going the opposite direction. "That's a long answer, and it gets mixed up with the promise I made your aunt."

"Which you can feel free to ignore anytime now," Barrie said, but even as she spoke, she knew she wanted Eight to be the kind of guy who didn't break a promise.

CHAPTER SEVEN

Barrie was digging for aspirin in her purse, so she missed Eight driving past the bridge to the mainland. She looked up to find that they had arrived on the outskirts of Watson's Point. Having found no aspirin, she threw the bag onto the floor and flopped back in her seat. Eight slowed the car almost to walking speed.

His eyes flicked between the road and Barrie, and she tried not to be embarrassed by how intently he watched her. Or flattered. "So, what do you think?" he asked.

She thought she had never really been alone with a boy like this.

She thought it was strange to take pride in being only a little afraid instead of terrified.

"Of the town," Eight said.

"I don't know yet." Barrie turned to concentrate on her surroundings. Elevated on pilings, the first houses of Watson's Point clung to the beach in a single file, the stark blues and grays of their clapboard sidings relieved by masses of roses and bougainvillea. The houses scattered onto residential side streets deeper in town, and colorful signs creaked in the wind in front of stores and restaurants. Shoppers strolled along the sidewalks in bathing suits, shorts, or summer dresses.

Barrie felt no connection to any of it, no pull of foundness or sense of recognition, not even as they passed the Watson Bank where Lula had worked for a couple of summers for her father—one of the few things Barrie's mother had ever mentioned about growing up. Eight drove nearly to the center of town, turned inland, and made a second right. Suddenly the car was on a collision course with a monstrous oak tree growing in the road.

"Welcome, ladies and gentlemen, to the one, the only, gen-u-ine tourist attraction in Watson's Point." Eight spoke in a theatrical announcer's voice. "I give you . . . the Devil's Oak." The *i* in "Devil" was stretched long in his usual Southern drawl.

Despite its name, sunlight shone through the canopy, outlining the hanging tendrils of moss, like fingers from heaven. The trunk was nearly the width of Eight's car. Several of the branches had grown so heavy, they snaked along the ground. The tree had to be older than the town itself. The road split to get around it, leaving room for a grassy knoll dotted with benches, tourists, and a soft-serve ice-cream stand. Eight parked on the shoulder across the street. Barrie wished she had her sketchbook, or at least her cell phone.

"Would you take a picture of me?" She reached for the door handle. "I want to send it to my godfather."

"Sure." Eight grabbed his phone from where he'd stored it in the ashtray, and loped around the front of the car to get her door.

He *had* to be too good to be true.

Still, Barrie waited in her seat for him to come around, and she couldn't help smiling as she stood up. He didn't look away. Time slowed, stretched like a rubber band, and snapped back into place when she stepped aside feeling breathless.

A sturdy tugboat of a woman had emerged from the side door of the soft-serve stand and came steaming toward them in a haze of pink: pink pants, pink T-shirt, and pink-painted lips clearly used to being pursed in disapproval. "Wadded-up tight," Mark would have called her.

"Eight Beaufort, is that Lula's little girl?" she called before she was even halfway across the road.

Eight's smile withered. "Hey, Emma Jean. I didn't know you were working the stand today."

"Not much choice, seeing as how Gilly's gone to the ortho-dontist." Emma Jean dismissed Eight with a wave of her hand,

and her eyes raked over Barrie. "Well, let me have a look at you. Gracious, you *are* a Watson, aren't you?" She shook her head, making it clear that being a Watson wasn't a thing to which one should aspire. "Gawd. Imagine Lula having a baby and never saying a word about it." She paused and her expression sharpened, her nostrils flaring like a hound that had caught a whiff of a scent. "How old did you say you were, sugar?"

"Seventeen." Pronouncing each syllable carefully, politely, Barrie stepped backward, but the car door behind her cut off her escape.

"Seventeen?" Emma Jean's eyes narrowed, and she studied Barrie's features even more closely, as if her sight were bad. "Not sure there's anything of my cousin Wade in you at all," she said finally. "Not a single thing."

The woman might have been talking about features, but given the question about Barrie's age, it was probably more than that. Maybe the Colesworths didn't even want Barrie to be related to them. She caught herself glancing at Eight, but she wasn't sure what she expected him to do. Play her knight in shining armor? Open doors and slay pink dragons? He hardly knew her.

She didn't need him to defend her. And she didn't need the Colesworths.

"My father was killed the night I was born," she said. "I never saw him, and I can't help looking like a Watson."

Emma Jean's ginger curls were sprayed so hard, they didn't budge when she shook her head. "Bless your heart, I know that. I don't mean any of this is *your* fault. It's just . . . none of this makes sense, that's all. Lula was supposed to have been dead since the fire. I keep telling Wyatt to calm down, that there's bound to be an explanation, but—maybe we've got it all wrong. Were you adopted? Maybe it was your adopted mama who died last week?"

Oh, for Pete's sake. "I wasn't adopted," Barrie said.

"Then where has Lula been?" Emma Jean gave the sort of cautious sniff someone might give a glass of milk that had probably gone sour. "You're telling me she's been alive all this time, with Wade's baby, and never said a word to anyone? Never got in touch? Don't tell me there isn't more to it than that. Trying to keep you away from us, most likely. That would be like Emmett, like all of them. Everyone around here will side with Pru Watson and Seven Beaufort, buy their version like it's gospel."

"There is no version!" Barrie's chest was squeezing tighter and tighter, and she pushed back against the car, letting it hold her up. Breathe out, then in. Out, then in. "And there are no sides," she continued more calmly. "Not where I'm concerned. My mother was hurt in the fire. Disfigured. She didn't want to come back here looking like that, and I can't blame her."

For the first time, Barrie could imagine what it would

have been like for Lula to face someone like Emma Jean, face any of the people who had known her before. Back when she'd been beautiful. Barrie let out a hitch of breath, little more than a hint of sound at the sudden memory of Lula on the floor, her wig askew, her scarred face exposed and still.

"Don't be upset, hon." Emma Jean's voice was softer. "I'm sorry. Everyone knows I talk too much, and Lord knows I don't always take the time to think before I open my mouth. I meant the situation was odd, that's all. Strange."

No arguing that. But it hadn't been all Emma Jean had meant.

Rubbing Mark's watch, Barrie wished herself back into the car. Wished herself back at Watson's Landing. Wished herself back in San Francisco.

"Wow, look what time it is. We need to get going, Bear." Eight peeled his hip off the fender and nudged her aside to pull the passenger door open for her. "Sorry, Emma Jean. I'm sure you'll be seeing Barrie around. I'll bring her back for ice cream." He hustled Barrie into the car and winked as she dropped into the bucket seat. "Emma Jean here makes the best ice cream in town."

"Is that right?" Barrie buckled her seat belt with a snap.

"Fourteen flavors fresh every day. Homemade. Every one of them." Emma Jean puffed up with pleasure and smiled, benign as a shark, watching while Eight trotted around to the driver's side and settled behind the wheel. She waved as he pulled slowly off the shoulder.

Barrie waggled her fingers in response, nodding a dazed good-bye.

"You all right?" Eight glanced sideways at her.

"Sure. Fantastic. That was fun." She blew out an exasperated breath, wanting to sock him in the arm. "What *was* that? First she implies that Wade wasn't even my father, and then she's acting like I was practically kidnapped by the Watsons. Psycho much? Why didn't you get us out of there sooner?"

"You were doing fine on your own. Anyway, you might as well get used to being grilled like a steak. There are plenty more where Emma Jean came from."

"Psychos?"

"Colesworths. And busybodies. Town's full of both."

Eight's thumb tapped the steering wheel in time to the music while he followed the road around the Devil's Oak. Barrie watched the families: camera-happy fathers, frazzled mothers, sullen teenagers, elementary schoolers with chocolate ice-cream lips. She and Eight hadn't gotten the photograph for Mark, but she didn't care. She'd had enough of questions she couldn't answer.

They turned on a side street, then doubled back toward the perimeter road. A cute girl in shorts emerged from a QuickMart carrying two green mesh shopping bags as Eight slowed to turn the corner. Spotting the car, the girl waved and called: "Hey, Eight! Is that her? Y'all come on over here!"

Barrie prayed Eight wouldn't stop.

He slowed until the car was barely moving. "Hey, Jeannie. It sure is, but we'll have to catch up with you later."

How was it possible to feel claustrophobic in an open car?

Barrie gave the girl a wave and concentrated on taking deep, slow breaths. Of course people would talk about her. She was the new girl. Mark had predicted this was how it would be. But it was early June, and in a few weeks she would be old news. By the time Labor Day rolled around and school began, the curiosity would have died. Until then she was trapped in hell and descending deeper.

They turned back onto the main road, and Barrie had to laugh. There in front of them, incongruous among the weathered clapboard storefronts, stood a black building with flames painted up the facade, perfectly mimicking her thoughts. A battered sign above the door read: THE RESURRECTION TAVERN: RIBS SO GOOD, YOU'LL THINK YOU'VE DIED AND GONE TO HEAVEN.

"Looks more like the devil's playground," Barrie muttered.

"What?" Eight glanced over.

"Nothing. I'm sensing a religious theme in town."

Eight grinned in a way that would have made Mark comment about the devil and temptation. "Besides it being hell to live in, you mean? There's a story for everything on Watson Island."

"And the story is?" Barrie found herself smiling back at him.

"The devil used to take a nap under the oak every day, until a thief came along and stole his favorite pair of shoes. Old Satan had to borrow the hooves from a goat to get home, but every summer, when it's as hot here as it is in hell, he comes back to dig for them—which accounts for the holes people find on the beach around here."

"Holes? Like someone's digging? But why?"

"Treasure hunting, for one thing—"

"Because Thomas was a pirate?" Barrie eyed him warily.

"A privateer." Eight gave her a slow, easy smile. "Our ancestors were respectable pirates, thank you."

"*Our* ancestors?"

"Thomas Watson and Robert Beaufort. Well, John Colesworth, too, but no one would call him respectable."

"That's kind of hypocritical, don't you think? Doesn't seem like we have any right to judge who's respectable."

"How well did you like Emma Jean?"

Barrie flushed and knew exactly how Pru must have felt in the kitchen with Seven the night before. Beauforts were infuriating. "Did you take me to the Devil's Oak knowing I was going to meet Emma Jean? Is that it?" She poked

Eight in the arm. "You thought I would reconsider meeting Cassie."

"Hold on." Eight threw her an incredulous glance. "I had no idea Emma Jean would be there. It's not just a question of respectability. Our ancestors may have been privateers, but Beauforts and Watsons have always been law-abiding citizens. The Colesworths sold guns to the Indians, ran slaves through the Middle Passage, and tried privateering again in the Civil War. They smuggled alcohol during prohibition. Wyatt's still running drugs, if you believe the rumors. He's not catching many fish on his boat, that's for sure."

"That all sounds like a bedtime story designed to scare little Beaufort and Watson children. If Wyatt is so dangerous, if he's running drugs, why haven't the police locked him up?"

"Because Colesworths have spent three hundred years learning how to hide in plain sight! Also there are a lot of Colesworth cousins around here, not to mention plenty of people willing to look the other way if the money is right. Especially if the drugs aren't sold here in town. Don't make the mistake of thinking Wyatt's innocent. Or safe."

Barrie stared out the window. It wasn't so much what Eight said that was hard to ignore as it was the absolute certainty in his voice. But everyone was supposed to be innocent until proven guilty. Shouldn't that go double for family?

On the left side of the car, a strip of beach dotted with

towels, coolers, and sunbathers led to a marina. On the other side, a pier stretched out into the ocean, and at its base sprawled a restaurant painted in vivid turquoise. Picnic tables shaded by red-and-white umbrellas crowded the deck around the building.

"That's Bobby Joe's there." Eight shifted the car into a lower gear. "You're still sure you want to do this?"

At least thirty cars filled the parking lot beside the restaurant, and a steady flow of customers shuffled in and out. So many people.

The familiar trembling started in Barrie's hands, but she dug them into the seat. "What's Cassie like?" she asked. "Besides being a Colesworth, is she nice? Smart? Pretty?"

"I don't know," Eight said flatly.

Barrie leaned back against the door and studied him. "You went to school with her."

"We didn't exactly hang out, and she's a grade behind me."

"The school can't be that big. So?"

"So she's both smart and pretty. I don't know how to describe her. The closest thing I can tell you is that she leaves a strong impression." Eight's face was wooden, making it impossible to tell if he meant a good impression or a bad one. Not that it mattered. Even in Barrie's class of sixty-four kids at Creswell Prep, there had been a couple of girls like that. They either attracted or repelled, but like the peacock at Watson's

Landing, they always fascinated. Barrie hadn't been friends with any of them.

She stared at the restaurant and reminded herself to breathe. It was so easy to clench up and forget, and then the panic would take root. "Maybe we ought to come back later. It's kind of busy. Cassie might not have time to talk."

"Well, damn," Eight said, narrowing his eyes across the lot at a pickup backing out of a parking space near Bobby Joe's. "It's bad enough what my dad will do to me for introducing you to Cassie. He'll tear a strip off me if I let you run into Wyatt."

"That truck? How can you even tell? It looks like every other white pickup we've passed."

"Wyatt's has a gun rack." Eight tapped the brake and slowed their approach to the entrance of the parking lot.

"Is that supposed to make me nervous?"

"It's supposed to be a fact."

There didn't seem to be any way to avoid a meeting, even if they didn't turn into the parking lot. The road ran straight on, with a sidewalk and a row of shops on the other side. No driveways. No side streets. Wyatt, if it was Wyatt, was going to get to the exit before they did, but not soon enough to pull out before he saw them.

The white pickup was still twenty yards from the road. Eight had the Mercedes slowed to ten miles per hour, practically crawling to give Wyatt time to exit. But a line of cars was stacking up behind them. One of the drivers honked. Two sharp blasts. Eight hesitated, glanced in the rearview mirror, then punched the accelerator.

The Mercedes surged forward. Still accelerating, they passed the entrance to the parking lot fast enough that Barrie got little more than an impression of a dark-haired man at the wheel of the truck and the shape of a rifle on a rack in the rear window. The truck pulled out onto the road after they had passed.

"Damn," Eight said again.

The truck followed thirty yards behind. Eight accelerated, but the truck kept pace, and soon they were well out of town, past the point with the lighthouse, past the public beaches. No shops, no side roads, just a long, narrow stretch of asphalt.

Barrie told herself it didn't matter. It was broad daylight, for Pete's sake. "Where does this road go anyway?"

"Past one of the old Watson rice fields and out to the edge of the woods."

"And after that?"

Eight tapped the top of the steering wheel with the flat of his hand, then switched to two fingers, as if he were playing rock-paper-scissors with the truth. "Marsh and trees and alligators. It runs into the creek that runs along Watson's Landing, and there's no bridge on this side." He rubbed the back of his neck and released a sigh. "This may have been a miscalculation. I figured Wyatt would go the other way."

"I'm not worried." Barrie burrowed her hands beneath her legs.

People didn't act like this. Stalk one another out of parking lots onto beautiful, lonely roads.

On Barrie's right, marsh grasses swayed in gleaming water. On the left, the ocean vanished behind a legion of sand dunes overgrown with sea oats, and a scant widening of the road allowed parking for access to the beach. In front of them, a heat haze slicked the asphalt. A yellow sign and a chain marked the end of the road, which dwindled into grass and brush descending the bank toward the creek.

Dead end. Not a soul around.

Eight cut a sharp U-turn, downshifted, and slammed on the brake. The car groaned to a halt along the sand, facing the white pickup that was suddenly a whole lot closer.

"What are you doing?" Barrie's heart rate kicked into a sprint.

"Give me a minute." With one hand on the gearshift, Eight stared through the windshield.

The pickup slowed, then stopped, just far enough away that the driver was hard to see through the glare on the glass. Still too close.

"Give me your phone," Barrie said.

"Hang on. Give him time to think. He'll figure out that I can get past him before he's breaking twenty miles per hour. He probably hasn't even figured out why he came after us. That's a Colesworth thing. They all act first and then engage the brain as an afterthought."

"You're crazy, you know that? What if he just runs us off the road?"

Even as she spoke, the truck lurched forward. Barrie snatched Eight's phone from the ashtray to call 911.

Eight held up his hand. "Wait. Look. He's leaving. I told you."

Eight's voice held as much surprise as relief, which didn't inspire Barrie's confidence. But he was right. With a belch of exhaust, the pickup shuddered into a three-point turn and screeched back the way it had come.

Barrie's spine surrendered. She slumped against the seat, clutching Eight's phone, and breathing, just breathing, until he reached over and took it from her.

"Are you okay?" he asked.

Her hands were trembling. She couldn't look at Eight, and she was done with Colesworths. She shook her head. "Sure. But let's go back to Watson's Landing."

"What about Cassie?"

"I can meet her later." When hell froze over.

Eight pushed his hair back and studied her with that odd,

fixed stillness of his. "I don't know. You might have been right in the first place. Better to get the introduction over with. Defuse Cassie—and all of them—by letting her know you went out of your way to meet her."

He made Cassie sound like a ticking bomb that needed to be disarmed.

Barrie shook her head again. Eight watched her another moment, then threw open the driver's door and stepped out.

"Come on. As long as we're here, I've got something I want to show you. You can tell Pru it was part of the tour." He set off toward the dunes without even waiting to see if she was coming.

Barrie's heels sank into the sand. She slipped off her shoes, tossed them into the back of the car, and ran after him. The smell of salt and the rush and roar of the ocean broke over her in waves of homesickness. When she reached the beach, though, it didn't look familiar.

Why did that surprise her? This wasn't the beach below the cliff at Lula's house. Barrie had no right to hope for a sunset-gold bridge that stretched from a shining city to low, green mountains across the bay. Yet its absence slapped her, woke her up like the cooling wind that came lashing off the water. It was strange to see a beach with no joggers, to find no one power walking or hunting for shells along the shoreline, to feel no sense that there were crowds and cars just out of sight. There were only gulls, and yards and yards of desolate sand leading to miles and miles of empty ocean.

She ran to catch up with Eight. "What are we doing here?"

He smiled infuriatingly and walked on, but it wasn't long before he pointed at a set of fan-shaped tracks, and turned to follow them as they led out to the water. Above the high-tide line, the tracks ended in a disturbed patch of sand.

"So that's your buried treasure?" she asked. "What is it?"

"Loggerhead nest. They're pretty common all down the coast in the summer."

"I thought they were endangered."

"Because only one in a thousand hatchlings lives long enough to lay eggs of its own." Eight's face suddenly looked pinched and serious. "They're tiny when they dig themselves up out of the sand—only two inches long—and then they have to cross the beach and make it to the ocean. Some days it looks like the whole beach is a feeding frenzy of crabs and seagulls, and hatchlings trying to reach the water. You have to see it to believe how impossible that trip must be." He shaded his eyes and turned to watch the waves coming in.

Barrie followed suit, her eyes narrowed while the wind whipped her hair. "Now what are we looking for?"

"Black pops breaking the surface. Those are loggerheads."

He lowered his cheek beside hers, so close the stubble he hadn't bothered to shave pricked Barrie's skin. So close she felt found again. She breathed in his calm. How could someone with so much energy be so calm, especially after the Wyatt run-in? How did he change moods so fast?

"There." He held up his finger so she could sight along it. "That's one. See it? And another there."

She squinted and finally spotted a shape where it broke the surface. "Oh, look! I see it."

Her voice came out in a squeal. She rolled her eyes at herself, but Eight laughed, a low rumble barely discernible from the ocean's voice. He dropped down to the sand and sat watching her with his hands hung across his knees.

"What are you doing now?" she asked.

"Nothing. You're interesting to watch."

Her face went warm, but she was smiling. A few minutes ago she wouldn't have believed she could feel like smiling. The thought sobered her again. She didn't want this feeling to end, not yet. Maybe it was the fear that had made the pleasure even sweeter, but for this moment, in this place, Watson Island wasn't bad. She wished she could stay right there on the beach with Eight, instead of having to go up and face the road down which Wyatt had followed them. She wished she had never heard of Wyatt. Or Cassie. What if her cousin was like Emma Jean?

And how many Colesworth cousins were there?

Barrie stared out at the ocean, and it seemed to her the

whole island was like the water out there, everything hidden beneath a layer of calm until some dark and unknown shape, some unknown relative or another of Lula's secrets suddenly broke the surface.

She hated to admit it, but Eight probably was right. The longer she waited before making friends with her cousin, the harder it was going to be to psych herself up for it. Obviously, he had brought her down here to make a point. Most of his hatchling turtles never made it to the water, but it wasn't because they didn't try.

Partly for Eight, but mostly for herself, Barrie didn't want to be the kind of person who never tried.

"All right," she said. "Let's go meet my cousin."

CHAPTER EIGHT

The parking lot at Bobby Joe's Beach Dogs was emptier than it had been earlier, but beachgoers in bathing suits and cover-ups still lingered at most of the outside tables. Reggae music trickled from speakers beneath the eaves. Barrie ducked under Eight's arm while he held the front door, and walked into a welcome blast of cooler air scented with grease and spicy mustard. Even more people occupied the inside tables covered in checkered cloths. But a girl chatting with the cook at the order pickup counter was the one who caught Barrie's attention—caught everyone's attention.

The girl's dark mass of curls was swept into a ponytail, her face tipped up as she laughed. Her back was arched and bare in a bikini top. That was the uniform, apparently; the other two servers wore the same kind of bathing suit top and cutoff shorts. Still, this was the girl you noticed.

Eight released the door. It fell closed behind him with a bang. The cook said something Barrie couldn't hear, and the girl's ponytail fanned out behind her as she spun to look at Eight. Every face in the room turned to look. The girl's attention moved to Barrie. Her eyes widened. Then she rushed across the floor littered with sand and peanut shells and caught Barrie's hands in both of hers.

"You just have to be my little cousin. Barrie, isn't it? I heard you were coming—in this town everyone knows everything!" She gave a laugh and pulled Barrie into a hug. "I am so, so glad to meet you."

This was the girl Pru and Seven didn't want Barrie to meet?

Barrie wanted to be the kind of a person who could throw her arms around a stranger and not feel self-conscious. But she returned the hug awkwardly, too aware of everyone staring at her. Closing her eyes, she forced herself to relax.

"Now tell me, did you come to eat or to say hello?"

"Both," Eight said at the same time Barrie answered, "I wanted to meet you."

"And I am so glad you did! Here." Cassie dragged Barrie toward a table by the window. It hadn't been cleared yet, but she swept up the cups, red baskets, and debris with a quick "Hold on a second," then rushed to drop them onto the counter by the order window. She returned with a fresh bucket of peanuts and a damp cloth, which she used to wipe the table. When she'd finished, she straightened with her cheeks slightly flushed.

"There now. Have a seat."

"Thank you," Barrie said, although she couldn't, because Cassie was in the way.

"You know," Cassie said, examining Barrie's face, "you don't look anything like the pictures I've seen of my uncle Wade." She turned Barrie to face Eight and dropped her arm around Barrie's shoulders. "What do you think? Do we look alike? Can you tell we're cousins?"

Barrie's face heated until, she imagined, she was the color of the crab shells hanging on the wood-planked walls. Even in her high-heeled shoes, she was almost a head shorter than Cassie. On top of that, her cousin had the kind of effortless confidence that came from being in-your-face gorgeous from the moment you entered the world. In their level of perfection, Cassie and Eight were a matched set. Barrie was nowhere near their league. She knew that. Seemingly everyone else did too. They were all still staring.

"You know what? It doesn't matter." As if she'd caught Barrie's embarrassment, Cassie gave a blinding smile and squeezed Barrie's hand again. "Look at this beautiful pale skin of yours! And bless your heart, look how skinny you are! I wish I had your figure. Now you sit right here. Sit. You order, and by the time your food is ready, I'll be able to sneak back and talk a bit." She pointed to a chalkboard menu hanging above the order window. "What can I get you? On the house, of course."

Barrie sat and tried to concentrate on the options, but there were too many combinations and hot dog condiments she had never heard of: the Blue Dog with blue-cheese slaw and sweet potato mustard; the Hottie Dog with chili, cheese, slaw, and spicy mustard; the Green Dog, which was tofu with mustard, ketchup, and onions . . .

"If anything seems too adventurous, you can always order the Bikini Dog." Cassie pointed to an item on the bottom of the listing. "That's just plain."

Eight slid along the bench, closer to Barrie. Her mouth was watering at the *idea* of sweet potato mustard; it sounded tangy and spicy and sweet all at the same time. "She'll have the Blue," Eight said. "Do you want sweet potato fries with that, Bear? And a Cherry Coke?"

"Sounds great." Perfect, actually, which bothered Barrie almost as much as the fact that Eight assumed he could order for her or casually give her a nickname as if he knew her. On the other hand, bears were strong, and she needed all the strength she could get.

She gave an annoyed nod, and tried not to notice the way Cassie stared into Eight's eyes while he ordered a Hottie Dog for himself.

"All right. I'll put this in and help a few more customers,

and then I'll be back." Cassie scribbled the last item onto her pad. "I can't wait to hear all about you and your mama and San Francisco—and well, just everything!" She gave Barrie a dazzling smile before departing.

The moment she was gone, a silence blanketed the room. A motionless silence. Then a bench scraped loudly a few tables away. A couple of teens hurried over, a boy and a girl with long legs and golden skin. The boy slapped Eight on the back and they introduced themselves, but Barrie didn't catch their names. Suddenly it seemed like *all* the benches were scraping back and the peanut shells on the floor were being trampled by every foot in the building en route to their table. Eight acted like it was no big deal, easy peasy, all these people, all those words, all the smiles and laughs and weighing, scrutinizing eyes. He sat on the bench like it was a throne and he was holding court, and the crowd made a half circle around their table, talking, elbowing one another out of the way to wave or hold out their hands in introduction.

Barrie smiled until her cheeks hurt. "Nice to meet you," she said at least twenty times, nodding and feeling like her head was as empty as a bobblehead doll's. Why was it so hard to think of anything intelligent or witty to say in answer to the questions thrown at her?

"How do you like Watson's Point?" someone asked.

"It's charming," Barrie answered.

"So you'd never met your aunt Pru before now?" an older man said. "That's what I heard, isn't it?"

"Nope, never met her," Barrie said. "But she's very nice."

"Sorry to hear about your mama passing," the golden girl said.

"Thank you." Barrie smiled even wider.

"Yeah, we sure were sorry to hear about your mama," someone else said. "A little confused about it, but awful sorry."

Barrie nodded again, feeling trapped and stupid. And so it went for a few more minutes, and though they were all very nice, she wished they would just go away.

"How long are you going to stay?" someone asked. "You moving back for good?"

Eight cleared his throat. "Y'all do know the girl just got here? We might want to give her some room to breathe or she's going to run out of here faster than a scalded haint. No need for her to meet the whole town in one swoop."

He didn't raise his voice. If anything, he spoke more softly than the others, but they heard him, laughed, and started to disperse. Barrie answered the last calls of "Well, welcome," and "Good-bye," and sighed in relief. It didn't escape her, though, that almost everyone seemed to pull out their cell phones before they had even gotten back to their tables.

"Everyone's going to race to make sure their friends know they met you first," Cassie said, coming back with their food.

"This place. I swear, you'd think no one had anything to do all day but gossip."

The front door banged and a middle-aged couple entered. As he passed their table, a man with a thinning thatch of hair stopped and gaped at them.

"Rolls the years back to see the two of you here like this," he said.

Barrie looked at him blankly. He seemed to give himself a mental shake and held his hand out. "Sorry. You must be Lula's daughter. Welcome back home, honey."

"Barrie Watson," Barrie said. "Thanks, and nice to meet you."

"Joe Goldstein." His smile was sheepish and sweet. "I edit the local paper. Heard you were back, of course, but I won't deny it caught me by surprise. I could almost think it was Seven and Pru back here, keeping one eye on each other and the other looking out for old man Emmett."

Cassie, rolling her eyes, excused herself and stepped back from the table. "Gotta get those orders," she said. "I'll be back."

"That's probably my cue to go sit down so I can tell her what I want to eat," Joe Goldstein said with a chuckle. "Sure hope I'll be seeing you again."

"So there *was* something between your dad and Pru?" Barrie whispered to Eight as the man threaded his way out the door.

"Must have been a long time ago." Eight reached across to Barrie's basket and stole a sweet potato fry.

Barrie slapped his hand away. "Quit."

"Mine don't taste as good as yours." He grinned, not the least bit repentant. "Hey, did you know your face gets pink when you're mad? Or embarrassed. Or confused . . ."

"Just for that, keep your hands off my food." Barrie slid her basket away from him, reached in for the Blue Dog, and took a bite. Sensory overload. "Oh, God. This has to be the best hot dog on the planet. Ever."

"It's the mustard and the salt air. And the company, of course."

"Shame you have such a case of self-confidence deficit disorder."

"Sounds dangerous. You should give me a compliment immediately to boost my self-esteem." Eight stole another fry, and frowned as the door opened and then banged closed behind a woman who stopped and scanned the room. "Heads up. Here we go again."

The woman who had come in was probably Pru's age, with a cute bob of dark hair and a pretty figure shown off in clothes that, while still elegant and expensive, looked about a size too tight. Spotting Eight, she smiled and marched determinedly toward their table. She was breathing hard by the time she reached them.

"No, no, don't get up," she said, clearly expecting they would. "Everyone is talking about how charming Lula's little girl turned out, so I had to rush right over here to say hello."

Eight stole another fry from Barrie as he stood up. "Barrie, meet Julia Lyons. She and her husband own the big boat shop across the parking lot."

"You just call me Julia. I was a friend of your mama's," Julia added. "Her best friend. I miss her like crazy."

"It's nice to meet people who knew her," Barrie said.

"Oh, honey. *Everyone* knew Lula." Julia laughed. "It was always more a question of who Lula was willing to know." Her eyes slid toward Cassie and rested there a moment before she gave a slight shake of her head. "I suppose the island always was too small for her. I shouldn't have been surprised when she and Wade ran off."

"Were they that much in love?" Barrie couldn't help asking.

Julia stilled momentarily, then sat down on the bench across from Barrie. "I've asked myself that question a million times. I never heard about it, if she was. But if Emmett forbade her to see Wade, she might have convinced herself she was in love with the boy. You couldn't ever tell Lula no." Julia glanced at Barrie and then at Eight with her eyes brimming. "Sorry. I've spent all this time wondering if I could have done something different when she left. I cried myself to sleep for weeks. You take things hard at that age—your age, just about.

I've gone over every moment of that summer so many times. I waited by the phone for her to call, and there was only the stupid letter." She tried to smile, and couldn't manage. "Now I find out she had a baby and didn't tell me. At least it explains why she had to leave so fast. Emmett would have locked her away for the rest of her life if he'd found out she was pregnant."

"My birthday's in September," Barrie said. "So I couldn't have been the reason she left. You said she sent a letter, though? She wrote to you?"

"Not to me. She sent me an envelope to give to Pru and scrawled instructions on a Post-it for me to make sure Emmett didn't see it." Julia twirled her wedding ring around her finger.

"Didn't Pru tell you what it said?" Barrie asked.

"She might have if I'd given it to her, but none of us could get past Emmett. He would tell me Pru wasn't there whenever I called or stopped by, and she never seemed to leave Watson's Landing unless he was with her. I kept waiting for a chance to slip it to her, but then we heard Lula was dead anyway. It seemed cruel to open old wounds."

Barrie leaned forward eagerly. "Do you still have it—the letter, I mean?"

"I haven't seen it in years, so maybe my husband threw it away. Or it got put somewhere. I don't know." Julia's eyes dropped to her wedding ring, and she twisted it around her finger as if she wished it could make her invisible, like Frodo's ring. "To be honest, the letter was the kind of thing I knew I shouldn't throw away, but at the same time, it was too late to do anything with it."

"So you never opened it?"

Julia shrugged, but her expression was vulnerable and almost pleading. "How could I?"

How could she *not?* Barrie held back a growl of frustration. When the answers were right there and all you had to do was open an envelope and read them, why would you not want the answer?

Julia's chin was starting to tremble, and she had stopped twisting her ring in favor of pressing her hands tightly together on her lap. "Lula and I were best friends. Best friends. We did everything together. And then she left without a word. She didn't even consider how I would feel. She left and then she died. It was impossible to think of Lula dead. She loved life so much."

Barrie wanted to reach across the table, take Julia's hand, and tell her it would be all right. Of course, it wouldn't be. It couldn't be, because Lula was still dead. The conversation withered into an embarrassed silence.

With a soft subject-changing sound in his throat, Eight got up and plucked his empty cup off the table to get a refill. "I saw Jack Sprague in front of the Wishy-Wash earlier, Miss Julia. Weren't you wanting to get your oven fixed? You probably want to catch him before he heads back across the bridge?"

Julia quickly rose. "Thank you for reminding me. Yes, I suppose I'd better go." She smiled as Barrie stood up too. "I hope we can catch up more. Come anytime."

Barrie nodded, but Julia was already hurrying toward the door.

Eight got the refill, came back, and dropped down beside her. "You haven't even touched your drink."

"I haven't exactly had a chance. And *you* should take up fortune-telling. How did you know about her oven?"

"It's Watson Island," Eight said, as if that explained it. "You had about enough? Why don't we get out of here?"

"No, you can't leave yet." Cassie came up behind them. She lowered herself gracefully to sit on the bench between Barrie and the wall. "What did I miss, Cos? I swear, it's been busier at this table than the kissing booth at the barbecue festival. Lord, I hate this place." Her eyes narrowed, and for a moment she looked very different, not pretty at all. "You may as well get used to everyone getting into your business if you're going to stick around. They think they own our families. Eight and I have lived here all our lives. We're old news. Imagine what it's going to be like for you with everyone watching to see what you do."

It was Barrie's worst nightmare. "I'm not that interesting," she said, staring hard at her congealing fries and cooling hot dog. "I'm sure they'll get tired of me pretty fast."

"You don't understand, do you? It doesn't matter how boring you are. They'll compare you to your mama, and her mama before that. They'll judge you because you're Emmett Watson's granddaughter, and Thomas Watson's great-great-great—who even cares how many greats—granddaughter. They'll shake their heads about Lula and Uncle Wade running off together, but in the end they'll forgive you because you're a Watson. Just like they'll blame me because I'm a Colesworth."

She said it so matter-of-factly, with almost no hint of bitterness. Barrie couldn't help but like her. How could anyone not like Cassie?

"Still, I'll bet they're wrong about you, aren't they?" Cassie's thick-lashed eyes narrowed in speculation. "You're not just a Watson. You're a Colesworth, too. I can feel it." She gave Barrie another dazzling smile. "But listen to me going on and on when I should be telling you how glad I am that you're here! Isn't it wonderful?" She threw her arms around Barrie and gave her a squeeze. "I can't believe I have a brand-new cousin. It's like Christmas in June. That's it exactly—you're my Christmas-present cousin. I just know we're going to be best friends. I can't wait for you to meet my sister, Sydney, and the rest of the family. Daddy hasn't talked about anything else since he heard you were coming. He's dying to hear all about you and what Lula told you about us—"

"Lula didn't tell her anything about *anything*," Eight

said. "She never heard of Watson's Landing until her mama died."

Cassie drew back to frown at Barrie. "Nothing at all?"

Something about Cassie's intensity made Barrie nervous. She resisted the urge to slide down the bench to give herself a little more breathing room. "Lula never talked about my father or where she came from. After the fire I guess it was too painful to think about it."

"Didn't you ever ask?" Cassie leaned over and took a couple of cold fries out of Barrie's basket. She chewed on them thoughtfully while Barrie shook her head.

Barrie wasn't about to admit how many times she'd asked, or tried to ask, Lula questions. Lula had been Lula. She hadn't talked about anything she hadn't wanted to discuss.

"Jesus," Cassie said. "Imagine showing up here and getting all this dumped on you. You have to be curious, too, I'll bet." She smiled, her foot tapping as if she were thinking. "My daddy's got loads of old photos back at the house. You should come over. Maybe after the play—" She glanced at Eight, and her mouth snapped closed.

An awkward silence hung over the table. Barrie struggled to think of something to say, but she'd never been good at that.

"I'm sorry." Cassie touched Barrie's shoulder, her face serious, her eyes big and wide. "This is exactly like me, jumping to conclusions. You may not even want to know anything about your daddy. San Francisco had to have been amazing. So much better than this suffocating town. Look at these gorgeous clothes . . . and your jewelry." She plucked Barrie's necklace off her shirt. "Are these Tiffany keys? They are, aren't they?" Almost reverently her fingers ran over the three keys with their tiny diamonds set in delicate platinum settings. "Are they real?"

Barrie barely resisted the urge to pull away.

"Need a refill yet, Bear?" Eight reached between her and Cassie for Barrie's Cherry Coke and shook the cup to see if it was empty. It wasn't, but the gesture made Cassie drop the pendants.

The way Cassie stared at the keys made Barrie want to tuck the necklace under her shirt or apologize for wearing it. She'd never thought about what the keys were worth. Not in terms of money. They'd been Lula's gift to her for winning the state and national Scholastic art awards, one key for each of the three prizes, which had been the first time Lula had shown any interest in Barrie's work. Barrie had given up pushing drawings under Lula's door in kindergarten. She liked to think the keys had been Lula's way of making up for that.

Sadness swelled inside Barrie's chest, filling her up until she thought that she would burst.

"Come on, Bear. We'd better get you back." Eight unfolded his legs and made the table wobble as he rose. "Your aunt will cut off my visiting privileges if I keep you out much longer."

"You don't have to leave so soon, do you?" Cassie bit her lip. "My shift is almost over. I can run you home. Or wait"— she reached over and grabbed Barrie's hands—"I'm meeting some folks at the Resurrection later. You could come. We can have dinner, and I can introduce you to a few of my friends. It's my last free night until Monday. Please say yes! It'll be so much fun!"

Barrie stood up slowly. She should want to go with Cassie. But she didn't.

Eight shook his head at her as if he wanted to *will* her to say no. Why was he always telling her what to do? Meeting a few friends would be manageable. Cassie deserved at least that much. And the more people Barrie met before school started, the fewer stares she would have to face in the halls and cafeteria on the first day of class.

Hadn't she promised Mark she would have adventures? Put some wear on her shoes? She needed to push herself. "Thank you," she said, "that sounds like fun."

Cassie gave her a quick, tight hug. "Great. I'll pick you up at six."

"No need. I'm already coming back into town for dinner around then. I'll drive her," Eight said, with a smile that wasn't as much a smile as the promise of impending argument.

CHAPTER NINE

It was strange for Barrie to raise her voice, let alone to have a no-holds-barred fight with someone she had never even heard of twenty-four hours before. She and Eight argued all the way to Watson's Landing in a way that reminded her of Mark and Lula's fights. By the time they reached the small bridge over the creek, Barrie felt as though every word in her vocabulary had been wrung out of her body. She turned up the radio to drown Eight out. He had the bass turned too high again, and the beat pounded along with her headache. She stared out the open window.

"Dinner with Cassie is a stupid idea. Dumb as a box of rocks." Eight turned down the volume again. "Admit it. What if Wyatt shows up? Running into him before might have been an accident, but by dinnertime Cassie will have had time to tell him you'll be with her at the Resurrection."

"Which is a restaurant. A place full of people. So, what is he going to do? Anyway, Cassie is great. She's family. *My* family. Do you have brothers or sisters?"

"A sister—Kate. She's sixteen. She's at camp, or we would have brought her over. But you'll meet her soon."

"You love her; I can tell by the way you said that just now. Do you see how lucky you are? I don't have a sister or a brother. Cassie and Sydney are the closest things I'll ever have to that— and Cassie is asking me to dinner in a public place, not hauling me off to a secret lair to be tortured by her minions. How am I supposed to say no? Anyway, you're the one who thought it was a good idea to introduce us."

"To introduce you. Not to have you think you're going to be best friends. Because trust me, that isn't what she wants."

"And how do you know what Cassie wants, Commander Beaufort? You know what *everyone* wants—"

"Don't be an ass. You don't understand—"

"So tell me! What don't I know?" Barrie turned to him and waited, but Eight set his jaw and stared out the windshield. She flounced back against the seat. "That's exactly what I thought."

"I promised I wouldn't say."

"Then it isn't up to you to tell me what to do."

She was sick of people telling her what to do. She would have loved to tell Eight she didn't need a ride either. But she didn't know how to drive . . . and Pru wasn't likely to take her to the Resurrection. Too bad she hadn't thought faster and told Cassie to go ahead and pick her up. Maybe it wasn't too late. Maybe she could find Cassie's number and call her.

The gate stood wide open when they reached Watson's Landing, and Eight drove straight through. Barrie hadn't even realized how much tension had built up inside her, until it vanished in the dappled light beneath the Watson oaks. She wished they were at the house already so she could go curl up on her bed, but Eight slowed to a crawl behind a blue mini-van with New Jersey license plates. He practically kissed its bumper. Which was Eight's problem right there. He was pushy.

"Back off a little, can't you?"

"They're going ten miles an hour." He flicked her a mad-deningly good-natured look.

"They're probably looking around. That's kind of the point."

The family in the minivan weren't the only ones doing that. Closer to the house a young mother was trying to cor-ral a pair of toddlers who were chasing the two peahens that had wandered too close to the family picnic. A white-haired man and his pink-skinned wife leaned on each other as they hobbled away from the parking area toward the tearoom.

Apart from the tourists, the scene gave Barrie a lurching

sense of déjà vu. Pru's ancient car stood in the same place as when Barrie had first arrived. It looked forlorn without its peacock hood ornament. Pru was out front again, too, teetering on a ladder, trying to fix the fallen shutter. Barrie ran to hold the ladder as soon as Eight slid the car to a stop. Even so, he somehow managed to get there first. What was it with him?

"Here, Miss Pru," he said. "Switch places with me."

Not, *Can I do that for you?* Just *Switch places with me.* Pushy.

"He has no business telling you what to do," Barrie said, loud enough for him to hear.

"What? I was hoping he would offer." Pru handed down the shutter and followed after it to trade places with Eight. "What's wrong, sugar? Didn't you have a good time in town?"

"I met my cousin. Cassie." Barrie injected extra enthusiasm into her voice. "She was great. Fantastic. But I barely got a chance to talk to her, so I'm going to have dinner with her tonight to meet some of her friends. As long as you don't have any special plans, I mean." Barrie peeked at Pru from beneath her lashes, hoping she wouldn't see refusal. Or rage. "It's okay, isn't it? Please say yes. I'd really like to go, and I promise I'll get up early tomorrow morning to help around here. I know I've been useless so far."

"I don't need your help. That's one problem you don't

have to worry about." Pru handed the shutter up to Eight. "Having dinner with your cousin, though—"

"She couldn't have been nicer! Honestly. Eight said there are . . . well, issues . . . between the families, but I have to go to school with her."

Pru glared at Eight. "I told you. I told you, and your father told you. But you didn't listen."

"Hey, don't look at me." Eight shrugged and frowned at Barrie. "I tried to talk her out of dinner. Good luck talking her out of anything she thinks she ought to do."

Barrie refused to let him draw her back into the argument. She was already mad at herself for allowing him to spook her about Cassie. Not to mention Wyatt, who had probably seen her with Eight and wanted to introduce himself. Eight was the one who had driven off like a crazy person. No wonder Wyatt hadn't known what to do once they'd reached the beach. Or maybe it hadn't been Cassie's father at the beach at all.

"Can we please stop arguing?" Barrie heaved a sigh. "I hate it. Especially with you, Aunt Pru. But Cassie and her family are my family too, and I want to know what my father was like."

"Be careful what you wish for, sugar. History isn't always what we hope it will be. You aren't going to believe what the Colesworths are like until you see it for yourself, though, are you?"

"I need to do this," Barrie said. It felt good to take a stand. To make a decision.

"Fine." Pru waggled her finger at Eight. "I'm holding you responsible, Eight Beaufort. You keep an eye on her and see she doesn't get in trouble."

"That's just it. I can't. Dad and I are having dinner at Harrigan's Steak House. The recruiter has flown all the way out from California, so I can't reschedule—"

"Who asked you to?" Barrie snapped. "I don't need a babysitter! Cassie's going to introduce me to her friends, not the local Mafia."

Eight used the base of the screwdriver to knock a shiny screw loose from the shutter. "You met kids at Bobby Joe's today. Nice kids."

"They didn't exactly invite me anywhere, did they?"

"Because you just got here. They were trying to be respect-ful." He took the box of screws from Pru, stuck one into the old hole, and twisted it in. Just exactly like he always dug around in people's heads, twisting their thoughts until a person didn't know whether up was up, down, or sideways.

Well, *screw him*.

"You know what? I'm done arguing with you. I was sup-posed to call Mark hours ago. Excuse me, Aunt Pru." Barrie let herself in through the front door and headed toward the stairs.

She was on the landing before she remembered she didn't

have her phone. Retracing her steps, she stomped back to the first floor, pushed through into the kitchen, and nearly ran over a woman carrying a tray of empty plates and glasses.

For a shocked moment they stared at each other. Then the woman laughed and set the tray on the table. "You have to be Barrie," she said. "Have mercy, aren't you a sight?"

Her voice had a faster tempo than Pru's and Eight's, and her words were more musical, the high notes climbing toward the end of the sentence before dropping again like the cabdriver's. She was sixtyish, with graying hair slicked back into a bun, and fine features highlighted by smooth, sooty skin. Her posture made the dark slacks and white blouse look elegant.

"Come here, child. Don't stand there gaping. Miss Pru warned me 'bout you lookin' like your mama, but I swear, you're the spittin' image."

Barrie smiled awkwardly and said hello, only to find herself pulled into a hug. There was no awkwardness to that. Maybe because there was no one to see, or maybe Barrie was getting used to being hugged, or maybe it was the woman herself. Mary, presumably. Who else?

"I know you're probably thinking all this is strange," Mary said, releasing her. "The house and Miss Pru and all. You're gonna like it here just fine. Miss Pru will love you, and you're gonna love Miss Pru. It'll be good for you both to have each other. She's missed your mama awfully bad." She stepped back and smoothed her blouse with a wink. "Now, I'd better get back to the customers, or we'll be in a real fix. Folks get downright mean when they're hungry."

Barrie hadn't had time to explore the tearoom yet. She was spending more time away from Watson's Landing than she was in it.

"You go 'head and eat some of them sandwiches, if you want." Mary nodded toward a half-full platter on the table. She picked up a tray of delicately frosted tea cakes, which were more miniature works of art than food, and bustled back through the butler's pantry into the tearoom.

Once she had gone, Barrie paused to regain her wits before searching the kitchen. Her phone had to be there. She'd looked everywhere else. Moving systematically, she opened and closed drawers, checked cabinets, and looked under the table. She felt nothing but a few inconsequential tugs here and there. The only phone she found was an old-fashioned rotary one hanging on the wall, which she used to dial her own number, and then listened for a nonexistent ring. She was considering her next move when Mary came back carrying another tray of dirty plates and cups.

"You look like you're fixin' to try to think your way through the floor, child."

"You haven't seen my phone by any chance? It has a white case with a pair of eyes painted on the back. I need to call my godfather—" Did Mary know about Mark?

It was always hard to explain who Mark was in terms of his relationship to Barrie and Lula. He *was* the closest thing to a friend Lula'd had in seventeen years, and he was also Barrie's godfather. But as Lula had liked to remind him on a daily basis, she paid him to live in and take care of Barrie. Barrie wasn't sure if Pru knew that. She hoped not, and somehow the idea of Mary knowing it was even worse.

Mary set the dishes beside the sink. "I haven't seen it," she said. "There's one on the wall you can use, or in the library. That's down the hall and to the right, 'bout halfway to the stairs."

Barrie poked her head into an enormous dining room and a parlor before she found a room with floor-to-ceiling book-shelves, a heavy mahogany desk, a pair of wingback chairs, and an elaborately carved wood-framed sofa. A thin-lipped man peered at her unpleasantly from a life-size portrait above the fireplace. His iron-gray hair matched the grim color of his business suit.

Seven Beaufort positively radiated joy by comparison.

Equally unpleasant was the violent pull of a lost object inside the room. It drew Barrie inside, but at the same time something about the room and the man in the portrait made her want to keep her feet firmly planted in the hall. Heavy velvet curtains blocked any light from the windows. Even after she had switched on the lights, shadows clung to the corners, and years of neglect coated the floor and the furniture.

After crossing to the desk, Barrie pulled the squat antique phone toward her, lowered herself into the chair, and paused with her hand on the receiver. Whatever was lost in this room, the pull came from one of the desk drawers. It made her head pound. She tried the handles, her fingers leaving trails in the dust. The drawers were all unlocked except the one where the pull was strongest. She had the top drawer halfway open to search for a key, but then she stopped. This wasn't her desk, and she had upset Pru enough already. What she needed to do was talk to her aunt about the Watson gift.

Not only was it strange to have anything lost at Watson's Landing, but also there was something strange about *how* and *where* things were lost. Why was the locked drawer the only pull of loss in the library? Despite the neglect, there wasn't so much as a tug from a pen or a missing paper clip anywhere else in the room.

But that was a question for another day.

She dialed Mark's phone number, reminding herself she had to focus on the conversation, do better than she had the day before. He needed to believe she was happy, that her life had become one big social whirl.

Weirdly, in a way, it almost had been.

"I've barely stopped all day," she told him when he asked

what she'd been up to. "I even went for a moonlit walk with the hottie last night after I talked to you. And I spent the whole day with him."

"You go, B. What's his name?"

"Eight," Barrie said, beaming happiness into the phone line. "Charles Beaufort the Eighth, and I probably owe Lula an apology. Turns out there *are* worse things than being named after a crooked street."

She expected Mark to laugh, or come back with one of his sharp-tongued observations. But he said nothing.

"Mark? What?"

"What do you mean 'what'?" His voice sounded pinched, the way it had the night of her first awards ceremony, when he'd worn Spanx to squeeze into a pink Chanel suit he'd accidentally bought too small on eBay. As pinched as Barrie's head felt, standing there beside the locked drawer with its pounding pull. She dragged the long phone cord with her, and edged around the desk to cross the room.

Still Mark hadn't spoken. "All right. What's wrong?" Barrie tried again. "Don't try to tell me it's nothing."

"Now, why do you have to go and keep asking me things like that?" He heaved a sigh that ended in a cough. "I'm here and you're there, and ashes of that damned, stupid, infuriating woman who named you are floating around the ocean somewhere, and I actually miss her skinny white ass. Which I never would have believed in a million years." Mark sniffed wetly. "Now no more morbid talk."

Barrie dropped herself onto the dusty chair and gripped the phone more tightly. "I'm not the one who was talking morbid. *I'm* not the one who sent me away."

"I need to know you have someone who loves you before I go. Is that too much to ask? Pru's good, isn't she? She's going to love you? Of course she is. She probably does already."

"I think so," Barrie said, unconvinced.

"Good. So tell me about this moonlit walk with your lucky number."

"Well, there was moonlight and there was walking." Barrie drew her knees to her chest to try to hold herself together. But there were more and more pieces of her heart splintering off all the time. "Then this morning he brought me a rose and took me to see sea turtles, and fed me the most amazing hot dog for lunch. A can't-do-better-so-never-eat-hot-dogs-anywhere-else hot dog, so it's a good thing I hate baseball, or I'd starve at the games. Have you ever heard of sweet potato mustard?"

"Sounds too good to be true," Mark said. "The boy, I mean, not the mustard."

Barrie thought of the way Eight pushed and acted like he knew everything, and she almost laughed. "Trust me, he isn't too good. He *is* picking me up in an hour, though, so I have to hang up. Oh, and I lost my phone. Call Pru's number if you need me." Mark was quiet so long, she thought she'd lost the connection. "Mark?"

"I'm still here. Quick, what shoes are you wearing?"

"Jeffersons." As always, Barrie named the first shoes that came to mind, which was how the game was played.

"Jeffersons? Huh. High and sporty. Kick-ass cute without making you seem like you're trying hard. You be very careful now, sweetness. You're not used to this, and the number's still just a boy. You've got places to go. No falling for him."

No worries.

Barrie didn't need that kind of aggravation.

"I met Lula's best friend today," she said. "Also my cousin Cassie, Wade's niece. Turns out my father had a brother. Turns out Lula running off with a Colesworth was quite the *Romeo and Juliet* reenactment."

Mark gave a snort. "Trust me, baby girl, that man was no Romeo."

"I thought you barely knew him?"

"Just because he didn't talk to me doesn't mean I didn't know what was going on in the next apartment. I know he was out all hours without Lula. That she had tear streaks down her face half the time when I ran into her at the mailbox or in the elevator. And I don't mean from her migraines."

"You never told me that."

"Lula had radar tuned to the sound of his name. No point talking about him at all. It's not like it was my business to judge before the fire. Or after. The minute I got to know your mother better, I realized she was about the most obstinate woman who ever lived."

Barrie nodded, then realized Mark couldn't see her. "I guess," she said.

"No guessing anything, baby girl. I did my best juggling you and Lula, and how much to tell either of you. As far as she was concerned, your father didn't exist. Easier to keep it that way."

Barrie wondered if she should tell Mark about Cassie. He'd be happy for her, wouldn't he? Still, something held her back.

"I better get going," she said. "The number is going to be here before I know it."

They said their good-byes and hung up. When she had put the phone back on the desk, Barrie couldn't help wanting to reach for the locked drawer again. Lost in thought, she startled at a movement in the doorway.

"Sorry." Pru stepped into the room. "I didn't mean to eavesdrop. Mary said she sent you in here because you still haven't found your phone. How is your godfather? How are you doing with his . . ."

"Dying?" Barrie put up her hand and turned away when Pru came to hold her. "I'm fine," she said.

"Oh, sugar." Pru paused short of the hug she'd obviously intended to offer. "I imagine you believe that. That's probably been your only option so far. Lula can't have been easy to live with. Sometimes, though, we let ourselves get so used to being 'fine' that we lose track of how 'not fine' we are."

She frowned at the portrait above the fireplace as she spoke, and Barrie suddenly saw the resemblance between the stern man and her aunt. It was there around the eyes, in the long, narrow nose. Remembering what Julia had said about Emmett, Barrie studied the portrait more closely. Her grandfather looked like the sort of man whose skin would have been cold to the touch even when he was still alive.

Was that why the library was so filthy? Because Pru didn't want to face her father even after he was dead?

"It's a coping mechanism," Pru said. "Telling yourself you're all right even when you're not. Maybe your brain and emotions go numb so you stop wanting what you can't have. But other people's darkness can drag you down."

Pru kept staring at the portrait. Then her chin came up. She crossed to the curtains and threw them open in an avalanche of dust. Moving around the room, she let the light in at every window, and then brushed off her hands and turned back to Barrie.

"I know what it's like to have to be 'fine' even when you're not. So don't you worry about that with me, that's all I'm saying. You go ahead and be mad about Mark and Lula. Be sad. Be whatever you want. It's okay to allow yourself to feel."

"I don't know what I—" Barrie began, but then stopped herself. "Did you ever read *The Bell Jar?* There's a line in it about watching Paris, the city, shrinking with every second, making you feel smaller and lonelier. That's how I feel. Mark used to be my Paris, and he's slipping farther and farther away."

Backlit by the sun, Pru, too, looked smaller. Deflated. Barrie painted on a smile. A little one was all she could manage. If Pru could smile, though, so could she.

"You said Mary told you my phone was still missing," she said. "Did you find it?"

"No, honey." Pru moved toward the desk.

Did Pru feel the pull from the drawer? Barrie trailed after her to see if Pru would reach for the handle, but Pru came to an abrupt stop and turned back toward her.

"Are you still planning on going out tonight?"

"Yes," Barrie said.

"Then you'd better get yourself into the shower and get cleaned up. The Resurrection isn't fancy, but Cassie will be all decked out—she won't risk letting you outshine her. You make sure you put on something pretty. Hurry now. It's getting late."

CHAPTER TEN

Eight was in the parlor, tapping his thumb on the armrest of a striped silk sofa, when Barrie came downstairs. Dressed in a blue jacket and khaki pants, with his hair combed back instead of slouching in his face as usual, he looked older. Miles out of Barrie's league. The thought and the lit-up smile he gave her made it hard to breathe. Him all dressed up waiting for her, her all dressed up coming downstairs—it looked like a date. Her first date. But it wasn't. Eight was playing chauffeur and babysitter, that was all.

She didn't want to be glad to see him. And yet she was.

He came over to meet her. His gaze dropped to the bows on Barrie's red-and-white peep-toe slingbacks, the ones that resembled high-heeled Sperry's, then slid up past her jeans and blouse to linger on her lips. "Very nice," he said. "The Resurrection won't know what hit it."

"Thank you." Barrie tried to hide her blush-warmed cheeks while he held the front door open for her. Tried not to feel the heat coming off him when she stepped past.

But of course he had to spoil it. "You might need to rethink the heels, if you ever want to come sailing with me. They're not actually practical as boat shoes."

Barrie gave him her best withering glance and walked faster down the steps. There was no chance of her going sailing, with him or anyone else.

"Why do you want to be mad at me?" He easily kept pace.

"I don't want to be mad."

"You may not think you do. . . ."

Suddenly Barrie remembered exactly why she shouldn't be glad to see him. Because he was infuriating. "So now you're telling me what I think? What is it with you? You order my food. You tell me who I want to go out with. You tell Pru to let *you* fix the shutter, tell random people who they need to call, you even tell me what kind of shoes to wear."

"Wait. I *like* your shoes. I've liked all your shoes so far."

"You're pushy." Barrie shoved him in the chest. "Stop pushing me. And get out of my head. I know what I want."

"That's just it. You don't *listen* to what you want. You think you don't want to be mad at me, but you do. You thought you should want to go to dinner with Cassie, so you told her you would. And now you're going because you think you have to—"

"Stop doing that!" It made Barrie even madder not to be able to deny it. He was right, damn him, but it had nothing to do with Cassie. She pushed the car door out of his hand and dropped into the passenger seat.

He tapped the roof, once, twice. "Could we call a truce for tonight, Bear? Neither one of us needs to be upset when we get where we're going."

They drove in silence until Eight turned on the stereo again. With the convertible top up, the car had shrunk. Or Eight and all the things they weren't saying had grown too big for the space. The tension built between them, ratcheting higher so that by the time they left Watson's Landing, Barrie's headache was back again, as intense and sudden as if it had been outside the gate waiting for her all along.

Eight stopped the car before turning out onto the road. Leaning across her, he opened the glove box and tossed a new bottle of Tylenol into her lap. "Here. You'll be miserable at the Resurrection with a headache."

Barrie took it without comment. She had probably winced or rubbed her temple without realizing it—she was beyond questioning how Eight always knew what she was thinking. He didn't even need to be clairvoyant to know the Resurrection would be hard for her.

When they got there, music vibrated through the flame-painted walls. Barrie got out of the car in the parking lot, and with her mouth dry and her head pounding, she mumbled a thank-you and a good-bye and walked toward the entrance. She expected Eight to drive away.

Instead he followed her inside. Laughter, music, and the clack of pool balls knocking into one another bounced off the floor and ceiling, but conversation hushed and heads turned as she paused inside. Eight scanned the room. After catching her hand, he led her past the bar area and a dance floor where a graying grizzly of a man danced with a woman in a ruffled denim skirt, fishnet tights, and combat boots.

Barrie heard Cassie's laugh before she saw her. Flanked by two pretty girls, her cousin leaned against the pool table closest to the wall, but she might as well have been dead-center in the room. She commanded attention as if it were hers by right. In a white shirt with the collar flipped up, tight fawn-colored pants, and sky-high black suede heels, Barrie's cousin missed being a *Vogue* cover model by ten pounds in all the right places.

The bottom of her own cue stick resting on the floor, Cassie watched a muscled twentysomething wearing a camouflage cap turned backward line up the two ball with the corner pocket. She bent to speak into his ear, but her voice was loud enough to carry above the music. "You might as well quit, Grady. You're going to overthink that shot. You know you are. Any second now, you're going to wonder if it isn't a hair to the left, and knock it too hard."

The guy straightened and gave her a pleading look. "Have a heart, Cassie. Would you just let me play?"

"Am I holding you back?" Cassie looked around for support, her expression innocent except for the smile playing around her lips. "Do you see my hands on the boy, y'all? Or am I simply telling him what we all know is the gospel truth?"

Laughter rippled across the room, and a woman from the next table over called: "She's got you there, Grady. Course, she's got you in all kinds of different of ways."

Cassie raised her head to laugh and caught sight of Barrie. She straightened away from the table. "Well, there she is. Hey, y'all"—she waved and glanced around with a smile—"come and meet my pretty little cousin, Barrie Watson."

Every eye in the room turned toward Barrie, and she wished she could head right back out the door. Most of the kids in Barrie's junior class at Creswell Prep had been together since the first day of middle school. They might not have been her best friends, but they knew her.

She didn't know anyone here, but after Cassie's introduction, every soul in the poolroom gathered around. Cassie's friends, Grady and *his* friends, other kids, older guys who reeked of beer. The crowd itself attracted attention, and soon the waitress and the hostess from the dining room came in, along with older people from the bar.

"Hold on," Eight whispered to her. "It'll be over soon."

It was. Maybe because the crowd was younger, they hadn't known her mother, and so Barrie wasn't as much of a curiosity. She breathed easier when it was only Cassie, Grady, and the two pretty blondes, Beth and Gilly, left standing with her. And Eight, the solid bulk of him forming a foundation at her back.

Both Beth and Gilly seemed more interested in him than Barrie. "So when do you have to leave for school?" Beth asked.

Eight cut a glance at Barrie. "Not sure yet."

"You have to be excited, I'll bet. Imagine being out in the middle of *everything*. Hollywood. The beach."

"We've got plenty of beaches around here," Eight said.

"That's right." Cassie threaded her arm through the crook of Barrie's elbow. "Beaches and cookouts and all sorts of things." She gestured to include Beth and Gilly. "We are going to have so much fun! And the best part? Summer's barely started. We'll have loads of time to hang out before school starts."

"I don't know." Beth looked Barrie up and down. She was taller than Gilly and less round, and she looked both elegant and casual, dressed all in white. "Barrie doesn't look like she gets to the beach much. We'll have to get some color on her first."

Barrie glanced at Eight. She couldn't help thinking of his cheek against hers while he'd pointed out turtles in the water. He wasn't always aggravating.

"I like the beach," she said. "I've just never been one for lying out."

In the background the jukebox had clicked over to Lady Gaga's "The Edge of Glory," the heartbeat opener with its simple voice building up to sax and soaring hooks. The song was one of Mark's favorites. Barrie had sung it with him so many times, karaoke style, hamming it up and laughing like crazy by the end. The notes flowed through her, loosening her shoulders. The plastic smile she'd been wearing started to feel more like her own.

Beside her Eight stepped closer, his breath hot and chill-inducing against her skin. "I've got to get going, but you're okay now, aren't you? You'll be fine on your own." He leaned in even more. "Just don't let Cassie bully you."

He pulled away, and Barrie felt it like a loss.

Cassie's lips slid into a potent curve aimed dead at him. "You sure you can't stay, love? Come on. Cancel your dinner or whatever. Get out of that jacket, and stay. I promise we're a whole lot more fun than whatever you have planned."

"I can't. Sorry," Eight said, not sounding it. He caught Barrie's gaze, and hesitated, then leaned in as if—

As if *what*? What was Barrie even thinking?

"Say hello to your father for me," she said sweetly.

A muscle worked along Eight's jaw. He opened his mouth, but Cassie tugged Barrie toward the dining room before he could speak. "His loss, right, Barrie? We won't worry about him. You're going to be fine with us. We'll go eat, and then maybe we'll dance. Or shoot some pool. You play, don't you?"

Barrie pretended she didn't care as Cassie led her and the other two girls away, but she was aware of Eight standing and watching them go.

Beth waited until he was out of earshot before catching Barrie's shoulder. "What *is* the matter with you, girl? Eight Beaufort was about to kiss you, and you sent him away looking like a dog without its supper."

"I'll be happy to take him off your hands, if you don't want him," Gilly said.

Beth frowned at Gilly with an ugly little twist of her lips. "As if."

"You want him, you can have him," Barrie said, but the thought carved a small pit of emptiness inside her. She studied the scratched wood floor. "Not that he's mine to hand over."

Not that she wanted him to be.

Cassie led them to an empty booth and gestured for Barrie and Gilly to slide in first on either side. Gilly gave Barrie a slight eye roll as she wedged herself in against the wall. Despite being plump, she was beautiful. Like Cassie, she had the magical kind of beauty that had little to do with individual features. Technically, proportionally, Gilly's mouth was too far from her nose, and her eyes were too wide apart. Studying her across the booth though, Barrie wished she had brought her sketchbook. Taken as a whole, Gilly's features transformed into a paintable and intriguing face. Had Cassie not been in the room, it would have been Gilly turning heads.

Gilly was pleasantly unself-conscious too. Leaning over the table, she shouted to be heard above the music spilling from the bar. "You have to try the barbecue, Barrie!"

Barrie nodded, her head throbbing in time to the beat. "The Edge of Glory" had faded into a set of Springsteen songs, as if someone had a thing for saxophone. Cassie plucked four menus from the stand at the edge of the table and passed them around. "They make a mustard sauce here that'll make your mouth want to dance."

"Is it spicy?" Barrie asked as a song ended. The words came out too loud.

Cassie smiled broadly. "You can use a little spice, sugar. Heat to bring out some color on that porcelain skin."

"Seems to me she's doing fine in the heat department." Beth tipped her head at Gilly. "Better than *some* of us, and she's barely been in town a day."

"Well, it wasn't like either of *us* was ever going to have him." Gilly buried her face behind a menu.

"Stop it, you two. It's not like the boy can help himself. It's the Beaufort-Watson thing pulling them together. Watsons and Beauforts are always together," Cassie said.

Beth turned to gape at her. "What are you talking about?

I've never so much as seen a Watson and a Beaufort in the same building."

"Not now, maybe. But that's not the way it's always been—Watsons and Beauforts used to run this town together and to hell with anyone else." The waitress had come to take their order, and Cassie glanced around the table. "Y'all are ready, aren't you?" She lowered her menu but didn't wait for anyone to answer. "I'll have the Boil and my cousin will have the Barbecue and—" She broke off and let the menu fall to the table, her expression wary and at the same time closed-off, as if the shutters had slammed on a house, hiding whatever lived within. "Daddy?"

"Hello there." Wyatt ignored his daughter and focused in on Barrie. "You've got to be my niece."

CHAPTER ELEVEN

Wyatt Colesworth was a big, forbidding man, and his dark hair and dark clothing melted into the shadows of the dim restaurant lighting. "Don't get mad," he said to Cassie. "I'm not going to crash your girls' night out, but I had to come by and say hello to Wade's little girl." He stopped beside the booth, and his slack skin and craggy features turned warmer as he smiled at Barrie. "Come here and give your uncle Wyatt a big old hug. Get up now, Beth. Let her out."

Barrie rose, but even from a yard away Cassie's father smelled of fish, with undertones of some beverage stronger than beer. His teeth were stained and all the same size, like little squares of yellow gum. Barrie wanted to stay right where she was, but Beth slid off the seat and left her without a choice. In the booths around them, people had turned to watch as if this were part of the evening's entertainment. Barrie gave Wyatt a quick squeeze and pulled away.

"It's nice to meet you—"

"You call me Uncle Wyatt, you hear? We're family, aren't we? Your mama and Wade and me went back a long way together. I imagine she probably mentioned me to you?" His eyes were hooded, but beneath the heavy lids he watched her sharply. "She probably talked about me a lot. She always liked telling stories."

Barrie's pulse and the throb in her temples hammered together at the undertone in Wyatt's voice that didn't match up with the friendliness of his words. Was he going to say anything about following them to the beach that afternoon? Should she say anything about it?

Maybe it had been someone else, or maybe he was embarrassed about it now. He had lost his brother. Of course he would hope that Lula had passed on some final message.

"I'm sorry." What was Barrie supposed to say? "Lula didn't really talk about living here."

"You see, Daddy? You're making Barrie uncomfortable." Cassie threw him a stare, then smiled at Barrie. "Excuse us a second." Grabbing her father's arm, she marched him away so that her furious whispering wasn't audible.

"Don't worry," Beth said. "They're always like that. The man's a piece of work, but Cassie knows how to handle him."

Wyatt pointed back toward Barrie. Cassie shook her head. Wyatt started to step forward, and she put her hand on his arm and spoke to him with the kind of body language a parent used with a child who was about to do something unreasonable. It was an odd exchange, stranger still because Barrie couldn't hear it.

Cassie must have won. Wyatt waved at Barrie and strode toward the exit, and Cassie returned to the table.

"Sorry about that." She slid back into the booth with a blinding smile. "Your daddy was his only brother, so he's been anxious to hear all about you and Lula. I told him I wanted you to myself for tonight. There'll be plenty of time for you to come over and catch up on family history. Daddy's got lots of photographs of Uncle Wade to show you."

Wyatt probably knew a lot more about why Lula and Wade had run off than anyone else in town, and Barrie should have jumped at the chance to see photographs of her father. She should have wanted to say she would love to go to Colesworth Place. But her warning radar was stuck in the on position. Which was stupid. Wyatt had been more than friendly. The wrongness in the pit of her stomach had to be a leftover effect from the afternoon and the things Pru and Eight had told her. It didn't make Barrie proud to realize she had bought into their paranoia about the Colesworths.

She leaned back as the waitress brought their Cokes and

passed them around. After scrunching the paper wrapper down her straw as tight as it would go, she eased it off and dribbled a few drops of water over it. The paper unwound like a snake, as unruly as Barrie's tongue, which still refused to cooperate. She couldn't make herself say she wanted to spend time with Wyatt when she didn't.

"You're not worried about my daddy, are you?" Cassie eased forward on her elbows, watching Barrie. "I can tell you didn't like him. Please don't let him put you off! You've probably heard stories about him, haven't you? The only people you've spent real time with so far are Watsons and Beauforts, so you're bound to have the wrong impression of us. Daddy can be a little odd sometimes, I'll admit. But the thing is, we're all dying to know."

"Know what?" Barrie asked.

Cassie made a face that stopped just shy of an eye roll. "Which family trait you ended up with. What did you get? The Watson gift or the Colesworth curse?"

Goose bumps ran along Barrie's skin. Cassie mentioned the gift so casually, out in the open, in front of the other girls. And they only looked at Barrie with idle curiosity. As if *of course* everyone knew about the gift.

Or maybe the shiver came from the other word.

"What curse?" she asked.

"You don't know? Really?" Cassie's expression hovered

somewhere between scorn and disbelief. "Didn't your mama tell you? Or Pru—or Eight?"

"Why don't you tell me?"

Cassie seemed to surge with energy, as if someone had turned a three-way bulb up a click. She jumped to her feet. "Let's move outside. I can't shout over the music." She winked at Barrie. "Plus we need better atmosphere."

Gilly and Beth gathered up their silverware, so Barrie did the same. Cassie tossed a five-dollar bill onto the table, paused to tell the waitress they were moving, then hurried out to the back deck that overlooked the water.

A fire crackled in a circular brazier, like a campfire on the beach. Old sails draped from end to end created a canopy overhead and fluttered in the wind, while music filtered at a more bearable volume from the windows.

They settled onto a bench at a table in the far back corner. The fire painted Cassie's face in a blend of shadow and light that made Barrie's fingers crave a sketchpad, and when every-one was seated, Cassie leaned forward with the air of someone about to tell a secret. She spoke in a theatrical half whisper that carried over the noise. Even so, Barrie found herself tipping close to listen.

"It all started," Cassie began, "with three younger sons of good English families: Thomas Watson, Robert Beaufort, and John Colesworth. They went to the Caribbean to make their fortunes, and since piracy was legal then, as long as you had a letter of permission from the king and you only went after England's enemies, they became privateers on a ship called the *Loyal Jamaica*. They collected a huge treasure before the ship ran aground near Charleston on a supply trip. With nice manners and plenty of gold, they weren't unwelcome, and the governors of the Carolina colony gave them grants to settle in the area. Then one night before the land deals were official, Thomas Watson had too much to drink and lost half his share of the gold while gambling with one of the governors." Cassie raised her eyebrows at Barrie. "Are you following all this?"

"The man who built Watson's Landing was a pirate, a drunk, and a gambler. Yes," Barrie said dryly, "I think I've about got it."

"Now, don't take offense, sugar. They were *all* pirates. I'm sure they all drank and gambled, but Thomas Watson had a bad night, and he accused the governor of cheating. Robert Beaufort and John Colesworth saved him from pistols at dawn by apologizing, but the governor was still plenty mad. He gave Thomas Watson land on a haunted island to get revenge."

"Haunted?" Cold etched itself deep into Barrie's bones. She thought of the sphere of fire and the dark figure by the river. Maybe what she had seen last night hadn't been a dream or a product of her imagination.

Did that make her feel better or worse? She wasn't sure.

The waitress came with their food, but Cassie talked on as if she didn't care that the woman would overhear. *As if everyone already knew the story.*

"Yes, haunted. Thomas Watson's island was inhabited by the Fire Carrier, the ghost of a Cherokee witch who had cleared his tribal lands of malicious spirits, *yunwi*, and pushed them down the Santisto until they'd come to the last bit of land surrounded by water on every side. The Fire Carrier bound the *yunwi* there, and kept them from escaping, with fire and magic and running water."

"Excellent," Barrie said. "Pirates, gold, *and* evil spirits."

"You can laugh. Thomas laughed too. At first. Until every brick of the mansion he tried to build disappeared every night, and every field he plowed or seeded was flooded or trampled. He spent most of his gold on the plantation, with nothing to show for it. He was about to give up, leave his friends, and go home to England, when John Colesworth offered to get one of his slaves to trap the Fire Carrier and force it to make the *yunwi* behave."

"How would he do that?"

"Voodoo," Cassie said with a narrow smile.

Well, that wasn't what Barrie had expected. "Seriously?"

"A lot of the slaves came from the West Indies. This one was a voodoo priest. He trapped the Fire Carrier at midnight when the spirit came to the river to perform his magic, and he held the Fire Carrier until the witch agreed to control the *yunwi* and make them leave Thomas Watson alone. Then Thomas replanted his fields. He built a new house that stayed up, but by then he was out of money. He couldn't afford a mansion as nice as Colesworth Place or Beaufort Hall across the river. So he and John Colesworth trapped the Fire Carrier again, and this time they made him let Thomas Watson get back what he had lost. The plan worked better than anyone had expected. The *yunwi* returned what they had stolen, and the governor gave back the gambling money."

"But that isn't how it works!" Barrie exclaimed.

"So you *do* know about it." Cassie pounced. "You have the gift, don't you? I was sure you did."

Barrie felt her face burning, but at the same time, a cold ache spread through her stomach. She pushed the dull knife through her sandwich—pulled pork with sauce on a white bread bun. She speared a forkful of coleslaw and made a show of chewing while she arranged her scrambled thoughts.

"I didn't say I had it. Or knew about it. What I meant is the story isn't logical. If the Fire Carrier gave Thomas Watson the ability to get back what he had lost, why would that pass on to his family as a gift, or let him find things other people had lost?"

"It might not have, but that isn't the end of the story." Cassie edged back, and in the shadow of the canvas sails overhead, her expression was impossible to read. "Robert Beaufort fell in love with a woman from town, a woman who was already in love with John Colesworth. Robert didn't care. He and Thomas Watson trapped the Fire Carrier again without John Colesworth this time, and demanded the witch help Robert win the woman's heart."

Cassie paused to let the story sink in. "From then on, Robert Beaufort knew how to give his love whatever she wanted most. He brought her jewels in the perfect color to match her gowns, rebuilt Beaufort Hall so she would love it, and he always told her exactly what she wanted to hear. Little by little, she stopped loving John Colesworth. Finally she agreed to marry Robert instead."

The moisture wicked out of Barrie's mouth.

Robert Beaufort had known *what someone wanted*. He had *known*.

Cassie veiled her eyes with heavy lashes. With her hands folded on the edge of the table, she studied the way her thumbs formed a cross, almost as if she were warding off some sort of evil but didn't want anyone to see the gesture.

Suddenly she looked back up at Barrie. "John Colesworth put up with all that betrayal as long as he could," she said. "But the night before Robert Beaufort was supposed to marry the woman John loved, John snuck back onto the island and trapped the Fire Carrier a fourth and final time. All he wanted was to get back what he'd had before. Except the Fire Carrier was done with being trapped. His magic overwhelmed the priest. And instead of giving John his wish, the Fire Carrier cursed the Colesworths in generations yet unborn to be poorer and unhappier than the Watsons, who would always find what was lost, and the Beauforts, who would always know how to give others what they wanted."

The sun was setting. In spite of the fire and the humid night, Barrie felt like she might never warm up again.

Thomas Watson had chosen sides between two friends and betrayed John Colesworth by forcing, *tricking*, a woman to love Robert Beaufort. That was the foundation of Eight's gift. And of hers.

Cassie's features tightened until her high cheekbones were blades and her beautiful eyes shone like glass. "No one has ever inherited more than one magic from the Fire Carrier. So which one do you have? Gift or curse? Are you a Watson—or a Colesworth?"

Barrie picked up her napkin and dabbed her mouth to buy a moment to respond.

It was just a story, she told herself.

Only, it didn't feel like a story. Not to her and, judging from the gleaming expressions of the other girls, not to them, either. They had stopped eating, and sat looking back and forth between her and Cassie the way RuPaul, Mark's Siamese cat, used to watch Mark and Barrie playing Ping-Pong on the deck.

And Barrie had seen the Fire Carrier herself. She had the Watson gift. Everyone on the whole island seemed to know more about what that meant than she did. Why not just admit it?

Something held her back. She crumpled her napkin and dropped it onto her plate. "I don't believe in curses," she said.

"Really?" Cassie coiled like a snake prepared to strike. "You don't *believe*? Look across the river when you get home. Colesworth Place is a ruin, but not Beaufort Hall or Watson's Landing. They're still standing as good as the day they were built, and we are forced to—" She bit her lip, swallowed, and started again. "The Watsons could have helped us protect our house, our *family*, during the war. Your mother could have helped us get our fortune back. Instead she stole Wade away and ruined his life, ruined my daddy's life. And it sure wasn't Lula who died the night of the fire, now was it?" Cassie's breath came fast and ragged. "Lula *Watson* got out, and my uncle didn't. Watsons are always lucky. The Colesworths aren't. Now you tell me that's not a curse."

Barrie thought of her mother's life, of Lula's scars. She considered telling Cassie exactly how *lucky* Lula had been. But the idea of perfectly lovely Cassie feeling sorry for Lula made her fingers curl.

149

"You have the gift. Don't you?" Cassie pushed back her silky hair from an unscarred face and smiled at Barrie. "You do. I can see you don't want to admit it, but you have to help me. We're family, and you're the only Colesworth ever to have any Watson blood."

"What is it exactly that I'm supposed to help you do?" Barrie asked tiredly.

"I keep forgetting you don't know anything." Cassie cast a *Help me* look at Beth and Gilly. "I want you to help me find what's left of the Colesworth fortune! My great-great-great-whatever-uncle Alcee buried all our valuables before the Yankees burned Colesworth Place. We've been looking for them ever since. Or we should have been looking for them." Cassie spread her hands and gripped the edge of the table. "Look, you *have* to help me. If I—*you*—could find the treasure, I could get out of this ridiculous town. I would give anything to get out of this town. Will you please, please help?"

Getting out seemed to be a popular refrain. First Eight, now Cassie. Still, the desperation of Cassie's tone was undeniable, and how was Barrie supposed to turn her cousin down?

"Sure," Barrie said. "When?"

"You see? I knew we were going to be good friends." Cassie flashed Barrie an approving smile. "I have to work the lunch shift at Bobby Joe's tomorrow, but my theater group and I do *Gone with the Wind* at night, in front of the ruins."

150

"I thought that was set in Georgia."

Cassie gave a graceful wave. "Doesn't matter. The tourists pay money and lap it up. Still, it's a good production. Please come. You can feel around, do your Watson thing, see if you sense anything. My sister, Sydney, is dying to meet you, and Daddy has the photographs for you. You can bring Eight, too, if you want."

Barrie had plenty to say to Eight. About his gift and everything he hadn't bothered to tell her. An invitation wasn't in there anywhere. Unless it was an invitation to his own funeral, because she was going to have to kill him.

The least he could have done was warn her that her cousin was going to ask her to trot out the Watson gift like some kind of freak in a circus sideshow. But he'd been too worried about keeping his own secret to consider how she would feel.

CHAPTER TWELVE

In the parking lot outside the Resurrection, Eight opened the passenger door of his car for Barrie. She slammed it shut again. She wasn't going anywhere with him just yet.

"I can't believe you didn't tell me about the Beaufort gift! And you used it on me. That's cheating."

Eight leaned back against the fender. "It might be cheating if what you wanted and what you think you're supposed to want were remotely the same. But reading you is like trying to pitch a no-hitter blindfolded."

"I don't even know what that means."

His body was too close to hers. He was so present and *alive*, he threatened to suck her in. Even out in the open, he made it hard to think straight, to be as mad as he deserved. Needing distance, Barrie headed across the parking lot toward a clump of pines beside the beach.

Eight trailed after her. "You know what your problem is? You're the least self-aware person I've ever met. What you actually want is buried under so many layers of what you think you're supposed to do, I'm amazed you can ever make any kind of a decision. And when you do decide something, it's usually at your own expense. You've got no sense of self-preservation."

Barrie spun to face him. "Are you done telling me what's wrong with me yet?"

"You're the one who seems not to know it's okay to be yourself. To want something for yourself."

And what was there to say to that? Everything Barrie wanted was impossible.

She and Eight both fell silent. The moon hung so low over the ocean, it practically touched the water, as if it were wading in to wash itself clean.

"So what did you tell Cassie about helping her?" Eight asked, looking grim.

Barrie stopped and braced her back against a tree. "I said I would."

"Pru will pitch a fit when she finds out. Come on. Admit it. Even you don't think it's a good idea."

Maybe not, but Barrie wasn't about to say so. Anyway, how could she avoid helping Cassie? "You're going to come with me," she said. "You owe me."

"Do I?" Eight took a step toward her and then another.

Barrie was surprised at how brave she felt, how close he was, how aware she was of him, how his eyes shifted from anger to intent. She tipped her chin up and glowered at him.

"You don't scare me," he said. But then he smiled. Bracing his arm above her on the tree trunk, he held her gaze and leaned in, his head angled for a kiss as he bent closer and closer—

And Barrie chickened out.

"We'd better get back," she said, ducking under his arm. "Pru will be expecting me."

Eight stood very still. "Fine," he said.

In the awakened silence of the long ride home, Barrie went over the moment, that almost-moment, ten, twenty, a hundred times. She wondered whether she had wanted Eight to kiss her. Whether she had wanted to kiss him. Maybe she just wanted to know why *he* wanted it.

With a hurried "Good night" she rushed out of his car as soon as he pulled up to the house, and she didn't look back when he called her name. Even sitting in the kitchen while Pru prepared miniature quiches to serve the next day in the tearoom, Barrie thought about that almost-kiss.

Pru, on the other hand, was focused on the fact that Barrie was going to Colesworth Place even after hearing Cassie's story. She stopped chopping green onions at the kitchen counter and pointed at Barrie with the knife.

"Are you even listening to me, sugar? I understand you mean well, wanting to help Cassie and all, but it's Colesworth property, and Wyatt is going to be there. Seven suspects Wyatt is going to do something about trying to get custody of you so they can get their hands on Lula's money. Colesworths always have some kind of an agenda. Believe me, Cassie isn't telling you even half the truth about whatever she thinks is buried over there. And why on earth would she expect you to want to help her?"

"She's my cousin. Why wouldn't I want to help her?"

"Because the gift is evil."

Barrie's eyebrows shot up into her hairline. "Evil?"

"That story Cassie told you is a fairy tale. Nothing good's ever come of playing with voodoo and witchcraft. Cherokee or otherwise. Look at Lula."

"What about her? She didn't think using the gift was evil—"

"Look what that got her! Look at her life." Pru stared down at the knife in her hand as if she didn't quite know what to do with it. Carefully she set it on the cutting board and came to join Barrie at the table. "Growing up, I was the twin who

155

sat and waited for things to happen. Lula was the wild one, the curious one. She went out and made things happen—and dragged me along with her. Right up until the year before she left. That year the gift made her strange. We'd both had a little of it all our lives. Daddy insisted we ignore it, and since neither of us liked it when he punished us, we stopped reacting to the pull of lost things. After a while the gift became background noise. For me, anyway."

"But not for Lula?"

"No. For her the gift was impossible to ignore. It gave her headaches if she didn't do what it demanded."

Barrie went very still. "You're making the gift sound alive. As if it thinks. Decides."

"Maybe. I know Lula tried to tell Daddy what she felt. He only preached more fire and brimstone and said she would burn in hell if she used the gift."

"Cassie's story didn't make it sound evil either."

"Cassie's story is a Colesworth story. She told you what she wanted you to know."

"What's the Watson story?"

"Daddy never said. Seven Beaufort once gave me the Beaufort side. I don't remember many details, but I know there wasn't anything about trapping the Fire Carrier. It was an out-and-out bargain. A deal with the devil."

If the devil had a painted face and carried fire.

Barrie waited for Pru to go on, but her aunt returned to the counter to distribute diced onions among tiny muffin cups lined with dough, and when Pru spoke it was with her back still turned so that Barrie couldn't see her face.

"I'm sure you think I should have told you all of this," Pru said. "But we've barely had any time to talk, and I wanted to wait to see if you needed to be told. I wasn't even sure you had the gift. If you didn't, what would have been the point of bringing it up?"

"Because everyone in town knows more than I do? I had to hear about it from Cassie."

"That's exactly why you need to reject the gift. Don't you see? All it does is make people like Cassie want to use you." Pru came over again and put her hands on Barrie's shoulders. "I know you want to help your cousin, sugar, and I know you already agreed to help. Just promise me you'll think about what I said. There's still time to change your mind about going over there." She waited until Barrie nodded. Then she kissed Barrie's forehead and went back to cooking.

Barrie sighed. "Good night, Aunt Pru."

"Good night, honey. Sleep on what I said."

Barrie wasn't sure there would a lot of sleeping going on that night. As she got into her pajamas, she found she couldn't think about the gift as being something evil. The ability to find things had been a part of her for as long as she could remember.

She paced the room, and her mind kept going back to Eight and the Beaufort gift.

What would it be like to know what people wanted? She couldn't imagine it. Eight was right: half the time she didn't know what she wanted.

She should want to help Cassie, for instance. Yet deep down she didn't. It had been hard to drum up enthusiasm to argue with Pru and Eight and pretend that she did.

Her reluctance had nothing to do with evil or even the story Cassie had told. It wasn't because Wyatt made her nervous. It wasn't a rational objection. Presumably there would be a crowd of tourists at Cassie's play, and helping her cousin's family get their fortune back was the perfect solution to end the Watson-Colesworth feud. There wasn't a downside, really. Barrie knew what it was to feel trapped by walls and by expectation.

Downstairs the grandfather clock chimed midnight. She listened to the last knell and let herself out onto the balcony. She walked toward the farthest point, half-hoping, half-dreading the sight of fire lighting up the trees in the woods. Already an orange glow lit the trunks of the knot-kneed cypress trees, casting macabre shadows that raced along the line of trees.

The Fire Carrier emerged into the open marsh. He was a silhouette, more of a suggestion than a shape as he waded hip-deep into the water beyond the marsh grass and spilled threads of fire across the water.

Flames rushed gold and red, upriver and down. Remembering Cassie's story, Barrie imagined the fire circling the island, hugging the shoreline, blazing up the creek that separated Watson's Landing from the rest of Watson Island.

How long had the witch performed this same magical ritual here, night after night? Three hundred years at least.

The burning globe in the Fire Carrier's hands grew smaller as he released the last strands of fire onto the water, leaving only an orange glow in his hands and occasional purple-blue spits of flame crackling across his palms. He turned to face the balcony where Barrie stood.

She squeezed the railing, grasping for something she knew was real. Clinging to the hope that it was all a hallucination. It had to be. But every detail of the scene was clear. Clearer even than it had been the previous night. There was the scent of sage-thickened smoke that she hadn't smelled before, and details she shouldn't—couldn't—have seen across the distance between her and the witch. The glistening war paint on his naked chest, the feathers in his cloak and headdress stirring in the breeze created by the flame behind him.

The red-and-black mask painted across his features, that was still the same. Behind it the Fire Carrier's eyes bored into hers. Barrie *felt* him watching, wanting, waiting for something from her.

Each beat of her heart thudded in her ears. Every ragged, shallow breath seared her lungs as if she were breathing fire. And still he watched her.

"What do you want?" she whispered.

He turned away. Hands cupped in a receiving gesture, he stooped toward the water. Where the fire had spread across the river, it raced back to him in strands of flame, and he spooled them up like a ball of yarn. Without giving Barrie another glance, he carried the burning orb back into the woods.

She took a shuddering breath when he had vanished among the trees. Her chest ached and her eyes blurred. At the edges of her vision, streaks of shadow raced behind the Fire Carrier, leaping and darting away toward the woods so fast, she couldn't be sure they were there. But abruptly she knew they *were*.

She had seen shadows like that before. Had noticed them without *noticing*. Shadows moving among the trees and beneath the bushes in the garden. *Yunwi.* That was what Cassie had called the spirits the Fire Carrier guarded on the island. The *yunwi* were still here too.

Shivering, Barrie went back to her room and latched the balcony doors behind her. Quietly, she crawled into bed. Curled on her side beneath the quilt, she lay awake going over everything Eight, Cassie, and Pru had told her about Watson Island, and coming up with five questions for every answer.

She hadn't asked if any of them had seen the spirits or the Fire Carrier themselves. She hadn't asked nearly enough questions. What if the Fire Carrier or the *yunwi* were the real reason Lula had run away? That made more sense than the romantic elopement Barrie had been envisioning. After all, if Lula and Wade had planned to run away together because they'd been in love, wouldn't Lula have confided that to Pru? Or to Julia? Maybe Lula hadn't planned to leave at all. Maybe something had scared her enough to make her run away in the middle of the night.

Sleep eluded Barrie most of the night. She woke bleary-eyed in the morning, with a bitter taste, like overbrewed tea, inside her mouth. Already the air was hot. The balcony doors she had closed had popped open again, letting the jasmine-infused humidity seep inside. She got up to shut the doors, only to have the latch come off in her hand. And the bedpost, which had been perfectly sturdy the day before, wobbled in her grip while she slipped into her shoes.

No wonder Pru had screamed at the poor old house. It had to be impossible to keep up with all the things that broke all the time.

The thought reminded her that she still hadn't confessed to Pru that Lula's furniture was going to be delivered.

With a sigh, she dressed and made her way downstairs. After hugging the wall to avoid the broken banister, she found Pru shaking a cast-iron skillet of shrimp and stirring a pot on a back burner of the stove. Mixed in with the faint ocean odor of the shrimp and a hint of bacon, Barrie picked out the scent of yellow and green onions; serrano, bell, and red peppers; paprika, and a few spices she couldn't place. The effort of sorting the scents reminded her of Mark. She cupped a hand over his watch, wishing more than ever that he was with her.

"This here's the low-country breakfast of champions. Otherwise known as shrimp and grits." Pru turned to Barrie with a determinedly cheerful smile, as if their argument the night before had never happened. But then her focus sharpened. "You don't look like you slept much, sugar. Do you feel all right?"

Barrie opened the avocado-colored refrigerator, still unsure what she wanted to say, or how to phrase it. She pulled out the pitcher of orange juice.

"So, um . . . I went out on the balcony to watch the Fire Carrier last night," she said.

Pru turned very slowly to face Barrie, and her lips were tight, her brows drawn into a furrow. Of worry or anger, not surprise.

Barrie set the pitcher on the table with a thud. "You've seen him too, haven't you? You know he's still here. Why didn't you tell me that last night?"

"I haven't seen the fire in years, so I couldn't know you would. And we were caught up in the Cassie argument." Pru reached behind her, anchoring herself against the edge of the stove. "Most people see a glow on the water and assume it's a will-o'-the-wisp in the marsh or reflected moonlight."

"How do you stop seeing it? It's not like a fairy. You can't just stop believing."

"I don't know if 'believing' is the word you're looking for."

"Then what?"

The grits began to scorch, and Pru snatched up the pot and scraped the mixing spoon against the bottom. Barrie straddled the nearest chair. Hands draped across the back, she waited, letting the silence grow until Pru finally looked up.

"I've been thinking and thinking what to tell you," Pru said with her back to Barrie. "The trouble is, I don't know how much you are like your mother. Warning Lula about danger only whetted her curiosity."

That didn't sound like Lula. But then, none of the things Barrie had heard since she'd had arrived at Watson's Landing sounded much like Lula.

"I'm not reckless," she said.

"You didn't believe me when I said the Watson gift is evil." Pru turned with the spoon in her hand. "Sugar, you can't play around with magic. Or magical beings. At best you appease them, and you stay clear. I don't know how to make you understand that. Your mama didn't believe in the danger either, and the gift almost tore her apart."

"What do you mean?"

"Lula didn't want to turn her back on it; she liked the idea of having something magical of her own. She couldn't stop thinking about the gift and where it came from, worrying over what the Fire Carrier wanted. Not using the gift started to hurt her physically, and the whole situation made her crazy. She got it into her head that if she could find the Fire Carrier and speak to it, she could convince Daddy he was wrong— that there wasn't any reason not to use the gift. She tried to talk me into going into the woods with her one night, but I wouldn't, so she went alone.

"Of course Daddy caught her. He took a switch to both of us, screaming that the Fire Carrier would kill us as sure as we were breathing. I was half-afraid Daddy was the one who was going to kill us. Fear twists people, makes them do things they normally wouldn't do. Lula usually didn't back down about anything, but she was different after that night. I don't know if it was the pain from the beating, or if she didn't want to see me punished for what she did, or if something Daddy had said finally convinced her, but she never went back to the woods again."

Barrie's eyes stung. Her throat ached for both Pru and Lula. How could Pru talk so matter-of-factly about being beaten? And how could she think the *Fire Carrier* was the villain in that story?

The Fire Carrier hadn't seemed vicious. Or dangerous. Not last night, and not the night before. He'd seemed . . . sad. Wistful and disappointed.

The doubt must have registered on Barrie's face.

Pru gave a *fffffft* of exasperation and flung the wooden spoon back into the pot of grits. "Your mama wore that same stubborn expression every time Daddy told her to quit poking at things she didn't understand."

"I thought you said she stopped going into the woods."

"That didn't keep her from going out onto the balcony to watch the fire. I could see her need to understand, all bottled up inside her."

"Does that mean you were out on the balcony with her?"

"Not to watch the Fire Carrier. I had other reasons."

"You did see him, though. The Fire Carrier. What did he look like? What did you *see*?"

"A ball of flame. A witch light. That's all that's left of him." Pru spooned grits and shrimp with sauce into the two bowls she had waiting on the counter and brought them to the table, gesturing for Barrie to eat. "You need to leave all this alone, sugar. The whole situation is more complicated than gifts and curses, more complicated than what little Cassie told you. Maybe it's more complicated than what Daddy said too, or what the Beauforts have passed down in their family—"

"You said you didn't remember what Seven told you." Barrie picked up her fork without any hint of appetite.

"I remembered some last night. Enough to know that the Fire Carrier will be here as long as the *yunwi* are here, and that as long as he guards them, the Watsons are supposed to stay to protect Watson's Landing."

"How?"

"That's where the gift comes in. It's so we don't have to sell off the land."

Barrie gaped at her aunt. "That makes so much more sense! If that's what the gift is for, then why on earth wouldn't we use it? Don't you see? We're supposed to help the Fire Carrier—"

"You're assuming that it's right to try to keep the *yunwi* on the island. What if it isn't? What if the Fire Carrier *is* evil and we should let the *yunwi* go?" Pru shook her head. "Sugar, your mama was just as sure as you are that Daddy was wrong about the gift. Don't make the same mistakes she did. I don't know if the gift had anything to do with what happened to her, but it sure doesn't sound like her life turned out well. Why take the chance? I don't think we should be taking sides between the Fire Carrier and the *yunwi*, and that's what you're doing every time you use the gift."

They were going around in circles. Barrie held in a sigh

and sat back in her chair. "Tell me about the night Lula left, Aunt Pru. What do you remember? Was she upset? Excited? Scared? Was she acting any different from normal?"

"I wish I knew. By the time I got home that evening, she had already locked herself in her room. Daddy sent me to bed, and the next morning Lula was already gone. That's all I know. Now eat your breakfast before it gets cold."

The tilt of Pru's head and the set of her chin were so much like Lula's. Barrie's mother had never wanted to talk about anything emotional either. Barrie glared down at the grits and the pink shrimp swimming in gravy on her plate, and she tried to decide if she should tell Pru what Julia had said about Lula's letter. Would Pru be even more upset to know that Julia had kept it all those years and never given it to her?

More questions. There were always questions.

Barrie was fed up with tiptoeing around everyone else's feelings. "I'm sorry, Aunt Pru. No matter what you tell me, I can't ignore the gift. I won't. I can't ignore the Colesworths. They are my family too. I can't throw them away over something that happened three hundred years ago. Some incident that no one even remembers clearly. I *am* going to go to the play tonight, and I'm going to help Cassie if I can. I need to do that."

She second-guessed herself the moment the words were out. Pru was, after all, her new guardian, and Barrie was living in her house. Lula had never been shy about using every weapon in her arsenal, from silent guilt to weekly threats of firing Mark if things didn't go her way.

Instead of flaring up in a fit of temper, Pru dabbed her lips delicately with her napkin and took a sip of coffee. Barrie waited, and the silence stretched, and stretched, until it became denial.

"You can't pretend a problem doesn't exist," Barrie said, reaching over to touch Pru's wrist. "Ignoring me—ignoring Cassie—isn't going to work. You keep talking about my cousin like she's a horrible person, but at least she had the courage to tell me about the Fire Carrier."

"Because she wanted something from you! Don't mistake that for friendship or affection— Well, shoot." The tremble of Pru's hands and the shine of her eyes gave away how hard she was fighting for control. She dropped her utensils with a clang. "I promised myself that I was going to let you make up your own mind about going over there tonight. So go. Do what you need to do to satisfy your curiosity."

"Thank you," Barrie said, but the victory felt like a Coke left open too long. All the fizz was gone.

Pru caught both of Barrie's hands. "I don't know why Lula didn't tell you anything about her life with Wade, but she must have had a reason. It may have been for your own protection, did you ever think of that? She may not have been the best mother, but she was still your mother. She loved you."

"She *never* loved me!"

"Of course she did!" Pru's face softened in sympathy, and she let out a breath. "Sugar, I'm mad at Lula too. Madder the more I hear about your childhood. But the Lula I knew would never, *never* have wanted to live the way she ended up living. Some people aren't cut out to be mothers. I'm not sure she was."

"Then she never changed much."

"She was all about living for the moment. For glamour. For fun. Being scarred and ugly and being invisible?" Pru looked up toward the ceiling, then she shook her head. "Don't you see? If Lula chose to get out of bed, if she chose to survive that kind of hell, there is only one reason: you. Be mad at her if you want to. Anger's a normal part of grief. But don't you ever—ever—doubt that she loved you."

Pru, the table, the whole room swam before Barrie's eyes. She had never thought of it that way, and she should have. She had known what the doctors had said, how the odds had been against Lula. She had heard how many people with those kinds of burns chose not to keep on fighting.

"I'm sorry. I . . ." She shrugged, not knowing how to go on.

"Don't keep apologizing for what you feel." Pru pushed away her unfinished plate. "Just don't let grief and thinking

Lula didn't love you push you toward the Colesworths, that's all I'm asking. They are never going to get over the fact that you're a Watson to love you for yourself. And damn, I've done it again, haven't I? Look at us. We're a fine pair, aren't we? I'll make you a deal. I'll try to let you make up your own mind about Cassie and her family, and you stop apologizing for feeling things you have every right to feel. I suspect it will be an uphill battle for us both."

Pru's words were hopeful, but the bleakness in her expression still reminded Barrie of the way she had looked sitting on the steps that first afternoon. Lost, as if the vastness of the world were dawning on her now that life was pulling her out of the cocoon she had lived in since the day Lula left.

What had Pru done all these years in the house with no one to talk to? Barrie couldn't imagine that Emmett had been any kind of company. Given the choice between him and Lula, Barrie would have taken Lula in a heartbeat. At least Lula'd had a reason for her sudden rages.

Heading upstairs to brush her teeth, Barrie mulled over what her aunt had said. Something *had* kept Lula alive all those years. Something had pushed her to survive the fire, the burns, surgery after surgery. All that pain.

Abruptly Barrie was thankful that she would have her mother's belongings. Sorting through them, touching them, trying on Lula's clothes, her shoes, holding the small pieces of her life, might paint a fuller picture now that Barrie had some context of who her mother had been growing up.

Barrie still hadn't told Pru the furniture was coming. Her aunt was trusting her about going to Cassie's. The least she could do was trust that Pru would understand she hadn't meant any insult when she'd asked Mark to send everything to Watson's Landing.

CHAPTER THIRTEEN

Pru stood at the sink, staring out into the garden. Heartache was etched in every muscle of her defeated shoulders. Turning as Barrie stopped short in the doorway, she dredged up an unconvincing smile. "You're back down awfully fast. And you look like you swallowed a river's worth of questions."

"I did something I'm not sure you're going to like, and I'm so, so sorry for not telling you sooner." The words tumbled out. "I was feeling homesick, and Mark and I were talking about Lula's furniture and clothes, and I couldn't bear the thought of her belongings being auctioned off to strangers. So I asked him to send it all here instead. I know there's plenty of furniture here already, and I don't mean to say Lula's things are better. I would never say that, but maybe there are some pieces we could use, and we could sell the rest or give it to charity."

"We're not going to sell Lula's—your—things." Pru's voice was firm. "We can make room."

"I don't want you to give up your furniture."

"Honey, half the pieces in this house are worn, and the other half are broken. And nothing here has ever been mine. Lord knows our ancestors have always bought whatever caught their fancy. You should see the attic crammed full of who knows what." Pru gave a nod. "Yes. It's past time we clear out the junk. Sweep out the cobwebs, open up the windows. We can make a project of it. I'm sure Lula's things are nicer anyway. Too nice." Her gaze locked on the cabinet door that she had fixed; Pru was always making repairs.

"How can anything be too nice?" Barrie asked.

"The Fire Carrier isn't the only spirit on the island. That's part of Cassie's story I know for a fact—"

Pru cut herself off, but Barrie's brain was already whirling around and around like a top, facts spinning ever more slowly until finally they settled.

"Are you saying the *yunwi* are making the house fall apart?" she asked.

Pru flinched as if she hurt to hear the words aloud. "I don't know exactly what I'm saying." She glanced at her watch. "Look, sugar, it's getting late, and the tearoom is open today.

You'd better scoot upstairs and get ready, if you're going to come out to help me. At this rate I'll never have the garden done before Mary gets here."

"But—"

"Go on now. We'll talk about it later." Pru's tone was the one Mark used when a subject was off-limits.

Barrie trudged upstairs, brushed her teeth, and slathered on a coat of sunscreen. When she came down again, she found a pair of gloves on the kitchen counter, along with a wide straw hat and a note.

> *You'll need these for the sun. Come on outside*
> *when you're ready to work.*

Twisting her hair up, Barrie picked the hat off the counter and settled it onto her head. A screwdriver that had been half-hidden beneath it rolled a few turns before it came to rest. It reminded her that Pru had to have been up at dawn to have started breakfast and repairs so early, and her aunt had still been up when Barrie had gone to bed. When did Pru ever have time for herself? She was constantly fixing one problem or another.

A swell of half-hysterical laughter pressed up through Barrie's chest. For all of Pru's seeming frailness, she was so much stronger than Barrie would ever be. Or maybe it was a matter of perspective. All Barrie could see was problems. Look at all the assumptions she had made since she'd arrived at Watson's Landing. She had assumed the house was falling apart because Pru couldn't afford to fix it. She had assumed Pru would be upset about Lula's furniture showing up. She had let Pru and Eight make her nervous about meeting Cassie and Wyatt. Even Wyatt had turned out to be not so terrible.

The *yunwi* and the Fire Carrier and trying to find Cassie's lost fortune? They all seemed like problems now, but Barrie would find solutions.

Pausing at the bottom of the terrace steps, Barrie spotted Pru picking up the mammoth blue bowl from beside the three-tiered fountain. Despite its size, Pru lifted the bowl easily, braced it against her hip, and lugged it toward the far edge of the maze, where roses and carefully tended flowers edged the boxwood hedges.

Barrie went to join her. "What's that bowl for?"

"Cuttings." Pru lowered the bowl to the ground and knelt beside it to trim a rose from the bush with her pruning snippers.

Barrie lifted an eyebrow and swept a glance down the neat rows of blossoms along the hedgerows. There wouldn't be a single flower left if Pru filled a bowl that size every day the garden was open to the public.

"Exactly how many tables are there in the tearoom?" she asked.

Pru sucked in her cheeks. She studied the bowl as if she had never seen it before, then slowly raised her eyes to meet Barrie's gaze. "The bowl isn't only for cuttings. I also use it to leave nuts, fruit, and honey for the *yunwi*."

"*That's* what you meant by appeasement?"

"It doesn't matter what I call it, so long as it keeps the spirits happy. I feed the *yunwi*, and they maintain the garden. That's one less thing I have to worry about."

"Is it? If the *yunwi* are so happy, why are they taking the house apart?"

"I don't know!" Hunching her shoulders, Pru looked away.

Barrie blew out a breath of exasperation. "I'm sorry, Aunt Pru. I don't understand any of this. How can you be afraid of the Fire Carrier and not the *yunwi*, when he's basically only here to guard them?"

"The fact that he locked them up doesn't mean he's necessarily any better than they are." Pru used the green-handled snippers to gesture around the garden. "Look around. How could I possibly keep up with all this by myself? Daddy fired the help after Lula left. He holed up in the library until he died. Watson's Landing started to fall apart, and no matter how hard I worked, I couldn't keep up. I'd come out here in the evening and eat a sandwich while I did the weeding. Then one night, I was too tired to eat. I came back the next morning, and the sandwich was gone, and so were all the weeds." Her chin rose and her eyes grew defiant. "I suppose that's the bottom line. The *yunwi* have never bothered me. They were willing to help me, and Daddy wasn't."

Daddy sounded like a piece of work.

For the first time Barrie took inventory of the garden: the gravel paths unsullied by weeds, hedges neatly trimmed, lawns manicured and unmarred by a single leaf. Everywhere flowers bloomed.

Her aunt and her mother really were alike. Pru had made her peace with the *yunwi* and taken refuge in the garden, never mind what happened on the rest of the property. Lula had hidden inside the house, inside herself, inside her pain.

Pru seemed to be finished talking. She settled down to work with her back turned to Barrie, and her humming and the *snick* of the shears and the *shush* of the river all combined into a lulling rhythm. Barrie was too tired to dig for information anymore. It was easier to lose herself in the simple, repetitive task of cutting flowers, and not to argue.

It was only after she had been lost in thought awhile that she noticed the shadows skittering at the periphery of her vision. They vanished when she turned her head, and returned when she went back to the flowers. More curious than worried, Barrie sat back on her heels, pretending to concentrate on cutting flowers. Sure enough, the shadows sprang back to life. As long as she didn't look at them, they danced and swayed in time to Pru's melancholy humming. Watching them, Barrie didn't see the snake until her hand was nearly on it. She shrieked and scrambled back.

The snake slithered deeper into the lilies and stopped with a snip of tail exposed.

Appearing beside Barrie, Pru patted her on the shoulder. "It's only a rat snake. You scared it as much as it scared you."

"I highly doubt that." Barrie removed a glove and wiped the sweat dampening her hairline.

"It never hurts to be cautious. Just because that one was harmless doesn't mean it couldn't have been poisonous. There are copperheads, water moccasins, even rattlers around here. The dangerous ones mostly have triangular heads and elongated pupils. You'll learn to tell them apart soon enough."

Barrie had no intention of getting close enough to look any snake in its eyes.

The snake shimmied the rest of the way into the clump of lilies, and from there rustled away beneath the hedge, presumably to chase mice somewhere else. Assuming there were mice to chase. So far, Barrie had seen only birds, squirrels, and insects—including a few bird-size mosquitos—and, of course, the fat, pink earthworms the peahens were always chasing. She'd heard frogs from the marsh and seen the nearly human-shaped footprints left by raccoons—or maybe that was the *yunwi*, for all she knew.

Barrie raised her eyes to the shadows darting across the green expanse of lawn to the edge of the woods. She tried not to focus on the pull coming from somewhere amid the trunks and tangled underbrush, but the more she tried not to feel it, the more she felt the compulsion calling her from deep within the trees. She sat back on her heels.

"Leave those woods alone. I can see you looking at them." Wiping her forehead with the back of her wrist, Pru left a smudge of dirt behind.

Barrie struggled to spool in her awareness, the way the Fire Carrier spooled the flames after they'd been spread across the water. "Don't you feel the draw from in there, Aunt Pru? How can you not feel it?"

"Feel what?" Eight's voice came from a few yards away.

"Nothing." The denial was automatic, uttered before Barrie remembered she didn't have to hide her gift from him. Or from anyone else on Watson Island. It was too new a feeling to provide much relief.

She stared at Eight resentfully. She hadn't heard the growl of his car or the *slap-slap* of his flip-flops, but that was because he was wearing rubber-soled boat shoes. He needed to wear a cowbell around his neck to warn her when he came over. And why did he and Seven worry about someone sneaking in through the front gate, when the two of them, or anyone else for that matter, could walk up from the river anytime they liked?

Eight's green eyes gleamed with amusement. "I came to invite you out on the boat. I promised Dad I'd pick up steaks for dinner tonight, so I'm heading into town." He turned to Pru. "You need any groceries from the farmers' market?"

"I'd love to save Mary a trip. I'll make you a list." Pru flicked a warning glance from Barrie to the woods and tugged off her gloves.

"What was that about?" Eight asked, watching Pru hurry toward the house.

Barrie started to say something biting about how he should know what Pru was thinking, but it wasn't worth the argument. "Long story," she said.

He studied her a moment. "I've got time if you want to tell me. I'd hoped you'd be done being mad at me about the Beaufort gift."

"I'm not mad." Barrie started off after Pru.

Although, suddenly, she was. Of course she wanted to tell him what Pru had said, but she wanted him to ask because *he* wanted to know, not because *she* wanted to tell him.

"How can I tell what's real between us when you are always eavesdropping on what I want?" she asked. "If I can't keep anything private from you, I'm not sure we can be friends. That's not an equal relationship."

"Knowing *why* someone wants something is always more interesting than knowing that they want it. I can't know the why unless you choose to tell me."

Barrie stopped on the path and turned to face him. "So share one of your secrets. What's the most important thing *you* want? And tell me why you want it."

His eyebrows dropped, and his mouth opened and closed without a word. Barrie waited. But when Pru came out of the house with her list, Eight practically loped off to meet her.

Barrie's hands curled into balls of frustration. Eight could have given Barrie an answer. Any answer. Instead he'd chosen to avoid the question. The Beaufort gift would never give her that luxury. Eight would always know what she wanted. Just once, someday, it would be nice for them to have a conversation that didn't devolve into her wanting to shout at him.

He and Pru met Barrie on the path, and she snatched the grocery list from him and stuffed it into her pocket. She marched toward the dock.

"Come on. Don't be like this." Eight kept pace beside her.

"Then stop using your Beaufort gift."

"Stop in general?" He raised his brows. "Or stop using it on you?"

Barrie considered that a moment. "*Can* you stop? Because Pru claims she quit using the Watson gift—but then, she says her gift was never as strong as Lula's. And mine got stronger when my mother died."

"It's more of a first-born thing. My sister still sees what people want, but it's easier for her to decide if she wants to act on what she knows. I have a harder time not giving in to people. It's a constant battle for me, and I think it's even worse for my dad."

"Exactly." Barrie nearly sighed in relief that he understood. "Pru doesn't want me to use the gift, but the compulsion just gets stronger if I try to ignore it. She doesn't understand what that's like. The woods, a drawer in the library, the closed-off wing upstairs—the pull keeps getting more intense. I can't imagine living like this for years or even months."

"What are you going to do?"

Barrie ignored him. "My grandfather told Pru and Lula the gift is evil," she said.

"What do you think?" he asked in a neutral tone.

The crushed white shells on the path were blinding in the full morning light, which made it all the more strange to see how the shadows chased one another. Barrie raised her eyes to the river, where the dock and the tall reeds gave way to a channel of coursing water.

"You may as well ask if a snake is evil because it's venomous," she said. "Is it wrong for the snake to defend itself or kill to eat? Like you said, the *why* always matters. We can use our gifts badly, or we can use them well." That was even more true for Eight than for her.

"Are we still talking generalities, or about you and me specifically?"

Barrie shrugged, curious to see what he would answer if she didn't specify.

"It's hard to choose not to help someone when I know what they want," he said, "but what I decide defines the kind of person I want to be. What people want isn't always good for them—or for other people."

The path and lawns sloped toward the water, and the shadows playing at the edges of Barrie's vision seemed more agitated the nearer they came to the dock. She hadn't been down to the river yet. From there, the old Watson and Beaufort rice fields sprawled to her right on both banks, mirror images in tangles of thick, green foliage. Alligator territory.

Downstream, the broken columns of Colesworth Place rose like clenched fists against the sky, while behind them puffed-up McMansions marked where the Colesworth fields used to lie. Maybe that was proof enough that the Watson gift was necessary. Without it, would there be enough money to keep Watson's Landing from being parceled off into tiny lots?

Barrie cast Eight a sidelong glance. "Did you know Pru leaves food out for the *yunwi* every night?"

Eight stopped on the dock. "What? Why?"

"So you know about them too. And you didn't think to mention that last night either."

"That's not the point. Why is she feeding them?"

"Because they help her in the garden. On the other hand, they also seem to be taking the house apart, which makes no sense. According to what Cassie said, the Fire Carrier is supposed to stop them from doing that—"

"'According to Cassie' being the operative phrase. Nobody knows much about the *yunwi*."

"Somebody has to know something. Will you help me? Ask your dad, or look up '*yunwi*' on the Internet? I would do it myself, but Pru doesn't have a computer, and I don't have my phone."

Eight read her for a moment. "If I say I will, can you promise you won't do anything stupid?"

Barrie bristled. "Stupid?"

"Hunting for answers where you shouldn't." He strode toward the boat as if he knew he had made her mad and was getting out of firing range.

She stepped out onto the long, floating portion of the dock. The boards swayed and the water flowed through the rushes all around her. Apart from one summer of lessons, Barrie had never learned to swim. And while Eight's boat looked bigger than it had from the balcony, it rocked precariously beneath her feet as Eight helped her on board.

He dug a life vest out of the seat compartment. "Here, put that on," he said. "And would you grab a couple of Cokes from the cooler in the cabin while I untie the dock line?"

The sun-bleached vest smelled of fish and salt. Barrie buckled herself into it before she leaned into the tiny cabin and rummaged in the cooler. Icy condensation stiffening her fingers, she brought up the two Cokes as Eight jumped in. The boat pitched with the sudden movement, and she had no way to hold on.

Eight set down the can she handed him. "You doing all right?"

"Fan-damn-tastic." She settled herself on the bench.

Smiling faintly, he focused all his attention on her another moment before ducking under the horizontal arm of the mast to settle beside the motor. He pulled the cord, one long, sharp movement that made his muscles flex. How had Barrie not realized how strong he was? The motor sputtered and spat water before finally kicking in.

She hadn't seen the boat under sail yet. She wasn't sure if she was disappointed not to see it now, either.

"No point trying to go without the motor when the wind comes straight over the bow like this," Eight said, reading her again. "You'd spend the whole time ducking while we tacked— turned—to keep the sails full. Which is what makes the boat go. Sailing, get it? There's a reason they call that a boom." He grinned and pointed to the arm extending off the mast.

"Go ahead. Laugh." Barrie tugged on her life vest strap to make it tighter. "I've been on a boat exactly once before this."

It wasn't until she looked down that she realized how much her hands were shaking at the memory of her mother's funeral, of the boat rising and falling in the swells beneath the Golden Gate Bridge. Was it only a week ago that she had leaned over the side and done her best not to throw up as she'd scattered Lula's ashes? She slid her hands beneath her thighs. This wasn't Lula's funeral. Lula's ashes were long gone, drifting somewhere in the Pacific, a continent, a lifetime away.

"I thought you wanted to come with me." Eight's tone went flat. "I know you did."

"I do."

Worry and hope stirred in Eight's eyes. He didn't move, but he suddenly seemed closer. Closer, the way he had been in the parking lot when he had almost kissed her. Barrie turned to look out across the water to break the spell.

"You're exasperating sometimes, you know that?" Eight said. "Also, I've been sailing my whole life. You're perfectly safe."

"Which is exactly what someone always says in the movies just before the disaster hits."

"This isn't a movie, and it happens to be true. Anyway, the river isn't deep. You can trust me."

Barrie turned her face into the wind and the fine spray

kicking up from the bow. The chug of the motor drowned the shush of the river. Eight steered out into the current and turned the boat downstream.

Like a switch turned from off to on, a sudden ache of loss hit Barrie, along with a sharp pain in her head. She looked back at the dock and house, waiting for the pressure to abate. It didn't, though. Come to think of it, it had subsided yesterday only when she and Eight had returned back to Watson's Landing. Unlike her normal reaction to a lost object, the pull and the headache hadn't diminished with distance. Instead, like now, they had grown stronger, and no amount of rubbing at her temples released the tension.

She tried not to panic. There had to be a reasonable explanation.

They passed the Colesworth dock, and she looked up the low hill to the eight jagged columns. Set farther back, the ordinary two-story house where her cousins lived was overshadowed by the size and eeriness of the ruins.

She distracted herself by kicking her feet against the bench. "Do you suppose there could really have been something valuable buried there all these years?" she asked.

"Why not?"

"How can they know it's there and not know where to find it? Isn't it more likely that whatever valuables they had were looted by the Yankees?"

"Listen to you, sounding all Southern already." Eight laughed as Barrie rolled her eyes, and in the sun and wind he looked like the boy she had seen playing with his dog across the river that first day. It was only now that she realized she hadn't seen him that carefree since.

"Treasure hunting is practically a Southern pastime," he said. "Seems like half the families in Georgia and the Carolinas have ancestors who buried the family jewels and silver when they knew Sherman's army was heading in their direction. If the men were killed and only children or women or slaves survived to tell the story, exactly where the stuff was hidden never got passed along. How something might have gotten lost at Colesworth Place isn't what worries me. I'm more concerned with what happens if there's nothing for you to find. Don't kid yourself. Wyatt came by last night for a reason. If he's that eager for you to find their lost fortune, what's he going to do when you don't?"

Barrie dropped her eyes. "I got the feeling it was all Cassie's idea."

"Then why did Wyatt follow you to the Resurrection?"

"Maybe for the same reason I want to go to Colesworth Place. Have you been there? Aren't you the least bit curious?" Barrie turned back to watch the columns receding. "And maybe I'll get a chance to talk to him about the night Lula left."

"If he'll tell you."

"You suppose Cassie's play is any good?"

"It doesn't have to be good. You've met Cassie. She could hold an audience captive reading a nutrition label."

Of course she could. Barrie stomped down a jealous pang and reminded herself she was the one who had asked for Eight's opinion. Girls who looked like Cassie owned a room the moment they walked into it. Eight might claim he didn't know Cassie well, he might not trust Cassie's family or her motives, but he wasn't indifferent to her. How could he be?

And how could it already matter this much?

The wind swept Barrie's hair into her face, but she didn't bother to hold it back. Colesworth Place vanished as the boat puttered around the bend. Here the river emptied into the sound, and the smell of the water changed.

"You never answered me before," Barrie said, "about what you want."

"What I want changes all the time."

"Not the important stuff. Come on. You owe me."

Eight adjusted the rudder, and they detoured around a sandbar exposed by the outbound tide. He was silent so long, Barrie started to think he wasn't going to answer at all. But he knew so much about her, and she deserved at least a crumb.

"All right. Two things," he said. "One, I hate the Beaufort gift, and two, I'd get rid of it if I could."

"Neither of those count. I'd pretty much figured them out already. Tell me something personal. Something real."

"I didn't want to like you as much as I do," he said. "Is that real enough for you?"

Barrie turned her face back into the salty spray and tried to decide if Eight's declaration was an insult or something to celebrate.

CHAPTER FOURTEEN

Barrie's expression must have registered her confusion. Eight shook his head and leaned toward her with one hand still on the rudder. "Hold on. I phrased that wrong. What I meant was more that I wasn't expecting to like you as much as I do. Which implies I wasn't expecting to like you at all, and I wasn't. I mean, I didn't have any expectations." He sighed and gave her a rueful grin. "I'm still not saying it right, am I?"

The boat rocked in the choppy water, and the spray on Barrie's face now carried the sting of salt. "What are you trying to say?"

"That I like you, but I'm going to California at the end of next month." He steered toward the marina in front of the lighthouse. "I've wanted to get away from Watson Island for so long, I can't remember not wanting it. Now, for the first time, there might be a reason to stay, and it's too late."

Too late? That summed it all up, didn't it?

They were passing the strip of beach where Eight had shown her the turtle's nest. Beyond it, the sound turned to ocean, and a jumble of umbrellas and tropical towels dotted one of the public beaches, echoing the chaos in Barrie's mind. Turning back to Eight, she caught him in three-quarter profile: his straight nose, his stubborn chin, his eyes wary on her as if he weren't sure what she would do. She wondered what he would look like in the dead of winter when his tan faded and his hair darkened. But she wouldn't see him then.

Last night he had talked about meeting someone for dinner, but she had been too focused on seeing Cassie to pay attention. "You mentioned a recruiter," she said.

"Yeah, I got a baseball scholarship to play at USC— Southern California, not South Carolina. Around here those two are easily confused."

"Free hint. California's a whole lot farther away." Too far.

But Barrie refused to feel dismay. She refused to want him to stay. That would confuse things further. She had only just met him, and he was being nice to her because . . . Oh, who knew why? Because of the Watson-Beaufort connection Cassie had mentioned, maybe.

"And after college? Are you coming back?"

"If I did, Dad would want me to join the family business.

I'm not cut out to be a lawyer." Eight said the word as if it had four letters. "I was lucky to get the minimum grades for my scholarship, which I needed so Dad couldn't threaten not to pay when he found out what I was going to do. . . ."

Barrie waited for him to continue, but he didn't. "Does it matter that much? Aren't there other jobs you could do here?"

"Not for a Beaufort. Law goes with our gift the same way finding investment opportunities goes with yours. Beauforts know how to negotiate settlements, pick juries, make deals." Eight steered the boat toward the harbor, and pointed suddenly off to their right. "Look," he said.

Barrie turned in time to see a dolphin glide back beneath the waves and reemerge. One, then two, then five or six sleek gray bodies arced and knifed below the surface, again and again, until they were only splashes in the distance.

"I wish it were that easy to get away. This place makes me claustrophobic," Eight said. "I'm dyslexic. You know what that is?"

Barrie nodded. "It makes it hard to read because you see the letters jumbled."

"It's not that I couldn't manage if I wanted to. Plenty of dyslexic people are doctors and lawyers and whatever. But that just isn't me. I don't want it enough to work that hard, and the whole town expects things from me that I can't deliver. My dad expects things. If I stay, I'll always be a failure when I don't meet those expectations, and I'd rather do something I am good at. Something that makes me feel good about myself."

The longing etched into his expression just then, the defiance and the slight hoarseness in his voice . . . those more than the words made Barrie want to reach out to him, to touch him and somehow know the right thing to say to make him feel better. But her mind was a mess of elusively swirling words.

Unlike her, Eight wore confidence like a second skin. How could she have missed seeing that he had the same insecurities she had? Maybe if she had bothered to look beneath his beautiful-boy exterior, she would have seen his doubt. Recognized it.

His intensity, the set of his shoulders, the thrust of his jawline, all looked suddenly different, like a deceptively simple piece of abstract art that revealed new layers of meaning and emotion when considered from an alternate angle.

She wanted to tell him she knew how he felt. How she had never been enough to interest Lula. Never been enough for Lula.

"Why baseball?" she asked instead. "Or is that just to get through college?"

He gave her a smile so wide, it was as if she'd given him a present on Christmas morning. "Thanks for not telling me why I'm wrong. I hate pity. And, no, it isn't just for college. It's not a lifetime career, but I want to play in the majors, then open a restaurant when I retire. Maybe I'll be a celebrity chef and feed people exactly what they want." He grinned even wider. "There's no right and wrong in fish or chicken, and in baseball everyone knows what everyone wants. A run or an out. Maybe a walk. When I'm on the pitcher's mound, people are too far away for me to read. I don't have to worry what's fair or unfair. I don't have to decide if I should try to help them get what they want."

Barrie had never stopped to think whether she *should* find an object once she became aware of it. At least not until she'd arrived at Watson's Landing.

"I thought the gift didn't give you a choice?" she asked.

"That's another downside to growing up in a family of lawyers. You learn to twist the gift so you give people what they want in a way that helps you instead."

"So you're saying that you manipulate people."

Eight slowed the engine to a purr and pulled into the marina. "If Dad can't argue you into doing what he wants, he'll maneuver you into it. I try not to be that way, but I can't not know what I know."

That was probably the closest he was going to come to giving her an apology. She couldn't really blame him for his gift—which didn't make it any easier to live with.

"What you need," she said lightly, "is a twelve-step program. Mind Readers Anonymous."

Eight darted a glance at her, and then he nosed the boat into a slip and jumped out to tie it off.

Barrie stowed the life jacket and stood on shaky legs. Her head pounded, and she was grateful when Eight reached down to help her up onto the solid dock. She kissed him. Just a peck, but he would have known she wanted to do that anyway. She wasn't sure which of them was more surprised, but she wasn't sorry. What he had told her couldn't have been easy for him to say.

They wound through the marina. Sailboats and a few big tourist yachts bobbed gently on one side, separated from the working vessels on the other. Rows and rows of fishing boats bristling with antennas and radar dishes looked rusty and weathered. Except for one just preparing to pull out, which was conspicuously sleeker, cleaner, and more powerful. Wyatt stood on its deck, talking to a man with a tattoo of a face on the back of his head. Wyatt fell silent when he caught sight of Barrie and Eight. His stare held none of the friendliness he had shown the night before.

"Come on." Eight took her hand and pulled her down the dock.

They left the marina and turned along the boardwalk, then walked a few blocks to a clapboard building hung with a green-and-gold sign: RIVERBANK FARM AND MARKET. Red-faced toddlers reached through the bars of a corral to pet a trio of miniature horses, while a shaved llama with a puffball face chewed its cud from behind a chain-link fence. Along the side paddock, older children lined up for rides on a pair of ponies decked out in straw hats that had been slipped over their ears.

"I thought we were picking up steaks. Do we have to kill the cow?" Barrie tried to ignore the fact that people were gaping at her the same way the kids looked at the animals on display.

"No worries. The stuff inside is dead already, apart from the odd crustacean and the fish-eyed locals."

Curiosity followed them into the building. Strangers stopped and chatted, gossiped, pried. At the meat stand an old woman in a yellow housedress, brown socks, and sandals counted out change for her purchases one coin at a time, while the younger woman with her watched Barrie and Eight with open speculation.

The old woman plunked the coins down onto the butcher-papered counter. With a last glance at Barrie, her companion loaded their white-wrapped packages into a bag.

"Come on, Granny," she said, catching the old woman's elbow. "We'd best get back."

The old woman hobbled a few steps, then peered at Barrie. "I heard Lula's daughter was coming home," she said, drawing out every word. "You are a welcome sight."

"It's nice to see you, Mrs. Price." Eight spoke more loudly than usual.

The old woman waved her hand at him without shifting her attention from Barrie. "I thought I was going to have to come up to the Landing to get a look at you, honey. Not that I'd have minded. Don't see near enough of your aunt." She paused and gave a wide, nearly toothless grin. "But of course, you don't have any idea who I am, do you? I taught Pru and your mama both. Every one of the Watsons for two generations. Broke my heart to think Pru was going to be the last of you, her ending up alone, dying alone in that prison of a house."

Goose bumps prickled down Barrie's spine.

"Granny!" The younger woman cast an apologetic look at Barrie. "Gawd. Don't mind her, now, sugar. She's eighty-seven and as stubborn as a cross-eyed mule. It's hard to rein her in sometimes, and her mind gets stuck back in the past. Glory days, you know."

"You hush up, Lily Beth. I'm not back in diapers yet." Mrs. Price pulled her arm out of her granddaughter's grasp.

Lily Beth leaned closer, but her voice was still loud enough for everyone around them to hear. "Watch what you say, Granny. You'll give the poor girl the wrong impression about her family, and she's only just arrived."

"It's fine." Barrie glared at Lily Beth, but the woman was too oblivious to notice. "So you taught my grandfather, too?" she asked.

"Along with his brother, Luke, and your grandmother." Mrs. Price nodded at Eight. "And your great-aunt Twila, matter of fact, Eight Beaufort. Although sometimes I doubt I taught any of them much. None of them could concentrate on anything except each other."

"Twila and Emmett, you mean?" Eight asked.

"No, dear." Mrs. Price gave a slight, delighted shake of her head, her eyes twinkling as if she enjoyed the gossip. "Twila was in love with Luke Watson from the beginning. Course Luke was always a little wild. Not bad, mind you, just needed settling down. Emmett, on the other hand, he could never bear for Luke to have anything for himself. Didn't matter if it was a football or a pencil. If Emmett couldn't have it, Luke wasn't going to have it either. The man might as well have been a Colesworth."

"Granny!" Lily Beth's face reddened, and she wound her arm around Mrs. Price's elbow. "Come away now."

Mrs. Price looked back at Barrie. "Your grandmother was too good for Emmett. And your aunt Pru, she was a saint for staying all those years. You tell her I said hello. Tell her to come and see me, when she has a chance." Mrs. Price snatched Barrie's wrist and regarded her intently. "Remind her Emmett's dead and gone, and it's time she started living."

Barrie gave an uncomfortable nod, and Mrs. Price dropped Barrie's hand. "I always did like Pru best, you know. People

199

may pretend they liked Lula, but Pru was always the kind one. Like Luke. Funny how there was one in every generation. I can't help wishing it was Pru who had gotten away and Lula who was the one chained to that house."

Barrie was grateful when Eight wrapped his arms around her.

"Not *actually* chained," Lily Beth hurried to explain, as if Barrie and Eight were dense. Her fingers dug into the paper-thin skin of Mrs. Price's arm. "Come on, Granny. This is *Lula's* daughter you're talking to. Apologize and let's go."

"It was a metaphor, dear." Mrs. Price winked at Barrie. "I taught English for nearly fifty years. You'd think my own granddaughter would understand figurative language. Still, it's true enough. Emmett lost Luke, Twila, and Lula. He was damned if he was going to lose Pru, too. Never mind he was the reason they all stayed away in the first place, you mark my words. Dead to Emmett might as well be dead to everyone. The pompous old ass."

"You all right?" Eight's chin rested lightly on Barrie's hair as they watched Lily Beth pull Mrs. Price away. His warmth felt good against her aching head.

"Do you mind if we come back for the steaks later?" she asked.

"What did you have in mind, exactly?"

Briefly, Barrie wondered if he already knew, if it was even worth explaining. She decided not to think about it. If she spent all her time trying to analyze what Eight knew and what he didn't, the extra brain-drain would make her even more conversationally challenged than she already was.

"It seems to me that if Pru ended up being punished when Lula left, she at least deserves to know why Lula ran away. I want to go see if Julia can find that letter."

CHAPTER FIFTEEN

Julia's house, a two-story home set on stilts, was close to the beach on one of the palm-tree-and-rhododendron-dotted side streets. She answered the door dressed for tennis, her face and hair windblown and damp as if she'd recently finished playing a match.

"Oh, it's you." She held the screen door open an inch, apparently unsure whether she wanted to invite them in or close it in their faces.

Barrie put on her most winning smile. "I'm sorry to bother you, but I keep thinking about that letter you got from my mom."

"You'd better come in." Julia's voice came out with a sigh. "I was going to call Pru later, only . . ."

"Only what?" Barrie prompted.

Julia led the way into a large family room with pale blue paneled walls and white furniture that matched the Wedgwood plates hanging on the walls. "Have a seat," she said, waving them toward an overstuffed sofa crammed with pillows. "Can I get you a lemonade? Sweet tea? Cheerwine?" She smiled at Barrie's confusion. "That's a soda. Cherry flavored."

"No, thank you," Barrie said, but Eight nudged her with his foot and raised his eyebrows at her. "Or maybe . . . could I have a glass of water?"

"Me too," Eight said.

Barrie waited for Julia to disappear into the kitchen. "What are you kicking me for? I thought we'd get this over with quick."

"She hasn't made up her mind what she's going to tell you."

"You think she found it?"

"She wishes she'd never remembered the letter or mentioned it to you. I don't know if she found it or not, but why else would she wish we weren't here?"

"Maybe she's having an affair with the tennis instructor and he's hiding in the kitchen," Barrie said. "Come on. Put yourself in her shoes. Losing something so important and worrying about confessing to Pru, and how Pru's going to react . . . Can't you see why she'd hesitate?"

Julia came back with the water and a plate of oatmeal

raisin cookies. "I baked these earlier. You're probably getting hungry, aren't you? My kids are always ready for a snack about this time of the morning." She lowered herself into the love seat kitty-corner from the sofa, and picked at a cookie.

"I lied when I said I was going to call Pru, you know. The truth is, I probably wasn't going to call at all."

"So you found the letter?" Barrie leaned forward and braced her forearms on her knees, wishing she was positive she wanted the answer to be yes.

"I got to thinking about places I don't normally get into," Julia said, "and I remembered the box of birth announcements and congratulations cards I'd put away after my son, Devon, was born. That was about ten months after Lula's funeral." She shook her head and looked up at the ceiling. "It's still so hard to believe. That she could have been alive all this time. I wish I'd seen her even one more time."

Barrie rubbed Mark's watch and told herself to be patient. "So was the letter in the box?"

"Yes. I opened it. Steamed it open. I figured I could glue it again if I needed to, but I thought it would help me decide whether or not I should give it to Pru. I'm still not sure. Maybe I'll leave it up to you." She reached over and pulled open a narrow drawer in the coffee table. "Here," she said.

Barrie sat with the envelope in her hand—a plain white envelope with Pru's name written in Lula's handwriting. Definitely Lula's handwriting, the letters flamboyant and flowing. Yet there was no sign of the shaky effort that marked everything Lula did after the fire. Barrie's own hands shook.

"You don't have to open it now," Eight told her gently.

"No. Not at all. Take it with you." Julia sounded relieved. She stood up and smoothed the tennis skirt over tanned legs that were just starting to show her age.

Barrie barely managed a choked thank-you as Julia saw them out. Descending the steps to the sidewalk, she clutched the envelope tightly in her fist. Eight walked with his hands in his pockets, glancing at her now and then.

"That was a crappy thing for her to do," he said finally.

"Steaming it open or leaving it for me to decide?"

"Steaming it open isn't much different from eavesdropping. But you're not sure if you want to read it now."

"It's not a question of want. I need to. Ought to." Barrie turned back toward the marina, which suddenly seemed impossibly far away. "I just don't know Pru well enough to make that kind of decision for her."

"Come on then." Eight caught her hand and led her toward the thin strip of sand in front of Julia's house. Winding between the low wooden fences that kept the vegetation from getting trampled, they walked until they reached a jetty.

One hand in his and the other still fisted around the letter, Barrie clambered across the rocks until they were almost at the end. She plopped herself down on a wide rock, pulling her legs up to sit cross-legged while she shielded the envelope from the wind sweeping off the water. When she pulled it out, the paper waivered in her hands like Lula's ghost.

Dearest Pru—

Can you forgive me for leaving without you? I wasn't thinking clearly, thinking at all, and by the time I climbed down from the balcony, it was too late.

Wade and I are in Oklahoma waiting for you. Why Oklahoma? I don't know. It's far enough from Wyatt and Daddy. Too far. It's making me sick to be away! I've tried and tried to call, hoping I'd get you or Mama, but Daddy always picks up. I bought a cell phone this morning, though. Can you believe it? 918-555-2207. I'll sleep with it beside me. Call and I'll explain everything. In the meantime, whatever you do, stay clear of Wyatt Colesworth!!!! And don't make Daddy mad!!!! Call soon and don't let him catch you!

It was signed with Lula's round-looped signature. Barrie turned the paper over, hoping there would be something more. An explanation. A reason. There was nothing.

"What does it say? Anything helpful?"

She handed Eight the letter. Judging by his scowl, it didn't make any more sense to him than it did to her.

He folded it, put it back inside the envelope, and returned it to her. "Are you going to give it to Pru?"

Barrie had no idea.

Hours later when she knelt near Pru in the attic at Watson's Landing, Barrie still hadn't made up her mind. They had been sorting and photographing junk: museum-quality junk, plain old eBay junk, garbage junk. And each piece was a leftover from someone's life. She and Pru worked companionably enough sifting through it, but Barrie's thoughts refused to arrange themselves into any kind of order.

If she gave Pru the letter, Pru would finally know Lula hadn't meant to abandon her. At least not at the beginning. But later? Lula'd had almost two decades to contact Pru. Surely she could have gotten hold of her, if she'd been trying. Wouldn't giving Pru the letter only bring back all those years of pain? Disappointment always hurt worse after a little bit of hope.

"Sad, isn't it?" Pru looked up from the clothes she was refolding. "All these remnants discarded or left behind when people died."

"Exactly what I was thinking." Barrie folded the quilt she had just photographed and laid it on top of the others in the cedar-lined trunk. Her fingers trailed across the intricate needlework that someone, many someones, had labored over, sewing unwanted scraps of shirts and dresses into a work of art.

But whose work of art?

"It's like that old question about the tree falling in the woods," Barrie said. "If you don't leave any achievements behind, did you really live? Does it count if you create something beautiful but no one knows it's yours?"

She spoke without thinking, but Pru's indrawn hiss of breath reminded her that Pru, like Lula, had existed more than lived. Imprisoned. Chained. Figurative or not, Mrs. Price's words were accurate. Pru's life had been stolen from her.

Was it possible to hate someone you had never met? If so, Barrie hated Emmett.

"I wonder if it's too late to do something with my life. Maybe I'm too tired to try."

"You *have* accomplished things. You took care of your mother and your father. You started the tearoom. You've kept Watson's Landing going. It's still here because of you, Aunt Pru."

"All these years," Pru said. "I've been waiting to start living." She looked around at the stacks of paintings leaning against the walls, at the rows of chairs and tables, the dust-swathed towers of trunks. "It's better now with you here, but . . ."

"But what?"

The effort behind Pru's smile was obvious. "When Lula's

lawyer called to tell me she had died and your godfather was dying too, all I could think was how you must feel. That *of course* you had to come here. *Of course* I'd take care of you. I made myself call Seven, and he arranged everything. But the thought of you overwhelmed me. Getting your room ready was about the only constructive thing I managed to do myself. Then suddenly it was the day you were supposed to arrive, and I was in the car, only I didn't know how to get to the airport. I found a map in the glove box, but then it dawned on me that I hadn't been to Charleston since before Lula had left. I hadn't been off Watson Island. Not once in eighteen years. I couldn't believe I'd let things get that bad.

"I started shaking. The more I thought about leaving, the more I shook. I couldn't breathe. There were spots in front of my eyes, and I thought I was going to pass out if I didn't get some fresh air. So I staggered to the steps . . . Then I couldn't get back up. I lost track of the time—"

"I understand, Aunt Pru. It's all right," Barrie said, but the words couldn't begin to convey how much she understood. She wished she were better at expressing how she felt.

"I was going to be an architect," Pru said. "Did Lula tell you? No, of course not. Why would she? I'd almost forgotten it myself. I did have plans, though. I was going to go to college and graduate school. Then I was going to come back, and Seven and I, we—well, never mind. Maybe not all lost dreams are worth regretting. I hadn't even thought about any of that in years until I was on the step. I couldn't tell which made me more furious, the fact that I was too scared to leave the island, or the realization that all the time I'd been locked up at Watson's Landing waiting to start a life, Lula had been out in the world living one without me."

"If you hated it here, couldn't you have made yourself leave?" Barrie whispered, suddenly afraid.

"It's not so much that I hated it." Pru stared down at the shirt she had been folding. "But Daddy wasn't about to lose me, too, not after Lula left. He drove me to school, and picked me up when it was over. I never got the chance to go anywhere else. College applications came and went, and I filled them out and he, *we*, never sent them.

"At one point I thought I would at least work at the bank like Lula, but then Mama got sicker, and Daddy wouldn't have anyone in, so I had to take care of her. Before she passed, Daddy was already crippled. When he died three years ago, I went on doing what I'd always done. Tending to the house took up most of my time, and I started the tearoom—mostly for Mary's sake, since Daddy had let her go. So you see, I never had much of a chance to leave the island, and I didn't need to go. Whatever I needed, I could get it here or order it in.

"Looking back now, I realize I've spent two decades on the same few square miles of dirt. Maybe Watsons are meant to stay. Daddy never left much either. Lula was the only one who got away."

"And Luke."

"And Luke. Neither of them came back."

Barrie bit her lip and shifted her weight backward. "Did Lula have a fight with your father the night she left?"

"What?" Pru stared sightlessly across at the gabled attic window for several beats. "Yes . . . how *could* I have forgotten that?"

"Forgotten what?" Barrie prompted.

"Lula was locked in her room, I think I told you that. I'd been out with—"

"Seven," Barrie said, half-smiling.

Pru blushed a little. "All right, yes. I wasn't supposed to be seeing him, but I'd told Daddy I was with a girl in town. When I got home, I hurried upstairs to tell Lula about it and the knob wouldn't turn when I tried her door. I could hear her inside. I asked her what was going on, but before she could answer, Daddy stormed out of his room and sent me to bed for coming in past my curfew. I was still half-dancing on the moon from being with Seven, so I let it go. But I hadn't been late, and Daddy'd already been all riled up."

"Then you barely saw Seven again."

Pru's whole body folded in on itself, deflating as if all the strength Barrie had seen in her was suddenly gone again. "Mama was so heartbroken after Lula left she took to her bed and stayed there until she died. By that time Seven had long since married Eight's mama. He got tired of waiting for me, I guess. Not that Daddy would ever have let us be together, the way he felt about the Beauforts after Twila and Luke ran off."

Barrie went and hugged Pru, but she had no idea what to say. How could she explain that her heart ached at the loss of Pru's dreams, at the stolen pieces of Pru's life? How could she tell Pru she understood the kind of fear that seized every muscle and made the world so big that it was easier not to leave your small corner of it. Fear could become an ocean that swallowed you whole.

Barrie knew how panic felt. Anything new, any place unfamiliar or crowded still seemed overwhelming, because she'd barely left the house most of her life. But she'd had Mark, who from the moment he'd taken her home from the hospital had been everything from her own nurse and godfather to Lula's caretaker and personal assistant. For Barrie's sake he had walked the fine edge between ensuring she had whatever she needed and keeping Lula happy enough not to kick him out. If Mark hadn't sided with her, insisted that she needed more freedom this past year, if he hadn't dragged her to restaurants and sights around San Francisco . . . Barrie couldn't imagine what the past few days would have been like without that preparation. The airport, the plane ride, the wraiths of panic she had felt, her breath coming in shallow pants, all the people closing in around her.

Pru must have felt all that sitting on the steps. Panic coming in waves and waves.

"I'm not sure I *can* leave Watson's Landing," Pru said. "Maybe it's force of habit, or Daddy reaching out from the grave, or the migraines. . . . Maybe the *why* doesn't even matter. But I'm stuck here, and that's no kind of life for a girl your age."

"I'm fine. *We're* fine," Barrie said.

She laid her head against Pru's shoulder, surprised again at how insubstantial her aunt felt, as if Pru, too, could slip away any moment. She should encourage Pru to chase her dreams, should let her know it wasn't too late to do whatever she had hoped to accomplish. But it hit Barrie that she didn't want anything to be different from how it was right now. If only she and Pru and Eight could all stay here, exactly the way they were, she wouldn't have to lose anyone else. But that was the kicker of having goals and dreams—achieving them meant something had to change.

"Maybe newness is like a muscle that needs to be built," she said. "We worry and worry anytime we're about to go somewhere new, do something different. It all seems impossible until it's over, but then it turns out not to have been so hard, and facing the next challenge becomes a little easier. Maybe that's the solution, Aunt Pru. We should get you off the island so you have that experience behind you. So you can see that you're stronger than your fear. We could go to Charleston, or at least drive across the bridge."

She smiled at Pru encouragingly as she spoke, but her own heart beat faster, as if she were absorbing part of Pru's panic herself at the thought of leaving. Maybe that was what panic attacks were, caged hearts fluttering their wings, trying to fly but unable to go anywhere.

Pru looked out the window across the river. She slowly shook her head.

"All right." Barrie sat back on her heels. "I won't push you to do anything you don't want to do, I promise. I shouldn't have brought it up. I'm sorry."

"You have to stop apologizing, sugar. Especially when you're right." Leaning in, Pru kissed Barrie's forehead. "Turns out Lula and I were a pair all these years after all. Funny, isn't it? Lula was holed up in San Francisco, and I was holed up at Watson's Landing. Luke was the only Watson who managed to actually escape."

She gestured toward the trunk she'd been sorting, full of men's shirts, sweaters, slacks, and navy uniforms. Tucked along the side of the trunk, Barrie spotted the spine of a book embossed with silver lettering: *Beauregard High School 1969*. A yearbook?

"May I?" Already reaching for it, she glanced at Pru for permission, then opened it gingerly and flipped to the index in the back.

Watson, Emmett, pgs. 3, 16, 21

Watson, Luke, pgs. 3, 16, 18, 19, 26, 39, 41, 47, 51

It had been a small school, so picking the Watsons out of the first photograph was no trouble. They were clearly brothers, but already Emmett showed hints of the iron-grim man whose portrait hung in the library. He stared into the camera with his chin tilted, as if daring it to take his measure and find him wanting. Luke laughed in every photo. He'd played football, basketball, and baseball. He'd been president of the senior class and the student council. Emmett had been vice president of the junior class. Barrie flipped through all the photos and backtracked to a candid shot of the brothers and Twila Beaufort. Luke and Emmett were talking to each other. Emmett had his arm around Twila, but it was Luke whom Twila watched.

"She wrote to Luke years later when the navy sent him to Vietnam." Pru touched Twila's face with the tip of her finger. "It's a beautiful story, really. Or horrible, depending on how you look at it, because Twila was engaged to Daddy. She wrote every day, and Luke wrote back. They fell in love, and when he came home for your great-grandfather's funeral, he and Twila ran off to Canada together. I guess he couldn't bear to go back to the war, and she couldn't bear to stay after she broke off the engagement. Daddy never did get over it. Twila was always there between him and Mama as if she had never left."

Barrie couldn't even imagine how awful that must have been, being with someone who loved someone else. "What was your mother like?"

"Pale." Pru took the yearbook and flipped through until she found a photo. "Not like this," she said, frowning at the picture. "Of course she was older, but she was sadder, too. She was always sad. I suspect it was hard to live with all of Daddy's could-have-beens."

"Would you rather know what you'd missed?" Barrie tried to think how to phrase the question. "I mean, if you were your mother, would you have wanted to know that Emmett loved Twila? Or would you have rather wondered why . . ."

"Why he didn't love *me*?" Pru finished for her.

Telltale warmth crept into Barrie's cheeks. "Yes."

"I think she knew all along. Everyone did."

"Hypothetically, then. Would you want an answer even if it was going to hurt you to know it?"

Pru set the yearbook aside in the "keep" pile and closed the trunk. "I'm not sure how I would have answered that this morning, but someone with a lot of insight reminded me that it's the *not* knowing that makes it impossible to move on from where you are."

Barrie hoped those weren't just empty words, but now at least she had the answer she'd been needing. She pulled Lula's letter from her pocket and handed it to her aunt.

CHAPTER SIXTEEN

Pru went parchment pale as she read the letter. She reread it several times, then folded it slowly and put it back into its envelope. "Where did you find this?"

"Julia had it. She tried to get it to you, but she couldn't get past Emmett." Barrie watched Pru warily. "Can I do anything for you, Aunt Pru?"

"It's after seven o'clock." Pru rose to her feet. "I know you're eating with Eight, but do you want a snack? It's Mary's night to stay late, so she can whip up something before you go get ready."

"I'll wait to eat, but I don't have to go at all. If you want me to stay—"

"No." The word was clipped, and after a moment Pru softened it with a tug of her lips. "I'm all right. Honestly. I just need a cup of tea and a little time." She crossed to the attic stairs, leaving Barrie to follow more slowly.

It was seven fifteen when Barrie reached the second floor. Eight was picking her up in less than an hour, and she was caked in grime. She hadn't even talked to Mark yet, and right then she needed to hear the familiar sound of his voice even more than she needed a shower.

Downstairs in the library, either Pru or Mary—Pru, most likely—had been busy, scrubbing the whole room clean. She had removed the heavy velvet curtains from the windows, tied new floral chintz slipcovers over the two dusty armchairs, and left a stack of paperback books on the round table near the fireplace. Most telling, though, she had placed a seascape above the mantel where Emmett's portrait had hung. The room hadn't been so much cleaned as exorcised.

Only the locked drawer remained unchanged. Barrie rattled it as she sat at the desk to make her call, and while the phone rang on Mark's end, she pulled open the top center drawer to search for keys. Then she closed it, realizing Pru could come in any second. Neither of them could take any more surprises. She pulled the phone with her and settled into one of the armchairs by the window. Mark's voice came through the receiver along with a burst of noise and music.

"I can barely hear you, Mark! Are you watching *Veronica Mars* again?"

"Hold on!" Mark shouted back. "I'll go out into the hall. I'm having a decorating party with the nearly-dead-and-departeds at the hospice. Turns out they're all fabulous! Say hello to my Barrie, everyone!"

"Hello, Barrie!" The greeting came in a chorus of voices, bass to baritone, and then the sound of music and chatter died away. "Is that better?" Mark asked.

"Much. It's wonderful to hear you having fun. And you sound better. Are you feeling better?"

"B, you know I won't get—"

"What are we decorating?" Barrie interjected. "Don't tell me you finally got tired of bordello-Gothic?"

"I'm going for a whole new look: red silk and zebra print. I found pillows and the cutest throw rug."

"Wow, that *is* different. *Nothing* like your polar bear rug."

Mark's room had always looked like the Moulin Rouge had thrown up, pink and black satin, a throwback to his drag show days when he'd been going to be the next RuPaul, the next José Sarria. BTF, as Mark always called it. Before the Fire.

"Send me a picture when you're finished," Barrie said, "and I want a group pic with everyone there. No, wait. Damn. I still don't have my phone, and there's no Internet."

Mark coughed again, a rattling cough. Was he crying?

"So you'll never guess what I ate this morning," she announced. "Shrimp and grits."

"Shrimp for breakfast?" Mark asked damply. "That sounds hideous."

"I'm sure there's a place where you can order it too. You're eating, aren't you?"

"Yes, Mother."

Barrie pulled her legs up and curled them underneath her on the chair. Her throat turned raw and tight. She listened to the wet, labored sound of Mark's breathing while she sorted through everything she wanted to tell him. It came down to: "Thank you, by the way."

"For what?"

"For being *my* mother. For putting your life on hold to raise me. For putting up with Lula's baggage so that you could stay."

Silence swept down the phone line, and then Mark cleared his throat. "You know, I was looking out my window at the bay earlier, and telling myself that some of the water flowing in the river outside your window will end up here. Drops of *there* coming *here*. Drops of *here* going *there*."

"In a million years maybe."

"You're always too literal, B. Who says time moves in a line? Could be it's all mixed up like the water. Like souls and karma. Could be a million years is only five minutes from now, and it won't be long before I see you. Oh, damn. Now I'm making my mascara run. Quick, go grab a Kleenex."

"Why?" Barrie wiped her nose with the back of her hand. "I'm not the one wearing mascara."

"Then how do you expect to hook that hottie of yours, baby girl? Mascara is a girl's best friend. Right up there with a great pair of shoes. What do I keep telling you?"

"Many things, and I ignore most of them. Also, the hottie is strictly catch and release. In a couple months, he's going to school out in California."

Mark's fingernail tapped the phone, two, three, four, five times. He always tapped when he was thinking. "So you like him then. A lot."

"A little," Barrie insisted.

"Then forget what I told you about not falling for him. You go after him, baby girl. Have a fling. Everyone should have a fling. You'll probably be sick of him anyway by the time he reaches his expiration date."

His expiration date.

As if Eight were a carton of milk that would sour at the end of summer. Everyone in Barrie's life seemed to have an expiration date. She sighed and couldn't think of a thing to say.

The silence grew until Mark broke it: "Speaking of time, did you get the package I sent you? I expected you would call me."

"Package?" Barrie wrapped the phone cord around her

fingers. "I'm sorry. Pru probably has it. It's been hectic around here."

"Oh . . . Well, call the minute you get it. In fact, call me before you open it."

"I will." Barrie tried to inject some enthusiasm back into her voice. Compared to everything else, Lula's shoes, or whatever Mark had put in the package, didn't seem important. Still, he had made the effort.

She hated to leave him disappointed. After she'd hung up, she stood with her hand on the receiver and tried to think of a funny moment she could call him back to share, some story that wouldn't worry him or make her bring up Eight again. But Eight was the only lightness she had found since she'd arrived. Being with him was the only time she'd laughed.

Upstairs, the air was hot and stifling. She flung open the doors to the balcony and dropped into the armchair to pull off her shoes. The chair pitched forward, tipping Barrie out. She stumbled to her feet.

One of the legs had fallen off. Not broken. Not sheered. Unscrewed.

She had been kidding—or half-kidding—when she'd said the house was out to get her.

"What did I ever do to you?" She stooped to pick up the leg so she could reattach it, and she shook it at the ceiling, realizing only halfway through the motion that she was shouting at the house the same way Pru had shouted at it, back when she'd thought Pru was crazy. And what was the deal, anyway? If the Fire Carrier had made a bargain with Thomas Watson, why wasn't he keeping it? He was supposed to make the *yunwi* behave. Did voodoo wear off? Was that the problem? Because she had no intention of trying to find a voodoo priest. *That* would be a conversation to have with Pru.

Barrie tried to tell herself she was being silly as she showered and dressed. She didn't bother to dry her hair, but the grandfather clock was already chiming eight o'clock when she knocked on Pru's door at the end of the hallway.

But Pru didn't answer, and there was no sound of movement from inside. Barrie was just thinking that Pru had to be really upset to have stayed up in the attic all this time, although she could have just gone straight down to the kitchen.

The doorbell rang. Eight was right on time. Why didn't that surprise her? Barrie couldn't drum up any annoyance, though. Her heart gave a glad little thud and then sped up to near-panic speed when Pru's voice floated down from the attic, the words too far away to be distinct. What if Pru had changed her mind about letting her go to Cassie's? About going there with Eight?

Maybe she shouldn't go. Maybe she should stay with Pru.

Yet the idea of not seeing Eight, of not keeping her promise to her cousin . . .

She ran toward the stairs, shouting, "I'm leaving, Aunt Pru," as she went.

Eight had let himself in by the time Barrie neared the landing. He stood at the bottom of the steps in red shorts and a clean, white shirt, looking so alive, it made Barrie's blood rush and her breath catch as if she'd been slapped awake.

Mark had been right—he usually was. What was the point of protecting her heart from expiration dates? So what if Eight, or Pru, or even Watson's Landing, were temporary islands of *found* in a sea of *lost*? Life wasn't going to come knocking at her door. It wasn't going to drag her out of bed while she buried her head beneath the covers, cowering. Living was going to be messy. She was bound to get scuff marks on her shoes.

She stopped on the last step, but Eight didn't move aside to let her pass. They stood eye to eye, only a hand span apart.

"Are you sure you still want to do this?" Eight asked, and Barrie thought he was reading her heart again, until he added: "We could still go somewhere else. Somewhere fun. You don't owe Cassie anything, you know."

Barrie swept around him and headed for the door. "Aren't you even a little curious about the treasure?"

"Frankly, my dear"—he gave her a heartbreaking grin—"I don't give a damn."

"Funny," Barrie said, but she couldn't help smiling back.

He leaned in closer. His eyes dropped to her lips and lingered. "As long as I'm channeling Rhett Butler, there's something I've been wanting to do ever since last night."

His voice was so soft, it was more like an echo as he bent toward her. His hands reached for hers. Their fingers brushed, and the *returning* clicked again, so loud even he had to hear it. How could he not hear it? The usual root beer and cherries smell of him mingled with the scent of salt on his skin. Barrie thought only for a second about how much breaking one heart could bear, but then his lips were almost warm on hers, almost touching . . .

"Barrie, sugar, are you still here?" Pru called from up the stairs. "Hold on, I'm coming down."

Pru reached the second-floor landing as Barrie turned. "I told myself I wasn't going to ask you to be careful," Pru called down. "Be careful anyway."

Barrie's pulse *thud-thud-thudded* like wheels on cobblestones, and she nodded, not really listening. Eight had almost kissed her, and even almost had been amazing. She wanted to press her hands to her cheeks to hide the rush of color she knew was there.

Boys didn't usually—ever—hang around long enough to want to kiss her. The finding gift or Mark or Lula or something always ran them off. Of course, Eight didn't really know her yet. There was still time for him to run off screaming.

"Thanks, Aunt Pru." She gave her aunt a vague wave and dismissed the thought that she should stay, that Pru might need her.

Eight waited until the front door had closed behind them before he turned her toward him again. "You have a smudge of dirt on your nose."

"I do not." She'd just had a shower, after all.

He gave her a slow, wicked grin. "Are you going to argue now?"

He brushed her nose with the edge of his finger and stepped closer, his eyes broadcasting that he was going to kiss her. But out there in the daylight, in the open, Barrie couldn't. Mouth dry again, she stepped away. The sun vanished behind a cloud overhead, and she shivered. "Um. Maybe I should get a sweater."

"All right." Eight frowned down at her, looking confused.

Barrie managed a dignified walk back into the house. Once inside, though, she raced across the foyer and up the stairs, her thoughts flying in every direction. Halfway to the landing, a step pitched suddenly, throwing her shoulder-first into the wall as her feet slipped. Her hip smacked the edge of the tread. She landed three steps down, and her elbow hit the step above her.

"Damn," she said, out of breath and choking on outrage.

"Are you all right?" Pru poked her head over the railing

again. "Hold on. Don't move until I get there." She sprinted down the stairs.

Barrie pulled herself up to sit on the step. The sound of Mary's footsteps running down the corridor blurred into the rush of Pru's descent.

Mary barely came into view before she started scolding: "Didn't you hear your aunt?" she asked. "Don't you go gettin' up until we've had a look at you."

Barrie rested her shoulder against the wall, and Pru dropped to the step beside her. "That's twice you've almost killed yourself on this staircase."

"Three times," Barrie said. As soon as the words were out, she wished she could take them back. There was no point in worrying Pru, but it couldn't be coincidence. The house, the spirits, the Fire Carrier . . . something was out to get her.

Seeing Pru and Mary exchange a look filled with horror, Barrie suspected they had reached the same conclusion. Mary's finger twitched as if she wanted to waggle it at Pru, but she folded her arms and glared at her instead.

"I told you," Mary said.

"You didn't tell me she would fall down the stairs."

"I told you they're gettin' worse."

"What am I supposed to do," Pru snapped, "replace every screw and nut and peg in the house with iron? It would look hideous, and they'd only find something else to break."

"You mark my words, you or the child—someone's gonna get hurt. You can't just keep hoping they'll stop if you ignore 'em long enough."

"But *why* are they doing it?" Barrie asked. It made no sense.

Pru and Mary turned to her with matching expressions of surprise.

"It's not like they're doing any real damage," Barrie continued. "Except to me. Dismantling one stair at a time, one shutter . . . That seems more like a message than taking the house apart. Plus, if you're still feeding them, why are they acting up at all?"

Mary stiffened like a corpse and narrowed her eyes at Pru. "Tell me I didn't hear that right."

Conveniently letting her hair fall to hide her face, Pru bent to examine Barrie's elbow. "Does this hurt bad, sugar? How hard did you hit it?"

"Don't you go pretendin' you didn't hear me." Mary poked Pru on the chest. "Haven't I told you and told you to leave 'em *plat eyes* alone?"

"*Plat eyes?*" Barrie pulled her arm away and tucked it behind her back, peering from Pru to Mary and back again. "What are *plat eyes?*"

Mary's lips fused into a stubborn seam, and Pru heaved a sigh. "They're what the Gullah—the descendants of the

West Indian and Angolan slaves here on the sea islands—call the spirits of the unburied or carelessly buried dead. Mary insists that's what the *yunwi* really are."

"No insisting 'bout it. I've seen 'em, haven't I?" Mary said. "Not that I wanted to. One look in their fire eyes, and they'll grow and grow till they swallow you whole. What we need around here are some bottle trees. Then we trap 'em before they make more trouble."

"Bottle trees?" Pru glared back at her. "Even if that worked, don't you think the Fire Carrier would mind just a little if we did that?"

Before Mary could answer and the argument could escalate—which it was going to, Barrie could tell already—the door opened and Eight leaned inside. "Are you about ready, Bear? We've got— Hey!" He crossed to the stairs. "What happened?"

"Nothing. I'm a klutz, in case you didn't get the memo," Barrie said. "And I still need to get my sweater." Mindful of the broken step, she hurried upstairs, grabbed a sweater from the armoire in her bedroom, and ran back down to find Eight alone in the foyer. "Where did Pru and Mary go?"

"That way." He pointed down the corridor toward the kitchen. "They were arguing like a couple of hissing geese. So now are you going to tell me what happened?"

Barrie debated whether to say anything at all; she was

so tired of all the half answers. "Have you ever seen the Fire Carrier?" she asked. "Actually seen him?"

Holding the door for her, Eight paused. "Why do you want me to have seen him?"

"Don't answer a question with a question. I'm onto you." Barrie slapped him on the arm.

He stayed a step behind her so she couldn't see his face. "A lot of people have—or claim they have. Anyone with Watson or Beaufort or Colesworth blood. Anyone sensitive to ghosts or psychic events. Not to mention the frauds who come down and make a production of it. We've even had a guy from MIT insisting it's some kind of freak weather phenomenon around this part of the island."

"But what do you see? What does the Fire Carrier look like?"

"Like a witch light moving through the woods and a wash of red and orange on the river, like sunset by moonlight. Except it happens even when the moon is covered." Eight held the passenger door, then went around to start the car. "I looked up the *yunwi* like you asked, by the way."

"Did you find anything helpful?"

"If by 'helpful' you mean 'confusing,' sure. If you're hoping I found an article titled '*Yunwi*, Instructions on Exorcism of,' then not so much."

Barrie swallowed a sigh. "And?"

"The word means 'people,' which, unhelpfully, doesn't distinguish between living or dead, human or supernatural. The Cherokee believe there are both *yunwi* water spirits and something called 'little people,' who either torment you or bring good fortune, depending on how you treat them and what kind of person you are. Hold on." He held up his hand as Barrie opened her mouth. "Before you say 'And?' again, that's it. That's all I've got."

Barrie swallowed the urge to slap him. But then she processed the rest of what he'd said. "So I must really be a horrible person," she said. "Or I accidentally did something to piss them off."

"Why do you think so?"

"Because they're dismantling pieces of the house again."

The engine revved, and Eight shifted into a lower gear. "Dismantling, like taking the screws out of shutters and the security chain off kitchen doors, you mean?"

"Also banisters and steps and chair legs." Barrie nodded. "But there is a better question. How do we make them stop?"

CHAPTER SEVENTEEN

Behind the stage the eight lighted columns of Colesworth Place rose like the skeletons of the dying South against a bloody sky. A fitting backdrop for Cassie's play.

A high school boy in a Confederate uniform led Barrie and Eight through a small crowd of tourists fanning themselves with programs. In the center of the front row, he picked up a pair of RESERVED signs from the folding metal chairs.

"Enjoy the show," he said. Giving them a smart salute, he clicked his heels together and turned back to the ticket table.

Barrie took her seat, but the pull of something lost drew her attention beyond the columns to where the mansion had stood. Something *was* buried there; Cassie was right. Something big. The pressure made Barrie's head ache even worse. At the rate she was going, she'd need to buy stock in whatever company manufactured Tylenol.

"It's nice that Cassie is so modest about taking credit." Eight leaned closer and tapped the thin program in Barrie's hand.

Barrie scanned the text. *Written by C. Colesworth based on a novel by Margaret Mitchell, Produced by C. Colesworth, Directed by C. Colesworth, Starring Cassandra Colesworth and the Santisto Players.*

"Who are the Santisto Players?" she asked, shrugging off Eight's sarcasm.

"The high school drama club." Eight stretched his legs alongside hers, close but not quite touching. "The principal won't let them say so because Cassie stole the story to write the play. He doesn't want the school to get in trouble."

"So all these kids are Cassie's friends?"

"I wouldn't go that far."

Barrie turned to look around. The seven rows of seats were filling up, and again, she and Eight seemed to be the main attraction. In the area to the right of the stage marked *Actors Only*, girls in hoopskirts and boys in bow ties and formal coats took turns peering at her from the gap between the curtains. People in the audience cast her curious glances. A curl of annoyance tightened in her chest, but she pushed it down, told herself she was fine. She just wished the play would hurry up and start.

"It's only a few more minutes," Eight said. "Are you hungry yet? I could go get our food." He pointed at someone carrying a small wicker picnic basket from the concessions stand.

Food was the last thing Barrie wanted. Or the second to last thing, because having Eight leave her alone with all these people staring at her would be worse. On the flip side, eating would give her something to do with her hands.

Before she could make up her mind, Eight turned to smile at a dark-haired girl in a pale pink costume who was coming down the aisle. "Hey, Sydney." His greeting was friendlier than he had ever been with Cassie. "You here to meet your cousin?"

"I was hoping to," Sydney said. Her smile was tentative, and she lifted both hands to call attention to the picnic basket and the steaming bowl she carried. "I brought y'all some food."

Barrie set the program on the seat beside her and rose, only to stand there with no idea what to do. Cassie had made this part of their introduction easy, sweeping her into a hug and eliminating all the awkwardness. Sydney, clearly, wasn't as outgoing.

"I'm so glad you came over. Is it okay if I give you a hug?" Barrie asked. "It's amazing to have cousins."

"Sydney?" Cassie's head turtled out from behind the curtain. "What are you doing? Come back over here."

Sydney gave Barrie a bobbing nod. "Sorry! I've got to go." She pushed the food at Eight and turned to hurry away. After a couple of steps, though, she ran back and threw her arms around Barrie. "I'm so glad to meet you." Barrie barely had time to return the squeeze before Sydney rushed away, calling over her shoulder, "There are sandwiches, drinks, and cookies in the baskets, plus cocktail sauce, napkins, and utensils."

Eight and Barrie slipped back into their seats, and he handed her the steaming bowl.

"What is it?" Barrie asked.

"Frogmore Stew. Otherwise known as low-country boil. Try it."

"There aren't any actual frogs in it, are there?" Barrie drew the line at eating frogs. Or snakes. Or insects, for that matter. She could make a list. But as Eight laughed and shook his head, she had to admit the dish was delicious to look at: pink shrimp, white clams, red-skinned potatoes quartered to show the creamy middles, bright hunks of yellow corn on the cob, and some kind of sausage. It could have been a still-life painting of *Bounty from a Cornucopia*, but it had no relationship to stew. There wasn't a real sauce, for one thing, and how was she supposed to eat it gracefully?

"Don't bother with the knife and fork. That's what napkins are for." Eight retrieved a stack from one of the baskets and spread them several layers thick on the ground for the husks and shells. Then he squirted cocktail sauce into one section of the bowl.

Barrie nibbled a potato wedge. The flavors bloomed on her tongue, and she let her eyes flutter closed as she concentrated: "Lemon, salt, celery seed, onion, pepper, cloves, bay leaves—"

Eight bent closer, his breath warm on her cheek. "What are you saying?"

Her eyes flew open. "Nothing." She hadn't even realized she was speaking aloud. "I was separating flavors into ingredients," she admitted. "It's not a game, exactly, more an experiment my . . . godfather and I used to do at home." The thought of Mark left her with a pang of loneliness.

Eight's lips twitched into a grin. "You cook?"

"Yes." Barrie felt warm and breathless from the way he looked at her.

A slow drumroll made them startle apart. Two football-player types dressed in Confederate gray marched onto the stage. Pulling on ropes hidden behind the broken columns, they raised a sheet of canvas to create a backdrop and turned to stand at attention. Four more boys carried in a framed front door, a small table, and a pair of swinging benches. They all saluted the audience and walked off in step with one another. The stage and columns went dark, leaving only the sunset to illuminate the grounds.

The beat of the drums faded, and the first mournful notes of "Dixie" ghosted through the trees. Behind the audience a light snapped on, projecting the porch of a plantation house onto the canvas backdrop. The front door in the image aligned perfectly with the prop onstage, which opened on a creaky note to admit Cassie and two boys, all of them in aristocratic costumes. They were followed by a girl dressed as a slave, who balanced glasses and a pitcher of lemonade on a tray.

"There'll be war soon." One of the boys posed at the edge of the stage with a hand in his pocket. "It's comin' here, too, I reckon."

"War." Cassie settled herself on a bench and spread out her skirts. "Ah'm sick to death of everyone talkin' 'bout the war." She gave both boys a flirtatious glance. "Tell me somethin' ah don't already know."

"All right." The other boy put a foot on the bench beside Cassie and hooked his thumbs into the armholes of his vest. "I bet you didn't know Ashley Wilkes is announcin' his engagement to Melanie tomorrow at the Twelve Oaks ball."

Cassie's face lost color. Then she raised her chin, giving the impression of looking down her nose at the boy even though she was sitting and he was standing up.

"You're lyin'." Her voice hit the perfect tone of careful rage. "You're lyin', and ah don't appreciate the jest. Ah want you to go." She pointed an imperious finger. "Leave. Go on.

Go home, Brent Tarleton, and take your brother with you."

The boys glanced at each other, shrugged, and went down the steps at the edge of the stage. Cassie watched them leave as if she were about to call them back. Barrie *felt* the warring rage and longing in her cousin as if it were her own. She held her breath as Cassie waited, hoping, until the boys were out of sight. Cassie picked up the lemonade from the tray and hurled it after them. The pitcher arced perfectly and crashed with the sound of breaking glass.

Eight leaned closer, his shoulder brushing hers, his warmth and scent grounding Barrie in the present while the play tried to sweep her into the past. Neither of them moved again until the audience gasped when Rhett Butler came on stage, played by a light-skinned African-American boy.

"Oh, that's brilliant," Barrie whispered. Everyone around her whispered too, but then the magic of the play took hold again.

Cassie was astonishingly good. Her every word deepened the magic that held the audience and didn't let go until the final backdrop faded from the projection screen.

"I don't know if that was nerve or genius," Eight said into Barrie's ear while the cast took their bows and curtsies and the audience rose to their feet.

"Both." Still caught up in the play, she turned toward him. He was unexpectedly close. His eyes locked on hers, and the returning click shuddered through her to settle in her chest. Eight breathed faster as if the same energy that pulled her toward him was pulling him to her. But the tap of high-heeled shoes hurrying across the stage reminded her where they were. She turned and found Cassie watching her—watching the two of them—with a fixed, unnerving scrutiny that wasn't the least bit friendly.

The impression was gone in an instant. Cassie's smile seemed genuine enough as she ran down the steps, holding up the hoopskirt of her beautiful red gown, her curled hair bouncing and her face still flushed with praise. In that moment, as much as during any part of the play, she *was* Scarlett running down the steps of Tara.

She swooped in and took Barrie's hands. "So? Did you love it? Tell me you loved it!"

"Of course I loved it. Who wouldn't?"

Cassie's laugh was delighted, deep, and breathy. She turned to Eight, her mouth open to speak, but then she stiffened and took a half step backward, her hand flying to her throat.

Wyatt emerged from behind the concessions stand. Barrie smiled wider than probably necessary. "Hello, Uncle Wyatt."

"What did you think of our girl up there? She's something, isn't she?" Wyatt bared his teeth at Barrie. Eight, he ignored so completely that it could only have been on purpose.

"They were both terrific." Barrie nodded at Sydney, who had materialized behind her older sister. The younger girl was pale, less vivid than Cassie, like a print from an engraving plate used once too often. Sydney's hair wasn't as dark; her skin wasn't as tanned; her eyes were a more watered-down shade of blue.

Ignoring his younger daughter, Wyatt dropped a hand on Barrie's shoulder. He stank of cigarettes and alcohol. "I 'spect your aunt wants you home soon. Cassie, Sydney, you go get changed. You have cleaning up to do."

"I invited Barrie to stay a bit," Cassie said.

Wyatt's frown pinned his daughter until she squirmed. "Now's not good," he said. "You've got work."

"But I was going to show Barrie around. I can clean up later—" Cassie broke off and seemed to shrink as Wyatt's expression deepened into a scowl.

"I'm happy to come back another time," Barrie interjected before Cassie could argue any more. Getting Wyatt upset wouldn't do any of them any good. The whole point of coming was to find the treasure and end the feud. Why didn't Cassie explain that to her father?

"Come on, Eight. Let's head home." Barrie caught Eight's arm to pull him away.

"Don't go yet," Cassie said. "You may as well look around since you're already here."

Wyatt's expression grew darker still. "Not now, I said."

Eight had been watching the exchange with apparent fascination. He shifted closer to Barrie but made no move to leave. "Cassie, didn't you tell your daddy about asking Barrie to help you find whatever y'all lost in the war? You're probably all excited about getting it back."

"Of course." Cassie darted a look at Wyatt and licked her lips. Then she wound her arm through the crook of Barrie's elbow, pulling her to the left of the stage. "I thought we could start where the tunnel collapsed. I'll bet it won't take any time at all."

The lights had come up again as the audience had begun to depart, but on the far side of the stage, the moon stole all the color from the landscape. Aside from the columns, marble stairs and three half-tumbled chimneys were the bulk of what remained of the mansion. Where walls had once stood, grass had grown over remnants of broken brick, making it treacherous to walk.

Cassie barely seemed to notice. She steered Barrie away from the source of the loss toward a fenced hole in the ground at the side of the ruined foundation. "This fell in four years ago," she said. "We didn't even know it was here. Or at least, we didn't know *where* it was."

"What is it?" Barrie asked. Grass and weeds had done their best to colonize the sides of the hole that went down some fifteen feet, but here and there brick and mortar showed through, suggesting a structure underneath.

"It used to be an escape tunnel to the river. All three of the founding families' houses had them. It's a big deal, apparently. Not something that you find on most plantations. We had archaeologists over here practically wetting their pants, begging Daddy to let them excavate."

"Why not let them?" Barrie asked. "Wouldn't that have solved your problem?" She stole a glance back at Wyatt, who had followed them. He looked sulkier and somehow larger, as if his anger were making him swell.

Cassie followed Barrie's gaze, and her eyes held her father's. Surprisingly, he was the one who looked away. Even then, Cassie watched him as she answered: "The tunnel cuts underneath the columns. If they fall over, we don't have much left to draw the tourists."

It seemed to Barrie there was plenty to see at Colesworth Place apart from what remained of the mansion. Eight had mentioned that Wyatt was restoring the plantation. Elaborate signs in front of several structures near the main house foundation marked the kitchen, smokehouse, and stables. Near the parking lot and the smaller, modern house, a chapel stood intact beside a cemetery enclosed by wrought-iron fencing. Closer to the river, a row of brick slave cabins near the woods looked like they were in perfect condition, along with a larger cabin that might have been an overseer's house.

A second tug of loss came from that direction, lighter and less important than the brooding ache that called to Barrie from beyond the columns. She rubbed her temples and took a few steps toward it.

Wyatt cut her off. "Where are you going? This is no time for bungling around. The moonlight may seem bright, but it's easy to lose your footing and hurt yourself."

"Daddy, just let her do her—"

"You and I are going to discuss this later, Cassie. But now, she needs to leave."

Barrie tried not to look at Eight. "I'm sorry, Uncle Wyatt. I don't know what I did—"

He whipped his attention back to her. "Didn't you hear what I said?" The tone of his voice had lost any pretense at civility. "You're as nosy as your mother, and just as sure everyone is going to welcome you wherever you show up. Entitled bitches, the both of you. But this here isn't Watson property. It's mine, and I decide who gets to stay. You want to be friends with my girls? I'll tell you when you can be friends. Just as soon as you have them over to visit at Watson's Landing. As soon as you stop lying about where you've been all these years. Your mother killed my brother! You think I want you over here sniffing around?"

Stricken, Barrie glanced at Cassie, and then at Sydney, who had frozen like a rabbit behind her father and her sister, as if she hoped neither one would notice her if she didn't move. Barrie wanted to retort that both her cousins could come over anytime, but she recognized she couldn't. Pru would have a fit. And what did Wyatt mean about Lula killing his brother?

"Come on, Bear. Let's go." Eight put his arm around Barrie's shoulder and drew her toward him.

"Daddy, stop. You don't know what you're saying." Cassie stepped in front of Wyatt, facing Barrie, her palms together in a pleading gesture. "Please don't leave mad, Barrie. He doesn't mean—"

"I damn well do mean it—"

"No, you *don't*! You know how our lives would change if we could find what Alcee Colesworth hid."

Wyatt stilled, the kind of stillness that had a weight all its own. "We can't find what doesn't exist," he said.

"But it does. I know it does!" Cassie turned back to him.

His hand caught her across the cheek. "You don't know that, and finding it damn sure wouldn't change things."

"Hey!" Barrie shouted.

Cassie gasped. Her hand flew to her face.

Eight moved between them. "Are you insane?" he said to Wyatt. "Or just drunk?"

Barrie willed Eight—wished him—to shut up. Wyatt's

face was red, and he was breathing hard. A vein bulged in his forehead from his hairline to the bridge of his nose. His hands fisted, anger pouring off him like sweat. "Get out of here, both of you. Go on now. Get!"

Cassie mouthed, "Just go," and Sydney nodded.

It was impossible to think of leaving her cousins with Wyatt. But Barrie also couldn't stay. She recognized Wyatt's anger, and challenging her mother in this kind of a mood had always ended in disaster.

She wrapped her arm around Eight's waist. "Come on. Let's go." Standing on her toes, she whispered into his ear: "If we stay, we'll only make it worse for Cassie."

Judging by the expression on Wyatt's face, though, they couldn't make it too much worse.

CHAPTER EIGHTEEN

Turning her back on Wyatt's anger made the hair rise on the back of Barrie's neck. She shivered as she took the first step toward the parking lot.

"Damn stupid crazy bastard," Eight muttered, moving with her. His voice was soft.

But not soft enough.

"What did you call me, boy?" Wyatt shoved Barrie out of the way.

Eight whipped around. "Get your hands off her."

Wyatt's face was ugly: skin red, eyes slitted, lips peeled back from his teeth. Deliberately he snatched at Barrie's arm and pulled her toward him. Eight grasped her other hand. Caught between the two, Barrie felt like a rope in a tug of war.

Her heart revved, and her brain spun as she tried to think of a way to get them both calmed down.

Eight let her go. He pushed up his sleeves.

"What is wrong with all of you?" Barrie wrenched her arm out of Wyatt's hold. "We were trying to *leave*. Come on, Eight. Let's go."

Eight didn't budge. Cassie and Sydney reached them and tried to pull Wyatt back, but he only shifted his weight to the balls of his feet.

Every movement around Barrie, every detail, her every thought, grew crystalline. A fight between Eight and Wyatt wouldn't be any kind of contest. Wyatt was too big. Eight would get hurt—badly hurt—and it would be her fault. But neither of them was going to back down.

Do something, Barrie. For once don't be useless.

"Eight, give me your phone," she said, already reaching into his pocket to retrieve it.

He ignored her.

Wyatt didn't. "I told you not to bring her here," he snarled at Cassie. "Now she's calling the police."

"She won't call anyone." Frantically Cassie shook her head at Barrie.

"He *hit* you." Barrie just about had the phone fished out.

Wyatt was chin-to-chin with Eight. He shifted toward

Barrie, but Eight blocked him. Wyatt's eyes darted between them, then slid to Cassie. "You fix this," he barked. "You're the one who made the mess."

Cassie cast Barrie a pleading look. "Daddy didn't mean to hit me, Barrie. I swear he didn't. He's not like that. But if you call the police, it will get bad for us." She looked down at her hands. They looked pale against the brilliant gown, which suddenly looked theatrical and out of place. "Please. Daddy has to work. You don't understand—"

"How's she going to understand?" Wyatt curled his lip. "Look at her, standing there with her gold watch and her diamond necklace. Throwing it all up in our faces how much class she has, how she's better than anybody else."

All of Cassie's color seemed to have bled into her dress, and Sydney looked like she wanted the river to sweep her away and drown her. Forcing a deep breath, Barrie dug for some semblance of calm. "I'm not throwing anything in anyone's face. But if you'll leave Cassie alone and let us go, I won't call the police. I swear it. Eight promises too."

"Watson promises don't mean jack shit. And Beaufort promises mean even less."

"Then what do you want from us?" Barrie was shaking again, shaking and desperate. "We can't prove a negative. Cassie's the one who got hit. If she doesn't want me to call the police, I won't. But don't think I'm doing you any favors, because I don't owe you a damn thing." She tugged at Eight's shirt, and when he didn't budge, she spun around and strode away without looking back—her shoulders stiff with the effort. All she could do was hope he would follow.

She never should have come. She should have listened to Pru and Eight when they'd warned her. She should have—

She paused, relief flooding through her as she heard Eight's footsteps coming after her.

Fists balled, every muscle broadcasting his fury, he brushed right past her and didn't slow.

Running to keep up, Barrie didn't say anything until they were almost to the parking lot. When she looked back, Cassie had her hands wrapped around Wyatt's arm, holding him anchored, talking fast. Sydney just looked miserable.

"Go ahead," Barrie said to Eight. "Tell me you told me so. Get it over with."

"Jesus." He stopped walking. "You think I expected *that*?"

Barrie gave a shrug. "I don't know. But I'll give you a free 'I told you so' anyway. Last chance. Going once . . . Going twice . . ."

"I'm not an ass," Eight said, grinning in spite of himself. "Well, okay, maybe I am. Some of the time—just not right this second. What the hell was with him?"

"Besides booze?"

"Not just booze. He was higher than a treed raccoon."

"What does that mean? Drugs?"

Eight cocked an eyebrow at her. "You did lead a sheltered life, didn't you, Bear? Yes, drugs. His pupils were as small as his brain."

Pressure was swelling in Barrie's chest. Stupid, stupid tears. Cassie had been nice to her, and so had Sydney. Barrie had wanted so much to be friends with them. And she hated the idea of her cousins having Wyatt for a father.

"No, hey. It's all right." Eight pulled her closer, winding his arm around her waist. She let her head drop against his shoulder as they followed the path through a clump of trees toward the parking area.

"I didn't want to believe you," Barrie said.

"On the bright side, it could have been worse."

"What, he could have fed me to the alligators?" She blinked up at him. "But thank you."

"For what?" He stopped and turned her to face him.

"For coming with me. For not saying 'I told you so.' For not being an ass. At least not right this minute."

His hands slid down her arms until their fingers tangled together, his eyes bright on hers. Barrie's heart went dizzy. The parking lot was empty, the tourists gone. The night was silent except for the rustle of the wind in the branches of the wooded path, the river's distant whisper, and the ever-present insects. For a stolen instant they were the only two people in the whole wide world, and right then being safe with Eight was all Barrie wanted. They leaned against each other, not moving, not needing to move, until the slap and crunch of footsteps running on gravel made them turn to look.

Holding up the front of her hoopskirt, Cassie emerged from the trees, breathing hard. She stopped midstep, and her face flushed an angry red. "Didn't mean to interrupt. Sorry," she said, not sounding like she meant it. "I wanted to apologize for Daddy. Honestly, he didn't know what he was saying. He's a mean drunk, and that's not your fault."

"You shouldn't apologize for him," Barrie said.

"Well, someone has to." Cassie's chin trembled. "You don't know what it's like feeling you'll never amount to anything. Knowing the whole town thinks you're not good enough. That's what it's like to be a Colesworth around here. That's how Daddy's felt all his life. Just give him time to cool off. He's mad because he thinks you're going to look down on us, on him, for not having a house like yours. And I guess he's not really over losing Uncle Wade, but he'll come around. He wants to get to know you and hear all about Lula, hear what she told you about Wade and all. He'll cool off, and it will all be fine."

"It won't." Eight pushed Barrie toward the car. "And you're insane if you want Barrie to forget how he acted just now."

"Don't put words in my mouth," Cassie snapped. She turned back to Barrie, doe-eyed again. "All I want is for the two of us to be okay, Cos. You were right. We're family. I can't help what Daddy says. I can't change him, but you matter to me. You don't have to look for the treasure—"

"I don't think whatever is down there is what you think it is anyway," Barrie said. "It's sentimental. Important but not necessarily valuable."

Cassie's jaw dropped, and it took her a second to gather herself. "You don't think our valuables are *sentimental*? Our house used to be as nice as yours. The damn Yankees didn't let anyone keep anything. Paintings, photographs, jewelry, keepsakes. History. Dignity. Civility. They took it all away. What's buried down there could give us a little of that back."

Barrie could have told her that *things* wouldn't make Wyatt civil or dignified, but what was the point? She sighed and turned to go.

"No, wait." Cassie's tone shifted back to pleading. "I swear, I don't know what's wrong with me. I didn't come out here to talk to you about the treasure. I swear I won't bring it up if you don't want me to. It's just that I hoped it could finally fix things for us. Just tell me we can still be friends."

The longing on her face was so intense, Barrie couldn't bear to see it. She knew what it was like to feel you were seen for where you came from instead of who you were.

People had always judged Mark. For being too gay, or not gay enough, or not transgender the way some expected. How many times had people presumed she would apologize for him being who he was? She had always refused. But she'd been able to walk away because those people hadn't mattered. Those people weren't family.

"Of course we're still friends," she told Cassie, trying to ignore the way Eight growled. "I'll talk to you soon."

Once they were in the car, Eight slammed the door and started up the engine. He was spectacularly mad driving out of Colesworth Place. Barrie almost wished he would go ahead and yell. Get it over with. He turned onto the main road with a squeal of tires.

"I'd prefer it if you didn't kill us, if you don't mind." Barrie kept her voice nice and even.

"I'd prefer to strangle you, and I *do* mind. How can you fall for Cassie's crap again? She doesn't want to be friends with you."

"Don't you feel sorry for her at all?"

"She was the one who put you in that situation! And you should never have admitted you felt something lost on the property. Of course she's going to ask you to try to find their fictional valuables again. She was lying when she said that wasn't what she wanted."

The Beaufort gift again.

What would it be like knowing whenever someone lied? Barrie decided she wouldn't take that "gift" if someone served it up to her with a side of chocolate-hazelnut torte. How many times a day did people lie? Or twist the truth until it wasn't recognizable anymore? How could you trust anyone, or even like them, if you always knew what was in their hearts?

When it came down to it, the only absolute truth was loyalty. Family. The people you chose to stick by no matter what.

"I'm not going to blame Cassie for a situation beyond her control," Barrie said. "Don't worry, though. I'm not going to let her push me into anything."

"How has that worked out for you so far?"

"About as well as minding your own business has worked for you." Barrie bit her lip as soon as the words were out, but it was too late to call them back. And maybe she didn't want to. The whole night had left her in the mood for a good argument, no holds barred.

Eight shot over the bridge and turned in the opposite direction from Watson's Landing.

"Home is to the right, in case you've forgotten, baseball guy."

"Thanks, but I don't need your Watson senses to tell me that."

"I see you're back to being a jackass. Are you going to turn around?"

"Since I'm being a jackass, no. I'm not."

"Fine." Barrie flounced back against her seat.

·"Fine."

The car sped up. Eight was still accelerating as they bar-reled through town, and Barrie half-expected to see flashing lights appear in her side mirror.

"Do you mind at least telling me where we're going?" she asked.

They passed the entrance to Bobby Joe's parking lot. "We're going to go forget about Cassie and Wyatt. Screw them if they don't like you for you."

He sounded like Mark.

Drained by the aftereffects of anger and adrenaline, Barrie found herself breathing in Eight's recklessness, swept up in it, and suddenly it didn't matter where they were going or what he planned to do. His moods were contagious, dangerous to her equilibrium.

He stopped at the beach, the same beach where they'd seen the turtle nest. Neither of them said a word while Eight retrieved a musty-smelling towel from his trunk and caught Barrie's hand, lacing their fingers like they were made to fit.

They ran barefoot over the dunes and through a break in the pickets that held back the sea oats. The moon turned the white sand to diamond dust, and Eight laid the towel down above the high-tide marker of shells and seaweed and damp, dark sand. He sat down and drew her against him, her back against his chest. His arms wrapped around her, and she leaned into the solidness of him. His heartbeat washed through her like the waves, until she didn't know whether the pounding of it was hers or his.

When she sighed and relaxed, he eased her down and leaned over and finally kissed her until she felt like she was going to fall. She reached for him, kissing him more deeply. His lips were scalding on hers, leaving her tingling and whole instead of so, so alone. She wanted the feeling, the moment, to never stop.

Only when she came up for air did the word "love" enter her thoughts. She pushed it away, but maybe by the time any girl thought about protecting herself, keeping herself from falling for a guy who was going to leave her brokenhearted, it was already too late. Maybe it had been like that for Lula with Wade, and instead of being Prince Charming, Wade had turned out to be like Wyatt.

"Why do you suppose my mother was afraid of Wyatt?" Barrie rolled and rested on one elbow to look at Eight.

"Apart from what we saw tonight, you mean?"

"I assumed it was about the feud. Because she was a Watson and she'd run off with Wyatt's brother. But it felt more personal."

"Feuds are always personal. That's what makes it hard to

break the cycle. Everyone lives locked inside their own anger until someone is finally brave enough to step outside themselves to see the view from the other side. It's why I need to get away from this place."

"But you're not stepping out for a different view." Barrie tipped her face up to the stars so she wouldn't have to look at him. "You're stepping out to run away."

He was silent, and she was suddenly afraid. Afraid that she had said too much, presumed too much, hoped too much. She rolled her capris as high as they would go, then ran toward the water. She didn't look back until she was knee deep, which was as far as she dared. He was right behind her, his face gleaming in the kind of light that turned beautiful boys into gods. He caught her, and held her, his skin so warm and alive, she couldn't help but melt.

"Why did you run?" he asked.

"To see if you'd come after me."

"It scares me how willing I am to run after you. We're both doing too much running."

"So kiss me again."

Her hands crept around his neck, tangling in his hair to keep him closer, even though she knew that beautiful boys with expiration dates couldn't be held, only borrowed for a time.

CHAPTER NINETEEN

The gate at Watson's Landing was open its usual inch when Eight pulled up. He hit the brake and slammed the gearshift into park. "Your aunt needs to stop doing that. It's the middle of the night."

"What is Pru supposed to do if she can't get to the phone?" Barrie asked. "She's probably gone to bed and wanted to be sure I could get back in. Also? Stop nagging. I don't want to spoil the mood with an argument."

Shadows spilled through the iron bars onto the roadway, swirling around Eight as he did his usual shuffle with the gate and the car. In the flickering light of the gas sconces on the posts, it was hard to tell if they were real shadows or *yunwi*. Barrie still felt like she had stars in her eyes that made it hard to see, and as they passed through the gate, the relief of coming back to Watson's Landing was like ten pounds of weight had lifted from her.

Eight shut his door and put the car back into gear. "You know, if we argue, we could make up." He shot her a grin steeped in mischief. "Especially if your aunt's gone to sleep."

"I don't know if she has. I hope she isn't waiting up for me," Barrie said with a pang of guilt.

It had been selfish to leave, especially since she knew her aunt would worry. It was funny: Barrie had spent so much of her life trying to keep her mother from panicking at the thought of being left alone, but it was Pru who'd never had anyone. And Pru would be alone again when Barrie left for art school next year. *If* she left. Did Pru feel as anxious about that as Barrie felt about Eight leaving?

Barrie stared out the window, watching the gleam of the river from between the live oak trees. All her life she had drifted around on currents of other people's making. She didn't want to be a drifter. She ought to be more like Cassie, who, right or wrong, made life happen. Cassie went after what she wanted. Eight did too. He seemed to navigate all his decisions as easily as he guided the car to a stop in the circular drive beneath the white-columned portico.

"You're dangerous when you get quiet." Eight walked her to the door. "What do you have brewing in that head of yours?"

"Like you don't already know."

"The head and the heart are different."

"Sure they are. Good night, baseball guy."

He kissed the tip of her nose. "Why do you feel like you have to fix everyone's problems, Bear?"

"I'm not fixing anything for you."

"Pru will love you even if you leave. People are going to like you even if you don't try so hard."

"You think that's what I'm doing?"

"Isn't it?"

"Must be nice to be you. Always having all the answers." Easy to make people love you when you could give them exactly what they needed, what they wanted so deep in their hearts that they didn't even know it themselves.

Was that what he was doing with her? How much of what she felt for him was genuine, and how much was he using his gift to make her like him?

She was going around in circles, and it was enough to make her crazy.

"Aaaand she's mad again." Eight stepped back and tipped her face up to look at him. "*Now* what did I do?"

She turned her head away. "Do me a favor? Teach me how to drive a car?"

He studied her and pushed his hands into his pockets. "Driving won't give you control of your life, you know. It may seem that way."

"It's a start."

"Anyway, how do you not know how to drive? Didn't you need a car in San Francisco?"

"The things I don't know would amaze you."

"So make a list. We'll do them all."

How was it possible to feel so much for him already? Barrie had only known him a few breaths in the comparative span of a life. It had to be the Beaufort gift. Grabbing two fistfuls of his shirt, she pulled him closer and rose onto her toes to kiss him. Because kissing Eight was the kind of magic she liked. As long as his lips were on hers, as long as they shared breath between them, most of her worries, her question marks, disappeared.

Until he pulled away again.

"When do you actually leave?" she asked. "The exact date."

"You're adorable when you're mad."

"I'm not mad, and that is one of the cheesiest lines ever invented by stupid boys."

"Maybe I'm the one who's mad, then. Because I've been stuck around this island my entire life and nothing interesting has ever happened. Now here you are."

"Here I *go*. That's my cue to say good night."

Before he could say anything she couldn't be sure he meant, Barrie let herself into the house, leaving him standing on the step looking almost as confused as she felt. Maybe that made her a coward, but she needed time to think. Falling for a guy was hard enough. She didn't need extra complications to make her doubt herself. She stood for a minute, leaning back against the door, shoring up her strength. Then she headed into the kitchen.

She had hoped it would be deserted, but Pru stood at the counter slicing the crusts off a loaf of thin, white sandwich bread. Her eyes went straight to the wind-tangled mess of Barrie's hair. "Is everything all right, sugar? I was getting worried. You were gone so long."

"Eight and I went to the beach to talk after the play was over." Barrie washed her hands and got another knife and a cutting board from the cabinet. After stacking eight slices of bread on top of one another, she took pleasure in hacking off the crusts. She looked up to catch Pru watching her with the same expectant kind of silence Mark had always used to get her to talk. Go figure. Maybe there was some sort of secret parental interrogation manual. She stacked more bread and guillotined the crusts.

Pru cleared her throat. "How was Cassie's play?"

"Fantastic," Barrie said brightly. "They did this thing where they projected the scenery behind the stage, and Cassie was excellent."

Pru waited another couple beats, then prompted: "So you didn't have any trouble?"

Barrie reached for another stack of bread.

"If you don't mind my saying so, you don't look like a girl who had a good night." Pru came over and put her hand over Barrie's. "Is it Eight, honey, or did something happen at the play? Wyatt wasn't there, was he?"

Barrie felt as if all the air had been sucked out of the room, and she searched for a way to answer without resorting to an 'I don't want to talk about it.' "Wyatt was there, but it wasn't . . . Oh, who am I kidding? He was awful."

Pru went still. "He didn't hurt you, did he?"

"N-no." Barrie hated the catch in her voice. "No. Not me," she said more firmly.

After a moment of continued stillness, Pru got a glass and poured herself a shot of brandy from a bottle in the cupboard. Then she went and sat down at the table. "All right. I'm ready now," she said. "Tell me all about Wyatt."

And what was the point of keeping quiet? By tomorrow Eight would have told Seven everything.

Barrie put down the knife and went to sit in the chair across from Pru. "He really was horrible," she said, resting her elbows on the table. "He accused me of going over there so I could look down on them, and he told me I was nosy, just like Lula. I don't even know what made him so mad. He seemed nice enough last night."

"I wonder if something happened between him and

Lula before she left. She did mention him in her letter."

Barrie looked up sharply. "Like what kind of something?"

"Lord only knows." Pru took another sip of brandy. "Lula was always liable to say whatever popped into her head. If she had her heart set on leaving with Wade, and Wyatt tried to stop them? I don't know." She set the glass down with a *thump*. "I should probably call Seven and ask him for help."

"Help doing what? Nothing happened that a lawyer can fix. Anyway, I think Cassie calmed Wyatt down." Barrie wasn't going to let anyone else fix her messes for her anymore. Not Eight, not Pru, and certainly not Seven.

Pru gave her a sympathetic look. "I'm sorry. I know how much you wanted to be friends with the girls. It's a shame that won't work out."

It had to, though. Barrie owed Cassie that much. She had to make Pru understand.

"It has nothing to do with our being friends. None of this is Cassie's fault—and Sydney seems genuinely sweet. I feel really bad for them. Wyatt hit Cassie, right in front of us. In front of her sister."

Pru rose, wiped her hands on her apron, and went back to the counter before she said anything. "Was Cassie all right?"

"More embarrassed than hurt, I think. But I can't help wondering how often that happens." Barrie's throat knotted. "You see why I can't *not* be friends with them, right?" She glanced at Pru. "What kind of person would I be if I walked away when Cassie and Sydney were nice and it was only Wyatt who was horrible?"

Pru gazed back at the brandy she'd left on the table as if she were contemplating drowning in it. She picked up a block of cream cheese instead and opened it meticulously. "So let me make sure I have this right. You're saying I should let you be friends with Cassie because you know her father is violent, even though I thought it was a bad idea when we only suspected he was violent."

"Well, if you're going to put it *that way* . . ." Barrie blew out a breath and smiled. "Yeah, that's pretty much what I'm saying."

Pru dumped the cream cheese into a bowl with an emphatic *splat*. "Just promise me one thing," she said. "Promise you won't go anywhere near Wyatt. Or anywhere he might show up. I'll talk to Seven, too, and we'll see if there's anything he can do."

"Cassie begged me not to call the police. I think that would make it worse for her." Barrie crossed the counter and picked up a peeled cucumber from the counter, and started cutting it into nearly transparent slices. Her burst of energy seemed to be draining from her.

"None of this is easy, is it?" Pru came over and kissed her on the cheek. "I know you're trying to do the right thing. It's not always obvious what that is."

Smiling sadly, she turned back to the counter and began combining cream cheese, mayonnaise, dill, salt, and pepper together into a cream. Barrie finished slicing the cucumbers and put them into a bowl with salt and lemon juice.

"We'll leave the assembly for tomorrow," Pru said. "Otherwise the bread gets soggy." She covered the plates and bowls in plastic wrap and stored them all in the refrigerator, then hung her apron on the hook in the butler's pantry. "There. That went faster with your help, even with our conversation."

"Thanks for not being mad, Aunt Pru."

Pru's eyebrows rose. "Why would I be mad at you?"

They locked the house together and went upstairs. The dim light of the corridor sharpened the hollows of Pru's face, making her look much older, as if Barrie's arrival had woken her from a magical sleep and the years had caught up to her. Barrie felt a twinge of guilt for making her aunt worry. Then the guilt was swallowed by rage—at the circumstances, at Wyatt, at Lula, at Cassie, and most of all at herself for feeling guilty.

Too many emotions were all crammed inside her. That and the pressure from the empty wing made her feel like she was going to burst as she neared the top of the stairs. She couldn't control Wyatt's violent temper, or Eight's leaving, or that Mark was dying. Whatever was lost down the dark corridor, though, and in the library or anywhere else in the house, that much she could fix. Pru didn't need to know.

She paused outside her door. "Good night, Aunt Pru."

"Sleep well, sweetheart." Pru gave her a quick kiss before continuing to her own room at the end of the hall.

CHAPTER TWENTY

Barrie pulled on clean pajama shorts and a thick pair of fuzzy socks, but she was too restless to read or sketch, let alone to sleep. Leaning on the balcony railing, she let the night sounds blanket her thoughts until a movement upstairs at Beaufort Hall claimed her attention. The distance couldn't disguise the silhouette of Eight's body in the window. He always moved as if he knew exactly where he was going. Barrie needed more of that.

It wasn't quite midnight yet. She peeked into the hallway. No light seeped under Pru's door, and there was no sound when she laid her ear against the wood. She crept toward the staircase. Every creak and groan of the time-warped floorboards made her wince and pause, and she let out a sigh when she reached the top of the steps. Then it occurred to her that she couldn't turn on the light in the corridor to the empty wing, not without the risk of Pru seeing it through the crack beneath her door. She would have to save that section of the house for daylight. In the meantime, there was still the library.

Even clean and exorcised, Emmett's sanctum was grim, as if it had absorbed the man's personality over the years. Barrie already knew enough about her grandfather to know she was glad she had never met him.

His keys, surprisingly, were in plain sight in the top-right drawer of the desk. There were eight on the ring, three of them too large and ornate. Four were too small. Barrie went straight to an old-fashioned brass key that looked about the right size to fit the bottom drawer. The lock *snicked* open on the first try, but the drawer was empty.

That made no sense. The finding pull clearly came from that drawer, and the sense of loss was stronger now that Barrie had it open. She leaned forward in the desk chair, sliding her fingertips across the smooth sides and top of the empty recess, probing until a pinky-size section released.

A panel at the back of the drawer popped open. Barrie reached inside the cavity, half-expecting to feel spiders skittering up her arm or the cold steel of a loaded gun. Something as unpleasant as Emmett himself. Instead paper crackled in her grasp, and she pried a bundle of yellowed envelopes out of the drawer. They were held together by an ancient rubber band that broke into several pieces as soon as she touched it.

Frowning, she stared at the envelope on top. It was five years old and addressed to Pru in Lula's familiar combination of flamboyance and pain-racked, shaking script. One by one, Barrie flipped through every envelope, through eleven years of postmarks, eleven years of letters addressed either to Pru or to Emmett. All of them had been neatly sliced open across the top by a letter opener or a sharpened knife.

The envelope on the very bottom had been mailed months after the fire, the same month Lula had finally been released from the hospital. Every letter had a return address.

Barrie felt like the room was spinning around her, faster and faster, and she didn't know how to make it stop. Someone—Barrie's grandfather?—had known exactly where Lula had been all along. And who else could it have been, aside from Emmett? It was his library, his locked drawer. Barrie couldn't imagine Pru ignoring Lula or pretending Lula were dead if she knew it wasn't true.

Pru had never seen these letters. She hadn't known her twin was alive, because Emmett had hidden that knowledge from her, the same way he had hidden it from everyone else on Watson Island.

What kind of father did that?

Barrie's hands shook. The yellowed paper rasped as she pulled the oldest letter from the envelope.

Daddy,

I understand what you said, and I'm not questioning. I'm not accusing. I haven't told a soul, I swear. I never will, because I'm a Watson as much as you are. There's also Barrie to think of now. She looks exactly like me. Like I used to look. I didn't realize how important family was until the first time she looked up at me from her bassinet. The doctors say I should be able to hold her soon. Maybe I will.

You can't mean it about not letting me come home. Tell everyone the funeral was a mistake. Tell them you didn't know I survived. Yes, it might be safer if Wyatt thinks I'm dead, but it's killing me to be away from Watson's Landing anyway. There are medical bills, too, and I have at least three surgeries left to go. How am I supposed to get through that and manage to take care of a baby?

Don't keep hanging up on me. Please! Please? Let me talk to you, or at least to Pru or Mama. You have to help me.

The letter wasn't signed or dated. Barrie dropped it onto the table and flipped through all the postmarks again, hoping the letters were simply out of sequence and she would find the first part of whatever discussion Lula had already had with Emmett mixed in somewhere. But the letter she had read was the oldest correspondence. She picked up the next one and pulled it from the envelope with fingers that felt too clumsy. This one was even shorter.

> *Daddy,*
>
> *Thank you for the money and instructions. No, I can't prove Wyatt was here, but if you would just tell the police on Watson Island, I'm sure they could find a reason to arrest him. Then maybe the police <u>here</u> would believe me, and I could finally come home. If you won't do that, at least let Pru come to me. You know how it hurts to be away. I'm in too much pain to bear it. Please! You have my promise. I swear I will keep your secret. What more do you want from me?*

Barrie's throat burned as she tried to swallow her rage and frustration. No signature again, and no real information. *What secret?* And what kind of secret would have anything to do with Wyatt?

She rammed the letter back into the envelope and threw it onto the desk as the *gong* of the grandfather clock sounded in the hall. Her blood quickened with each hour it counted.

Midnight.

Already flames lit the trees, and the sky outside the library window was brightening. The fire called to Barrie, drew her to her feet. She gripped the top of the chair and told herself to be sensible, but a moment later she was hurrying down the corridor into the kitchen, tearing the chain off the jamb again in her rush. In the night air, the pull grew stronger, more compelling.

She raced across the terrace and down the steps. The gravel and shells on the path bit through her socks, tore into her skin. But the Fire Carrier had reached the river already, and Barrie's feet swept her forward as if she couldn't stop. She entered the maze and kept running, approaching the fountain and the point where the path drew closest to the trees.

The woods had a pull of their own. Just past the fountain, the competing sense of loss hit her like a fist and slowed her long enough for sanity to intervene. She stopped to rub her head, to catch her breath.

What was she doing? She hated stupid horror movies where the characters did things like this. In what universe was it a good idea to be out here at midnight? Alone? Chasing after a ghost—worse, the ghost of a *witch*? Except she *felt* the Fire Carrier wanting—needing—something from her.

Sure he did. Her skin maybe. Wasn't that one of those voodoo legends? That dead things could steal a person's skin?

At the farthest edge of the marsh grass, the shadowy form of the Fire Carrier bent low over the water, fire spilling from his arms across the river. He hadn't seen her yet.

He straightened. Any moment he would turn and catch her watching, the way he had every night at this part of the ceremony. Barrie backed toward the house. But she tripped over something—the ceramic bowl Pru had left out beside the fountain. It clattered against the stone. She fell, and caught herself on her hands, slicing the heels of her palms.

The Fire Carrier spun toward her. His dark eyes searched for her, eyes she felt more than saw.

She made herself stand up. For Pete's sake, all she needed to do was start screeching as she ran away, and she would qualify as the heroine of some horrible B movie. The kind who inevitably died.

The Fire Carrier watched her, neither threatening nor advancing. Barrie's hands stung where she had cut them, and they were sticky and caked with grit. She rinsed them in the fountain.

In the glow of the river fire and the moon, her blood sent red ribbons unfurling in the water. Ribbons that eddied in the current and sank slowly toward the bottom.

Barrie's head swam. The edges of her vision blurred. The fountain grumbled, gurgled, then flowed faster and higher, as if more pressure had rushed into the pipes.

Everything around her surged with intensity. The babble of the fountain, the susurrus of the river, the crackle of the fire, the screech of frogs and insects—they were all too loud. The air throbbed with a war-drum chant, words Barrie couldn't understand, and sage-scented smoke assaulted her nose, mixing with the loamy earth and the briny tannin odor of the river. All around, the night glittered as if she were looking at it through a prism. Even the knee-high shadows darting around her were clearly human-shaped. Their eyes left fiery contrails of orange behind them.

Fiery eyes. Wasn't that what Mary had said?

Barrie reeled from the onslaught of noise and scent and light. She felt, too, as if something watched her. Not the Fire Carrier. He still stood like a rock in the river, the fire and the current eddying around him. He was clearer than he had been, almost solid enough to be a living man. Beneath the mask of war paint, his features were proud and somber, flickering in the light of the flames he held in his arms. But as Barrie met his eyes, he raised his hand and pointed behind her at the fountain.

Reluctantly Barrie turned. The movement itself took a hundred years, long enough for the hair on her arms and the back of her neck to rise, long enough for all the air to squeeze out of her lungs.

From the top basin of the three-tiered fountain, a figure

stared back at her. Not a person. Another spirit of some kind, a woman with translucent hair cascading around shoulders that melted into water drops and the moonlit dark of night. Her fingers were rivulets pouring into the basin, her legs and hips and torso a streaming column of water. She watched Barrie with ancient eyes, evaluating her. Judging. Yes, that was the word. Barrie felt she was being judged.

"W-what do you want?" Barrie croaked.

The voice that answered was a whisper of water and a breath of wind. It came from inside Barrie's mind and from everywhere around her. "You have given blood," it seemed to say.

"Given?" Barrie swayed on her feet. She grabbed the edge of the fountain to keep from falling.

"We accept the binding."

The pronouncement echoed. Before it had fully faded, the woman collapsed in a froth of water. Then the water calmed, and the fountain was only a fountain again.

Had the woman been there at all? Barrie wanted to believe the spirit had been an overdose of emotion or imagination, but she'd spent days wishing Lula's death and Mark's announcement had been a nightmare from which she could wake. Wishes didn't come true. Not for her.

She rubbed her arms as if that could warm up the chill that had taken root inside her. Her palms were slick with blood again. The sweet copper taste of it sprang to her tongue as if she had licked her skin, which she hadn't. Which she wouldn't . . . *She* wouldn't.

But the fountain had. The water had. The water that probably came from the river, where the magic of the Fire Carrier created a barrier to keep the *yunwi* confined to Watson's Landing.

Barrie stared at the smears of blood on her arms. She grabbed the bottom of her shirt and scrubbed at the drying streaks until she had scoured off every trace from her skin, and then she wiped her hands, too, over and over as if she could get rid of the water and the taint of whatever she had done.

Stories of water sacrifices crowded her thoughts, lessons learned in history class, on museum visits, in books of mythology. So many stories about sacred wells and objects dredged up from lakes or rivers: swords, knives, daggers, bowls. Things that might have once held blood.

Blood magic. The oldest magic.

Barrie's heart threatened to pound through her ribs. She met the Fire Carrier's silent stare. "What did I do?" she whispered.

His features didn't change. He didn't say anything. Yet Barrie got an impression of a deep and weary sadness as he nodded and turned his back. Bending low, he spooled the flames back into a ball.

Barrie wrapped her arms around herself. She glanced around again, half-dreading, half-hoping to see the woman there again, but she found plain water splashing into the basins as usual. She bent and righted the ceramic bowl that she had tripped over, setting it back beside the fountain, where Pru had left it.

Sleep, that was what she needed, she told herself. She needed to burrow under her covers and forget. Maybe she would wake up and find it had all been some crazy nightmare inspired by frogmore stew and an overdose of Colesworth dramatics.

She limped toward the house. Her feet stung where she had cut them on the shells, now that the first flush of adrenaline was fading. Her socks were damp, and she was leaving pinkish footprints on the gravel. Shadows swarmed behind her as if the blood attracted them. Barrie felt their curiosity, their need, their *want*. That was even more appalling than the rest.

Oh, what the hell, why not?

"Have these, too, then." She peeled off her bloody socks and threw them down. "Enjoy. Eat up."

But then she had a thought and snatched the socks back off the ground. She felt a chorusing howl of outrage. Felt the howl as if it tickled her skin instead of her eardrums.

"Ours. Ours. Ours," it seemed to say.

"I'll give them back to you." Barrie forced the words past cracked, dry lips. "But you'll have to trade for my phone and anything else you've taken."

The vibration of silent voices shivered through the air, making Barrie's skin erupt in goose bumps. Burning eyes and flashes of shadow rushed toward her from all directions and then sped away again. She waited, fingers curled tightly into her palms, not sure what kind of reaction she was expecting. It was silly to think they would listen or even understand what she had said. Ridiculous, really. Clearly they didn't understand, because one by one they all milled around her in a circle some fifteen feet in diameter.

So, that was it. Barrie turned and started back toward the house—and nearly stepped on her phone, which lay on the path. Her shaving razor was there too, along with her copy of *The Night Circus*, her sketchbook, two pens, and the cap to her hair gel. She hadn't even realized any of that was missing. The pile of knobs, nails, wooden pegs, and shiny screws was at least more expected, though larger than she could have imagined. She didn't even want to think where all those had come from. The stairs and shutters, the broken chair leg.

"No more breaking things!" she yelled. "No more taking my stuff. Anyone's stuff."

She threw down the socks, scooped up her belongings, and made a makeshift bag to carry them in by doubling up the bottom of her bloody shirt. She left the rest of the items where they lay gleaming in the moonlight. "And put those back where you found them," she added more quietly.

With as much dignity as she could muster, she stomped toward the house on her lacerated feet. The shadows provided her an escort, running alongside, racing ahead, and doubling back as if she were moving too slowly for them. Barrie squashed down a small thrill of triumph. In the scheme of things, getting them to listen to her was a very small victory, and she wasn't sure exactly what it meant.

Something had changed tonight, of that she was certain. She had changed something. But she had no way of knowing if she had changed it for the better or made it worse.

CHAPTER TWENTY-ONE

The scream of the peacock startled Barrie from an exhausted sleep. The sun was still painting the clouds lavender and orange, and she lay disoriented awhile before memory flooded back. Bolting upright, she checked the desk. Her phone was safely charging, and her book, sketchpad, and razor lay beside it. That was a good sign.

On the flip side, her elbow hurt, her palms were scraped, and her feet were sore and tender. And shadows stirred to life in every corner of her room as if they, too, were just now waking.

God, she needed coffee. She wasn't ready to deal with shadows.

They milled about her as she dressed hurriedly, and ran around her down the hallway like a herd of little children. It was almost cute until they darted into the unoccupied wing. The loss that usually clung to that section of the house rushed out to meet Barrie even more grotesquely than before. But that was another question that needed to wait until she'd had her caffeine.

Turning toward the staircase, she found her aunt kneeling below the broken step with a hammer in her hand. Pru beamed at her. "Well, hello, sugar. Isn't it a wonderful morning!"

"Is it?" Barrie was reserving judgment. "Then why were you scowling at the step?"

"Oh. That." Pru frowned again, climbed to her feet, and dusted off her knees. "I woke up full of energy and decided to whip the house into shape. But see this?" She jumped on the step, which didn't budge. Next she tried to shake the railing. It didn't so much as wobble. "I don't suppose you got up in the middle of the night and hammered everything back into place for me? And found the missing knobs and drawer pulls and put them back in the kitchen?"

Barrie resisted the urge to turn and stare at the shadows as she trailed her aunt down the steps. "Maybe the *yunwi* have started fixing the house instead of breaking it," she said.

"Wouldn't that be nice. Although I suppose it's as good an explanation as any. It doesn't matter, I'm in too good a mood to worry about it." Pru stowed her tools in the closet under the stairs and wrapped her arm around Barrie's waist. "Come on, sug, let's get some breakfast."

After Pru had swung the kitchen door open, Barrie paused to squint against the light. She could smell the ripe summer scents of honeysuckle, roses, and bougainvillea even through the sharp tang of the scones Pru pulled from the oven. Low notes of music trickled from Pru's radio on the counter, and marsh birds called to one another over the soft lapping of the water against the dock. She shouldn't have heard so much. She shouldn't have smelled so much. And yet she did.

"Are you coming down with a bug, honey?" Pru gestured for her to sit at the table, which was already set for two. She dropped a sour-cherry scone onto Barrie's plate. "I may have gotten in a good night's sleep last night, but you surely didn't. Those bags under your eyes could pass for suitcases."

Lovely. Barrie managed a feeble smile. She swallowed a sip of orange juice, and then winced at the aftertaste of toothpaste and oranges and the suspicion that she was about to ruin Pru's effervescent mood.

"Out with it," Pru said, pausing beside her. "Something's bothering you. Are you still worried about Cassie?"

Barrie broke off a piece of scone and stared down at it. "I found my phone last night."

"You did?" Pru dropped into her chair as if her knees had given out. "That's . . . wonderful. Where was it?"

"In the garden, where the *yunwi* left it after I told them to give it back. I also asked them to return the pile of nails and wooden pegs and kitchen cabinet knobs, and I told them to stop breaking things." Barrie ventured a glance at Pru from beneath her lashes.

Pru looked as if Barrie had hit her with a plate of grits. "You asked the *yunwi* to fix the house. And they fixed it."

"Well, I was mad. And I figured it wouldn't hurt." Barrie gave a hunched-shoulder shrug.

Pru laughed, a rusty creak of a laugh that built until Barrie couldn't tell if her aunt was laughing or crying or some combination of the two. She picked at her scone and watched warily until Pru finally mopped her cheeks with the corner of her apron, took a shaky breath, and leaned across the table to take her hands.

"Thank you," Pru said. "I'm sorry, sugar. I know this isn't funny. It's just that, Lord knows I've asked them to stop often enough, and they never have. It didn't occur to me to ask them to fix things. Maybe I should have. More than likely they'll start dismantling the house again tomorrow, but I don't care. I'll take whatever good news we can get. You can't imagine what it's been like this past week. I thought I was going to go crazy."

"Wait. It's only been a week since the *yunwi* started acting up?" Barrie hadn't expected that. "Was that before or after Lula died?"

Pru sat back, and her smile faded. "They stopped for a bit when Daddy died, and then started up again a day or so before the lawyer called me." She shook her head. "How could I not have made that connection? Mary was right last night: I did bury my head in the sand, hoping that if I ignored the problems, they would all somehow go away." She crossed to the kitchen sink and stood with her back to Barrie. "It's too much, you know," she continued. "All of this. Watson's Landing. The *yunwi*. Wyatt. I've been exhausted with worry, and while it's nice to think the mischief might be over, I'm not sure I like the idea that they listened to you and not to me. Or that it started when Lula died. What if they do something worse than the steps? I can't let anything happen to you." She turned back, and her expression hardened with determination. "Yesterday, going as far as Charleston seemed an impossibility, but I could do it now. I feel like I could leave. Migraines and panic don't matter when it compares to your safety. You want to go to art school next year anyway. Pick a place, sugar. Pick a place you want to live, and we'll go. Tomorrow. Today. Right this minute if we need to."

Barrie's chest seized into a fist of panic. "No! We can't leave."

"You can finish high school just about anywhere."

Barrie got up and paced across the kitchen. "We're supposed to be here. *I'm* supposed to be here."

Saying the words only made her realize what her heart knew already. The fountain and the Fire Carrier had bound her to Watson's Landing. How else could she explain the claustrophobic feeling she got at the *thought* of leaving? It made no sense, and yet it did. She felt the opposite of Pru's newfound lightness.

She couldn't leave.

"What would we do with Watson's Landing?" she asked, fighting to stay calm. "We can't sell it, and we can't just leave it to rot. Anyway, I don't want to go." Which was the simple truth. The realization scared her spitless. She didn't want to end up like Pru. Like Lula. She didn't want to wake up and find that she had waited, endured, half her life away.

Locked in a prison—wasn't that what Mrs. Price had said?

What was Barrie going to do? Between her arrival and last night, Watson's Landing had imprinted itself into her DNA. Now the plantation belonged to her and she belonged to Watson's Landing.

The land itself seemed to welcome her as Pru coaxed her out into the garden on the pretext that they both needed to get some air. More likely, judging by the worried glances Pru kept sending her, her aunt expected her to have a hysterical meltdown any moment and didn't want her to be in reach of any plates she could throw. Either that or Pru was trying to issue a not-so-subtle reminder of how much hard work it took to keep Watson's Landing going, in the hope that an apartment somewhere in Rhode Island or New York City would sound more enticing.

Being outside had the opposite effect. The slow music of the river sang through Barrie's blood along with the rustle of reeds and brush and branches. Her chest finally loosened and her shoulders relaxed. She refused to let herself think about anything except weeding as she and Pru worked side by side in the flowerbeds. But even that simple task seemed to have been altered by the binding. Barrie's fingers went unerringly to the tiniest buds of alligator weed and spiderwort; the weeds practically leaped out of the earth before she touched them. The white peacock wandered around beside her and pecked up a worm before settling into a meal of weeds. In spite of her best intentions, Barrie's thoughts drifted to the fountain and the Fire Carrier and gifts and bindings and—

Oh, God, Lula's letters! She had left them out last night. What if her aunt found them in the library before Barrie had a chance to prepare her? Barrie hadn't even decided whether Pru should see them at all.

"I'll be right back, Aunt Pru."

Dropping her gardening gloves into the flowerbed, Barrie hurried toward the house. With her head down, she almost bumped into Eight before she registered the finding click that always preceded him.

"You need to quit doing that." She pressed a hand to her chest, while her clueless heart flopped over in capitulation like a dog exposing its belly just because Eight had smiled at her.

His smile faltered. "And here I brought you a present."

"Another rose?"

"Better." He pulled a black-and-silver box from a shopping bag. "It's a new wireless receiver for the gate. We can program it so you, Mary, and your aunt can all call it from the house phone or your cell phones. Genius, right? I even picked up a cell phone for you, Miss Pru." He raised his voice as Pru drifted toward them. "Dad said you didn't have one. He said to tell you 'lawyer's orders.'"

Pru glared at the box as if it were full of rattlesnakes. "That man thinks he runs the world."

"Must be a Beaufort thing," Barrie muttered.

Eight laughed, his eyes brightening. She couldn't be mad at him. This wasn't a simple intercom just any store in Watson's Point would carry. He had to have driven all the way into Charleston first thing to be back with it this early. Even then, he and Seven had to have called in special favors. The whole gesture was typically bossy and presumptuous—and very sweet.

It was also useless. The stirrings in Barrie's subconscious finally coalesced into a semicoherent thought. The gate wasn't what worried her. Wyatt could come across the river anytime.

He wasn't rational, and who knew what innocent encounter or idle bit of gossip from town might set him off? They needed to defuse him, to use Eight's word for it. They—*she*—needed to find a way to end the feud.

Eight slipped the box back into the bag. "What's the matter?"

"Nothing." Barrie frowned absently at the shadows peeking from beneath the bushes.

"Nothing. Right." Eight shook his head and tucked the bag beneath his arm. Then he turned back to Pru. "Is it okay if I borrow your car, Miss Pru? I promised Barrie a driving lesson, which would be easier without a stick shift. I thought we could drive up to install the receiver."

"Of course," Pru said. "The keys are probably still in it, I suspect. Oh, and Eight? Thank you. And thank your father for me." She softened her tone for Eight, but she sounded as if she hoped Seven would choke on her thanks.

Eight draped his arm over Barrie's shoulder and cheerfully led her away until they were around the corner and out of sight. Then he bent his head until his lips were poised a hairsbreadth above hers.

"Now you can thank me properly," he said.

She kissed him briefly and ducked away, running toward the car to escape the disoriented feeling she got whenever she was close to him. He caught up and, infuriatingly, seemed unperturbed.

"Did you ever find out what went on between Pru and your father?" Barrie asked.

"A crowbar couldn't pry that out of Dad." Eight climbed into the driver's seat and pulled the car out of the circle until it was facing the straight shot down the oak-lined lane. They switched places, and he pointed out the controls and pedals, leaning in close, too close. Barrie relaxed when he drew back and finally let her get the car rolling. She pushed on the gas too hard.

"Easy. All you have to do is go straight. Practice slowing up and stopping to get a feel for the brakes and the accelerator."

"It's fine. I've got it."

"What is it with you this morning?" He frowned over at her from the passenger seat. "I hoped you would be glad to see me, but I can't tell if you are or aren't. It's like you keep changing your mind."

Which was exactly what she was doing. "I need to think."

"About what?"

"Many things. Us. Wyatt and Cassie. The Fire Carrier. Pru and Lula—oh, hell."

"What?"

Barrie sighed. "We have to go back to the house. Right now. I found a packet of letters my mother wrote to Pru, although I don't think Emmett ever let Pru see them. And like an idiot, I left them out in the library. I don't want her to find them like that."

"We'll be back before she even comes in from the garden. Don't worry. Besides, there's no place to turn around until we get to the gate."

Barrie sighed and gave him a sidelong look. "Emmett did know Lula wasn't dead," she said. "He gave her money and told her to stay away."

Eight's eyes widened. "Why? That makes no sense."

Concentrating on keeping the steering wheel and the car's speed steady, Barrie wondered how much to tell him. If she explained that Lula had mentioned Wyatt, Eight was likely to pitch a fit if she had anything else to do with Cassie. And Pru, too, for all her understanding the night before, was likely to balk.

"Talk to me, Bear." Eight turned his shoulders and studied her profile, hard enough that Barrie felt the scrutiny and felt the flush rising up her cheeks. "Tell me why you're mad and why you don't want to tell me about the letters."

"I told you, I'm not mad. I just need time to think things through."

"And how long are you expecting that will take?"

"As long as it takes."

His jaw tight, Eight unclicked his seat belt before she had even slowed the car at the gate. The Mercedes was practically prehistoric, so there wasn't much to driving it. Barrie only pretended she needed to focus as she lurched to a stop, and she pretended she didn't mind when Eight slammed out of the car and strode toward the gatepost. She leaned on the fender while he took out the old receiver and installed the new one, watching the way the muscles played in his forearms and knotted in his calves, the way his Achilles tendon stretched when he crouched on his heels. The sun picked up both blue and copper lights in his hair that made it look like the fire on the tannin-laden river. He glanced over at her and grinned when he saw her watching.

He was perfect. Not perfect in an only physical way, more in how who and what he was shone out of him. Maybe he was perfect just for her, Barrie thought, making a memory sketch to preserve the moment. Even the *yunwi* didn't scare her as much as he did. They could only hurt her physically, but Eight could break her heart.

He paused, the blade of the screwdriver poised in the air and his shoulder braced against the gatepost. "Is there a reason you look like you want to murder me?"

"Not particularly. You have that effect on people."

"I've heard that." He nodded solemnly and came over. Placing his hands on the hood on either side of her, he leaned closer until her back arched. "I feel an irresistible urge to kiss you," he said. "I wonder if this is how a crack addict feels."

"Can you get doped up on someone else's want?" She wiggled out from under him.

"You think I want you only because *you* want *me*?"

"Are you sure that's not the reason?"

"I have some self-control. If that was how it worked, I'd be pining after Gilly or . . ." He glanced away, looking sheepish.

"Or any of the dozens of other girls who want you," Barrie finished for him. "That's what you were going to say? Very nice." Her hands shook, and she folded her arms across her chest as if that would protect her heart from him.

What was she going to do? How had she ever, for even a second, thought it would be easy to have a fling? With Eight. A guy like Eight. She ought to strangle Mark for even suggesting it. For making her think it might turn out okay. She walked away a few steps and watched the glint of sun on water on the other side of the road. The landmarks were different, but the river itself looked much the same as it did from her balcony.

Eight swept the screwdriver off the hood and strode back to the gatepost. He continued installing the new intercom with an angry intensity, throwing tools into the toolbox with sufficient force to send the curious shadows skittering. When he finished, he packed up the empty receiver box and the old intercom parts and tossed them into the car without saying anything. The passenger door closed behind him with an emphatic *snick*, and he sat in the passenger seat staring straight ahead.

Barrie slid behind the steering wheel. "You don't get to be mad at me, you know."

"Why the hell not? Every time I think we're making headway, you find another reason to blow me off."

"What are we making headway *toward*? And what's the point?" She stared at the gearshift a moment, then pulled the knob from park to reverse. Looking over her shoulder, she started to back onto the grass to turn around. But the car went in the opposite direction than she expected, heading straight for the gatepost. She panicked and hit the accelerator instead of the brake.

"Other pedal." Eight grabbed the wheel.

She mashed her foot down, and the car stopped. "You're supposed to be telling me what to do!"

"You want to be in control. Isn't that the whole point?"

"You get training wheels on a bicycle. I should at least get instructions." She threw the car back into *drive*, pulled it forward, and then backed it onto the grass beside the gatepost more slowly. She felt ridiculously elated when she maneuvered onto the lane heading for the house.

"See?" Eight said. "You're doing fine."

"No thanks to you." She accelerated, and gravel pinged the fenders, dust pluming behind them.

"You might want to slow down a bit there, speedy."

"Now you're going to tell me what to do?"

"You know, at the rate you're going, you'll convince your-self you hate me long before I go anywhere." Eight stared fixedly out the window. Then he swore beneath his breath.

"What?" Barrie asked.

He didn't answer. Barrie had to concentrate on pulling into the circular driveway without running into Eight's car or flattening the peacock. It took her a moment to notice that Cassie was waiting for them, poised on the lawn as if the sun were her exclusive spotlight. In scalloped lace short-short-shorts and a flowered bikini top, the girl commanded as much attention as she had in her hoopskirt and Scarlett curls. She was like a reverse chameleon, making herself stand out no matter where she was.

Barrie slammed on the brake, and the car rocked to a stop.

"Hey, y'all! I tried to call you this morning, but no one picked up. I wanted to see if you were up for going to a cook-out." Cassie leaned her elbows on the edge of Eight's open window while she smiled across at Barrie.

"I'm supposed to be helping Pru," Barrie said. Which was what she should have been doing in the first place, instead of driving around with Eight. "Anyway, I thought you had to work today."

"My shift got changed. And I asked Pru just now. She said it was up to you if you wanted to come."

"Whose cookout?" Eight pushed open the door while

Cassie's face was still uncomfortably close to his. She backed up a scant step, but not enough to give him room.

"Your crowd." Cassie waved a hand and smiled up at him blindingly. "I figured you'd want Barrie to meet everyone." She held Eight's eyes a beat too long before turning to wait for Barrie to get out of the car. "I rowed over, but I thought Eight might sail us down. . . . Unless you're still mad about last night, of course? I've been hoping you meant what you said about being friends in spite of that whole silly argument with Daddy, because I couldn't stand it if you didn't!"

If she'd meant to deliberately play on Barrie's guilt, Cassie couldn't have phrased it better. Barrie couldn't imagine having Wyatt for a father. That would have been far worse than having no father at all.

"Of course I meant it. Eight?" She turned to him. "We can go, can't we?"

"If you want." His tone was flat, making it clear it wasn't his first choice.

Barrie couldn't tell whether that was because he was tired of arguing with her, or if he didn't feel like going to a cookout, or if he was reluctant because he knew she didn't really want to go. For that matter, he could have been picking up on something Cassie wanted.

Trying to understand Eight's gift was going to make Barrie nuts.

"I'd love to come," she said. "Although I think Eight has other plans—"

"Just you try to go without me." Eight's voice dropped to a growl.

"You'll need a bathing suit if you're coming," Cassie said. "And sunscreen. We wouldn't want you to get a burn."

How was it possible that Cassie managed to be infuriating even when she was being nice?

Barrie stalked up the steps. She looked back when she reached the front door, and Eight stood with his hands at his sides, tension etched into every line of his body as he said something to Cassie too softly for Barrie to hear. Cassie shook her head and snapped something furious in return. Then, abruptly, her body language changed. She stepped toward him, trailed a finger up his bare forearm, tipped her head, and smiled. Whatever she said next was obviously *very* friendly. Barrie waited for Eight to step away. But he didn't. And Cassie moved even closer.

An enraged ball of want formed in Barrie's chest. She wanted Cassie to stop, she wanted Eight to push Cassie away, she wanted it not to matter if neither of those things happened. She slammed the door and sped up the stairs. Shadows chased alongside her at knee level, leaping ahead, tumbling behind. Their shapes were still blurred and ephemeral, but Barrie could pick out long, thin limbs and eyes that watched her with a little too much curiosity.

Shivering at the thought, she rummaged through the armoire for the bikini Mark had told her was adorable, and for a plain, red tank dress to cover it up. She took off her necklace and Mark's watch and set them on the desk.

"Those had better be there when I get back," she told the *yunwi*.

Hearing herself, she rolled her eyes. She was getting too used to talking to shadows. Cassie or no Cassie, she needed to get away from Watson's Landing for a few hours. She raced back down the stairs, trying to ignore the breathless ache that came with the thought of leaving, and the small voice of doubt in her mind that wondered what would happen when she tried.

CHAPTER TWENTY-TWO

There was no rational reason why Cassie needed to go with Eight while he rowed her boat to the Beaufort side of the river. Barrie bit down a protest when her cousin climbed in, smiled at Barrie, and said, "We'll be back to pick you up in no time."

Barrie nodded. She sat and waited, dangling her toes off the end of the weathered dock. The water was bathtub temperature, but she felt cold watching Cassie's boat surge and slow with the rhythm of Eight's steady strokes, while Cassie leaned back, chatting to him.

It wasn't as if Barrie thought he wanted Cassie with him. Still, the way Cassie touched his arm as she got out of the boat at the Beaufort dock, the way she watched him while he pulled off his shorts and shirt and started to prepare the sails of his boat dressed only in his bathing suit. The way she stood on the bow like a figurehead with the wind blowing back her hair . . . How could Eight *not* notice?

"Is it bad for me to kind of hate her?" Barrie asked the *yunwi*. The shadows went still, as though they were listening, and then pressed in around her as if to offer comfort.

Eight's boat drew closer. For the first time Barrie noticed the name painted on the side: *Away*.

She refused to register any kind of reaction. Swinging her legs up onto the dock, she rose and dusted off the back of her dress. Shoes and bag in hand, she waited for Eight to pull in close enough to help her into the boat. He raised an eyebrow in a silent *Are you doing okay?* check. Barrie gave him a *You bet* smile and settled herself on the seat.

It surprised her that she *was* okay. Part of her, a big part, still didn't want to leave Watson's Landing even for a cookout, but she wasn't panicking at the thought of leaving. Maybe whatever she had done last night wasn't going to be so bad.

Eight adjusted the lines until the sails went taut. The boat pulled out into the river. Shadows raced with them along the shore, but stopped at the head of the creek at the plantation's eastern edge, where they paced like cats afraid of water. Pressure built in Barrie's head, crushing her skull in a vise of pain as soon as the boat was past the boundary.

"Don't you just love sailing?" In the seat opposite Barrie's,

Cassie kept her face turned into the wind. "Skimming over the water is the next best thing to flying."

"Sailing is great because it's sailing," Eight said, sitting at the tiller behind them. "What's the point of liking something because it's almost as good as something else?"

"Because it's fun. Don't you ever do anything just for fun?" The purr in Cassie's voice made the words a challenge. An invitation.

Irritated, Barrie burrowed deeper into her life vest. The boat cut through the choppy water, and loss washed over her in waves of misery.

"You all right, Bear? Another headache?" Eight trimmed the mainsail to tack into the wind.

"I'm fine," Barrie said, although she wasn't. She'd had a headache every damn time she'd left Watson's Landing, but it had been nothing like this. Pru had mentioned migraines. Lula's life had been one long migraine, especially the past three years.

Barrie's stomach rebelled against every rising and falling motion of the boat. She swallowed down her nausea and squinted her eyes against the sun.

Cassie dug into her big straw bag and pulled out a pair of oversize sunglasses. "Try these. Might be the glare off the water. That does it to me sometimes."

Barrie could hide behind the glasses. Taking deep breaths,

she schooled her features until she thought she could fake some semblance of normalcy. Eight, fortunately, was too occupied with sailing to be able to pay much attention. The tide was out, and sandbars and round-backed swollen tree stumps protruded from the water as the boat neared the ocean. Eight crooked his finger for Barrie to come sit closer to him. Before she could move, Cassie started chatting again.

The mouth of the river opened wide in front of them. A fleet of boats, fourteen or fifteen of them—rowboats, dinghies, and sailboats smaller than Eight's—was anchored off a sandbar. The wind whipped strands of music toward Barrie, and on the bar itself the sand bristled with chairs and grills and coolers and teenagers dancing or baking in the sun. The partygoers all stopped as if someone had hit the pause button on a DVR when Eight threw in the anchor and Cassie jumped out of the boat.

Barrie hesitated, rubbing her wrist where Mark's watch would have been.

"Come on. Use the ladder. You'll be all right." Eight went ahead and held her steady.

Her feet stinging from the salt, Barrie waded to shore through thigh-deep water, holding the hem of her dress clutched tightly in her fists. Everyone gaped at her.

So much for not wanting to stand out.

"Hey, y'all." Eight pulled her forward through the last feet of surf. "This is Barrie."

As if someone had pressed play again, the crowd surged, pushing her and Eight together. "Do you want names," he asked, "or should I leave them out so you won't feel bad when you forget?"

"I'm happy to let my bad memory be your fault," she said, relieved when people laughed.

"It's always going to be Eight's fault. He's male, isn't he?" Cassie squeezed through from the edge of the group. "But what are y'all doing? We need to crank up the music, get the party started. Barrie's used to lots more excitement in San Francisco. We don't want her to think we're a bunch of hicks down here in the South."

Barrie nearly choked. "It wasn't very exciting at home," she said, which came out sounding condescending. Or like an outright lie. Way to start things off. "Not that I mean it isn't exciting here," she added hastily. "This is great. I didn't know there were places like this."

She ran out of steam, and the conversation lapsed into an awkward silence. The other kids shifted their feet, looked away. Barrie racked her aching head for something to say, something not completely lame.

"I loved San Francisco." A girl with a round, open face and a galaxy of freckles pushed toward Barrie. "My mama and I went out there last summer to visit her roommate from college. I couldn't believe the shops and restaurants. Fisherman's

Wharf and Sausalito and Chinatown. And Lombard, that crazy crooked street. I loved it. We crossed the bridge to Muir Woods to see the redwood trees, which was awesome in the literal sense. You forget what that word means until you see something that actually leaves you struck with wonder."

Barrie opened her mouth to say she knew exactly how that felt, but Cassie cut her off with a throaty laugh. "My cousin has trees of her own, Jeannie. Acres of them. You know, at Watson's Landing?"

Why wouldn't Cassie please shut up?

"Ours are nothing like Muir Woods," Barrie said. "But then you've got the Devil's Oak here in town, and that's as amazing as any redwood."

"Not when we grew up climbing all over it. I guess it's harder to feel awed by something that you've draped with toilet paper at two o'clock in the morning." Jeannie grinned as everyone laughed. She moved with an athletic, unconscious grace in her bikini as she wound through a couple kids to stand with Barrie. "The Devil's Oak is pretty to look at, but walking through Muir Woods? That was like walking straight into a cathedral from Jurassic Park."

Barrie nodded, Jeannie's words settling over her with a sudden, throat-closing rightness. She remembered Mark's reaction to the place. He had worn his new wedge sneakers, which had been his idea of appropriate footwear for tromping through the woods, and he'd complained the moment they'd left the rental car that he wasn't cut out for "any nature shit." Then they had reached the trees. He had fallen silent, walking with his head tipped up to take it all in, and for the first time in Barrie's life, he hadn't seemed gigantic.

"So what else did you do while you were in San Francisco?" she asked Jeannie. "What was your favorite place to eat?"

"Don't judge, okay? Bubba Gump's at the Wharf." Jeannie smiled, the kind of smile that said she didn't mind whether people laughed with her or *at* her. "I love the Tom Hanks movie. I ended up getting a *Stupid Is as Stupid Does* T-shirt and eating enough popcorn shrimp to make myself sick. We watched sea lions—there must have been fifty of them—climbing all over one another on a floating raft. One would get pushed off; then he'd get back up and shove another one off—"

"Barrie, you're probably starving," Cassie interrupted, linking her arm through Barrie's. "We should go get food. The grill's right over there."

Barrie pulled away and rubbed the elbow she had knocked on the steps. "No. Thanks. Not yet." She gave Jeannie an apologetic smile and looked around for Eight, who had snuck off without her realizing it. He was splashing through the surf with a cooler and a stack of folding chairs. "I ought to go help Eight," she said.

"He can handle it by himself," Cassie said. "He's a big boy. Or haven't you noticed?"

Jeannie's face twitched into a grimace. "We're sitting over there. Why don't *you* and Eight come sit with us when you're ready?"

The emphasis had been very clear. Cassie looked like she'd been bitch-slapped, but pulled herself together as Jeannie walked away. She cut a look at Barrie and stalked toward the grill.

"Drama queen," someone muttered as she went.

"What's she doing here any—" someone else said, the last word cut short as if by an elbow to the ribs.

Barrie couldn't tell who had spoken. The faces around her all looked friendly.

"You doing okay?" Eight dumped the cooler and chairs into a pile on the nearest stretch of empty beach. "Would you mind setting up the chairs? I've got one more load."

Barrie didn't get the chance to tell him about Jeannie's invitation. She would have to run after him. And he had left their things at the edge of the crowd, so now she stood by herself.

It was her own fault for feeling out of place, she knew that, but it brought back memories of standing at the edge of the playground while the other kids played, and trying to pretend she didn't care.

Which would be worse, setting the chairs up where Eight had dropped them or carrying them over to where Jeannie was sitting? And what about Cassie?

Cassie saved her the trouble of deciding. She unfolded a chair, spread a towel over it, and lowered herself to sit. "You're looking a little green there, Cos," she said too loudly. "You're supposed to be sick *while* we're sailing, not after you get off the boat."

Heads swiveled toward them. Barrie had a picture of herself once school started, going to classes with Cassie clinging to her side, Cassie driving everyone else away until it was the two of them at the edge of the crowd. Then Cassie would transform back into the shining girl Barrie had seen at Bobby Joe's and the Resurrection. Barrie didn't mind not being the center of attention. She didn't *want* to be the center of attention. But she didn't want Cassie to be her only friend.

Eight would be gone, clear across the country when school started, and Mark would probably be gone then too. Barrie's head throbbed. Tears pressed against her eyelids.

Not here. She couldn't start crying. She refused. But her lip was already trembling.

Eight dropped the load of towels he was carrying. After hurrying the last few steps, he drew her toward him. "You can't cry in front of Cassie," he whispered, pulling up the fabric of Barrie's tank dress. "Come on."

Barrie tried to hold the hem down, but he grinned and flicked the dress over her head. In one smooth motion he picked her up, turned toward the water, and carried her as if she had no weight.

"What are you doing? Put me down. Right now. Eight! Stop it! I *don't want* people looking at me. I *want you* to put me down." Horror clawed at Barrie's chest as Eight carried her into the water. "Let me go back."

Waist-deep in the waves, Eight launched her into the air.

Water and panic closed around her, fast and dark. Arms flailing, Barrie opened her mouth to scream and ended up swallowing half the river. She kicked Eight in the chest before she realized it was help. Safety. He caught her and brought her up coughing and sputtering. She was mad enough that she almost kicked him again.

"Oh, hell. I'm sorry, Bear." He held her tight against him. "I thought it would help to loosen you up. You never said you couldn't swim."

"*Screw* you."

"I'm going to fix this. Trust me. Just go with it, all right?"

He lowered his head and kissed her before she could answer. Kissed her until she wasn't sure if it was him or the fear of almost drowning that was making her head spin and her heart whirl.

"There," he said. "That'll give everyone something else to think about."

"*That's* why you kissed me?"

"One reason." His grin was quick and lethal. "Cassie wants to be accepted. She's trying to make herself look good, and she'll use your panic to put you down. But you aren't weak."

He was right. Showing weakness was the signal for predators to pounce.

Was that how Barrie thought of Cassie? When had her opinion changed?

She started wading toward the beach, but Eight swept one arm under her knees and another beneath her back, and carried her out of the river to the accompaniment of whistles and applause. Bringing her head up, Barrie flashed a brilliant, carefree smile, and when Eight kicked open a chair and dropped her into it, she kept one arm wrapped around him, grabbed a towel, and threw it over his head. While his eyes were covered, she dug a handful of ice out of the cooler and pressed it to the back of his neck, wishing she were the kind of girl who would dare to put it down his shorts. Cassie would have.

"You know I'll have to get even now," Eight said, laughing at her with approval.

"Not if you can't catch me."

Barrie spun away, feeling suddenly wild and unlike herself. Her footsteps pounded the sand in time with the pounding of her head. She refused to be prey.

She grabbed the hand of a blond, bare-chested boy who

stood nearby. "Dance with me," she said, forcing a laugh. "I need protection."

She didn't know where the nerve had come from, or what magic made the boy follow her to a bare stretch of sand at the water's edge. The song had lyrics about zombies, and a heavy, monotone beat that pulsed right through her. She figured she looked half-dead anyway, so she went with it. The boy chuckled and joined in, stiff movements, arms outstretched, head bobbing and all, and before she knew it, other couples were zombie-shuffling on the sand beside them.

Eight pulled up a chair. He gave her an encouraging nod. Then Cassie leaned over to whisper something. He shrugged, but didn't answer.

Barrie danced. When she was dancing, she didn't have to talk to Cassie. She didn't have to think. Didn't have to feel anything except her loss-heavy body moving and the ache of the music. She could ignore that what she wanted most right then was to be back exactly where she had been earlier: with Eight at Watson's Landing, driving under the cathedral canopy of oaks that, to her, was even better than the redwood groves. At Watson's Landing she felt connected to Eight and to the earth and sky and trees, to Pru and the *yunwi*. To the Fire Carrier and the water that wrapped Watson's Landing in a veil of magic.

At Watson's Landing she felt found instead of lost.

Despite the piercing stab of the music and the sun that lanced through her eyes straight into her nerves, even through the dark sunglass lenses, she danced through lunch. She was long past the point of being tired, but she danced with the blond boy and with Eight, and with more boys than she had ever thought she would dance with in her life. She surprised herself. But all of it was killing time until she could safely ask Eight to take her home.

Cassie tanned alone in her chair at the edge of the party. Finally she must have tired of waiting. She shimmied up beside Eight, her long limbs oiled and dangerously graceful. While her body was angled toward Eight, it was Barrie she addressed.

"You look like you could use another swim to cool down, Cos. Or a comb. Did you remember to bring one? If not, I can loan you mine."

Cassie, of course, looked beautiful. All she had to do was flip that switch inside her that made her shine, and she became the center of attention.

Then why had she been sitting alone?

"Thanks, but I'm all right," Barrie said.

"Well, I hate to cut in on your fun. Are y'all about ready to go? I have to get back into my Scarlett slippers. I have another performance tonight." Cassie turned to the group dancing around them and raised her voice to be heard above the music. "Barrie and Eight came to see my play last night."

The temperature chilled again, and this time Barrie knew it was Cassie and not her making everyone uncomfortable. What had happened to the Cassie she had seen at Bobby Joe's and the Resurrection? The Cassie who'd seemed so comfortable. Now Cassie seemed to be trying much too hard. Was she nervous? Or was there something else going on?

Barrie closed her eyes, disgusted with herself. Here she was, already pulling away from Cassie because that was easier than standing up for her cousin. "The play was great," she said, speaking as loudly as Cassie had. "Have you all seen it? You should go. Cassie did a fantastic job writing and directing, not to mention acting. She ought to go to Hollywood."

"Oh, she's going," Jeannie said. "Hasn't she told you? She's sure told everyone else. She's leaving the second she graduates, if not sooner, and she's never coming back."

Barrie couldn't help stiffening. She managed not to look at Cassie. Or Eight. How was it neither of them had mentioned that he and Cassie would be minutes away from each other in Los Angeles, or that they shared a desire to get away from Watson Island?

"Maybe I won't go after all." Cassie's eyes flashed with something Barrie couldn't read. "I'm feeling more like sticking around here lately."

There was no mistaking the bitter note in her voice. For a

moment everyone fell silent, and Barrie had a feeling she was missing something in the conversation. Then Cassie laughed and made a dismissing motion with her hand.

"Now, what about that ride, Eight Beaufort? Are you going to take me home, or am I going to have to swim?"

She walked off to get her things without waiting for an answer, which left Barrie and Eight with the awkward choice of following her or ignoring her. "Come on," Barrie said. "Let's go." She grabbed Eight's hand and waved to everyone. "It was great to meet you all."

"That's 'y'all,' around here, sugar," Jeannie said. "Or even 'all y'all.' But don't worry, you'll catch on. I'm having a cook-out at my house tomorrow night. Come on by for more lessons. Six o'clock, all right? You and Eight." She didn't look at Cassie, who clearly was not included in the invitation.

"We'll be there," Eight said, without waiting for Barrie to agree. He snatched up the chairs and cooler and left Cassie still pulling clothes over her swimsuit. While her cousin combed out her hair, Barrie grabbed their stray towels and the bag Eight had left on the sand, and held them chest high while she waded into the surf. Eight dropped his own armful over the side, swung himself into the boat, and reached over to help her up.

"You do know Cassie asking for a ride isn't about her needing to get ready for the play, don't you?" he whispered into Barrie's ear. "She wants you to go back with her to search again."

"Permission to come aboard?" Cassie called from beside the boat. A second later the top of her head appeared at the ladder. "I'm not interrupting, am I?"

"And there's my cue to cool off before I tear her apart." Eight swooped in, gave Barrie a quick kiss, and did a cannonball off the side of the boat into frighteningly shallow water.

Barrie held her breath until he came up shaking his head, spattering sunburst drops of water everywhere. It was the same way he'd shaken himself the first time—no, the second time—Barrie had ever seen him. That felt like a lifetime ago, and as good as he'd looked to her then, he looked a thousand times better now.

She settled herself and pulled on her cover-up while he climbed back into the boat and went to get the anchor. Partway there, he stopped suddenly to study Cassie, making no attempt to disguise the fact that he was reading her. Then he rubbed the bridge of his nose and shook his head. Barrie figured she might as well get it over with. She leaned back and watched as Cassie came and sat beside her.

"This was fun, wasn't it?" Cassie dug a tube of gloss out of her bag and offered it to Barrie, who shook her head, before shrugging and applying it to her lips. "It's not really my crowd, but maybe next time Beth and Gilly can come."

Barrie exchanged a look with Eight.

"I was thinking," Cassie continued, twirling the gloss between her fingers, "that we could maybe go back over and have you try the Watson gift again, since we were interrupted last night. Daddy's out with the fishing boat tonight, and he won't be home until after nine, so the timing is kind of perfect, if you come right now. You wouldn't run into him." She gave a smiling, embarrassed little shrug. "I wouldn't ask, but you saw how everyone was today. They treat me differently than they treat you and Eight. But if we could find the treasure, they would finally see us like we matter. Daddy could rebuild the old house, and we wouldn't always have to feel like we aren't good enough. . . . You see that, don't you?" She leaned toward Barrie and put a hand on her arm.

Barrie stared at the floor of the boat. The rocking motion churned her stomach as Eight got under way. She looked longingly at the seat beside him, trying to think how to answer Cassie. Because she still hadn't decided. She stood up as Cassie dug for something else in her bag.

"I need to think about it," she said.

"What's there to think about? I swear, Daddy won't be there. I promise."

"Don't push me, all right? Now excuse me. I need to go tell Eight something." She went and sat beside him before Cassie could say any more.

"I take it she asked you." Eight kept his voice soft. "What did you tell her?"

"Nothing yet. What did she want just now, when you read her?"

"You wouldn't believe it if I told you, trust me. You know, this whole afternoon has been surreal. Cassie talked baseball to me the whole time you were dancing. In her own way, she really made an effort."

"Baseball?" Barrie wrinkled her nose, happy to talk about anything but Cassie.

"Not a passion of yours?" Eight laughed at the expression on her face. "I can see I'm going to have to convert you before I leave for school. I can't possibly date a nonbeliever."

"Baseball wasn't a religion, last I checked. And who says we're dating?"

"Do you kiss many guys you aren't dating?"

"Not many, no."

"Are you intentionally trying to pick a fight?" Eight leaned in closer. "Nice try, but it doesn't get you out of telling me what you plan to say to Cassie."

Barrie smoothed the fabric of her dress across her knees. "I don't think I have a choice. You know she's not going to stop asking until I show her what's there. To be honest, I'm not sure *I* would stop asking if I were in her shoes. It shouldn't take me long, though, and Wyatt's out until late tonight."

CHAPTER TWENTY-THREE

Eight steadied the boat so Barrie could jump out. "I'm not going to argue with you," he said.

"There's a first." Barrie kept hold of his hand until her feet were firmly back on the Watson dock. She closed her eyes in relief, and the shadows danced around her, grabbing at her dress as if they were vying for her attention. She ignored them and glanced back at Cassie, who was still rowing downstream from the Beaufort dock back to Colesworth Place. "You didn't have to brush her off so obviously, by the way. It *would* have made more sense to drop me here first."

"I didn't want to be alone with her any more than you want me to be alone with her."

Barrie adjusted the bag on her shoulder and looked away. "Are you sure there isn't a history between you two I need to know about? Something's different between yesterday and today."

"You and I are different." His eyebrow quirked at her in a way that was maddening and sexy all at once.

"Okay, and what does that have to do with Cassie? Wait. Why are you looking at me like I'm as dumb as a box of rocks?"

He slid his arms around her waist and pulled her closer. "You are awfully cute when you're clueless, Bear. Let me spell it out for you. The curse makes Cassie want what we want. So . . ."

"She's interested in you because *I'm* interested?" Appalled, Barrie watched Cassie climb out of the rowboat and tie it off at the dock beneath the columns. "You're saying she doesn't have a choice?"

"I don't know exactly how it works. I do know you need to hurry up if you're going to be back here in half an hour. I'm not going to let you risk having Wyatt catch you over there."

"*Let* me? Hold on, buster—"

"That didn't come out right." Eight held his hand up in surrender. "What I meant to say was: I'm going to call the harbor and make sure someone lets us know the second Wyatt is coming back with the boat, so we have time to avoid him. If you'll go put on your reasonable shoes and do whatever else you need to do, I'll be back to pick you up."

"Were you born this bossy, or is it something you culti-vate? Because seriously, it's not your most attractive quality."

"I'm going along with your crazy scheme, and you're calling me bossy?" Eight gave her a mournful shake of his head. "You pick a mean fight, Bear. But I'm a Beaufort, remember? I know what you really want." Tightening his arms, he bent his head and kissed her, briefly at first, but even as he started to pull away, he seemed to change his mind and deepened the kiss instead. Barrie wound her fingers in his hair as his hands moved to cup her face. His eyes were dark and dilated when he finally pulled away. "I'll tell you a secret," he said. "This all scares me, too." Without looking at her again, he jumped back into the boat and grasped the rudder.

Barrie watched the boat slip away. His words, the fact that her migraine was gone, and the relief of being back at Watson's Landing all rolled through her with a rush and made her almost giddy. Her feet quickened to a run, and she raced the shadows toward the house. Mary was clearly afraid of them, but Barrie didn't find them sinister. They seemed more like naughty children playing pranks. In an odd way, they were even comforting.

Letting herself into the kitchen, Barrie nearly barreled into Mary, who was carrying a three-tiered serving dish loaded with miniature tarts, scones with butter and jam, and sliced cucumber sandwiches. A scone bounced onto the floor. Mary pushed everything else back in order.

"I'm so sorry." Barrie retrieved the scone and wondered what to do with it.

"Throw it away. I'll get another one." Mary's lips thinned, and she looked Barrie up and down. "It's 'bout time you got back. I heard you were runnin' round with that Colesworth girl again. Nothin' good is goin' to come of that. And you're makin' your aunt crazy. She's been holed up in the attic all afternoon."

Great. Guilt. Because Barrie didn't have enough of that.

"I'm sorry," she repeated. "I know I haven't been here much. But I can't stay to talk. I've got to go back out again."

She tossed the scone into the trash and hurried out of the kitchen toward the stairs. The corridor was brighter than normal, with a sharp beam of sunlight falling through the open library door and leaving a rectangular patch on the floorboards.

The library. Lula's letters. God, Barrie had forgotten about them again. Forgotten them all day.

How could she have been so stupid? She stopped on the threshold with a twist of dread.

The room smelled of rubbing alcohol and vinegar, and the windows were newly sparkling. And of course the top of the desk was empty.

Barrie sagged against the doorframe. The distractions were no excuse. Pru must have been shocked to find and read the letters—and she would know Barrie had found them first and not given them to her. Not even mentioned them.

Unless Mary had found them. But what were the odds she wouldn't have given them to Pru? And Mary hadn't seemed upset.

On the off chance Mary might have put the letters away, Barrie searched the desk drawers anyway, and checked the floor in case they had fallen. Knowing it was hopeless, she fumbled inside the secret compartment. Then she startled Mary out of six years of her life by bursting back into the kitchen.

"Did you go into the library today?" she demanded.

Hand on her chest, Mary peered at her as if Barrie had lost her mind. "Now why would I be goin' in there, child?"

Crap. Poor Pru.

Barrie took the stairs two at a time, without having a clue what she was going to say to her aunt.

Really, what could she say? All she could do now was to listen, provide comfort, and let Pru vent. As awful as she felt, the damage was already done. Wouldn't giving Pru a chance to talk about her feelings only stir them up again? Obviously that would have to happen at some point, but Barrie couldn't leave with Eight if Pru was an emotional mess. And once Pru had read those first two letters, the chances of her ever letting Barrie go to Colesworth Place were slim to when-ice-cubes-froze-in-hell.

Barrie slowed when she reached the second floor, and she continued up the next flight of stairs on tiptoes. She wasn't sure what she expected to hear. Sobs? Tantrums? That would have made her decision easier—she couldn't leave Pru alone like that. But listening at the attic door, she heard only silence.

Deciding to let Pru be, she backed quietly away. Creeping to the second floor, she retreated to her room, wishing she could just lock the door and stay there. Forever. Because all of this? Dealing with history and secrets and the mess of moving into a brand-new life was like diving headfirst into a garbage disposal. Her emotions were being shredded.

Crossing to the armoire, she threw down her bag and tugged the tank dress over her head. After digging out a top and shorts, she turned toward the bathroom. A purple-and-orange FedEx envelope stood propped against the pillow sham on the bed. The package Mark had been excited about. Another thing Barrie had completely forgotten.

She threw on her clothes and yanked a brush through the snarls in her hair. The girl in the bathroom mirror stared back at her, unaccustomedly tanned and wild, dressed without an ounce of style. Barrie could practically hear Mark asking her what she was doing, what she was *thinking*. There was nothing about herself she recognized anymore. She stalked back to the desk, snapped Mark's watch back onto her wrist, and pulled the necklace Lula had given her over her head.

Screw Wyatt—or anyone—if they thought she was showing off. Wyatt's jealousy had made her not wear the two things that were most important to her. She wasn't going to change the way she acted for anyone anymore. And she was full-up on guilt. Jealousy, hers and Cassie's, had made her hurt Pru today. From now on, she wasn't letting herself get distracted from what was important.

She picked up the FedEx envelope from the bed and tore off the pull strip to find a sketchbook inside. Not one of her own sketchbooks. This one was old and yellowed, filled with drawings of Watson's Landing executed in a bold, intensely emotional style. Drawings of the house from the long oak lane, drawings of the lane itself and the reflective strip of river flanked by marsh grass, drawings of Beaufort Hall perched like a crown on the hill, and the Watson woods lit by fire and moonlight. The sketches were so alive. They made Barrie feel the sway of the dock and the spray of the fountain. She could almost smell the shrimp and grits cooking in the kitchen, and imagine trailing her fingers over the architectural details in the carved wood paneling, fleurs-de-lis and roses, leaves and the faces of strange bearded gods.

There were studies of Pru as well. Many of them. A

different Pru, younger and carefree, racing up from the dock with a Seven who looked more like Eight. Pru and Seven holding hands, looking at each other instead of where they were going. Looking at each other as if they would never stop looking. Despite the fact that Emmett had hated the Beauforts. Despite the fact that they could never be together.

Pru and Seven had missed out on a life together because of Lula. Because of Emmett.

Barrie pressed her knuckles against her eyes. More than ever she wanted to run upstairs to Pru, to hold her. For them to hold each other. It had to be getting late, though. She stopped at the balcony doors and looked across the river. Eight was already starting down the slope of the Beaufort hill toward the *Away*.

Throwing the sketchbook into a drawer in the desk, she dislodged a bloom of bougainvillea and ruffled the tag that hung from the handle of the sweetgrass basket. The same label Pru used on all the gifts she sold in the tearoom. The sketch of Watson's Landing on it was almost identical to one of Lula's drawings in the sketchbook. Same view, same style, same artist.

Barrie dialed Mark's number as she left the room. "How could Lula not tell me she could draw like this?" she demanded before he could say hello. "She never commented on a single piece of artwork I did."

"She didn't tell me, either, baby girl. Trust me. I'd strangle the woman, if she weren't already dead. I knew you'd be hurt, and I wasn't sure if I should send it to you. But I know you. Ten minutes from now you're going to be studying every line of her sketches and figuring how she got so much passion in there. It looked to me like she hated the place as much as she loved it."

Barrie thought back to the drawings. Yes, there had been both love and hate in all of them. Light and darkness. It seemed to be a theme with Lula.

"Does the place still look like that?" Mark asked.

"Yes." Barrie pushed down the sick sense of outrage and started down the stairs. "How are you feeling?"

"Not dead yet." Mark did his usual Monty Python impression, but he sounded tired. And weaker. "Hold on," he continued. "We're still on you. Are you going to be okay? You know Lula not telling you about her art wasn't personal, don't you?"

"How is it not personal?" Barrie shoved through the swinging door into the kitchen. "Whatever talent I have came from her. When I think about all the sketchbooks I left lying around accidentally on purpose, hoping for her approval—"

"You had her approval, baby girl. She was proud when you won those prizes."

"She never said so."

"Lula was never good with words."

"I just wish she'd told me." Barrie let herself out onto the terrace and turned to wave at Mary in the tearoom before heading down the stairs. "Or shown me. Anyway, how could she stop drawing? Some of those sketches are good enough to go in museums."

"Artists need to go places," Mark said gently. "See new things. She probably got tired of drawing the same view from different windows."

Barrie hurried past the fountain, shivering as it misted her skin. She started down the slope to the river, where Eight and the *Away* were approaching the Watson dock.

"So," she said to change the subject, "you remember the hottie?"

"Your hottie?"

"Well, he might be mine. You'd love him. Except he plays baseball and he's bossy. Bossier than Lula. But he kisses very nicely, thank you."

Mark sputtered into a laugh that turned into a deep, guttural fit of coughing that went on too long.

"What's with the hacking?" Barrie asked when he finally stopped. "Aren't you taking care of yourself at all?"

"Don't you nag me too. One of the nearly-deads gave me a cigar, that's all. I figure I may as well enjoy new vices while I can. Now tell me, are we talking literal baseball or second base, third base kind of stuff?"

"Literal, of course. Who do you think I am? I've known him about five whole minutes!"

Which was crazy. Certifiably insane.

Eight waved at her. Barrie raised her hand and felt herself smiling.

The silence on the other end of the phone was the ominous kind. The kind that suggested Mark was trying to find a way to "save" her, the way he had used to try to "save" her, back when she'd been small enough and stupid enough to tell him about every stolen lunch, hurtful whisper, and so-called friend she'd lost. Except Mark's "saves" usually involved him rushing off to call the principal, a teacher, a parent, because *he* needed to do something. His "saves" usually made things ten times worse, but also a hundred times better because he loved her.

"Earth to Mark?" Barrie said. "I told you I kissed a boy. Aren't you going to say anything?"

"I warned you about falling in love with him, didn't I? I told you to have a good time. Have a fling, I said. Why don't you ever listen?"

Barrie's lungs deflated. "Who said a thing about love?"

"You don't need to say it. But so we're clear here: I told you not to fall for him."

"And I told you orange was not your color, but you still ordered that Isaac Mizrahi dress. Don't give me I-told-you-sos."

"The dress had bows that tied at the elbows. How was I gonna pass that up?"

"Easy. You could have moved on to something better."

"That's exactly what *I'm* saying—"

"This is a boy, not a dress!"

"Which only makes him harder to return!" Mark took a deep, long breath that ended in another cough. "All right. Clearly you've already fallen for your number boy. So you might as well figure the pain is coming and make sure the crash is worth it."

"What do you mean?" Barrie stopped where the path ended and the dock began and turned away so Eight couldn't see her face.

"The things I regret right at the end of my life aren't the ones that left me hurt. I regret all the things I never had the courage to do."

"You have more courage than anyone I know."

"Overcompensating for being scared isn't the same as being brave, baby girl." Mark sounded so tired that Barrie wanted to crawl through the telephone line and wrap her arms around him. "I was scared of being myself, so I put on a show. And I kicked ass, but it wasn't real. When they put you in my arms at the hospital and you looked up at me . . . that was my one true act of courage. I told myself I had to choose between you and the show. I told myself I was being brave because I fought to stay with you through all of Lula's bullshit—and don't get me wrong, I wouldn't trade a second with you. But I was still cheating. Deep down I knew no audience was ever going to love me the way you did. I should have tried harder to give you a better life."

"You gave me a great life."

"I never taught you not to be afraid. Maybe too, if I had ever left the house for more than a few hours, Lula would have been forced to step up and be your mother. That's what I'm realizing now. It doesn't matter how great your shoes are if you don't accomplish anything in them."

Barrie glanced back at Eight. If leaving Watson's Landing meant living in the kind of pain she'd experienced today, she wasn't sure she had the courage to go too far. In her heart she didn't want to try. Mark was her core. Without him, bound or not, all she had left was here at Watson's Landing.

Which raised the question: What was she going to do about Eight and Cassie? Because one way or another, her happiness here was tangled up with them.

CHAPTER TWENTY-FOUR

Sneakers squelching in the mud, Barrie followed Cassie from the Colesworth dock uphill toward the columns and shattered chimneys of the old plantation house. Although Cassie's family maintained the upper portion of the property for the tourists, they didn't bother with the area by the river.

"Careful." Eight steadied Barrie when she stumbled for the second time on what had once been a gravel path. Where thick trestles dug into the hillside formed steps on the steepest portions, the wood was splintering and rotten. Weeds, mud, and stagnant puddles of water colonized the rest.

Barrie paused to get her breath and her bearings. The Colesworth property was only a few acres across, with thick woods bordering the Beaufort land on one side and the sub-division on the other side. The foundation of the old mansion was far enough away that the sense of loss Barrie had felt after the play hadn't reached her yet. From under the creeping green vines of ivy and wisteria that blanketed entire trees and buildings near the restored slave cabins, though, she felt an ache and something ugly pulsing at her temples.

"Can y'all please hurry up?" Cassie stopped above them on the path. "What are you looking for? Did you see a boat?" Shielding her eyes, she turned to scan the river.

"Expecting someone?" Eight didn't bother disguising the contempt in his voice.

Barrie dug her elbow into his ribs. "Hey. Be nice. You agreed to this."

"Yeah, but why is she so jumpy," Eight asked quietly, "if Wyatt isn't coming back until tonight?"

Cassie did look anxious. Her face had taken on a gray cast that had little to do with the dappled shadows from the overhanging cypress branches. She stood with her hands on her hips, and her usual languid grace was missing.

"I'm sure it's fine," Barrie said with an inward sigh. "Your friend said he would call if Wyatt's boat came in." She wished it were all over with so she could get back to Pru and Watson's Landing. Blood or no blood, if she never saw Colesworth Place or her uncle again, it would be too soon.

Eight made a show of crooking his elbow and holding it out to her in invitation. "Well, shall we?"

With a mock curtsy, Barrie linked her arm with his. He bumped her with his shoulder playfully and set off, keeping her close, the warmth of his skin on hers both distracting and reassuring. Barrie freed herself as they reached a steeper section of the path.

"You go ahead," Eight said, moving aside as the steps narrowed.

Barrie concentrated on where she set her feet, until a slither of brown serpentined across the path a couple feet ahead and vanished into the reeds. Startled, she jumped back and landed on the edge of a rotting trestle. The wood crumbled out from under her. Arms windmilling, she clipped Eight's jaw and knocked herself sideways. She landed on her knee with a heavy thud, her foot twisted underneath her.

"Bear!" He lunged too late to catch her. "Are you all right?"

She shook her head, caught in the blinding pain of a twisted ankle. She hoped it was only twisted. After edging around to sit, she braced the ankle with her hands and tried straightening her leg.

Eight crouched beside her. "What can I do? Tell me what hurts."

Everything. Her pride mostly. "There was a snake," she said. "It looked poisonous."

"Sure it did." His lips twitched. "But never mind that. Did you break anything?"

"Give me a sec." Barrie winced as she tried to move her foot.

Behind her the sound of footsteps from up the path announced that Cassie, too, was coming to be amused at her expense. And in case sitting on her ass in the mud wasn't humiliating enough, her ankle was already swelling around the top of her sneaker. Didn't it just figure she would break her leg the one time she actually wore "sensible" shoes?

The path up the slope suddenly looked daunting. They had to have steepened it on purpose somehow. This was ridiculous. Why had she ever agreed to come?

"I told you it was a stupid idea." Eight pushed his hair back and let his arm drop with an endearingly helpless motion that almost kept Barrie from wanting to strangle him. Almost. "You don't owe the Colesworths anything," he said, glaring at Cassie over Barrie's head. "And you aren't going to fix the feud no matter what you do."

"I never said she owed us," Cassie said.

"Both of you stop it. It's only a twisted ankle. Eight, help me up, and I'll be all right."

Eight slipped his arm around her waist and supported her as she straightened. "Careful," he said. "There's a difference between brave and pointless, and I think you've crossed the line."

"Drop dead, would you?" Barrie bit her cheek. She took a

quick inventory: ankle, throbbing; knee, skinned and aching; seat of her shorts, covered in mud. Pain shot up her leg when she tried to put weight on it, and her elbow still twinged from falling down the stairs the night before. But that was nothing compared to the shock wave of finding pressure that hit her as she took a step. Her head felt like it was filled with shards of glass pressing on her brain.

"That's it," Eight said, watching her. "You're done. We're out of here." He bent and, one arm beneath her knees and the other on her back, swung her off her feet.

"Hey, hold on," Cassie said. "Where are you going? You don't have to leave. Just take her up to the house. I'll get her some ice, and she'll be fine in a minute. It always hurts like hell when you first twist your ankle."

Every small and large hurt in Barrie—her foot, her head, her elbow, the loss, even her scraped-up feet—all fused into an overwhelming, exhausting ache. She dropped her head against Eight's shoulder. "I can't, Cassie. Not now."

Eight threw Cassie a look that might as well have been a weapon. "Are you seriously this selfish?"

"But it wouldn't take her any time at all! And who knows when we'll have another chance with Daddy . . ."

"With Daddy *what*?" Eight prompted. "What is going on that's making you so paranoid?"

Cassie's head snapped up. "Nothing. I'm frustrated, all

right? You can't leave me hanging like this again. Just carry her up there. Let her show me where the treasure's buried, and we'll be done for good. It'll be—"

"Stop!" The word exploded from Eight and made Barrie flinch. "Look at her. Can't you think of someone other than yourself for a change? Christ, grow up, would you?"

Cassie'e eyes glittered, and her face, her stance, her whole being radiated fury. She looked like she had looked onstage when Ashley had walked out on her after she'd confessed her feelings for him. She looked as if she wished she had a lamp to throw.

The memory of Cassie's theatrical outrage and jealousy brought back what Eight had said about the Colesworth curse. Barrie's own emotions, what she wanted, had been such a roller coaster that she couldn't imagine throwing anyone else's desires into the mix.

Her anger at Cassie melted away. That afternoon, she would never have believed she could feel sorry for her cousin again, but how could she not feel sorry for Cassie? Living here, with the carcass of Colesworth Place lying in pieces all around her, all the time knowing, hoping, there were remnants of her family's wealth and dignity hidden somewhere that would let her escape and live a different kind of life. Or stay here and live a different life. How frustrating must it be to have believed, all these years, that the Watsons in their big house across the river could find the Colesworth treasure if they wanted to, and thinking that Lula, Emmett, and every other Watson had simply refused to help. And here Barrie was, doing just the same.

"I'll come back another time," Barrie said. "I swear I will."

Cassie nodded and stared at the ground, then bent to tie her sneaker with her face angled away, as if she couldn't stand to have Barrie see her disappointment and frustration. She had stood up again by the time Eight crossed the dock. Hands on her hips, she stood with her hair blowing in her face. The white fabric of her shirt looked almost ghostly against the dark background of oaks and hollow-shadowed cypress. Then Eight stepped onto the *Away*, and Barrie's head splintered beneath another wave of pressure that made her vision blur.

CHAPTER TWENTY-FIVE

Eight docked the *Away* at Watson's Landing and carried Barrie to the house. The door of the tearoom burst open as they reached the terrace, and Mary came rushing out.

"Eight Beaufort, what'd you do to the girl? Lord, honey, look at your foot! It's the size of an elephant. We'll need to get that X-rayed."

"No." Barrie'd already had too many headaches and heartaches for one day. "I just want to go upstairs. I'll ice it and I'll be fine."

Eight frowned down at Barrie. "She's a little bit stubborn,"

"You can put me down anytime now," Barrie told him sweetly.

Mary glanced from one to the other, rolled her eyes, and

held the kitchen door open wide for them to pass. "I'll go get Miss Pru. We'll let her decide."

"There's no need to worry Pru," Barrie said, but she might as well have saved her breath. Mary hurried straight to the attic as Eight carried Barrie upstairs. Barrie smacked him on the shoulder. "Thanks a lot."

"What? Mary's a smart woman. Unlike you. Now, where's your room?"

"Down there." She pointed him down the hall, but resisted when he crossed toward the bed in her room. "There's no point getting the quilt dirty. Put me down in the bathroom so I can clean up."

"You are the most stubborn— Stand right here and do not move." He set her down beside the bed, disappeared into the bathroom, and came back with a couple of towels, which he spread on top of the quilt while Barrie balanced on one leg, holding on to the bedpost.

"Help me get my shoe off, would you?" she said once he'd settled her on top of the towels.

"Prince Charming at your service."

"You've got that backward, baseball guy. *He* was trying to put the shoe back on."

"Taking things off is always more fun."

The tears that spilled over caught Barrie totally by surprise, and she wasn't even sure why she was crying. Emotional exhaustion maybe, and the damn pain in her head, which was even worse than her ankle. She turned away so he wouldn't see what a wimp she was, but he swore softly, and the bed sagged as he sat beside her and gathered her against his chest.

"Why do you even like me?" she whispered into his shirt. "I am clearly a total dork."

"Because you fell? That could have happened to anyone."

"No, I'm serious." Barrie thought of all the times she had started to be friends with someone, only to discover that they didn't get her relationships with Mark and Lula—or get *her*, after the Watson gift had shown up a few too many times and made her obviously weird. The thought that Eight could get scared off once he knew her, really knew her, felt like someone had kicked her in the stomach.

"Hold on. Are we back to the Beaufort gift again?" His chin rested on the top of her head. "I thought we'd covered that."

"You don't know me at all. You think you do, but you don't. I'm a klutz—clearly—and I have this strange Watson thing—"

"And I have my Beaufort thing."

"I yell at you all the time."

He leaned back so he could see her face. "Little-known secret about guys, Bear. The girls who flirt and pant all over us are the ones we want to ignore."

"So you're interested in me because I'm mean to you?"

"I'm interested because you're interesting. And unpredictable and a little bit magic."

"I'm not sure 'unpredictable' is the way you want to go here," she said.

"On the bright side, unpredictable is never boring." Leaning forward again, he cupped her chin and turned her toward him. "You want to know why I like you? All right. I like that feeling sorry for yourself pisses you off. I like that you love wearing sexy shoes but you don't walk in them like you're trying to be sexy. That you look for the best in people, even though you think you don't."

"That's not me. You're seeing qualities that aren't even there."

"No, you're not seeing yourself clearly. You're looking at the individual pieces of yourself, looking for the bad things, and I'm looking at *you* and enjoying the view. You've even made me see this place—all of Watson Island—from inside your heart, and it looks better from in there than it does from out here. You're shaking things up. Shaking me up."

"They have these natural disasters called earthquakes out in California. You're going to love them."

"Before I met you, I used to know where I was going."

And there it was again. Long before she came along, he had made plans to follow his dreams away from Watson Island. Even the thought of leaving made Barrie sick.

He would go and she would stay.

"I can't leave," she said.

"I know. But you can come to USC once you graduate. It's only a year." He smiled at her, that *You are the most important thing in the universe* smile he gave everyone, the one she wished he would only give to her.

"No, I mean, I really can't go anywhere. My head practically splits open every time I leave Watson's Landing, and it's getting worse. It didn't even stop completely when we came back just now. And I don't think it's just me. You know how Pru hasn't been in town much? She hasn't left the island because she gets migraines when she tries. Lula had migraines. In her letters she wrote how she couldn't stand to be away from Watson's Landing. At first I thought she meant she was homesick, but now I think she physically couldn't bear to be away."

"Daddy had the migraines too," Pru said from the doorway. Her face was ashen. "He did most of his work here instead of at the bank because of them, but the doctors never could find anything wrong with him. Maybe that was his problem all along. It's hard to be patient and kind when you're in pain."

"Don't make excuses for him," Barrie said.

Pru crossed to the foot of the bed. "My headaches are never as bad as his used to be. Maybe because I didn't have the gift as strong."

"Does your head hurt now?" Eight turned back to Barrie.

"Not too much."

"Good. We can work with that." From his expression and his voice, he could just as easily have been discussing the weather instead of something kind of cataclysmic.

She punched him in the shoulder. "Hey! Earth to Eight. I just told you I can't leave Watson's Landing. Did you miss that part?"

"No, I heard you." He made a show of rubbing where she'd hit him, as if she could ever dent something other than his ego. "What did you expect me to say, Bear? You're a Watson. Weird is part of the package, and I'm all in—"

"But you're leaving."

"We'll figure out why you can't leave. I've never heard about this part of the gift before."

"I never made the connection either," Pru said, "but I'm starting to realize I haven't been thinking clearly for a long, long time." She dropped an ice pack onto the towel beside Barrie's leg, and prodded at the swollen ankle before wrapping the ice pack around it. Drawing herself up and crossing her arms once that was done, she glanced from Eight to Barrie. "Now," she said, "which one of you wants to tell me what you two were doing back at Colesworth Place?"

Barrie flinched as the cold from the compress began to seep into her skin. "How do you know where we were?"

"I saw Eight's boat from the attic window."

"I didn't want to worry you," Barrie said, reminding herself that was true. Partly, anyway.

Pru shifted her gaze back to Eight, and it was as close to furious as anything Barrie had ever seen from her. "I think it's about time you headed on home. Seven's worried, and our girl here should rest a bit. Although, frankly, what she needs more than anything else is a dose of common sense."

Eight opened his mouth to argue, then evidently thought better of it. He dropped a quick kiss on Barrie's nose and headed toward the door. "I'll call you later, Bear."

While his footsteps receded, Pru sat herself on the edge of the bed. "You know what I'm going to say, don't you?"

None of the options were going to be any fun. "That you found the letters?" Barrie asked.

Pru gave a *tsk*. "I mean about going back to Wyatt's house. I would have told you that was the worst idea since low-fat peanut butter—even before I read the letters."

"Did you read them?" Barrie reached over and put her hand on top of Pru's. "Are you all right? I'm so sorry you found them like that. I was going to tell you, but I got distracted. I can't believe Emmett never gave them to you."

"Never mind me. What on earth was running through your head when you let Cassie talk you into going back there again? No, don't look surprised. You think I can't figure out that's what happened? Don't you have any sense of

343

self-preservation? Lula was afraid of Wyatt. Afraid. Don't you ever go over there again, do you hear me? Don't go anywhere near him." Pru looked down at her hands. "Lula and I—we were so alone. We were both alone. She was there and I was here, and I wish—I wish I had back even a few of all those years we wasted."

"Did she say why? What happened the night she left? Why wouldn't Emmett let her come home?"

"She and Daddy had some kind of agreement that wasn't spelled out. I went through them all, and she never even mentioned it after the first couple of letters."

"Then why did she write? Why would she write to *him*?"

"To connect." Pru got up off the bed. "We were Lula's people. Even Daddy, as imperfect as he was. We were family, and when things go bad, it's family you want. You'll have to read the letters to understand. They're mostly about you anyway. Your mama loved you. She might not have known how to say it or show it. Some people can't."

"Right," Barrie said, although Lula had never hidden anything she thought or felt.

"I guess you'll believe it when you're ready to believe." Pru reached over and squeezed Barrie's shoulder, smiling at her sadly. "I'll tell you what, sugar. I think that ankle is going to be fine with a little rest and some ice. We'll get you cleaned up. I'll run the tub for you, then bring up some supper and those letters, too. You can decide when—or if—you want to read them."

Barrie nodded, but now that she knew the letters were about her, she didn't know what to feel. What could Lula possibly have written about her? Did she even want to know?

She submerged herself in the warm water of the bathtub once Pru had gone, and tried to wash away a sense of loss she couldn't place. It was only when she started to scrub herself clean that she realized it wasn't just her mother she was missing. She dropped the washcloth and patted her chest, her neck. Her necklace, the chain with the three Tiffany keys Lula had given her, wasn't there.

CHAPTER TWENTY-SIX

The knowledge of what Cassie had done gnawed at Barrie while she dried off and put on her pajamas. She had been stupid to think her cousin's feelings could have been hurt by what Eight had said. Cassie had bent to tie her shoe only so she could pick up the necklace. The whole time Barrie had been feeling sorry for her—the whole time Barrie had been promising to come back to help her—Cassie had been in the process of stealing Barrie's necklace.

Family. What a joke.

It was all Barrie could do not to say as much when Pru came back and fussed over her, wrapped her ankle with a compression bandage, and fed her chicken soup—like chicken soup could fix strained muscles or ligaments.

"You need to eat, sugar," Pru said. "Is your ankle feeling

worse? Maybe we ought to take you in for an X-ray."

"I'm fine. I want to go to sleep, that's all."

Pru laid the back of her hand against Barrie's forehead, as if her rudeness had to be due to fever. It was almost funny. Rolling onto her side, Barrie buried her face into the pillow and let Pru assume whatever she was going to assume. It didn't matter.

"Call me if you need a drink or fresh ice—anything at all. And I'm leaving the letters on the desk for you." Pru kissed Barrie's forehead. "To be honest, I feel relieved having read them. I'm sad, too, and angry, and confused, and a lot of other emotions I haven't sorted through yet. But I've been living in a fog all these years, and now that I know what happened, that fog has cleared away. I want clarity for you, too. Read the letters. They'll make you feel better. I promise they will. Lula mentions headaches. You probably need to read that if nothing else."

Headaches. Barrie started to reach for the letters, but her hand shook and she couldn't make herself pick them up. Not if they were about her. Not after what Cassie—family—had done. She'd had enough family betrayal.

Even without the letters, pieces of the various puzzles were falling into place. By her own admission, Pru had been full of energy since that morning. Coming out of her fog probably had less to do with the letters and more to do with whatever had happened when Barrie had washed her bloody hands in the fountain and the water spirit had appeared to accept a binding Barrie hadn't meant to offer—a binding Barrie didn't understand. *That* was what had changed. It had transferred something from Pru to Barrie. The headaches that kicked in every time Barrie left Watson's Landing had been worse since then. So much had changed in the past few days, she hadn't recognized what her own gift had been trying to tell her after she'd fallen at Colesworth Place.

Cassie had stolen from her.

The necklace was the only sign of approval Barrie's mother had ever given her, the only acknowledgment that Lula had felt connected to Barrie's art at all. Barrie hadn't even begun to sort through what she felt about that.

Cassie had the necklace, Barrie knew it, but how could she prove it? All she could do was ask Cassie to give it back, and she could picture the smug look on her cousin's face, the way Cassie would feign innocence. If Wyatt hated Barrie now, she couldn't imagine what he would do if she accused Cassie of being a thief.

Still, she had to at least try to talk to Cassie.

She slept very little. The Fire Carrier came and went. Dawn paled the moon and tinted the sky in gold. Barrie eased out of bed, scattering the shadows around her. She tried out her bandaged ankle. It hurt, but it was tolerable. She hobbled to get her sketchbook.

Back on the bed with her foot elevated, she let her pencil drift with her thoughts: Cassie and Wyatt, Lula and Pru, the horrible old man from the library painting. The lines on the page took on a life of their own, the style growing thicker and bolder, more like her mother's than her own.

She went back to the desk to retrieve Lula's sketchbook and laid it flat on the bed for comparison. The oak alley. The fountain. The kitchen. The views from the balcony. It was funny how little Watson's Landing had changed. It was mainly the emotion behind the pictures that was different.

The drawings showed Watson's Landing as seen through Lula's heart. It was the first real glimpse Barrie had ever had into her mother's internal landscape, and she had never imagined Lula could be so passionate, so enamored with little details.

Had she ever known Lula at all?

Barrie's mind reeled through all the missed opportunities. The things they had never said, the never-hads, the never-woulds, the could-have-beens of her mother's death. Not just the landmarks of her life that Lula had already missed, but the moments Lula would never get to see. She wouldn't come to Barrie's high school graduation. She wouldn't even have the chance to refuse to go. Then college graduation. Assuming Barrie went to college—but how could she?

And a wedding? Marriage? She thought of Eight leaving,

and Pru's husk of a life here at Watson's Landing, Lula's life in San Francisco.

Barrie's phone was in her hand before she remembered it was still the middle of the night on the West Coast. Mark would have a heart attack if she called him now. He would expect that something horrible had happened.

She had to stop calling him, had to stop needing—to hear his voice.

She flipped back through the sketchpad, looking for any glimpse of Lula she could find in her mother's work. After the last sketch, there were at least a handful of pages missing, as if Lula had torn them out. Maybe she'd been bored with drawing architectural details. Barrie examined each sketch more carefully. Something in them nagged at her like a toothache.

At first glance she found nothing out of the ordinary. There were views of the river, of Beaufort Hall and Colesworth Place, of the gardens around Watson's Landing and rooms she had never seen, of the master bedroom with carved panels on the walls. Pru's room had framed photos of interesting building and bridges, and gauzy curtains blowing in the open windows. Lula's was a clutter of photographs and hair ribbons, tiaras and sashes hanging on the wall. Homecoming Queen, Homecoming Princess times three, Miss Glass Slipper Queen of Hearts, Miss Southern Grace, Miss Magnolia, Miss South Carolina BBQ Shag. Lula must have been proud of them. The letters were meticulously stenciled and readable in the sketch.

What had Lula imagined her life would be when she had walked across a pageant stage? Or waved to her admirers from the backseat of an open-topped convertible?

Barrie shoved the sketchbooks away and flopped back on the pillow. What was left of the dawn passed in restless thought and short gasps of sleep. She woke with her fists balled and her ankle aching when Pru came in at ten o'clock.

"Good morning! How do you feel? I brought you some breakfast. Also, Cassie's downstairs asking for you."

Of course she was. "Tell her to go away."

"She's on her way to work, but wanted to see how you are." Pru set the tray on the desk, then crossed to the balcony to open the doors. The air already held the promise of scalding heat. "We should soak that ankle in Epsom salts before I leave for the afternoon."

"Where are you going?"

"I have to see Seven for a bit and take care of some other errands. You should keep your foot propped up. Do you want me to tell Cassie you'll call her later?"

"Whatever."

Pru turned with the morning light behind her. "What happened between you two? Anything I need to know?"

"Nothing." Barrie retreated behind closed eyelids.

She tried not to think about Cassie when Pru had gone,

tried not to picture Cassie's alligator smile, her hand closed around Lula's necklace. What was her cousin doing with it now? Trying to sell it? Rejoicing in the fact that she had it and Barrie didn't? To think Barrie had been happy to have a cousin. To have more family. Rolling over, she chased sleep again and tried to quiet her racing thoughts, without much success.

Pru came back a couple of hours later with more ice and another tray of food. "Eight is downstairs asking to see you," Pru said.

"Tell him I'll call later," Barrie said, not ready to see anyone. Even Eight. Especially Eight. "Or here, he can call me if he wants. Give him this." She tore an empty corner from her sketch and scrawled her phone number on it.

"So I should give the number to Eight, but not to Cassie?" Pru peered at the scrap of paper, then at Barrie. "Sweetheart, you're going to have to tell me what happened last night. The whole story."

"Nothing happened—I wish you'd stop asking me. I'm tired, that's all."

Pru was silent; then she nodded. "All right," she said, sounding tired and hurt. "I have to go out again, but I'll be back as soon as I can. If you need anything, Mary's here until six. Call the house phone and she'll pick it up."

"My ankle isn't that bad. Honest. And I'm sorry I was—"

"You know you can trust me, don't you? I'm worried about you."

"I know that. Thank you, Aunt Pru." Swinging off the bed, Barrie tested her weight on the bandaged leg. Limping slightly, she went to give Pru a hug.

When her aunt had gone, she stood in the middle of the room, unsure what to do with herself. Eight's boat swayed gently at the Watson dock, and across the river, Beaufort Hall stood calmly on its hill. She took Lula's sketchpad to the armchair in the corner and flipped through it again. Lula's room, Pru's room—each of them reflected their owner's personality, but the pictures of the master bedroom showed little evidence that a woman had shared it with Emmett: a silver hairbrush on the vanity, a jewelry box on the dresser. Even the walk-in closet behind the bed looked sanitized and bare. Although Lula had drawn studies of the heavily carved paneling around the door, the room inside had no clothes or shoes, no jumble of belts and scarves, nothing but empty shelves. Why would someone put a closet behind the bed?

Unless it wasn't a closet.

Unless they didn't want anyone to find it.

And where was this bedroom with the heavy carvings on the walls? Barrie had opened every door off the corridor while looking for her cell phone. She thumbed back to the sketch of her mother's bedroom and examined that more closely too. The difference was there, now that she knew to look for it. Although she was used to seeing Beaufort Hall to the left when she stood on the balcony, Lula had drawn it to the right. The sketch of the view from Pru's room was nearly identical.

The family hadn't lived on this side of the house while the girls had been growing up. All of those bedrooms were in the wing with the terrible sense of loss.

Moving gingerly on her sore ankle, Barrie wriggled into a clean pair of capris and an orange shirt almost the same color as Mark's hideous Isaac Mizrahi dress. The color looked better on her than on Mark, but not by much, and yet it made her smile. She pulled her phone off the charger and dialed his number.

"I'm wearing that horrible melon shirt you bought me," she said. "I love it."

"Did I tell you, or what? What are you and your hottie up to today? Tell me something good, baby girl."

"I'm staying in for a change. Learning Lula's drawing technique. Trying to figure her out."

"Good luck with that." He coughed out a laugh. "Maybe in my next life, or the afterlife, I'll ask her what in the hell she was thinking all those years."

He sounded tired and small.

"I thought you were coming back as Cleopatra," Barrie

said, trying to picture him, to keep him from fading away. "You don't believe in an afterlife."

"Life looks different as you near the end. You want to have faith in something bigger than you are. And maybe my lack of faith was always more about me than God. I guess I thought if God couldn't believe in me the way I am, there was no sense in me believing in him." Mark's laugh cracked and turned into a splintered cough that went on so long, he told her he'd have to call her back.

Except he didn't.

Barrie waited five minutes, then ten. She redialed and got sent straight to voice mail. Redialing again, and then again and again, her emotions ricocheted between frustration and fear.

"Come on, Mark. Pick up." After the fifth try, she stuck the phone into her pocket. She needed to move; she needed to *do* something so she wouldn't panic. Because there was no reason to panic. Mark was fine. He was with the nearly-deads, and they had probably drawn him into a game of poker, or pulled him away to watch a DVD of *Veronica Mars* or *Buffy*. There were absolutely a dozen, a hundred, perfectly reasonable explanations why he hadn't called her back.

Barrie wished she could make herself believe any one of them.

CHAPTER TWENTY-SEVEN

After having left her alone for most of the day, the *yunwi* swarmed around Barrie, interested and eager as she emerged from the cocoon of her room. She limped into the abandoned wing, following the finding pull that drew her toward the end of the hall. Curiosity made her open all the doors she passed. The motion left half-moon streaks on the dusty floorboards. No one had been in any of the rooms for years, but there seemed to be nothing unsafe about them.

Lula's room was the third door from the end. Although Barrie recognized the furniture, Emmett had stripped the room of any personal effects or signs of personality, as if he'd been trying to stamp out every trace of Lula. Barrie closed her eyes, trying to feel Lula's presence. There was only a hairpin half-wedged under the baseboard, and a strip of pictures from a photo booth that had been forgotten behind the bed. Pru and Lula, side by side, their faces pressed together. Lula beautiful and undamaged, and looking so very much like Pru. Like Barrie.

Barrie closed her fingers around the hairpin. In the photos, Lula's hair was drawn back into a sleek ponytail. Had she fought with it the way Barrie did, caged it with pins to try to make it behave, while all the time she herself wanted to rebel? To break her father's rules? To run away with Wade?

The emptiness of the house swelled around Barrie. Pru wasn't back yet, and when Barrie glanced at her watch, it confirmed that the tearoom had closed and Mary would already have left. She stayed late only on Friday nights to prepare for the weekend.

Barrie had never been alone in a house, not once. But being by herself at Watson's Landing wasn't liberating. It was a thorny tumbleweed of a feeling that stirred up the need to scream, to play music with the volume all the way up, to run and kick the walls. Things she had never done, never could have done, in Lula's house. For as long as she could remember, Barrie had been a ghost in her own life, quiet to compensate for not being wanted, always tiptoeing around Lula's moods.

No, that wasn't fair. Mark, at least, had wanted her. Mark had fought for her.

Until he was dying, and having her around got to be too hard and he, too, pushed her away.

Wow. *Wow.*

The realization struck Barrie as if she had kicked a wall and it had kicked her back. Was that what she'd been doing sulking in her room? Pushing Eight and Pru away before they could hurt her too?

She hit redial, but Mark's phone still went straight to voice mail. "Dammit, Mark! Where are you? I'm worried. If you went off to Pier 1 for more throw pillows, I'm going to have to come out there and smack you." She paused and swallowed. "Please just call me. I love you and I'm worried."

She strode to the last door in the corridor and threw it open. Her head was splitting from the loss seeping from inside the room. Groping the wall, she found a switch, but the light from the dust-coated chandelier overhead did little to dispel the darkness. She stepped into the room to go open the green velvet drapes drawn across the balcony doors.

Something moved beside the bed.

The hair bristled on Barrie's neck, and her instinct to run was nearly as strong as the sense of loss clawing at her head. She tried to convince herself the white whisper of light was only the dust motes stirring. But the figure was too human-size, too translucent, too much like the woman in the fountain.

It moved as if it were falling to the floor. Then it disappeared, only to appear and fall again.

A spirit. Another spirit.

Barrie backed toward the door, but the *yunwi* rushed into the room to form a circle around the apparition. There were more *yunwi* than she had ever seen in one place. They stood, still as mourners, and the only movement came from the ghost. But unlike the water spirit or the *yunwi*, this one didn't react to Barrie. It was only the *yunwi* who turned and looked at her, their fire eyes pleading with her for something, wanting something from her the same way the Fire Carrier wanted something.

"What?" Barrie asked. "What is it you need?"

But they only stood and stared.

Barrie glanced desperately around the room, looking for some kind of clue. Didn't ghosts always want something? Wasn't that why they haunted a place?

She found no answers to her questions. Down to the stiff silver-backed brushes, the room looked the same as it had in Lula's sketches. It was hard for Barrie to think. Loss raked at her, making her head throb. It wasn't the ghost, though, or not just the ghost. There was something inside the dresser too, but the darkest, most nauseating sense of loss radiated from beyond the bed.

The carved paneling Lula had drawn was closed, leaving no sign that a room lay hidden behind it.

Barrie climbed up onto the dark mahogany bed. A seam ran from the floor to the ceiling where Lula had shown an opening, but no matter how Barrie pushed or tried to pry it apart, it wouldn't budge. Though there was no trace of a lock or lever, Lula must have found one to make the panel swing inward.

Or had she?

With the heavy bed in front of it, Lula couldn't have found the room by accident. Someone else must have left it open long enough for her to get a glimpse inside. Yes, that made more sense. If Lula had come back later, searching for a way to open the paneling again . . . that would explain why she had been fascinated enough by the individual carvings to want to draw them.

Leaning across the headboard, Barrie prodded at the fleur-de-lis, the roses, the bearded faces around the seam. She imagined her mother pushing at these same carvings, trying to reach the room beyond the wall, to follow the finding pull even though Emmett had told her to ignore it. Even though he had told her the Watson gift was evil.

What if Lula had stumbled on the reason he had said that in the first place? Emmett's warnings about the Watson gift and the Fire Carrier could have all been a lie to keep his daughters from finding whatever was in the room behind the bed. Maybe *this* was the secret Lula had promised her father she wouldn't share.

There had to be a pattern. Barrie went back and retrieved Lula's sketchbook. Then she sat cross-legged on the dusty bed, studying the carvings on the panel behind it and comparing them to the last drawing her mother had made, the bearded face—Pan or Zeus? Some god with his eyes closed. Lula had drawn the carving skewed slightly to the right, as if it were twisting open. That was clear enough. What Lula hadn't done was provide any hint to identify that one face from the hundreds of identical faces in the paneling all around the room.

Barrie's eyes blurred on the thick pencil lines and delicate details of Lula's sketches. She had been studying them too long. If there was a clue hidden in them, she couldn't find it. Maybe Lula had left a message on one of the pages she had torn out. That could have been part of whatever deal she and Emmett had made. But if so, then Barrie would never learn the truth.

No. That wasn't happening. Barrie wasn't going to live at Watson's Landing and leave that awful loss gnawing at her from beyond the wall.

She went back to studying the paneling. Rose, fleur-de-lis, leaves, bearded face. The same pattern as in the sketchbook. She knew the order, but where had Lula started? Barrie traced the lines of the sketch with the tip of her finger while staring at the nearest rose carving on the wall, trying to put herself into her mother's frame of mind. It was only then that she realized what she was seeing—and what she wasn't. The rose in Lula's drawing had a petal missing. She checked it twice more before she was certain.

She moved on to the next sketch in the book. The fleur-de-lis had an extra leaf.

Lula might have missed a petal, but she wouldn't have consistently drawn what wasn't there.

Her breath coming faster and her fingers tingling, Barrie leaned over the headboard, and finally . . . there. A rose with a petal missing. Followed by, yes, a fleur-de-lis with an extra leaf. All the way through the pattern, each carving had the same subtle anomalies that Lula had drawn, including a bearded man with an extra line between his brows.

"Gotcha," Barrie said.

The headboard dug into her ribs as she leaned over to reach the bearded face. She prodded it, and nothing happened, but when she twisted, the face swiveled to the right and revealed a keyhole. For a key Barrie didn't have.

The finding compulsion grew even stronger. Barrie threw down the sketchbook, sending the shadows scurrying along the floor. Climbing down from the bed, she followed the other pull of loss to the dresser, skirting behind the ghost and the yunwi gathered at the foot of the bed.

Surprisingly, clothes still filled the drawers. Men's yellowing undershirts and tightie-whitey underwear lay stacked in obsessive perfect rows. Starched, collared shirts in solids and conservative stripes were also precisely folded, and the sock drawer held at least thirty pairs of identical black socks. The only thing out of place was the Bible stuffed beneath four pairs of paisley pajamas.

Barrie pulled out the book. Her head spun with the loss roiling from its pages. Giving herself a mental shake, she opened the Bible, ruffled through it, and shook it out above the dresser. It fell open naturally. About three quarters of the way through, a section carved from the pages created a hollowed compartment. A locket and a diamond ring were nestled in the recess. An engagement ring.

She tipped both the necklace and the ring onto her palm. Her blood quickened. Beads of sweat dampened her lip and forehead. Prying open the locket with a fingernail, she found Luke Watson smiling at her from a faded photograph. Except for the navy uniform and the fighter jet beside him, he looked much as he had in the yearbook. Only now he wore a navy uniform and stood beside a fighter jet.

The shock of recognition rushed through Barrie. What was Luke's picture doing in a locket in Emmett's room?

She closed her fingers around the jewelry. Whose had it been? Not her grandmother's. Twila would likely have given Emmett back his ring when she'd broken off their engagement. But there was no reason he would have had her necklace, and his wife, Pru's mother, certainly wouldn't have had a locket with Luke's picture inside.

Her mind churning with questions, Barrie turned from the dresser. She came face-to-face with the ghost.

Not the vague, pale apparition she had seen before. A ghost who was recognizably Twila Beaufort, a Twila not much older or different from how she had looked in the high school yearbook. A ghost girl in a miniskirt and red, shiny boots, her arms raised as if she were dancing with a lover. Her head was tilted and her lips were puckered. Kissing. Twila was kissing someone. Then she whipped around, her eyes wide, mouth open in a silent scream.

Barrie nearly screamed. Horror had contorted Twila's face. She collapsed to her knees, reached out for something— or someone—on the floor. Half-turning, she screamed again, and threw up her hands to protect her head. She fell sideways to the floor.

Hand over her mouth, Barrie stared in shock.

Murder. Twila had been murdered.

At that moment Barrie hated Watson's Landing.

Twila had been kissing someone. Was that who she'd been reaching for on the floor? No. There would have been two ghosts if two people had been murdered. That seemed logical, if logic applied in situations like this.

The ring and the edges of the locket dug into Barrie's palm as Twila's ghost faded and began the cycle again. Twila kissing someone, screaming, falling to her knees, dying again, over and over like playing back a video, echoing the last moments of her life. With each repetition, Barrie hoped the scene would end differently. It never did. Twila must have been caught in this loop for forty—fifty—years.

Who had Twila been kissing here in Emmett's room? Luke or Emmett? Had Luke caught her here with his brother and killed her? Was that why he'd run away?

Shivering, Barrie drew a sad face in the dust on the dresser and brought her finger away coated in grit as thick and dark as everything else in the room. The murder sickened her, the stillness sickened her; the loss sickened her.

She had to find the key.

She slipped the ring and necklace into her pocket and searched the rest of the room. Opened every cupboard. Ran her hand under each piece of furniture, behind each drawer in case something was taped back there. Threw open the curtains out to the balcony and sneezed at the flurry of dust. Then she peered back around the room, trying to think.

Downstairs the grandfather clock chimed seven times, seeming to echo in the stillness of the empty house. Seven? It had been more than two hours since Mark had promised to call her back. Barrie pulled her phone out of her pocket. She still hadn't heard from him. She dialed his number again, and what his silence might mean slowly sank in.

She had to brace herself against a wall as she got the hospice number from information. She waited while the hospice transferred her three times before connecting her to someone helpful. The nurse was one she remembered meeting when she'd gone to look at the place with Mark—a heavy blonde who'd bracketed all her sentences in "wows" and exclamation points. *Wow, we're so happy to have Mark coming! Wow, he's going to love the place! Wow, fantastic shoes!* There were no exclamation marks now, only discomfort punctuated by the click of a pen.

"I'm sorry," the woman said. "We had to transfer Mark to the hospital early this morning."

"But I just talked to him a couple of hours ago. What's wrong with him?"

"Pneumonia. If you've talked to him, maybe he's feeling better already." The forced cheerfulness was already creeping back into her voice.

"Why didn't anyone call me?" Barrie asked. "I'm his emergency contact."

"He asked us not to call. He wanted to do it himself as soon as he heard what the doctors said. I think he just didn't want to worry you. You know how it is, honey. You have to keep a positive attitude, and Mark's the best. We love having him around here."

The pep talk grated on Barrie's nerves. She thanked the nurse and asked her for the hospital number before finishing the call. Then she dialed the information desk and hyperventilated through the transfer to Mark's room. Even when he picked up with a ragged "hello," she couldn't seem to take in air.

"What are you doing telling people not to call me?" she yelled at him. "I'm supposed to know if you are in the hospital! I should be there with you, not stuck out here not knowing anything."

"The doctors don't know anything either," Mark said. "You'd fit right in."

Barrie sank to the floor and hugged her knees. The smile was back in Mark's voice. Thank God. She took a deeper breath. "So what *are* the doctors saying?"

"Nothing. They're pumping me full of antibiotics and sticking oxygen up my nose. But it's no big deal. Trust me, baby girl. The old bats at the hospice were afraid of getting sued, that's all. I'm fine. I'm sorry for worrying you. I forgot to charge my phone last night, and the battery died so I couldn't call you back. Have you been calling?"

"No, not much. I have things to tell you, but I'll wait until you get out of the hospital. That will give you a reason to hurry up and get better."

"Do they have to do with your hottie?"

"Wouldn't you like to know? So chop, chop. Get out of there. I better hear from you tomorrow."

The line went so quiet, Barrie heard the faint hiss of the oxygen. "Maybe not tomorrow, baby girl. You know how doctors are. Anal. And not a McDreamy or a McSteamy in sight. This place is a whole wasteland of hotness."

Barrie sat in the center of the master bedroom after they'd hung up, watching the ghost rise and fall. The room seemed to spin, or maybe it was only her thoughts whirling. She couldn't stop picturing Mark lying by himself in a hospital bed, scratchy sheets and an IV drip, drip, dripping antibiotics into his arm. He hated hospitals. He didn't even want chemo or radiation. He didn't want to *be* in a hospital.

The lack of control made her heart stop, then race ahead as if it were trying to outrun the ache it knew was coming. The *yunwi* crowded around her, the same way they had crowded around the ghost. She wondered if they sensed her loss.

She couldn't just sit there. She had to *do* something.

The key to the panel behind the bed had to be somewhere at Watson's Landing. It had to be. And she was going to find it.

CHAPTER TWENTY-EIGHT

Pru was still out when Barrie retrieved the keys she had seen in the top drawer of the desk in the library. It didn't surprise Barrie to discover that none of them fit when she tried them in the keyhole of the master bedroom panel.

She thought of Mark in his sterile white hospital bed, of Pru stuck at the plantation all those years, of Lula's letters, of poor murdered Twila, and of Eight across the river practically packing up his suitcase. She thought about leaving Watson's Landing, about running *to* Mark, about running *away* from here. Again the thought brought a flail of panic.

She was damned if she was going to be like Lula, wasting her life without even trying to live. Or like Pru, locked up here stifling the gift. Or like Emmett, the bastard, who'd stuffed anything he didn't want to deal with into a drawer and pretended it wasn't there.

"This place doesn't own me," she said to the shadows that hovered at the edges of her vision. "You don't own me!"

If she was going to stay on Watson Island, it was going to be on her terms. She needed to separate what she wanted from what Watson's Landing wanted of her.

With the house still empty, she went room by room, searching for keys and simultaneously clearing out the clutter of misplaced things, tracking down every ping of loss, from an earring wedged behind a dresser to a mound of buttons, receipts, and hairpins. She even retrieved a silver fork pushed under the carpet in the dining room.

With the possible exception of the fork, every object she found was new. New*ish*. Nothing older than the prescription bottle she had found from 1969. Which confirmed what she had begun to suspect. Until Emmett had scared Pru and Lula out of using the gift, other Watsons must have used it. Emmett—she refused to call that man her grandfather—must have used it himself. Nothing of *his* was lost. Barrie didn't find so much as a tie clip.

Emmett had made his daughters suppress the gift and endure the pain of stifling it. He'd told them that the Fire Carrier would hurt them. He'd scared them, punished them— locked Lula in her room for finding the panel, and he'd beaten both Lula and Pru with a switch when Lula had gone into the woods.

The woods still contained something lost.

A few minutes later, dressed for snakes in a pair of Pru's rubber Wellingtons and jeans that made her skin itch in the heat, Barrie let herself and a horde of *yunwi* out the kitchen door. She'd barely set a foot on the terrace when she felt the warning click and saw Eight's tousled head appear on the staircase, his smile wide and blinding-bright when he saw her.

"That's a new look for you." He eyed the ugly green boots. "Going native?"

"Didn't you know? Swamp-chic is the latest trend." Barrie put one hand on her hip and the other behind her head and gave him her best runway strut, complete with unfashionable limp. "Now step aside. I'm on a mission."

Eight goose-stepped sideways and swept out his arm to bow her past him. "After you, *mademoiselle*. Where did you say we were going?"

"I'm busy. *Qu'est-ce que tu veux?*"

"Sorry, '*mademoiselle*' was it for me."

"It means 'What do you want?'"

"Sounded better in French. But what do I want? Hmm, let me think."

He spun her toward him, his eyes intent on her the way that only his eyes had ever been. His head tilted so his mouth came down on hers with just the right amount of lingering and hunger and expectation.

For a few blissful moments Barrie let herself forget Mark and the ghost and everything lost. She sank into Eight's kiss, melted into him the way the ocean melted onto the beach. He relaxed when she leaned on him, but he held her steady, held her up. Except, he wasn't someone she could count on. And she didn't want to lean on anyone anymore. She pulled away.

"Are you about done?" she asked.

He followed her onto the lawn. "Are we going to argue again?"

"Only if you want to disagree with me."

"All right." He slid his hands into his pockets. "So where are were going?"

"Into the woods."

Eight's eyebrows shot up into his hairline. "Why?"

"Because I'm looking for something. If you promise not to yap at me about it, I'll let you be all He-Man and beat off the snakes and alligators. There's still plenty of light, so no excuses. We're not going to see the Fire Carrier."

"Not so sure you can count on that."

"He wouldn't hurt me anyway. I think we have a deal."

Eight looked at her as if she had gone insane. "What kind of a deal, exactly?"

"Not a very exact one." Barrie allowed herself a smile.

"The short version of a long story is that I cut my hands and accidentally made a blood bond with a water spirit in the fountain, and I sort of on purpose fed blood to the *yunwi*. Now they want me to find something, but all I've found so far is your great-aunt Twila's engagement ring and locket, along with her ghost. Which is in the master bedroom, by the way, because that's where she seems to have been murdered. Probably by Emmett, who seems like he *could* be a murderer. He was definitely a total bastard. Except I think he really did love Twila. So maybe it was Luke who murdered her and ran away. Or Luke ran away because Emmett murdered her. That last bit's a little confusing, and I haven't worked it all out quite yet."

"Take a breath."

But now that she'd started, Barrie couldn't stop. "I also found a hidden room behind the master bedroom," she continued, "and I think whatever I'm supposed to find is in there, but I need a key to get inside. I've looked everywhere in the house, so the woods is the only place it might be. Which presumes Emmett didn't throw it away. I don't think he was the type to throw things away, though. He was the type to hide them somewhere close and obsess over them, like the way he kept Twila's ring and the letters my mother sent to Pru for *thirteen years*. Bastard, right?"

"Bastard," Eight agreed. "You have been a busy Bear,

haven't you? And when were you going to tell me about all this?"

"I just did." Barrie couldn't help a sputter of laughter at the smacked-dumb-by-a-two-by-four look on Eight's face. But the fact that he wasn't arguing about going into the woods gave her an extra boost of courage. Throwing her arms around the back of his neck, she pulled him down to kiss him on the lips. Then she sauntered away, or at least she did the best imitation of a saunter she could manage with a limp. "You coming?" she called back over her shoulder.

"Try getting rid of me before you've explained all that."

She told him while they walked, and he listened without— as far as Barrie could tell—trying to calculate the quickest route to the nearest exit. She left out only the part where Cassie had stolen Lula's necklace. That admission stuck in her throat, as if saying it aloud would make the betrayal real. As if keeping quiet would make it all less true.

Her hair snagged in tendrils of Spanish moss as she and Eight entered the woods. The tang of decaying leaves scented the syrupy air, and she paused to search for the source of the finding pull.

"It's this way, I think," she said.

The underbrush thickened, but the trees grew sparser. A few minutes later, the shadows of the *yunwi* hung back as if they had reached some kind of invisible barrier that kept them from going farther, and soon Barrie and Eight stepped into a clearing around a tree nearly as large as the Devil's Oak. Its trunk was easily eleven feet thick, gnarled with the weight of wide-spreading branches and the knotted remnants of long-dead limbs. The undisputed king at the heart of the woods, it had rooted out every tree for a good hundred feet around it.

Barrie pointed at the base. "That's where the pull is coming from."

"I've heard of this tree." Eight followed her toward it. "The natives around here used to call it the Scalping Tree and hang the scalps of their enemies on it."

The tatters of Spanish moss did look eerily like scalps. Barrie shivered despite the still-warm air. "Why?"

"I don't know. I don't even know which tribe it could have been. None of them, probably. The Fire Carrier was Cherokee, but since he brought the *yunwi* here from somewhere else, he clearly wasn't local."

Barrie edged closer to the tree and stumbled over a half-buried branch. Eight caught her and pulled her up. "Be careful, Bear."

"You're always saying that."

"Well, you're always falling on your ass."

She let out a pent-up breath, and scraping together the shreds of her dignity, she marched to the trunk of the Scalping Tree. The finding pull urged her toward the roots. A thick layer of leaves covered the ground, and she stooped to brush them away.

"Hang on." Eight caught her hand. "Snakes, remember?"

He found a stick and used it to clear the leaves, exposing a layer of rocks wedged into a recess between the roots. Flicking them away one by one, he paused when one gave a metallic *thunk* as it landed.

Barrie picked it up. While it had looked like an oval rock at first, it was actually a fist-size metal box. It clanked when she shook it, a loose rattle of metal on metal. A gust of wind played with her hair and rustled the leaves above them.

The finding pull let her go. Even the tree looked happier.

Excellent. Now she was having delusions of happy trees. Because talking to the *yunwi* wasn't bad enough. Watson Island was going to turn her into one of those crazy old ladies who doddered around having conversations with plants. Really, all she was missing now was an extensive cat collection.

Shaking her head at herself, she turned the box over and tried to open it. It didn't budge. She fought down a surge of disappointment and bent to hit the hinges with a rock.

"Hang on," Eight said mildly. "There's probably a screwdriver or something back at the house we could use to open it without maiming ourselves. Or damaging the key, if you think that's what's in there. Maybe you shouldn't get your hopes up, though. Why would Emmett—or anyone, for that matter—hide a key out here in an iron box?"

"Emmett hid everything. In the strangest places," Barrie said. "But you're right. Pru has a toolbox in the closet."

When they emerged from the woods, the *yunwi* were waiting for them. The spirits surged around Barrie and jumped to get her attention, but her eyes shot beyond them to where Cassie was hurrying up the path.

"There you are!" Long, dark hair flying like a banner behind her, Cassie gave a careless wave, as if it were just another evening, just another visit. A swell of finding pressure crashed into Barrie, a pull so strong, it made her vision blur and ripple. She staggered and grabbed Eight's arm. Cassie not only had Lula's necklace; she'd had the nerve to bring it with her.

Eight stopped and turned her to face him. "What happened between you two?" he asked quietly. "Besides being her usual self, what did she do to make you wish you'd never met her?"

Barrie shook her head. She couldn't decide which she wanted more, to run away before Cassie reached them or to march up to her cousin and slap her in the face.

"Hey, y'all. Barrie, sugar, didn't you get my messages? I've been calling and calling. I've been so worried— Hey, what's that?" Her eyes dropped to the box Barrie held, and she reached for it, because apparently she felt entitled to take anything of Barrie's that she wanted.

Barrie pulled the box away and handed it to Eight. "What are you doing here, Cassie?"

"I told you. You didn't answer any of my messages." Letting her hand drop, Cassie made her lip tremble in a good imitation of someone whose feelings were honestly hurt. Not that Cassie had an honest bone in her body. "I wanted to see if you were okay. You're not mad at me, are you, Cos?"

That was how she was going to play it?

"Is there a reason I should be mad?" Barrie asked. "Come on, Cousin. Think hard."

Cassie's face flushed crimson. Then the color drained away. "Oh!" she exclaimed. "I clean forgot. Wait. You didn't think—" She broke off, unclasped a chain from around her neck, and pulled Barrie's Tiffany keys from underneath her shirt.

Barrie snatched them back before Cassie could change her mind. The returning click went off in her head, and her eyes fluttered closed with the release of pressure.

"That was the other reason I've been calling you," Cassie went on. "I found your necklace after you left. The chain broke, but I've been wearing the keys so Daddy wouldn't find them. I wanted to keep them safe for you."

Even now, part of Barrie, a big, irrational part, still wanted to believe Cassie. "Then why didn't you leave it with Pru when you were here?"

"And when exactly did you find it?" Eight asked before Cassie could even answer.

Cassie shifted her balance, not looking at either of them. That was the problem with wanting to believe in Cassie. She'd had the necklace before Barrie and Eight had reached the boat. Anything that came out of her mouth now was going to be a lie, and Cassie had to know Barrie knew it. But she was counting on Barrie to be too stupid, or too naive, or too . . . weak . . . to call her on it.

It was time for Barrie to be smart. Screaming at Cassie wouldn't help. They still had to go to school together, so they needed to find a way to get along. Barrie tightened her hand around the necklace. She had it back. That was what mattered most.

"Thanks for bringing this back for me," she said, "but Eight and I have to be somewhere right now. Sorry." She grabbed Eight's hand and tugged him toward the house.

"I was hoping we could hang out." Cassie hurried after them. "Maybe get a hot dog or something. My treat. I traded shifts so I could come see you."

"Another time." Barrie walked faster than was comfortable with her ankle. But she wasn't going to limp in front of Cassie.

They reached the terrace. "What about later? Game of pool at the Resurrection?" Cassie asked.

"We have plans later too."

"What kind of plans?"

If Barrie had to look at Cassie's lying face another second, feel half-sorry for her another second, she was going to lose it. "Please, Cassie. Just go." She paused at the bottom of the steps. "I'm sure we'll figure it out later, but right now I need some time."

"So you are mad?"

"I'm not mad." Barrie started up the stairs, then spun back around. "What did you think was going to happen? You thought you could take my necklace, and I was going to let that go?" She held up her hand as Cassie opened her mouth to answer. She couldn't listen to any more excuses. "Just drop it," she snapped. "I have something I have to do, but I swear, I'll call you as soon as I can."

She was aware of Cassie watching her all the way up the staircase, and she didn't relax until Eight finally shut the kitchen door behind them. Judging from his furious scowl, though, the conversation was far from closed.

"Why didn't you tell me?" he demanded as she hurried across the kitchen. "Cassie had your necklace before we even left Colesworth Place, didn't she?"

"She had to realize I would know she had it. I don't get her."

Eight followed her through the swinging door and down the corridor to the closet beneath the stairs. "I'm sure she was

380

waiting to see what you would do. Waiting to see if she could get away with keeping it. The Colesworths all seem to operate on instinct and deal with the consequences later."

"So what do we do?" Barrie asked, speaking as much about how to open the box as she was about the situation with Cassie. Both seemed fairly hopeless.

"Let me see the toolbox." Eight rummaged around inside and pulled out a chisel and a hammer.

Barrie leaned back against the wall. "Cassie had to be worried I was going to call the police. Right? I'll bet that's why she's been calling."

"Hold that thought." Eight chipped away the last of the rust that had fused the seam of the box closed. He levered the box open triumphantly. Inside were two large iron keys. "Jackpot," he said.

CHAPTER TWENTY-NINE

The secret panel swung open, and Barrie scrambled over the headboard. Inside, the hidden room was empty except for a threadbare Oriental carpet and dusty shelves rising to the ceiling on every wall.

"Well, this is disappointing." Eight jumped in after her and looked around. "What do you think? Some kind of a safe room? I guess that makes sense, since the original Watson was a privateer."

"Pirate. Otherwise, why bother with a treasure room?" Barrie followed the finding pull and the *yunwi* to the back corner. Stronger and more sickening than ever, the sense of loss came from behind the paneling. She jiggled the nearest shelf, but it didn't budge.

"What are you doing?" Eight came and peered over her shoulder.

"There has to be another hidden panel. Here, help me figure out how to get it open. You take that far wall, and I'll take this one." She started at the corner and worked back toward the master bedroom, checking every shelf attached to the ornate paneling. The carvings were the same as in the bedroom, and she pressed and twisted each of them, looking for a keyhole. Eight watched her a moment, then started at the corner, checking the back wall of the room. They both startled as something clicked.

"Found it," Eight pointed to the button at the base of a fleur-de-lis.

The wall rumbled. A large section swung inward, revealing a steep flight of steps that vanished into darkness.

Barrie's stomach turned at the loss that pulled her down the passage. The light from the bedroom didn't reach the bottom, and she fumbled along both sides of the stairwell for a switch. Cobwebs tangled in her fingers, and rough brick scraped her skin.

"I remember a flashlight in the toolbox," Eight said. "I'll go grab it."

Barrie nodded. She waited for him just inside the hidden room, as far from the narrow staircase as she could get without obviously retreating. Whatever was down the stairwell made her want to crawl out of the treasure room, shut the secret panel, and ignore the whole abandoned wing the way Pru had managed to ignore it all her life.

As if they felt her reluctance, the *yunwi* crowded around her, trying to nudge her toward the stairs. When Eight came back, she let him go first.

"You just want me to clear all the cobwebs, don't you?" he said.

"Of course. Do I look stupid?"

Cold, stale air wrapped around Barrie the deeper they descended, and she tried not to wince as the steps made her ankle ache. The anorexic beam of Eight's flashlight didn't hold back much darkness. More and more of the *yunwi* who had followed her into the passage fell back, until only a handful remained. Even they lagged behind as if they were afraid.

Barrie trailed her fingers along the bricks and counted steps to keep herself from hyperventilating—192 stairs to the bottom. They had to be at least two stories underground. Three stories from the master bedroom. She closed her eyes at the thought of all that earth above them held back by a few bricks on the ceiling.

Eight ran the flashlight over an iron door with black cross-pieces. "You have that other key?"

Barrie dropped both into his outstretched hand. "I don't remember which one we used upstairs."

"Want to do the honors?" He glanced back at her, his eyes gleaming in the darkness.

"That's all right. I wouldn't want to deprive you of all the fun."

Something in her voice must have given away her panic. "It's going to be fine," Eight said. "Whatever's on the other side can't be that bad."

"Snakes and alligators," Barrie said, wishing that were all.

But it wasn't. The loss coming from behind the door raked her skull like nothing she had ever felt before. She took the flashlight so Eight could fit the key into the lock, but the light trembled in her hand. She squared her shoulders and tried to keep it steady.

The first key got the lock open, and Eight grinned back at her. "Fifty-fifty, right? Good omen."

He leaned into the door, and it opened with a groan of protest and a belch of something acrid and decaying. A few *yunwi* darted through the gap. The rest hung back by the stairs. Barrie glanced at them before stepping forward to shine the flashlight into the blackness.

Beyond the door, the walls curved to form an arch overhead, but the light didn't penetrate far enough to find the far end of the room. Eight pushed past Barrie and stopped a few yards inside.

"It looks like the escape tunnel Cassie was talking about."

He moved deeper into the chamber, looking around and shining the light at the walls and ceiling. At the edge of the flashlight beam, his foot connected with something that gave an echoing clank.

"What was that? Are you okay?" Barrie came up beside him.

"I'm fine."

They both bent to examine a black garbage bag that lay on the ground where Eight had kicked it. He tore through the knot in the plastic and pulled out a blackened teapot.

"Here, shine that flashlight closer." As Barrie sidled up beside him, he turned the teapot over and squinted at a faint maker's mark obscured by the layers of tarnish. "It's sterling," he said. He pulled other pieces from the bag: a tray, a creamer, platters, plates. "How much do you want to bet this is the stuff Luke supposedly took to Canada with him."

"I didn't know Luke took any silver."

"He was back from Vietnam for his father's funeral, so technically everything was his anyway. The oldest child has always inherited in all three families—to keep the plantations intact from one generation to the next."

So the master bedroom wouldn't have belonged to Emmett then. With his father dead, the room would have gone to Luke, and maybe he and Twila had come in to clean out his father's things. Or maybe Luke's father had left instructions for him about the secret room before he died.

The pressure in Barrie's head and the queasy feeling in her stomach hadn't lessened when they'd found the bag of silver. There was still something here she was supposed to find.

She shone the light farther along the tunnel, walked a few more feet, then looked again. The beam of the flashlight illuminated a leather suitcase, not much more than scraps and clasps and a handle made of brass. Eight went and nudged it open with his foot. The clothes inside had disintegrated, but there were buttons and zippers, a rusted razor and a plastic comb and toothbrush. But finding that didn't dim the pressure either. Barrie went a few more yards, aimed the flashlight deeper into the room, and almost dropped it as her fingers went numb and nerveless. Her other hand flew to her mouth to stifle a scream.

"Hey, a little light over here?" Eight looked up. Then he jumped to his feet as he saw her face.

Six or seven yards beyond the suitcase, a collection of bones lay on the ground. Barrie pushed herself forward on unsteady legs. And what had looked like one pile in the shaking light resolved into two. Two *skeletons*. The white flash of a ghostly hand rose from one skeleton and moved toward the other.

Eight pulled at the back of her shirt. "Hang on, Bear. You don't want to go there."

Barrie kept moving. She had no choice. The finding pull made her want to throw up. But the skeletons were why she was here.

"Luke never made it to Canada," she said.

"Doesn't look like it." Eight's voice was so quiet, Barrie barely heard him.

The few *yunwi* who had followed them inside stood in a row beside what was left of the bodies. Their heads were bowed, and they moved aside to let Barrie through.

The smaller skeleton lay on her back, still wearing her vinyl boots. The larger skeleton rested half on his side, as if he were reaching toward her. His ghost *did* reach for her, a spectral arm rising like mist from the yellowed bones. Though the fabric of the actual navy uniform had long since disintegrated, Luke's ghost still wore one, complete with gold pilot's wings pinned above four full rows of a hero's ribbons. He reached for Twila's face, but his transparent fingers touched bare skull.

Twila's ghost wasn't there. She must have died before Emmett had moved her body. She and Luke had been forever separated, Twila's spirit in the bedroom and Luke's there in the tunnel. Forever reaching for each other where they had died, and never finding comfort.

Luke's eyes fell closed. His ghostly hand slid away, as if he were too sad, or too weak, for his touch to linger. Barrie tasted salt on her tongue and realized she was crying.

"Christ. Oh, Christ." Eight pulled Barrie close and drew her head to his chest.

"Do you see him?" she asked.

"See who?"

"Luke's ghost."

Eight stiffened and then shook his head. Barrie didn't have the heart to describe what she saw.

She stooped beside Luke's remains and picked up the metal wings that lay on the ground along with a plastic name tag. A returning jolt shot through her, deeper and more electric than anything she had ever felt.

L. Watson. Luke, who was supposed to have deserted the navy, deserted Watson's Landing, but never had.

Barrie ran her fingers over the letters and felt the click again and then a lightness. A release. Peace. As if not only the spirits, but the walls, the ground, the very air around her sighed.

Luke's ghost vanished. Maybe recognition was all his spirit had needed to move on.

All this time, the Watson gift had been screaming for someone to find the bodies Emmett had wanted hidden. It couldn't have been coincidence that Lula had discovered the hidden room the night she had run away. The night Emmett had locked her up. What would Emmett have done to keep the secret of what he had done to Luke and Twila?

What was it Mary had said? That *plat eyes* were the spirits of the unburied dead. Barrie had assumed Mary was mixing up *plat eyes* and *yunwi*, using some Gullah superstition to explain what she didn't understand. But the way the *yunwi* had behaved, the way they had reacted to the ghosts, the way they stood now, looking at the skeletons so solemnly, they clearly wanted Luke and Twila found.

Emmett had stolen more than life from Luke and Twila. He had left them unacknowledged. Ungrieved and unremembered. He had left their spirits lost.

The wings and name tag from Luke's uniform dug into Barrie's fist. "Their bodies have been here all along," she said. "Luke was a hero, and Emmett made him look like a deserter. He and Twila were in love, and Emmett kept them apart even after they were dead."

Eight gathered her in again to drop a kiss onto her hair.

In the silence there came a sudden rustle of plastic and the clatter and clank of metal hitting metal. Eight spun around. "Who's there?"

Barrie dove for the flashlight. In its faded beam, her cousin's face shone furious and guilty. She was dragging the bag of silver backward toward the door.

"What are you doing?" Rage at her cousin bubbled up and made Barrie's voice harsh and clipped.

"I'm leaving!" Cassie pulled the bag of silver more quickly. Eight sprinted forward.

Barrie needed to create some kind of distraction to slow Cassie down. "Hold on a second," she said. "Tell me what you're doing. What is it you want?"

"Besides the silver, you mean?" Cassie shook her head. "I've spent my whole life not being as good as the Beauforts and the Watsons. But your grandfather killed his own brother! And look at the stuff he just threw away down here like it didn't even matter. Look at you. You strut in here with your gold watch and diamonds, acting so innocent. You've got Eight *and* Watson's Landing, when they've never—he's never—even given me a chance. You Watsons get away with anything. Even murder."

She stepped through the open door and pulled the bag through to the other side with a triumphant glare at Eight, who had almost reached her.

"Wait." Barrie struggled to find something to make Cassie pause. "Don't you see? Now you'll have the pleasure of telling everyone what Emmett did."

"That would be fun, but I'm going to help you cover up your murder and protect your perfect reputation instead. No one will ever need to know." Cassie gave a shove, and the door closed with a bang that bounced off the walls.

CHAPTER THIRTY

Reaching the door too late, Eight slammed both fists against the iron. Cassie had already locked it behind her. "Damn it, I left the key in the lock. What kind of an idiot am I?"

"The same kind I am." Barrie dropped into a crouch along the wall and let her head fall back against the bricks. "We didn't know Cassie was going to follow us. I didn't even think to lock the kitchen door to keep her out."

The *yunwi* had fixed the security chain, and she had left it dangling.

"*I* should have known what she was going to do," Eight said bitterly.

Barrie looked up at him. "Cassie probably didn't even know until after we had gone inside. But blaming ourselves is useless. Cassie's going to have to come back eventually, right?

She'll change her mind just like she did with my necklace. She gave it back as soon as she thought she was going to get caught."

"That's exactly why she won't come back. Taking your necklace was one thing, but locking us down here? That's a whole other level of stupid." Eight braced his forearms against the door and rested his head against the iron.

"She'll say it was a prank."

"Who in this town would believe her over us?"

"She wouldn't leave us here to die. Would she?"

Eight kicked the door again and didn't answer.

A dry, aching cold shivered down Barrie's arms and seeped into her bones. Her chest tightened, squeezing until there was no room for air.

No one knew this place was here. All Cassie had to do was throw Lula's sketchbook into the hidden room and close the panel behind the bed.

Given how resistant Pru was to using the gift, she proba- bly wouldn't even think to check the abandoned wing. Even if she managed to piece the clues together, she wouldn't have the key.

Barrie dug her phone out of her pocket. No bars. Of course. And screaming wouldn't help. No one was going to hear them this deep underground.

She shifted Luke's wings and name tag into her other

hand and dug Twila's ring and locket out of her other pocket. Holding them all together in her palm, she tried to think. She spun toward the *yunwi*, who still stood motionless, well away from the door.

"Do something, can't you? If you can dismantle shutters and stairs," she told them, "a lock can't be any problem."

Eight turned toward her. "Who are you talking to?"

"The *yunwi*."

"They've been here all along?" He looked around sharply when Barrie nodded. "Well, even if they are here, I doubt they can go near the door," he said. "I'll bet that's why it's made of iron in the first place. The screws I took out of the shutter for Pru were galvanized steel, but she had me replace them with iron. She probably thought that would keep the *yunwi* from working them loose again."

Pru had said something to Mary about using iron in place of wooden pegs, and most of the *yunwi* had fallen back before they'd reached the bottom of the narrow staircase. Iron had to hurt them, if it made them so afraid to touch it or even go near it. The few who had come into the tunnel with her must have been very determined to make sure she found Luke's and Twila's bodies.

Barrie cut the flashlight back to Luke—her great-uncle— and to the girl he had loved. Love had been written in every line of Luke's body, in the yearning of his spectral fingers as he'd reached out to Twila. Were the two of them back together now? Barrie tried not to imagine that she and Eight might be trapped down here long enough to turn to dust and bones. She played the beam of the flashlight past the bodies, but the floor just faded into darkness.

"This tunnel has to go somewhere. There has to be a way out." Barrie shone the light back at Eight.

His attention sharpened on the wall near the door. "Hold on. Shine the flashlight back over there."

Barrie trained the thinning trickle of light on a recess two bricks thick and two feet high. Inside it an old-fashioned lantern hung from a hook, with an age-stained tin box on the ledge below it. Eight picked up the lantern and examined it.

"That can't possibly work," Barrie said. "Come on. We're better off trying to find an exit before the flashlight dies."

"No, look." He sloshed the oil inside the lantern. "It's sealed up tight. All we have to do is get it lit, and this is a tinderbox. They did a demonstration with one at the Charleston Museum. They're not that hard to use."

"This isn't the time for a geek moment," Barrie said as he opened the box and held up a piece of rock and a wad of yarn scraps.

"Actually, it's the perfect time. The flashlight's going to give out any minute."

After placing the yarn into his left hand, Eight struck the

flint against the fire steel. A spark lit but missed the yarn. He let out a huff of breath, adjusted the flint, and struck again.

"I told you it wouldn't work," Barrie said.

But even as she spoke, a curl of smoke rose from the yarn. Eight blew gently to fan it. Barrie pulled the candle out of the tinderbox and tipped the wick into the yarn. It caught with a nose-stinging *pppfft* and lit the small triumphant gleam in Eight's eyes. He took the candle from her and used it to light the lantern. The flame guttered, then steadied. Reflecting in the mirror at the back of the lantern, it gave off a surprising amount of light. Eight blew out the candle, turned off the flashlight, and tucked it into the waistband of his shorts. He reassembled the tinderbox before sliding it into his pocket.

"Ready?" he asked.

With the light and triumph playing across his features, he looked even more beautiful than usual. Things, and people, were always more beautiful when you were afraid to lose them.

Barrie's throat felt raw, and she swept past him. "Man, I hate being underground. Let's at least hope this tunnel isn't collapsed like the Colesworth one."

"It looks pretty stable. Thomas or whoever went to a lot of trouble bricking it in."

"By 'whoever,' I take it you mean the slaves?"

"Why are you mad at me again?" Eight reached out and took her hand as he walked beside her. "I just meant you didn't have to worry. I know slavery was awful. I just meant that labor-intensive things tend to last. Think of all the building the Romans did underground that has held up all this time. The drinking fountains in Rome still feed from the original ancient aqueducts, which are two thousand years old. What's three hundred years compared to that?"

What was seventeen years in comparison? There were so many places Barrie hadn't been. She hadn't been anywhere, really. She didn't even have a bucket list. Dying without a bucket list was worse than dying without finishing one.

"I want to go to Rome before I die," she said.

"Fine. I'll take you. Or you'll take me. We can take each other." Eight squeezed her hand.

The *yunwi* milled around them for a while, subdued and harder for Barrie to see in the lantern light. She and Eight had been walking some five minutes before she registered that the tunnel had been sloping gently downward. Now it leveled out, and another lantern hung in a niche cut into the wall. She pulled free of Eight to retrieve it.

"We've probably got enough light already," Eight said. "Let's just go. We have to be close to the river by now."

"What if the tunnel goes straight under to the other bank?"

His forehead creasing, Eight peered ahead. "I doubt it. The whole reason for the tunnels would have been to get away during the Yamassee uprising. Or maybe other Indian raids before that. Or away from other pirates, if Thomas was paranoid. He would have wanted to escape on the river."

"You're not escaping if you are still on an island. As long as someone was going to all the trouble of making a tunnel this elaborate, why wouldn't they go all the way across?"

"You think it goes to Beaufort Hall?"

"I doubt it would go to Colesworth Place." Barrie started limping ahead with renewed determination.

Twenty yards ahead, the tunnel split. She walked a few steps farther, then paused to picture the geography aboveground. Eight tugged her toward the left. "This way should come out in the Watson woods. Apparently old Thomas believed in hedging his bets."

"Hold on."

The *yunwi* weren't with them anymore. Barrie turned back and found them standing a few yards behind where the tunnel branched, as if they had reached another invisible barrier they couldn't cross.

It was absurd to worry about leaving them. But they watched her so forlornly, and she was leaving them locked up here alone in the dark. Not that it would be for long. There had to be two ways out of the tunnel to choose from now. At least one of them was bound to work. Maybe.

"I'll come back and let you out," she told the *yunwi*, with more confidence than she felt.

CHAPTER THIRTY-ONE

The tunnel climbed steeply toward the surface and another iron door, which because of the sharp pitch, was more above them than in front of them. Eight yanked the handle. It didn't budge. He put his shoulder against the metal, and when that failed, he gave the door a kick. The angle made it impossible to get much leverage. He switched to kicking the iron hinges.

"You might want to save that foot for walking," Barrie said, trying to keep her voice from sounding hysterical. "Why don't we try the other tunnel before you put yourself in a body cast?"

He kicked one more time, then let her pull him away. He rolled his head on his neck.

"Feel better?" Barrie asked, wishing she could kick a few things too, but that would have been both pointless and painful.

Eight spun her toward him and kissed her, a long, deep kiss, until she thought she was going to pass out from lack of oxygen to the brain. "Now I'm better. You?"

"Yeah. Fan-freaking-tastic."

"Good, because we're going to get out of this. Look at me." He ducked his head so he was eye level with her, and laced the fingers of both hands through hers. He spoke so intently, it was hard not to believe him. Not to believe *in* him. "We will get out."

Maybe the human brain was hardwired to require faith. Some people believed in God. Others believed in sports teams. Some believed blindly in their own talent or intelligence, regardless of evidence to the contrary, and then there were those who believed in family no matter how often it betrayed them. The people who mattered were the people you chose instead of the people who were yours only by an accident of birth. Real family was heart as much as, if not more than, blood.

Barrie had grown so used to the returning click falling into place whenever she and Eight touched each other that she had stopped paying attention to it. But now in the middle of feeling lost, she felt found again. She was choosing him, and she was going to believe in him, and if she ever got out of here, she was going to believe in Pru the way she had always believed in Mark.

"Yes," she said, more certainly. "We are getting out." She pretended she didn't feel how cold Eight's hands were in hers.

They retraced their steps back to the main tunnel, and followed it beneath the river until the floor sloped up again. They passed three more niches containing lanterns, which let Barrie hope that someone who had put so much thought into preparing the tunnel would have thought to leave a spare key for emergencies. She almost had herself convinced it would be there, hanging on an old-fashioned hook beside the door on the Beaufort side. Or maybe the tunnel would come out where Eight's little sister or his father could hear them if they yelled.

She and Eight passed another branch in the tunnel that led up toward the river, but in silent agreement they walked straight on. Barrie kept hoping, picturing a ring of keys, imagining a door swinging open into some secret recess of the basement at Beaufort Hall. But the tunnel ended in a very solid oak door reinforced with iron. Eight couldn't kick it down, and no one answered when Barrie screamed until her throat burned raw.

She gave up before Eight did, and sank to the floor. The flame from the lantern cast shadows across the bricks, and the vaulted ceiling echoed the *boom, boom, boom* of Eight's foot on the door.

Why couldn't the wood have been water-soaked and

rotten? Or eaten by termites? After three hundred years, a few termites didn't seem like too much to ask.

Barrie's head jerked up. The iron door Cassie had closed at Watson's Landing and this door at Beaufort Hall were both protected from the elements because they were inside and underground. The door at the end of the branch tunnel Barrie and Eight had followed was still within the boundary of Watson's Landing. Blood rushed through Barrie's head while she chased that thought.

Everything that had been broken at Watson's Landing, every last thing, had been designed to get her or Pru's attention. As if the *yunwi*, whether at the request of the Fire Carrier or the spirits or by their own choice, had been trying to force the Watsons to use the gift and live up to the bargain Thomas had made.

The *yunwi* had wanted Luke and Twila found.

But they hadn't done any lasting damage anywhere.

The garden was still in perfect shape. The boards on the dock were sturdy. The roof wasn't blowing away or sliding off the house. Nothing had fallen on any tourists. No one had been seriously hurt.

Was it possible that the door at the end of the branch tunnel on the Watson side, maybe all of Watson's Landing, was protected from decay and rust by magic? Maybe by the same kind of magic that created whatever invisible barriers kept the *yunwi* on the island?

There was another door, though. There had to be one at the end of the branch tunnel she and Eight had passed on the Beaufort side of the river. And that door, presumably, wouldn't be underground or have magical protection. If it had been exposed to air and water all these years . . .

Barrie scrambled to her feet and took off at a limping run. "Come on! I have to see something."

Eight's sneakers were lighter and quieter on the brick than the heavy Wellingtons she still had on her feet, and his legs were longer. He caught up in a handful of strides. She had a stitch in her side by the time they reached the top of the Beaufort river tunnel, where she could see even at first glance that the oak door was definitely more weathered and water-darkened. Hope relaxed the grim set of Eight's jaw. He kicked the door, grinning expectantly. But it held.

Barrie hadn't realized how sure she had been that it would splinter, until it didn't. Now they had no more doors—and no more options. What were they supposed to do, just sit here and wait for someone to come find them? No one would have a clue where to begin to look. Eight's boat was at Watson's Landing, but Cassie might have done something with that, too. And who knew what kind of lies Cassie would tell to cover her tracks.

Eight must have come to the same conclusion. He was still kicking the door, with no sign of giving up.

"It's not going to break," Barrie said. "Stop. We should keep movement to a minimum, since we don't have any water. We need to hold out as long as we can. Give Pru and your dad as much time as possible . . ."

She couldn't finish the thought. All she could think of was Pru being trapped at Watson's Landing again. And Mark, expecting her to be here and never hearing from her.

She had to think of something.

Eight slumped against the door and hung his head. Barrie had never imagined he could look defeated. In the sudden quiet, their breaths and the light trickle of sand sifting to the floor were the only sounds.

There had to be a way out of this. There had to be.

She glanced at her watch. It was almost ten thirty. Pru would be looking for her by now.

Eight's steps scratched on the bricks as he came toward her, and she looked up as he wrapped his arms around her. His Adam's apple bobbed, and then she couldn't see anymore. His heart was erratic against her cheek.

"It's all going to be fine," he said.

"Of course it is. We should go back to Watson's Landing and wait. And we should bring all the lanterns we can find."

"In a minute. I'm still thinking."

"Then think fast, would you?" Barrie tried not to imagine their lives measured by an hourglass, marked by the slow whisper of sand. So many hours until the light ran out, so many days until they died of thirst in the darkness.

Why did she keep thinking of sand? Abruptly she pulled away from Eight and moved to the bricks beside the door. Stooping, she ran her hand across the ground flecked by grit that Eight's kicking had dislodged from the three-hundred-year-old mortar between the bricks.

"Give me the flint from the tinderbox, would you?" she asked. "I want to try something."

Eight handed her the sharp rock, and she ran it along the mortar. It bit through, and she pressed harder, dislodging more sandy material as the flint dug in and made a narrow trench.

She paid little attention when Eight's footsteps receded. Then his voice came from a few yards back, "I thought I'd get another flint, but there's no tinderbox in this niche. I'm going to go see if I can find one."

"Sure." The word came out a groan, because Barrie was using all her strength.

She heard Eight light the other lantern. They needed to conserve oil, but on the other hand, if he got the other flint, the work would go twice as fast. She let him go.

Her knuckles scraped raw against the brick as she dug the

flint as deep as it would go into the mortar. Then she switched to using the pointed end of the fire steel to go deeper. That was less successful because she didn't have the strength to push it through. Deciding to leave that job for Eight, she went back to using the flint. She started on another side of the same brick, working methodically until she'd done as much as she could on all four sides.

Eight peered over her shoulder when he came back. "Good work," he said with a nod of approval.

"Try using the fire steel to clear out the rest of the mortar where I've already done as much as I can do," Barrie said.

She stepped aside to let him try it, and he rammed the steel from side to side with pure, brute force, grunting with the effort. Then he suddenly jerked forward.

"I'm through," he said, stooping to put his eye to the new void between the bricks. "But I don't see any light."

"Maybe there's no moon tonight. Keep going."

She squeezed in front of him so they could work simultaneously. She felt the rise and fall of his chest, felt the heat of his body, heard the beat of his heart. Her own breath came faster, and not from exertion.

Grief made you think about sex; she had read that once in a novel. Did fear do that too? Or excitement? Hope? Whichever it was, Eight's scent, his warmth, his strong jaw and kind eyes suddenly made her want to kiss him almost as much as she wanted to get out of the tunnel.

"All right," he said a little later. "I think we need a break."

Barrie leaned back into the crook of his shoulder, and let herself pretend this was an adventure, that they were only experimenting to see if they could claw themselves out of a pirate tunnel.

Except it wasn't a game. Pru had to be panicking by now. And Mark. What if he had tried to call her back? Barrie attacked the mortar again, faster, harder.

Her knuckles bled, and so did Eight's. Drops of blood freckled the floor, and there were no spirits, no shadows to bargain with.

She and Eight moved a row at a time, working in silence because talking was too much effort. When they had five rows cleared, Eight pulled his arms from around her and nudged her aside. "Stand back."

He braced his hands on the wall. Then he kicked the bricks hard, once, twice . . . Where he and Barrie had cleared the mortar, the bricks fell outward and released a stream of mud and decaying leaves that rained back into the tunnel. Barrie jumped out of the way as the debris kept coming, splashing onto the floor and splattering her boots and legs until it finally stopped.

Eight pushed the lantern through the hole they had made. He poked his head out, but his shoulders didn't fit. "It's a covered stairwell. The crud that fell in came through spots where the lid above us has rusted away."

"So we have to get through another metal door?"

"It's corroded. I can see strips of moonlight."

Bits of hope. "All right." Barrie licked her lips and swallowed hard. "Let me try climbing through."

Eight looked at her like she had lost her mind. "You're not going anywhere without me. Let's clear the rest of this."

"It'll take too long to remove enough bricks for you to fit through. I can be back here with help before then. God knows what Cassie is doing, now that she's had time to think. And Pru has to be frantic." Barrie wriggled between Eight and the wall and kissed him quickly. "Can you give me a boost?"

He caught the collar of her shirt and kissed her, long and deep so that the warmth of his lips turned to fire and promises. He pulled away so slowly, she felt like there was still a live strand of energy running between them, holding them together.

"Be very, very careful." He brushed her cheek with the back of his finger. "I don't like you leaving."

"I'm not the one who's leaving, baseball guy."

"Maybe I've changed my mind. It's amazing how fast you figure out your priorities when you're under pressure."

"Meaning what exactly?"

"We'll work things out. Whatever happens."

Barrie's answering smile was shaky. It frightened her how much one person could matter to another, how a whole life could depend on a few simple words. "I thought you were going to stop reading me?"

"It's not always about what *you* want, you know." He kissed her again. "Now go on, Bear. Bring back the cavalry. Or at least someone with a reciprocating saw."

CHAPTER THIRTY-TWO

Barrie wiggled through the hole, and hunched nearly in half to keep from knocking her head on the lid covering the stairwell. Ankle-deep in mud, she tried not to think of snakes. Thank god for Pru's ugly rubber Wellingtons.

The cover didn't want to budge. Feet planted more firmly, Barrie pressed her shoulders up against the cover and used every bit of strength in her knees, thighs, and back to strain against the lid. It rose an inch, two inches. A piece broke off, and her left shoulder cracked through. The rest of the cover clanged into place again, and she was back where she'd started. Or maybe not. With the heel of her hand she hammered at the edge she had broken.

"Wrap this around your fist." Eight stripped off his shirt and threw it at her.

Barrie jabbed at the metal, and another piece broke off. She kept at it, hitting and prying until she had cleared a space big enough to fit through. Then she pushed herself out. Her tired muscles rejoiced when she could finally stand.

Under the heavy tree cover, it was hard to get her bearings in the moonlight, but she decided she had to be in the woods between Beaufort Hall and Colesworth Place. Leaves, mud, and thick underbrush hid the stairwell where she had just emerged. She could have walked over it a hundred times and never realized it was there. And how many people ever went into these woods? The demilitarized zone. Not the Beauforts, and probably not the Colesworths, either.

Some thirty feet through the trees, she saw the glint of the water and heard its murmur. Across the river, she could make out the Watson dock upstream, with every light blazing in the house and garden. No light shone from the Beaufort side, but the woods were thicker there. Anyway, Seven had to know Eight was missing by now. He was probably with Pru since Eight's boat was on the Watson side.

"I'm going to get Cassie's rowboat and go for help. Don't go anywhere." She tossed Eight's shirt back down to him.

"Where am I going to go?" The frustration growled in Eight's voice.

Underbrush clutched at Barrie's clothes and reopened the scrapes on her hands as she ran toward the Colesworth dock.

Twigs snapped, leaves crunched, and her breath came heavily, distorting her hearing. She hoped the racket she was making would at least scare away the snakes.

The trees cleared to a verge of grass sloping toward the river. Cassie's boat bobbed alongside the speedboat Barrie had seen her first night at Watson's Landing. She felt a renewed surge of energy and relief that almost cut through the familiar dread of having to navigate the water. She lengthened her stride.

A man jumped out of the boat with his arms full of small brown packages. He looked dead at her, and they both stopped short.

Barrie recognized him. She'd seen him talking with Wyatt at the marina. Moonlight gleamed off his shaven scalp, and she shivered as she remembered the tattooed face inked onto the back of his head. More tattoos snaked down his arms and up his neck from beneath the black T-shirt.

He shouted something in Spanish and threw the packages back into the boat. Then he sprinted toward her.

Instinct sent Barrie running back toward the trees. Which would lead back to Eight. Changing her mind, she cut toward the river instead, and managed to splash through five yards of shin-high marsh before iron-muscled arms lifted her off the ground.

Screaming, she kicked and twisted. Jabbed with her elbows.

The man's hand slapped over her mouth, grinding her lips against her teeth.

She tasted blood and smelled something vinegary and acrid. Wrenching herself sideways, she kicked harder, caught him in the knee, and screamed.

His fist slammed into her cheek. She fell and inhaled a mouthful of river. Jarred and breathless, with stars spinning behind her eyes, she came up coughing. She scrambled to her knees.

"What the hell?"

That voice. Wyatt's voice. Barrie's head shot up, trying to call out to him for help. The guy behind her jerked her back, his palm pressed against her mouth again. And what were the odds that Wyatt would help her?

Slim to none.

In the area beneath the slave cabins, Wyatt swung himself out of a hole and slammed the lid. He ran toward Barrie. The moonlight gleamed on a dark object in his hand.

A gun.

Barrie began to shake.

The tattooed man kicked her in the ribs and sent her back into the water. She came up sputtering, and he grabbed the back of her shirt and hauled her to her feet. Water blurred her eyes. She couldn't catch her breath. Not deeply enough.

"You really are like your mother, aren't you?" Wyatt

stopped in front of her, his face twisted into a snarl. "Can't stay the hell out of the way. I'd have figured you could take a hint."

The man holding her ground his thumb and forefinger into Barrie's cheek and spoke to Wyatt in heavily accented English: "You know this girl?"

Something like fear flashed in Wyatt's eyes. "She doesn't matter, Ernesto. Drown her. Shoot her. Maybe that will be more effective than fire. Hell, I don't know." Wyatt gave an exasperated wave of the gun. "She and her bitch of a mother should both have been dead seventeen years ago, but here she is. Take her out to the boat. We'll bring her with us. Do it fast. I don't like all those lights on across the river. We need to finish up."

Barrie aimed another kick at Wyatt's knee. Her foot connected with bone. He grunted.

Ernesto turned toward Watson's Landing. His hand slackened over Barrie's lips. She wrenched her head and bit down, teeth grinding on flesh, blood pooling metallically in her mouth.

"*Madre de dios!*" He snatched his hand away.

Barrie spat and darted toward the river. Ernesto tripped her. She stumbled to one knee.

"Hold it." Wyatt's voice was cold. "Don't think I won't shoot you right here."

His gun clicked. Barrie looked back, and his face was

emotionless. As if she didn't matter at all. As if she were only a minor inconvenience.

How loud was a gunshot? Would Wyatt really risk shooting her if he thought someone might hear?

Barrie's breath came in shallow pants of panic, and she'd broken out in a clammy sweat. Her legs didn't want to let her stand back up. She needed time to think.

"You're the one who killed my father, aren't you? It was you who set the fire." The words grated in her throat, what he'd said tonight and what Lula had written in her letter, the way Wyatt had wanted to know what Lula had said about him . . . The pieces had finally fallen into place.

Wyatt's head recoiled on his shoulders. "It wasn't me. You want to know who killed him? Your mother. Her damn Watson righteousness. Wade was too softhearted to take care of her. To do what had to be done."

"To kill her, you mean?" Hysteria hovered at the edges of Barrie's brain, but her breath was coming more easily. It shocked her how calm she sounded. How much easier it was to say "kill" now that she had said it before. She had to keep Wyatt talking. She waved her hand at the speedboat and whatever was hidden in the hole down the bank. "Lula caught you both doing *this*, smuggling drugs, didn't she?"

Wyatt shook his head slowly, more in disgust than denial. "You can't outrun the cartel. Wade was stupid to try." He glanced sideways at Ernesto, then pointed the gun from Barrie to the boat. "Walk," he said. "I'm not going to ask you again."

"You won't shoot me here," Barrie said, with no confidence whatsoever.

"Then I'll knock you out and carry you to the boat. Your choice."

There had to be a way out of this. Why wouldn't Barrie's brain *work*? She held her palms up toward Wyatt in surrender. "Let me go home, Uncle Wyatt. Please? I swear I won't tell anyone."

Wyatt snorted. "You think I'm that stupid, girl? But at least you're trying. I'll give you credit for that. All your mother did was scream."

"Until you shut her up," Barrie guessed.

"All I did was hit her. She howled like I was committing murder."

"And then?" She saw the answer in his face, the way his eyes slid away, the way his muscles thickened with strain. "Wade went after you for hurting Lula, didn't he? That's why you killed him."

"It wasn't my fault. Lula slammed herself into the bedroom, and Wade barreled into me—I had to defend myself. And the stupid candle of Lula's set fire to the curtain. I tried to drag him out, but the whole place was a firetrap. I barely got out myself."

"So you left him. You left him, and you left my mother in the bedroom." Barrie planted her feet in the middle of the dock. "You left them to die, and that's your idea of *not your fault?*"

"We could have had a sweet operation out there, Wade and me. If the bitch really loved him, she would have understood he had changed his mind."

"About what?"

Wyatt glanced darkly at Ernesto. "You don't quit on the cartel," he said.

Wyatt jumped onto the dock. Barrie's stomach lurched. Acid spilled into her mouth, and she barely bent over before she was heaving, the taste of bile chasing away the metallic sweetness of the blood from her lip.

Ernesto watched her in disgust. "Get her onto the boat," he said. "We have to go."

Wyatt moved toward Barrie. She opened her mouth to protest, and no sound came out.

"I'll shoot you if you scream. The shot won't be any louder than that." Wyatt raised the gun.

Barrie finally understood why deer froze in headlights. Her muscles weighed five hundred pounds apiece. Her legs refused to work. Wyatt gave her a shove, then jerked her arm behind her back, marched her to the end of the dock, and pushed her into the boat. She fell to her knees, her empty stomach heaving.

"Not in the damn boat." Ernesto caught her with his knee and knocked her head into the edge of one of the seats.

By the time she could see again, Ernesto had the engine started. Was the motor quieter than normal? Too quiet? Or was there something the matter with Barrie's ears?

She grabbed the seat and used it to pull herself to her feet. Ernesto picked up the last of the brown, plastic-wrapped packages he'd thrown into the boat, and tossed them into an open storage hold that stank like eighteen kinds of animals had peed in it. He dropped a false bottom over the drugs, threw in an anchor and a bunch of rope, closed the lid, and settled a seat cushion back on top.

Wyatt reversed away from the dock and out into the river. Barrie tried to calculate how close he would get to the Watson side before he motored the boat forward. She needed to minimize the distance she had to swim if she was going to have any chance at all. But maybe it was better to try while Wyatt and Ernesto were both still busy. Realistically, what chance did she have either way? The thought of swimming revved her pulse, and she took a deep breath that was laced with sage-scented smoke.

Smoke.

Midnight?

Heart galloping, Barrie looked toward the Watson woods. The Fire Carrier was coming. Already flames lapped at the shadows between the trees. She scrambled up onto the seat.

"Get down from there," Ernesto commanded. "Wyatt, get her down."

Wyatt grabbed for Barrie, but the Fire Carrier had reached the edge of the marsh, and he was looking straight at her. The paint of his red-and-black mask gleamed by the light of the flames he held. Barrie could feel him questioning. She had never wanted anything as much as she wanted to be at Watson's Landing right that moment.

The Fire Carrier gave a nod and spread his hands. Lines of flame streaked toward the boat.

Wyatt swore. Ernesto turned. "What the hell?"

Back by the Colesworth dock, someone shouted. Eight's voice? Barrie couldn't turn to look. The fire reached the boat, and she dove into the water.

Flames passed over her, through her, but where she expected to feel heat, she felt only water. She flailed and tried to propel herself upward. Pru's rubber boots had become dead weight, pulling at her swollen ankle. She struggled to get them off, and dog-paddled underwater, her every muscle stiff with fear. Her lungs seared with the half breath she had taken, and she pushed toward the surface.

An explosion rocked the air, followed by an even bigger boom. Something sharp hit her in the shoulder, knocking her forward. The water surged, swelled, tumbled her until she didn't know which way was up. Her left arm went numb.

Her ears rang. Everything was muffled. Opening her eyes, she stopped struggling. The churning water above her was lit with an eerie orange glow. She thrust upward, thrashing as she broke the surface and gasped for air. Was that blood pouring off her arm? Blood. *No, don't focus on the blood.*

She cringed from the heat of flames that had become very real, and she fought to stay afloat. Black smoke billowed in gusts, and the air smelled like burning fuel. Pockets of flaming debris floated on oil-slicked water from the remains of Wyatt's boat.

Where was she? She turned to look behind her.

She wasn't even halfway back across the river. A burning wall that loomed in front of her as though held at bay by some invisible barrier marked the midpoint. As if the Fire Carrier, having deviated from his nightly ritual to send actual fire streaking toward the boat, had then gone back and finished surrounding Watson's Landing in magical flames.

At least, Barrie hoped they were only magical. Otherwise how was she going to make it through them?

How was she going to make it at all?

But she couldn't let Eight down. Couldn't let Pru down. Or Mark. *Mark.*

I'm right here with you, baby girl.

She was going crazy. Mark's voice sounded so clear.

Don't you even think about giving in, you hear me? You're halfway there already.

Halfway. She *was* halfway—and suddenly the water was whispering the way it had in the fountain, and she was buoyant. The current carried her as though hands held her up. Crowd-surfing without the crowd.

If she survived, she was going to have to try that sometime. Experience an actual concert, feel the pump of the music for herself instead of watching *Rock of Ages* on her ass from the couch.

Swim, baby girl. Move your arms, kick your legs. You can do it. Fight now. Fight and don't you ever stop fighting. Mark's voice sounded stronger than it had in days. In weeks. That strength and the surge of the water pushed Barrie toward the shore until her feet touched bottom.

She broke the surface gasping, drinking in a mix of air and water. Choking. Coughing. Her eyes watered. Her ears filled with ringing echoes and muffled sounds as if she had cotton stuffed in her ears. Across the river, pieces of Wyatt's boat still burned, and the Colesworth dock had caught fire too, pluming smoke and spitting bursts of ash into the air. But the flames that burned on the waist-deep water around Barrie, the flames that touched her, held no heat. They licked her skin with barely a tickle.

She was back on the Watson side.

And Wyatt? Ernesto? Where were they?

She had to get out of the water. She stumbled toward the bank and pulled up short.

In the rushes before her, the Fire Carrier stood close enough that the war paint on his face and chest shone slick with grease. Veins stood out on his arms, and every lean muscle of his chest and stomach seemed defined and ready to spring into action. But apart from the feathers of his cloak and headdress stirring in the night air, he was motionless. He watched her.

Barrie had thought him older when she'd seen him from a distance. He wasn't much older than she was, though. Not much older than Eight.

"Thank you." Holding her injured arm to her side, she drew herself up to face him.

He watched her. His eyes reflected the fire and darkness. They looked sad somehow, and tired. Barrie thought of Luke's spirit reaching for Twila, hoping to touch her all those years. How long had the Fire Carrier performed his midnight ritual night after night?

He wanted something. She felt that with even more certainty now, but before she could find a way to frame a question, he inclined his head and turned toward the Watson woods. Fingertips skimming the surface, he waded through the water while flames sped toward him from across the river, running up his arms until he glowed as brightly as the moon.

It was only when he reached the bank that she realized she could almost see through him.

She wondered what would happen if she ran after him and begged him to tell her what he wanted from her, asked him to explain the binding and whatever bargain she had made. She splashed after him, but her body was shutting down, shock making her slow and lethargic.

Her hearing was coming back. Where before there had been only the ringing and the roaring silence, she now heard splashing behind her. She turned to look, and in the flickering light from the burning dock, she saw someone swimming.

Wyatt? Or Ernesto?

She struggled toward the shore, weighted down by mud, water, and panic. Exhausted and fighting to keep from sobbing, she pushed on, ignoring the shouts behind her. She wasn't going to get this far, only to have them catch her again. The Fire Carrier had disappeared into the woods, but shadows raced along the shoreline, and she threw herself toward them.

The splashing was closer, right behind her. Barrie pushed herself faster.

"Bear, wait. Wait! Hold up. It's me."

Almost to the shore, she stopped. It *was* Eight. He caught her and lifted her up, holding her as if he were never going to let her go.

CHAPTER THIRTY-THREE

Barrie barely felt the tug of the needle stitching through her shoulder as the doctor worked. She concentrated on answering another round of questions from the police as best she could. With the collar of Pru's heavy bathrobe pulled down to expose the top of her shoulder, she couldn't seem to get warm enough. The light in the kitchen shone too bright, and the room swarmed with people. At the same time, even with Pru beside her, she felt oddly alone. Eight stood leaning against the counter, answering questions from still more police. County sheriff, state police, military police, the DEA, the FBI. They were all here, crawling around the tunnels and the river, not to mention the Colesworth bank.

"There, that's finished," Dr. Ainsley said, securing a bandage over the wound.

He smiled at Barrie tiredly, and she wondered if he'd had any sleep before Seven had insisted the doctor come over. She felt guilty for that, but the idea of going to an emergency room, leaving Watson's Landing again after all she'd already been through, had been too much.

Dr. Ainsley fiddled in his bag and pulled out a syringe and a small bottle of clear liquid. "Now this is a dose of antibiotic," he said, drawing some out of the vial and filling the syringe. "Just as a precaution. I want you to keep those stitches dry for forty-eight hours, so take sponge baths and have Pru help you wash your hair in the sink. I'll give you a sling to wear until I see you in the office. Keep your arm as still as possible. And stay off that ankle for a few days too. A little rest wouldn't be a bad idea."

Barrie nodded, but she wanted nothing more than to immerse herself in the tub to get rid of the stench of the river and the night's events. She winced as Dr. Ainsley administered the shot.

A radio crackled in the hand of the nearest sheriff's deputy. He walked off a few feet, spoke into it, then came back, and his eyes met Pru's over Barrie's head. "They're bringing the bodies up from the tunnel now," he said.

Dr. Ainsley visibly went pale, his hand trembling as he put the used syringe into his bag. He was probably in his sixties. Barrie wondered if he had known Luke. But then, everyone seemed to have been shaken tonight. She shivered again; the shock waves kept hitting her.

Heroin and murder. So many murders. But Emmett was long dead, and Wyatt had died in the explosion. Neither of them were any loss. Barrie couldn't help thinking of Cassie, though, who was still missing like Ernesto. With a father like Wyatt, had Cassie ever had a chance to turn out well? Maybe that, more than anything else, was the Colesworth curse, passed down from generation to generation. The bitterness, rage, and willingness to take the easy way out. Maybe with Wyatt dead, Cassie and Sydney would both be better off.

Barrie pulled up the collar of Pru's thick bathrobe and burrowed deeper into the fabric. Eight nodded at something one of the FBI agents said, and peeled himself away from the counter to rejoin her. She met him as Pru went to talk to Seven.

Eight's clothes were still damp, but Barrie didn't care as he drew her toward him. She was just grateful to hug him. He could have died in the river. He could have burned, or Wyatt could have shot him.

She smacked him in the chest with the flat of her hand.

"Hey, what's that for?" He rubbed the spot as if it hurt.

"For being reckless and risking your life."

"We'll argue that one another time. I'm giving you a free pass for the rest of the night."

"There is no 'rest of the night,'" Barrie said. "It's light out already."

Pru came back, leaving Seven still talking to the group of police. "They're all done with you for now," she said. "Thank goodness." She peered closer at Eight and crossed her arms. "Lord, Eight Beaufort, your clothes are still wet. What is your father thinking, letting you stay here talking all this time?"

"I'm all right," Eight said, his jaw jutting stubbornly.

"You're not going to do Barrie a bit of good if you catch your death. At least go home and get into something dry. That won't take you long. Barrie can wash off meanwhile, and we can all have some breakfast together."

Food was about the last thing on Barrie's mind. "I want to call the hospital and check on Mark before I do anything else." She glanced back at Eight. "My phone is shot. Come down to the library with me."

Pru and Eight both went stiff, and Pru's eyes welled. "I'm sorry," Pru said. "I'm so sorry. I wanted to wait to tell you. Eight agreed that you've been through so much tonight and—"

"No," Barrie said, although she knew. Part of her had known in the river. Mark's voice had been so clear, so *Mark*.

He couldn't be gone. He couldn't.

Eight's arms tightened around her. He rested his chin on her head, cradling her against him.

"I'm sorry. I'm so sorry, sugar." Pru's hands fell in a helpless little gesture.

Barrie buried her face into Eight's chest and felt his lips brush her hair. "At least he won't go through any more pain. That's what you wanted, isn't it, Bear? It's what he wanted. The pneumonia was mercifully quick—his body just couldn't take it."

How could she take it? How could she be losing everyone?

"You aren't losing me. Or Pru."

"We're right here with you, sugar."

Barrie wasn't sure who she was crying for. Mark. Lula. Luke and Twila. Even her father. She had lost them all in the past few hours, lost them and found them and lost them again. Or maybe it was herself she had lost and found.

As if by some silent agreement between them, she found herself passed from Eight's arms into Pru's. "I'm going to let Pru fix you up," Eight whispered into her ear, "but I'll be back. You know that, right? I'll always come back."

She gave him a numb, silent nod and walked to her room with Pru holding her close. But as they approached the door, it occurred to her how much Pru, too, had lost. The hallway blurred around her, and the air turned to stars and prisms. There were too many shadows, too many ghosts of lives that could have been. She wanted to say she understood how Pru felt, but the words stuck in her throat.

"We should have a funeral for all of them," she said instead. "Mark and Luke and Twila."

Pru stopped in the doorway, and the sunlight from the balcony carved hollows into her face. "A service. For Lula, too. That's a wonderful idea, sugar." Her voice broke, and around her the house, the shadows, the whole universe seemed to give a final sigh. "Lord, all these wasted years. Because of what my father did."

She didn't call Emmett "Daddy" anymore.

Barrie wished she could take some of Pru's pain away. How hard did it have to be to know that your father, your own father, had murdered not one person but two people he was supposed to have loved? Murdered them and left them to rot like garbage. And he had stolen years or dreams from so many others: Pru, Lula, Wade, even Cassie. It made what Barrie had lost seem small by comparison.

"You lost Mark today," Pru said, "and I know you're afraid of Eight going away. But you can't lose someone you truly love. Love doesn't come with an on-off switch. It's made of too many threads of memory and hope and heartache that weave themselves into the very core of who you are. You carry all those shared experiences with you."

Wordlessly Barrie nodded. But love was so much more than shared experiences. Love was more alchemy than memory. Love was the kind of magic that made Mark beautiful to her and made her feel filled up inside when Eight was happy.

"So are you and Seven going to get back together now?" she asked, glancing at Pru with a telltale blush.

"Maybe it's inevitable." Pru looked toward the balcony and across the river. "I can't remember when I didn't love him. Your mama and I used to climb out on the balcony at night and talk until the river caught fire and lit the sky. Then Seven would come out and watch from the balcony on his side, and he and I would stay out there after Lula went in. I used to imagine the Fire Carrier was burning a path between us, from my heart to Seven's. I didn't expect that fire would ever go out. And it hasn't. Not for me. It just got banked down for a while. I think Seven feels it too. We've lost a lot of years, but you can't lose love. Not real love. It stays locked inside you, ready for whenever you are strong enough to find it again."

Pru rubbed her palm, staring down at it as if the lines there surprised her somehow. "I went into Charleston yesterday," she said quietly. "To see an antiques appraiser about the things in the attic. If I can do that by myself, I can do anything. Even go with you to a funeral, if you think you want to go to California."

Tears made rivers down Barrie's cheeks. More water. She thought of what Mark had said about rivers and oceans mixing. Her whole life, he had been her safe harbor when events, people, words, had broken her into flotsam and jetsam. Now he had set her adrift, launched her into the current again.

Pru got up and rubbed Barrie's cold hands between her own. "Breathe, sugar. I'm right here for you. You know that. And Eight is still here. Do you want me to send him up?"

Barrie shook her head. "You sent him home."

"He didn't go," Pru said. "He's still standing on the dock."

Barrie looked out the window. Eight stood staring at the *Away* with his hands in his pockets. She stepped out to the balcony and leaned across the railing.

"What are you doing?" she shouted, as if he could possibly hear her across the distance.

But he turned and waved.

His outline went soft at the edges, as if someone stood at either shoulder. Mark, in his favorite pink Chanel suit, pointing at Eight with a shimmy of delight and then turning to give Barrie a big thumbs-up. And Lula, dressed to the teeth, with no veil, and her hair a loose tumble blowing around her unscarred face, standing on the other side.

When Barrie closed her eyes, she could almost see Mark turning and walking down the long, gray dock with Lula beside him. There was no mistaking the swing of his hips, his elbow pushed out. Working it, as if the dock were a stage and he were off to take a bow after a great performance. Lula's stride was unfamiliar, fierce and free of pain. Was that how Lula had used to look?

Barrie wondered if she'd ever have the courage to read her mother's letters. For all she had lost that night, that week, Watson's Landing had given her back a family. The Fire Carrier had saved her life.

She had known since the moment she'd stepped out of the cab and touched the bricks on the gatepost that she had found where she was supposed to be. But there was a difference between being stuck and choosing to stay. Between being found and finding yourself.

Watson's Landing had bound her without giving her a choice. In the tunnel today she had chosen. She had chosen in the river, and she was choosing again. Now all she had to do was find a way to make Eight choose.

"We should start a restaurant," she said to Pru. "Out here, I mean." She wasn't sure where the words came from, but they felt right. It shocked her. Not only did she want to stay, but she was willing to invite strangers in. Turning to Pru, she gestured down at the garden. "I can picture it, can't you? People sitting out under the fairy lights, watching the water and the fireflies. We could float candles on the river to set the water on fire. Play romantic music. Put out dessert stations and let people stroll along the paths so it feels like they've been invited here as guests."

"Would people pay for that?" Pru looked at the garden with her eyes wide, as if she were seeing it too. "Yes, I think they would. We could catch our own shrimp and fish, dig oysters. We already have pecans, strawberries, and vegetables."

"Eight would always know what people wanted. When he wasn't off playing baseball."

Pru's smile dimmed a little, and she folded her hands together, her expression guarded. "What about art school, sugar?"

"I'll go someday, but not yet." Barrie leaned out over the balcony railing to take it all in: the landscape of her heart, and the spirits and the family she had chosen all around her. She stood a moment breathing in the silence. "Right now," she said, "I can't think of anywhere else I'd rather be."

Pru slid her arm around Barrie's waist and stood beside her. "Sugar, that's the whole point of being home."

Stay tuned for *Persuasion*,
the next book in the
Heirs of Watson Island series,
coming Fall 2015!

Acknowledgments

I owe boundless gratitude to so many.

To Doug, who believed this story would be the one, and who by example makes me want to work harder and be a better person every day.

To Hailey, whose perseverance and sheer grit inspire me, and who came running at one in the morning to tell me she had finished a book I *had* to read, kicking off our shared exploration of YA literature.

To Ryan, who has loved and hoarded books since he first used them to climb out of his crib, and who reminds me how important it is to try the things that scare me.

To my parents, who taught me the power of hope, and whose courageous journey led to a life filled with freedom, books, and intellectual curiosity.

To Kent Wolf, my stellar agent, who championed the book and made it more pyrotechnic than I could ever have made it on my own, and who continues to save me from myself all too frequently.

To Amanda Panitch, whose leap of faith started Barrie on her journey, and the team at LMQ, whose fabulousness knows no bounds.

To Annette Pollert, who *got* Barrie, Eight, Cassie, Pru, Mark, Lula, Julia, and even Mrs. Price more than I could ever have hoped, who wanted to call Barrie on the missing cell phone, who turned this first book into a series, and who coaxed more out of me than I believed I had.

To Sara Sargent, who never faltered no matter what I threw at her, and whose unfailing wisdom and patience are beyond price. I'm looking forward to the rest of the journey together.

To Bara MacNeill, who copyedited the manuscript and made me look better than I deserve.

To Patrick Price, who shepherded Barrie off on a solid start, and to Carolyn Swerdloff, Mara Anastas, Mary Marotta, Lucille Rettino, Christina Pecorale, Paul Crichton, Anna McKean, Hayley Gonnason, Emma Sector, Michelle Leo, Anthony Parisi, Katy Hershberger, Candace Greene, Katherine Devendorf, Sara Berko, Nicole Ellul, and the editorial, art, marketing, publicity, sales, and rights teams— all the magicians at Simon Pulse—who took in a dingy manuscript and made it a shiny book.

To Regina Flath, who took the time to read *Compulsion*, and whose design and cover created a wonderful invitation for the reader.

To Andrew Agha, whose patience and enthusiasm for answering my zillions of archaeological questions have been a gift. All mistakes (and liberties) are entirely my own fault.

To Jan, who has been my rock and best cheerleader, not to mention my fellow night owl, who does the work of ten mere mortals, and without whom this book and I would be a red-hot mess.

To Susan, whose words gave me strength when I had almost given up, whose insight and editorial wisdom are infinite, and whose heart is a bottomless well of kindness.

To Cici and Carol, the strongest, bravest, most kick-ass women I could ever hope to laugh with, who have been with me through every step, from the birth of this story and before.

To Kimberley, my lately discovered soul sister and fellow PID, who is quite literally a saint.

To Shannon, who has blazed trails and offered guidance that has kept me from making countless mistakes.

To Kari Stuart, Lorin Oberweger, Brenda Windberg, and Emma Dryden, whose expert advice and kindness have been instrumental, and to my beyond fabulous CPs and early readers: Lisa, Clara, Marco, Mariana, Chris, Vivien, Carolyn, Erin, and my beautiful (inside and out) sister, Alena, who have all made it possible for dreams to come true.

To my wonderful AYAP partners, YASI sisters, blogging friends, and fellow wanderers on what was once a solitary road, whose generosity, support, and enthusiasm have been the kick to my butt every morning.

To the authors whose books have given me human

connection, growth, hope, and joy throughout the years. Thank you especially to Cynthia Leitich Smith for igniting my daughter's love of reading and for rekindling my goal of writing. Thanks also to Kami Garcia and Margaret Stohl for reminding me how much I adore Southern Gothics.

To every librarian, bookseller, reviewer, and book blogger who encourages reading and who provides a foundation for those of us who write.

Last, and definitely foremost, to all the readers who bring books into their hearts and breathe life into them with the turn of every page.

Thank you, everyone, for your trust and faith and kindness.